Rachel

Rachel

Sue Ritter

NELSON WORD PUBLISHERS

RACHEL

Published in the UK by Nelson Word Ltd., Milton Keynes,
England, 1995.

ISBN 1-86024-033-X

Reproduced and printed in Great Britain for Nelson Word Ltd. by
Cox and Wyman Ltd., Reading

95 96 97 98 99 / 10 9 8 7 6 5 4 3 2 1

*To my sister Jean.
Unlike the sisters in this book,
Jeannie and I have always got
on like a house on fire! I'm
grateful for her 'input' into
this novel—we had a lot of fun
researching, didn't we?*

PART ONE

LABAN

Then Jacob kissed Rachel and began to weep aloud.
(Genesis 29:11)

CHAPTER

1

W hy do you bother Rachel?" Leah was sitting in bed with a huge silk pillow behind her head and a cup of fresh-brewed coffee in her hand.

Rachel was twenty one years old and very beautiful. Her hair was raven black, very long and thick. It hung gracefully from her proud head and rippled as she moved. Her eyes were a startling blue, strikingly set off by long black lashes which seemed to go on forever. It was hard to find a flaw and although her face gave the impression of being cleverly made-up, closer inspection revealed hardly any cosmetics at all. She could walk out of the bathroom after scrubbing her face, with her freshly washed hair still dripping in wet tendrils down her back ... and still look like a million dollars!—and that was before she smiled! When she did, her already strikingly beautiful face was, well, beyond description. People would do anything to see Rachel smile—and her nature inclined her always to make that happen. She was a selfless girl, a happy girl, and very fond of her sister.

Unfortunately, the feeling was not completely reciprocated by Leah—who was fairly ordinary, with hair being dark but not quite dark enough to give it a definite colour. It was neither curly nor straight and it tended to frizz out—unlike Rachel's which always fell in envious, wavy locks.

Leah's looks were not helped by her warped feelings towards her sister. She spent a great deal of time frowning and kicking out at anything that she felt was unfair. One could easily have felt sorry for Leah having to live in the shadow of Rachel's outstanding beauty, but somehow she didn't give anyone the opportunity. Life owed her one, and she was determined to get it.

Rachel looked into the vast framed mirror in Leah's room and brushed her hair vigorously.

"Bother with what?" she smiled, looking at her sister's reflection through the glass.

"Working, of course." Leah retorted. "Why on earth do you bother to go to that poky little office, with those tiresome clerks and awful secretaries? You know, you really could do so much better—I mean Father would give you a super job if that's what you really want." She picked imaginary fluff from the sheet. "Though I can't think why you want it."

Father was Laban Monklaast, a silver-haired authoritative-looking man whose air of command came from owning the world's largest broadcasting company—MBC, the Monklaast Broadcasting Corporation. His daughters, Leah and Rachel, were his pride and joy and he tried to spend as much time with them as possible, especially as his wife Elisabeth had sadly died when the girls were quite young. All the money in the world could not compensate for the love their mother had had for them, and even now, fourteen years on, they missed her terribly.

Laban tried to share his time between his daughters and his company, but as the main offices were in London, he found himself staying, more and more often at his Park Lane apartment, while the girls spent most of their time at Monks Lodge, his country home which nestled in the heart of Buckinghamshire, in the village of High Montley. It was hidden from the road by a sweeping drive almost half a mile long, serving its purpose well and excluding them from prying eyes and unwanted journalists.

This particular morning, Rachel was getting ready for work and Leah was watching her, which was a fairly typical start to their day. Leah spent a lot of her time looking at Rachel and won-dering why life had seen fit to give her the lesser slice of the cake.

"Oh Leah, I have to work. I'd get so bored staying at home." Rachel's face softened as she looked towards her sister.

"I do it." retorted Leah. "And I certainly don't have time to get bored, what with parties and shopping and ... oh!...." Leah's cup slipped from her fingers and splashed black coffee over the silk sheets. Rachel ran straight to the en-suite bathroom, grabbed a towel and began mopping up the coffee, hoping to prevent stain-ing the expensive silk sheets.

Leah snatched the towel away angrily. "For goodness sake! Even if you must be a working girl in London, you are not one here—we have servants to do that." She lifted the receiver by her bed.

"Blanche, there's coffee on these sheets, bring some new ones up. Now-immediately." The phone slammed down on its receiver.

"Honestly, what does Father pay these girls for?

Rachel sighed—her sister could be hard work at times. She knew Leah was resentful but could never really understand why. She lived in the lap of luxury and could have anything she want-ed and yet nothing seemed to be enough.

She continued to brush her hair, and her thoughts wandered to the small office in Byron Street where she worked as the per-sonal assistant to David Landers. He ran a small entertainment agency—one of many in the popular Soho area..Working in a small office might not be everyone's idea of fun, but she enjoyed being close to the people who worked there. They were real people, with homes and families. They travelled in on the Underground and laughed about ordinary, everyday things. The reasons she liked working there so much was probably because she had been brought up surrounded by 'big business' and wealth, and the agency added a little light relief to her life. She had never felt drawn to the hustle and bustle of her father's corporation, and even though Laban Monklaast had tried everything he knew to persuade Rachel to work for him, she always refused. He knew she would be a prize—even if all she did was decorate the office with her stunning looks! The fact that she was actually a hard-working, efficient PA just added to the frustration of her endless refusals to join him.

"I love you Daddy," she would say, smiling at him, "but you have hundreds of very clever people working for you already, and I can't see why you should want me. You know you can call if you really need me, but other than that–I am needed at the agency."

"The 'agency'—pah!" Laban tried to look upset with his daughter but failed, "That is no agency. It is a speck in a tiny complex in Soho—and what famous names do you have? Who can you boast of on your books—huh?"

It was true, there were no enormously famous people listed at Landers Entertainment Agency–but that, as she kept insisting, was the whole point. Landers existed to search out hidden talent and set people on the road to success, and once they were well-known they were usually snapped up by the larger agencies.

"It's a pointless argument Daddy," she laughed tossing her hair, "and anyway, Leah would help ..."

Here the conversation usually stopped. Leah would not help. She considered herself far above the menial tasks of 'the office' and only ever helped out when there was something in it for her— as when the current England goalkeeper graced them with a interview and press reception. She was there then. Cleverly holding onto his arm whenever she thought people were about to take a photograph; always asking questions by whispering in his ear so that people thought they were 'close'. It was this kind of behaviour that had made her father vow never to use her again, but it wasn't easy, the press were always snooping around, asking things like 'Why haven't we seen Monklaast's daughter around lately? Where is she? Is there a story here?' Laban had to be very careful. Newspaper reporters could quickly jump to conclusions. The press were as much a headache as they were a prize.

Rachel's thoughts were cut short when Leah suddenly sat up in bed and drew up her legs. Clasping her hands around her knees she said: "Daddy's trying to get Elliott Blaze."

Rachel whirled round in surprise. "Elliot Blaze? Wow!" she smiled delightedly. Blaze was one of the biggest names in the film industry at the time. He had classic good looks, the 'Greek god' type, all sun tan, blond hair and muscles—his photos and posters where everywhere.

He was famous for his breath-taking thrillers, where he spent the whole time rescuing dazzling women—with long flowing locks and bodies like Venus—without ever getting a hair out of place himself, but usually with an indecent amount of sweat falling from his face, onto his perfect body. That's all any fan wanted, and the producer made sure they got plenty!

Unfortunately, he was also famous for being the most obnoxious character ever, off-screen. He had never given an interview without walking off in disgust, in fact he had hardly ever given an interview at all. So for Laban to land him on MBC would be the catch of the year. Although the interview would be on radio, it would come hand in hand with a magnificent press reception—the stops would be pulled out on this one. There would be photos in every possible newspaper the following day and the publicity for MBC would be enormous.

"How near is he to succeeding?" Rachel asked.

Leah hugged her knees again and gave her a knowing look that actually meant she knew nothing.

"Well," she replied with an air of importance. "All I know is that Father has asked me to keep my diary free over the next month—and the name Elliott Blaze was mentioned."

She lay back on her luxurious feather pillows and looked up at the ceiling.

"What a catch!" she sighed and looked over to Rachel. "Pity you're so involved with your little office."

Her sister laughed at her fondly. "Honestly Leah, I do believe you are already planning the honeymoon! Give the man a break, he hasn't even agreed yet!"

"Ah but he will," replied Leah. "He will, our father can be very persuasive."

Sometimes Rachel worried about her sister. It seemed that she was determined to get married, and she didn't seem too particular who to! There had been a few near misses in her life—one, an executive, and another a rock star. The executive had been using her to get to her father's business and the rock star turned out to be already married. So, now in her mid-twenties she was starting to worry, and worse still, she was frightened of Rachel getting married before her. There was always a stigma attached to the youngest getting married first.

"I hear Elliot is getting bored with being single," Leah remarked.

Rachel giggled. "Honestly Leah, you're the end, you really are!"

Her sister threw back the covers and slipped out of the bed. She put on a midnight blue silk dressing gown and pushed her toes into small leather slippers. Wandering over to one of the three vast mirrored wardrobes in her room, she selected a Chanel suit in cerise and a severe blouse which didn't quite match.

"Want to try my cashmere with that?" smiled Rachel. She was trying hard to be diplomatic. "It's definitely more your colour than mine."

"I really don't see myself as the fluffy jumper type", retorted Leah as she swung into her dressing room.

Rachel turned back and carried on with her make-up. They had a strange relationship. Ever since they were very young they liked to be in each other's rooms; even though they had always been given superb single bedrooms, they spent most of their time getting dressed and made up in the same one. They loved to discuss things together and share each other's secrets—and yet there was always a strain, this underlying jealousy of Leah's that overshadowed the fun and laughter of being sisters.

There was a small knock on the door and Blanche came in with a pile of new sheets. She looked slightly agitated, but smiled on seeing Rachel in the room.

"Come in Blanche, how are you today?" Rachel's voice always had a lilt of happiness in it.

The maid put the sheets down on the bed. "Not too bad Miss Rachel. You're looking lovely today—just like your mother if you don't mind me saying so." She swept the coffee-stained sheets off the bed.

Rachel's eyes misted over at the thought of her mother. She seemed so young to be taken away from them, when they both still needed her so much. If her mother had been here now, Rachel could have talked to her about Leah and this obsession with getting married. She looked towards the ceiling and sighed. If there was a heaven—and she truly believed there was—then her mother was surely up there waiting for them.

Leah appeared from the dressing room and frowned at Blanche. "Well that's a bit late isn't it? I'm up now, so you might as well wait until you come to tidy the room. Off you go. Shoo!"

Blanche looked down at the floor and couldn't trust herself to say anything. She brushed past them both and quietly closed the door behind her.

Rachel sighed knowing there was no point in saying anything. She picked up a light cotton jacket from the back of a chair.

"Well, I'm off to my dreary little office," she joked, "So I'll be back later tonight. Have a nice time shopping."

She hurried downstairs and along the hallway to find the maid.

Blanche was furiously stuffing dirty sheets into a linen basket

as Rachel came up behind her. "Don't take any notice Blanche. You
know she doesn't mean it—she's just not very good with people
that's all." Rachel patted her shoulder and continued down the
hall and out of the house.

Meanwhile Leah finished dressing, she looked ready to kill,
dolled up to the nines and ready for adventure. Unfortunately, the
truth was ... she had nothing to do, although she would never ever
admit that to Rachel, especially after their chat this morning.

Her mind went back to the conversation with her sister about
Elliott Blaze. If he was really going to be her father's guest at MBC
it was time to get her act together! Maybe she should phone her
father and offer her services, before he had the chance to ask
Rachel.

She strolled back over to the bedside cabinet and picked up
the phone.

CHAPTER

2

The Monklaast Broadcasting Corporation was a huge important-looking complex in the centre of London. Walking past it, you'd be forgiven for thinking it was a large hotel. Its old stone walls rose solidly out of the West End and never failed to impress. The forbidding entrance was fronted by two uniformed doormen who gave the impression they were guarding the Crown jewels—but to be entrusted with the welfare of MBC was an equally weighty responsibility. No one got into the building without identification or permission, and even then they would only reach reception.

The vast area just inside the entrance was the domain of a battery of receptionists, porters, and security. On one side was a huge curved desk, an arc of marble which all visitors had to confront. There were four different-coloured phones, plus switchboards and computers, all furiously at work under the fingers of four receptionists. It was their job to sort out who was who—who could be pointed to the various lifts and who had to wait where they were for 'someone to come and fetch them'.

The waiting area was sparsely furnished with a few comfortable chairs and just one low table scattered with radio and media magazines. The idea, according to the designer, was to give the impression that you were only going to sit there for a few minutes, a technique which soon got rid of 'hangers-on' who quickly lost interest after they had sat around for half an hour. Thus the assortment of people waiting at reception was always a strange mixture. It usually included one or two journalists who had dubious 'appointments' to see certain producers or programme presenters; also three of four 'pluggers' from various record companies who were waiting to convince anyone who would listen that they had the next number one two weeks before its release date—especially for MBC. There was usually a glamorous-looking girl whom nobody could quite place or work out exactly why she was there. And then of course there would be some legitimate visitors, such as a fairly well-known star who was about to give an interview on one of the various chat shows—(such as David Wills' show, if they were lucky). The star would be accompanied by an agent or a manager and usually a young secretary.

In fact, this was just an ordinary day at MBC, and on the eighth floor Laban Monklaast was listening to a list of messages being competently read by his PA, Henry. Henry was actually a 45-year-old woman whose real name, Henrietta, had always irritated her. She was small and slim with immaculately coiffured blonde hair and she always wore smart, understated clothes. Her reasoning behind this was that although she was involved in some very big business deals, her job was to be invisibly in the background, picking up on any important details and storing them in her laptop computer. Then, later when Laban had forgotten the logistics of the deal, Henry would reel them off in a matter-of-fact way that made him feel he hadn't missed out on anything of great importance.

Henry's office was almost as large as Laban's, but where as his was filled with highly polished leather furniture, top of the range video and audio stacks, and a well-stocked drinks cabinet, hers was a mass of equipment—fax machines, computers and phone lines.

A brisk knock on the PA's door was quickly followed by the appearance of a wide smile, on the face of a very confident man.

"Hi Henry! How's my favourite blonde?"

This was David Wills. He was a law unto himself and managed to get away with it by being the most genuine person you were liable to meet. There was no malice or suggestiveness in his comment about his 'favourite blonde'—he was just being himself, a 35-year-old guy with the road to greater success stretched out before him, and a great admiration for the way Henry kept the Corporation under control.

Henry looked over to where David stood adjusting his tie, head bowed. His mid-brown hair was handsomely shiny, cut very short at the back but longer at the front. He struggled with his tie, (knowing that Laban paid attention to detail) and failed miserably. Henry arched an eyebrow and came to the rescue. No wonder she always found it hard not to mother him.

"Early as always David—I suppose that means you'd like something to drink." Without waiting for an answer, she turned to the filter machine that provided a constant supply of fresh coffee and poured him a large steaming cup, adding just the amount of cream he liked. David sat on the corner of her desk and picked up the cup.

"Any idea what this meeting's about?" he asked. "I hear that quite a few heads of department are involved. Come on Henry, what's going on?"

Henrietta smiled and sorted through a file on her desk.

"Now you know better than to ask me a question like that! I'm sure Mr Monklaast has his reasons for not telling you beforehand."

David laughed. He did know better—but it was always fun to try. As they carried on talking, Henry's office gradually filled with people. A meeting of heads of department was always quite volatile, since they were all so different—they had to be to do their jobs. Programme controller James Ledbury was a serious plodding type. He always felt that it was his sole duty to avoid the words 'new' and 'change'. This actually worked to his advantage, because the only 'new and innovative' things that got past him, were nearly always worthwhile and enhanced the image and reputation of MBC. So although one often felt that talking to James was like walking through treacle, the end results were worth the hassle.

In contrast trying to work with someone like Jane Hunter, press and PR, was more of a wrestling match that nobody won. Jane was fiercely possessive of her position and of the stars she publicised. Her red hair and explosive personality were well-known around Fleet Street, but one had to admit, she was very good at her job. That's the way Laban picked them.

Also present was Simon Darrell, marketing manager, characteristically wearing his Armani suit as an outshowing of the kind of success 'we at MBC' are used to. His goal in life was to be so good at his job that he became indispensable, and along with that came the company car, the 'on location' assignments and the trips abroad to 'see how the other broadcasting stations were doing'.

"Hi David!" He slapped their number one presenter on the back. They were old friends, having started at MBC in the same month more than eight years before. Simon had then been on Research and David started as a sound engineer. That was another of the good things about Laban Monklaast—when he saw talent he moved in quickly.

By now, Jeremy Sargeant, head of stations, had also arrived, mincing his way through the small group with that theatrical style he kept from his days 'on the boards'.

The only person still to arrive was the new boy. Laban had just taken on new talent in the person of Aaron Holloway. He was a DJ, young, fresh and a little naïve. Monklaast had decided to introduce Aaron to the team this morning, as well as talk to them about the visit of Elliott Blaze.

Aaron arrived, he looked around the office with his wide eyes—this wasn't the kind of thing he was used to. He had been spotted while working on a small local radio station where he was used to playing the records and making his own coffee, and now, all of a sudden, there were people to see to his every need.

Aaron was quite unconscious of the effect created by his handsome face, and the honey-coloured hair that fell so appealingly into his serious eyes, making him blink and push it away. As far as he was concerned he loved music and had the right voice for radio, so his looks could be of little interest to his listeners. (The talent scout who found him thought differently, and sang his praises to Laban. They would be sitting on a goldmine, he said!)

When Henry turned and saw Aaron making his way into the room, she came straight over to him. She was well aware of how newcomers felt entering this vast set-up.

"Hello Aaron, my name's Henry. We met the other day with Jonathan and Mr Monklaast." She smiled at him.

Aaron felt very relieved to have someone to talk to and his face lit up as he smiled.

"Yes, right, Henry. Phew, it's a bit of a place this, isn't it? I can just about work out which floor I'm on!" He relaxed a little and laughed, revealing immediately the potential that Jonathan had seen. This young man was going places!

"Would you like me to introduce you to a few of these people? They're quite nice once you get to know them." Henry waved to Simon Darrell and soon the pair of them were chatting away like old friends.

The large panelled door to the main office opened and Laban Monklaast stood surveying his staff. Almost as one, they turned and acknowledged him. The atmosphere quietly melted into one of great respect as they made their way through to the luxurious apartment that was Laban's office.

Mr Monklaast was a most compelling figure—a tall man, with silver hair, white moustache, a constantly healthy tanned complexion and grey/blue eyes that missed nothing. His expressive hands waved them to their seats around a large board table. In most offices, a board table would be a hard thing to miss, but Laban's office was so vast, that it seemed to occupy only a small corner of the room.

"Gentlemen ... and ladies (he nodded towards Jane) please be seated."

The team duly drew chairs from the table and sat down with their files and laptops in front of them. Aaron looked around anxiously. He had brought nothing.

Laban stood up and began the proceedings straight away.

"As many of you are aware, we have a new member—a very important member—joining MBC today." He smiled benevolently across to where Aaron was sitting. The rest turned to stare, some with a smile of acknowledgement and Jeremy with his usual curt nod, in Aaron's direction.

"Aaron Holloway," continued Laban, "will be joining us as from today and will be on the air in a couple of weeks. He will be joining our pop station 'Chart MBC'. We are expecting great things of him, and I'm sure he won't let us down."

Aaron laughed and pushed his hair out of his eyes. "I'll do what I can. I'm really looking forward to it."

Immediately the marketing and publicity heads noted his beautiful radio voice—a natural, and with that face—so photogenic, they were going to have to start on him straight away.

A rush of questions ensued and Laban had to hold up his hands to stop the flow.

"All right friends, I realise that you see the same great potential that I saw, but right now I have asked Aaron to join us because I have an announcement to make that will concern him as well as the rest of us."

He had their undivided attention. There was a scuffle as notebooks opened and many electronic beeps as the computers came to life.

Laban waited for silence and then continued slowly and precisely. "MBC has once again come through where others have failed." He looked around the table. "We have managed to sign and seal two 'on the air' live interviews, plus a major press reception with ... Elliott Blaze."

There was an astonishing gasp. This of course was not possible. Elliott Blaze would never give an interview, and definitely not 'live'. Simon Darrell's heart began to race, he knew people that would literally sell all to get a scoop like this. It would be worth millions in advertising, in features, in fact his mind couldn't cope with all the possibilities. He would probably have to get extra temporary staff.

Jane Hunter was already preparing her first press release. She would keep so close to him that no one would get a word out of him without her say so. (And actually keeping close to Elliott Blaze was an extremely attractive thought...!)

Laban brought their attention back to himself by waving a sheaf of papers in the air. "Everything you want to know for the time being is here in this paper. I want you to read it thoroughly —it contains the dates that Mr Blaze will be with us and a rough itinerary of expected events. You have just two days to come up with any proposals and I will need rough drafts from you all. That's it."

It was a very short meeting, but everyone understood the urgency of shooting straight back to their departments and getting started. Well, all except Aaron Holloway.

Laban went over to him and patted his back.

"Welcome to the firm, Aaron. I'm sure you are going to make a great impact. Young life, new blood, it's just what we need."

Aaron grinned, he liked this old man. "Thanks a lot. I can't wait to get going. There's just one thing I don't understand at the moment, though..." he faltered.

"What's that?" asked his boss.

"Why you wanted me in on this meeting about Elliott Blaze? I mean, he's hardly likely to grace the turntables of 'Chart MBC' is he?" He laughed at the thought.

Laban pulled at his moustache and looked down at this young eager face.

"Aaron, we think you are going to be big. We even think you might pull MBC's chart station back to the number one spot where it belongs. So what better way to start, than to have a complete mega-star on your show within a couple of weeks of your arrival?" The boy went to protest. "Think of it, from local radio to the country's most popular DJ! You are a class interviewer Aaron—we wouldn't give you the chance if we thought you couldn't do it."

Laban went to walk away, but the young DJ caught hold of his jacket. "You really mean this, don't you?" His eyes were at their widest, like huge smudged stars.

"This is your chance, Aaron," was all Laban said.

Aaron Holloway walked back through the door into Henry's office. He was so stunned that he didn't notice David Wills pick up his files and walk out behind him. He had been offered fame and fortune on a plate, and he was genuinely thrilled. He leapt up and punched his fists in the air.

"Yes!!" he yelled, much to the surprise of Henrietta who wasn't used to that kind of thing.

"Excuse me." A sombre voice spoke almost to the back of his neck. It was David Wills. Aaron whirled round in surprise.

"Oh, sorry. Hey, Mr Wills is there any chance I could get together with you sometime? I really could do with a lot of advice right now—and you're the best thing going."

Once again Aaron was just being himself and David looked at him with raised eyebrows. Was he being sarcastic? He had just been given Elliott Blaze as his first ever interview! But then looking at the eager face once more, he decided this young guy was actually on the level.

"Of course. I'm in room 7001 most of the time. Come up whenever you want." It was hard to be generous in the face of what could be opposition, but there was something about the boy that reminded him of himself.

Once all the fuss was over and everyone had departed from 'Upstairs' as it was generally known, Henrietta poured out two coffees, one for her boss and one for herself. If she had been the type, this is when she would have put her feet on the desk and lit up a cigarette; however being Henry, she just sipped her coffee and stared out of the window for a few minutes. This visit with Elliott Blaze was going to generate a lot of work, and if she wasn't much mistaken, a lot of cat and dog fights too.

"Well, that's certainly stirred them up!" Laban walked through and smiled appreciatively at his steaming coffee.

"They'll have their work cut out, Laban." Henry only called him this when there was no one else around—it didn't sound very businesslike in front of the staff.

"I know, that's why I'm working on a few plans," replied Laban.

'A few plans' in Laban's book could sometimes mean rearranging the whole organisation. Henry looked interested. "What have you in mind?" she asked.

"I need someone to look after Elliott while he's in our care, and I think if I gave him to Jane Hunter, she'd eat him alive! Anyway she will have more than enough to do keeping the press at bay. No, I need someone who will look after him graciously, show him around the town and take him to lunch now and again ..."

Henry cut in, "She won't do it, Laban, you know she won't."

Laban looked at his secretary with frustration. "Why are you always three steps ahead of me, Henrietta?"

"That's what you pay me for, sir!" she replied, laughing at him. "And your next question is going to be: 'can you persuade her?'

Really Laban, Rachel is a wonderful person, but she does have her own life to lead. And her own job, come to that".

"But this time I really do need her. And not only that, I have to find someone else. This is going to be a big job and I've been thinking for some time of creating a new position in the company. 'Liaison Officer' ... what do you think?" asked Laban.

"Job description?" enquired Henry with her pen poised.

Laban rubbed his chin. "Hmm ... I want someone who can communicate between all my departments. He needs to have his finger on the pulse all the time, so that he knows at any given moment what any department is up to. We've had a few *faux pas* in the past, with publicity doing one thing and press doing another—we can't afford to get it wrong with this one."

"That sounds like a highly paid job," replied Henry.

"To the right man ... it would be," said Laban slowly, his mind far away.

Henry looked closely at her boss. "You keep saying 'man', as if you already have someone in mind."

"You know me, Henry. I'll just keep praying about it!" Laban had a secretive look on his face. His PA always marvelled at the character of this man. He could hold the company together, wheel and deal with the best, and keep a fervent belief in God at the same time. She shook her head at the thought."

"All right, you're the boss," she replied. "But since you are feeling strong in your faith at the moment, how about me getting Rachel on the line, and you talking to her—Mmm?"

CHAPTER

3

Walking down Old Compton Street, Rachel always felt free. The sights and sounds of Soho were so alien to the rest of her life. Here, the hustle and bustle made you feel alive. There was still some camaraderie left between cafe owners and local tramps, between prostitutes and the regular office clerks. Although their trades were entirely different, each would still look out for the other. As she walked, she spied a bundle in a doorway.

"Morning Betty." Rachel stopped to talk to the lady.

"'M'ungry s'mornin," muttered the vagabond. Her grey hair was matted beyond control and she hugged an old blanket to herself.

"OK, I'll get you something. See you in a few minutes." Rachel wandered over to a local sandwich bar and purchased some hot food in a plastic container. It was pitiably sad that Betty wouldn't accept any help. Rachel had spent a considerable amount of time trying to persuade the old lady to seek some proper shelter, but she was terribly stubborn. Betty had been an entertainer in the theatre in the old days and when she grew too old to dance and sing, she just took to the streets. The only thing she ever asked for was food (she knew money would go straight on wine) and old copies of magazines with 'film stars in 'em'.

Everyone knew Betty, but there was only so much you could do for her.

After giving her some breakfast, Rachel walked on and turned into Byron Street. The small side street was already busy. The Landers Entertainment Agency was on the first floor, so she had to pick her way through an untidy stairway belonging to the out-fitters downstairs to get to her office. The glass door of the agency had the regular kind of gold lettering on it that you would expect from the entertainment world, but inside it was very comfortable. There were only three rooms, one of which she shared with Dean the talent scout and Sarah the secretary.

Dean was a good friend to Rachel and she very much liked sit-ting in the office hearing his tales of the disastrous acts he had sat through the night before. She often thought he should be on the stage himself—he had a likeable face, not handsome, but full of character; the kind of guy you laughed at even before he told the joke, because you knew what was coming anyway!

Sarah did just about everything else—made the tea, typed the letters, answered the phone and handled the artists. Because it was such a small company, it was necessary for everyone to know how everything worked. This was great for Rachel who realised that in the end, a company was a company, and ran the same way whether there were four people in it like Landers, or thousands as in her father's international company.

Rachel's title at Landers was Personal Assistant to David. It was a job she loved as David was more than generous in giving her a free hand to make decisions when he was away. It was a real reason for living. Back at home, life was almost surreal, for as Leah had pointed out, she didn't have to work, didn't have to lift a finger. What then? Leah was extremely keen on finding some rich influential guy to marry—but for Rachel, that would not be enough. She had often wondered if she would marry; she was cer-tainly not short of boyfriends—or offers, come to that. But Rachel treasured in her heart the thought that maybe there really was someone especially for her. Leah seemed to be ready to marry anyone at the drop of a hat, but Rachel knew she needed much, much more.

Maybe marriage would be enough, if this one person in her life really existed. She sighed as she entered the office and took her jacket off ready for work.

"That was a big sigh," remarked Sarah, already typing furiously and glaring at the computer screen.

Rachel shrugged and laughed. "Oh, you know how it goes. Sorry I'm a bit late today, I just saw Betty and went to get her some breakfast. She's looking very hollow, you know."

"Oh, she's OK." muttered Sarah, still looking at the screen. "But you know there's no need for you to get in early ... the entertainment business is rarely awake before eleven."

This was a fact. She knew plenty of people in the music business and most of them started work around ten in the morning. Of course the music industry didn't sleep in the evenings either, so although it was often a late start, it invariably dragged on until the evening.

"By the way," Sarah looked at her notepad. "Your dad rang."

Rachels' eyebrows drew together. "Did he say what it was about?"

"Nope. Just that he needs to talk to you, so can you ring him back?"

"Did it sound urgent, Sarah?" Rachel asked the secretary.

"Couldn't really say ... more like a favour if you ask me. You know, he was sounding really nice as if he wanted you to do something for him." Sarah was pleased with her detective work.

Rachel's hand went to the phone on her desk, although she had not yet sat down. Before she could make the call, Dean came flying into the office. He flung his coat over one of the reception chairs and threw a load of papers onto the coffee table. Thrusting a mug under the coffee machine and adding two sugars, he made his way over to the mirror where he patted his own face and told himself what a handsome devil he was.

"Morning, fans!" he turned to face them both. His comical expression and his out-of-control wavy hair made them both laugh immediately. He threw himself in a chair and put his legs up on the corner of Sarah's desk.

"Hey, listen!" he said, as if he were about to let them in on a big secret. "I went to Tony's last night. You know his new club The Closed Door? What a scream! He was trying to introduce the first act, when this rabbit—honestly, a real rabbit—ran out on the stage! Nobody knows what it was doing there—it must have belonged to a magician or something from a previous night! Anyway it ran round the mike stands, behind a set of drums—and the girl who was supposed to be singing wouldn't come out till they'd caught it! Oh, it was brilliant!" He grinned.

The girls were laughing loudly, not so much at the situation, but at the way he told the story and mimicked the actions of Tony and the rabbit.

"Anyway," he continued, "the girl was pretty useless after all—but I booked the rabbit an appointment for three o'clock this afternoon!" He thumped his fist on Rachel's desk as he reached his punch line.

"Really Dean, you're terrible!" Rachel began to giggle again.

"Oh well, while you're in a good mood, I suppose there's still no chance you'll marry me is there?" he countered with a quizzical expression on his face.

Rachel decided to snub him cheerfully and went for the phone again.

"Important call," she explained, waiting for MBC to answer.

"Drat! Another one bites the dust!" He glanced at Sarah, and pointed towards the door. "Is the great white chief in?"

Sarah nodded and Dean went through into the other office.

Meanwhile Rachel had got through to Henry, and finally to her father.

Sarah sat listening to a one-sided conversation.

"Daddy, I already have a job ... Yes I know ... What about Leah? ... That important? ... Who? ... Oh yes, of course I've heard of him ... How much time will this take? ... Oh Daddy ... yes, yes. All right, I'll see what he says ... yes, bye ... I love you too ... bye." Rachel sighed as she put the phone down.

"Full of sighs today," remarked Sarah, dying to know what was going on.

"My father wants me to work for him for a week starting in two weeks," she explained. "The trouble is, I actually think he does need me this time. He sounded quite desperate and it's a big scoop for him, don't want to let him down."

She toyed with a pen and started to scribble on a diary. "I suppose David would give me the time off. He's always insisted that I shouldn't neglect MBC if Daddy needs me."

Sarah interrupted her spoken thoughts. "What's so special? What's the scoop?" she leaned over her desk in anticipation.

"Oh, Elliott Blaze is coming over to do some interviews and press conferences." Secretly, it was more the fact of having to work with him that put her off. She had heard that he could be very arrogant and crude, despite his fabulous looks and successful films.

"Elliott Blaze!!" cried Sarah, jumping out of her typist's chair. "Rachel, why does it always happen to you? Does your dad need a secretary? A floor sweeper? Anything! Did you see his last film? I thought I'd die when he looked at her and said, 'Anywhere, as long as I'm with you.' Just imagine him saying that to you!"

Rachel waved her hands frantically to try and calm the secretary down. "Whoa, whoa ... this will be strictly business. The last thing I need right now is an involvement with someone like him! Anyway, it's a few weeks away yet so I think I'd better get some work done here first."

The rest of the day went smoothly enough. David Landers was

happy to let Rachel have a week off to help out at MBC. He appreciated the fact that Rachel worked for him at all, and could never really understand why she did. She was a marvellous person—he and his wife had met her socially on a number of occasions and she was always perfect. She was courteous, considerate, warm and relaxed. The nicest compliment she had been paid had come from Mrs Landers when she reached out her hand to Rachel as they left a theatre, and said 'You know dear, I'd even trust you with my husband!'

*   *   *

Rachel and Leah hadn't see each other for five days, as Rachel had been working late most nights at Landers and therefore staying at her father's apartment in London.

Although it was good to get back to Monks Lodge, sometimes it was just not possible, so Laban had purchased a wonderful apartment overlooking Hyde Park, with enough room for all the family to live there without getting in each other's way. Laban also had a small flat at MBC which he used when he wanted to stay even nearer to work—like the time the news broke on the Gulf War: there was really no way he could be out of the building when the news bulletins were coming in fast and furious all night long.

But tonight Rachel arrived home to be met by a sister who had been bored out of her mind for the past week, although of course Leah had no intention of letting Rachel know that.

A delighted Blanche opened the door as she heard Rachel's car purr up the driveway; life with just Leah for company was very heavy going for the maid.

"Good evening Blanche. Ooh—it's nice to be home! Is Leah in this evening ... or out on one of her social whirls?"

Blanche bit back the retort that Leah had hardly left the house and had been roaming around like a bear with a sore head. "I do believe she is in tonight, Miss. Would you like a light supper, or a full evening meal?" Blanche knew the cook would be happy to provide either for their favourite girl.

"Oh, something light would be wonderful. I seem to spend half of my life having very heavy meals with managers and agents at the moment." She waltzed past the maid and ran lightly up the stairs, hoping to catch Leah in her room.

They met on the landing. Leah had heard Rachel's car arrive and was determined to look unmoved about it. She also overheard the short conversation about lunching with managers and agents and was envious of Rachel's life.

"Leah!" Rachel's instinctively threw her arms around her sister. "It seems ages since I was home. You're not going out are you? I was hoping we could have a girls' night in." She was still holding on to her sister.

Leah shrugged her off, and examined her Cartier watch. "Well ... I was going to meet ... Oh never mind, I'll give him a ring and cancel. The stupid boy is crazy about me, so he can wait a night," she said.

Rachel grinned widely. "Great! I'll just slip into the bedroom and change. Blanche is sorting out supper for us."

Leah went downstairs and picked up the phone in the hall, but as soon as Rachel was out of sight, she put the phone back on its cradle again. Of course the 'stupid boy' didn't exist.

In a very short time Rachel was back down in the lounge, looking like a million dollars. In fact, all she had done was freshen up her make up a little and change into a pale blue shirt that hung over the top of well-cut trousers. She looked cool and relaxed, and was looking forward to eating food from a tray on her lap, and catching up with the news from her sister.

"Not dressing for dinner then?" was Leah's first remark.

Rachel took no offence, but understood her sister to mean that she was thinking of eating in the dining room.

"Oh no. Come on Leah, let's eat in here. It's so much more cosy and besides I want to chat."

Blanche arrived pushing a trolley laden with mouth-watering dishes. The silver salvers offered fresh salmon, wafer thin smoked ham, the cook's own pâté, prawns in home-made mayonnaise and every possible combination of salads and bread to go with it. It looked delicious and Rachel wasted no time telling the maid so.

"Wonderful Blanche! Do thank Mrs Hamilton for doing so much at such short notice!" She began to spoon the prawns onto a piece of home made bread, making an open sandwich.

Leah shot the maid a glance, and pointed at the trolley.

"Tell Mrs Hamilton I'll have a steak, medium rare," she barked. "I suppose I can eat some of this green stuff with it." She waved her hand as if to send Blanche back to her quarters.

Once again, Rachel did not take the bait. She cheerfully munched her sandwich and commented, "If I had another steak I'd look like one! Oh, these prawns are beautiful."

At the back of her mind, Rachel knew she had to approach the subject of Elliott Blaze. Her father had told her on the phone that he didn't want Leah involved to any great extent, but Rachel remembered her sister's comments about how she was hoping to be at the forefront. She was going to have to be very diplomatic about this. She curled up in the armchair, balancing her plate on her knees. This was not going to be easy.

She approached the subject carefully. "Still happy staying at home then Leah? We're so different, aren't we? I mean, I really enjoy my work and you really enjoy the social scene."

Leah gave her sister a sideways glance. What was that supposed to mean? Had someone told her sister that her 'social scene' was one big yawn? "Anything is better than working in an office," she retorted.

Rachel shifted uncomfortably in her chair. "Daddy phoned me at work today," she began casually.

Leah's steak arrived and her sister became preoccupied with barking instructions at Blanche.

"No, no! Not all over the plate, put the salad just here!—So," she paused, "what did he want?" Leah did not look up at Rachel, but started to cut the steak up into tiny pieces and then proceeded to eat it with a fork 'American style'. (Something she had learnt from yet another rich Texan who only stayed long enough to love her and leave her.)

"Well, you know how busy he gets at times. It seems he needs a helping hand for a week, soon, and he managed to persuade both me and David Landers that I could be spared for a short time." She waited for a comment from Leah, but her sister just carried on enjoying her steak and nodding in Rachel's general direction.

So Rachel continued while she was winning ... "It will be fun to work at MBC. I hear they have a new DJ, Aaron Holloway. Apparently he's going to be a new teenage sensation—that is, he's not a teenager himself, but the publicity office think he'll be on posters on every girl's wall by the end of next month!"

She was waffling—she knew that, waiting for her sister to ask the fatal question, but Leah just looked up with a sneer and said, "Aaron. Sounds too young for me. I suppose he's another pretty-faced guy that everyone wants to mother."

"I don't know," replied Rachel. "I haven't seen him yet, but Daddy seems to be pretty impressed, not just with his looks but his ability as a presenter. He's giving him some enormously responsible interviews within a few weeks of the show going on the air."

"So what's your part in all this?" Leah asked. "Has Father asked you to 'wet nurse' him till he knows the ropes—or have you just got to keep the millions of fans at bay?" She could be so flippant and sarcastic when she wanted to, and belittling anything Rachel did was becoming something of a hobby.

Rachel pressed her lips together and wondered how to tell her
sister the truth. She put her plate down on the coffee table and
laid her hands in her lap.

"I'm not there to work with Aaron—well not really, although
he will come into it." ('I'm waffling again,' she thought.) "Daddy
needs someone to help show Eliott Blaze around. They thought
of taking on extra staff, but Daddy thought it would be better if it
was someone he already knew. Anyway it's only for a week and
then I'll be back in my little office again." She spoke quickly,
trying not to give Leah any chance to interrupt before she'd
finished.

There was a silence. When Rachel looked up, she saw rage in
her sister's eyes.

"Rachel, how could you?" Leah's fury sent her tray crashing
to the floor, scattering plates and food all over the carpet.

Rachel said nothing. She knew she had to give her sister time
to calm down before she could ever hope to talk this through with
her.

Leah strode over to the window and stood staring out at nothing. Her arms were held tightly at her side and her fists were
white. She stared hard and willed the tears not to fill her eyes.
Why did this always happen? Why was life so damned unfair? She
pushed back the answers that clouded her mind—the thoughts of
how she was always the one to hit back, the one with the sarcastic replies ... She felt her sister's hand fall lightly on her shoulder.

"I'm sorry Leah, I am really. It wasn't my idea." Rachel knew
this was of no comfort to her sister, but she just couldn't think of
anything else to say."

Leah shrugged Rachel's hand away and moved to the other
side of the room. She swung round violently.

"He knew, Rachel! Father knew how much I wanted a piece of
that action! Why did he do it, huh? Why did he ask you and not
me!" To her annoyance, Leah found herself hanging her head like

a little girl who'd had her favourite toy taken away from her for being naughty.

Rachel moved over to where her sister stood, took her hand gently and guided her back to the sofa. Her heart went out to Leah. It wasn't her fault—they were just so very different. She sat her down and looked at her.

"Leah, I really am sorry. Do you want me to talk to Daddy and persuade him to let you do it instead? I know you like this Elliott character and I don't particularly fancy the job at all ..." This all sounded a bit pathetic. "Leah?"

Leah's thin lips drew to a straight line and determination took over.

"No, Rachel. You go ahead. I've heard he's murder to work with anyway ... I've ... er ... other things to do, as it happens. Excuse me." And with that, Leah walked out of the room, head held high. Life could only kick you down so many times before you had to take revenge. And that was the word at the top of her agenda.

Someday, she would have her revenge.

CHAPTER

4

The phone rang abruptly on Henry's desk. She was just about to leave for a lunch date and frowned at it, as if to make it go away. It rang persistently, even though the receptionist had been told to hold all calls until 2 p.m. Henry sighed and walked back to the offending phone.

"Mr Monklaast's office. Henrietta speaking." She tried not to sound too resigned. A very official female American voice cut through on the line.

"I need to talk to Laban Monklaast, like now!" it said.

"I'm afraid he's at lunch. I'm his personal assistant, can I help at all?" Henry sat down and grabbed a notepad.

"OK. This is Julie Redwing here, secretary to Elliott Blaze." The voice was changing now from the official 'get out of my way' attitude to 'secretary to secretary' mode. "We have a slight problem here. Mr Blaze is insisting on flying over tomorrow to meet Mr Monklaast. He wants to get the feel of the place and talk over a few details regarding press and general publicity."

Henry was aghast—their special guest arriving the next day. A thousand thoughts raced through her head.

Julie continued. "He will only stay for one night and will want the full co-operation of your organisation. It is to be a low-key meeting, with the absolute minimum of staff in the know. Are you with me?" she asked.

"I am," replied Henry, her shorthand gliding erratically across the paper. "Give me the times of arrival and I will get on to it

immediately." (Why did the American slang catch on so
easily?)

"So you think you can handle it?" Julie's voice was crisp
again, but this was mainly because she was so anxious for everything to go smoothly. Elliott was a real brute to work for and
didn't realise that things don't just happen. Someone has to book
planes and hotels and liaise between different countries.

Henry's mind was on overdrive. "Certainly," she replied with
a confidence she didn't feel at all. "I wonder if you could give me
an hour to filter this through to the right people and then I'll come
straight back to you and discuss the finer details?"

"I'll get back to you," Julie answered. "In one hour, OK?"

The phone went dead and the bedlam began on both sides of
the Atlantic.

*   *   *

The entourage hit the country the next day. A private plane
landed at Gatwick and dispatched Julie Redwing, an official photographer, a minder, a hairdresser, two publicity agents, a manager, a chef and of course Eliott himself, onto the tarmac. This was
as 'low key' as the American star knew how to get!

Laban had sent Henry to meet him with three chauffeured
limousines, and they were just about enough. Elliott Blaze insisted on riding alone, whilst Julie and Henry got to know each other
a little in the car behind. Henry was more than a little worried
about her 'responsibility' riding alone.

"He's always like that—don't worry, honey," assured Julie.
"We'll just make sure we are on his tail the whole time."

Julie Redwing was younger than Henry had expected. She was
in her mid-twenties, very polished with shining auburn hair and a
neat pointed chin. Meticulously made-up, her air of confidence
was astounding and every time she spoke, her hair swung

smoothly just brushing the shoulders of her deep maroon jacket. Dramatic hand gestures and highly polished fingernails completed the picture.

Henry decided she liked her. At least she wasn't some bimbo who would follow the artist around with stars in her eyes, giggling at his least remark.

The cars swept up the motorway and through the busy London streets until they finally parked outside the Dorchester, an hotel which never failed to impress Americans with its fountains and liveried doormen.

Elliott Blaze stayed in the safety of the limo, while his team made their way through the huge doors to the reception area. Naturally they were expected, although Elliott had been checked in as "Edward Blane", to prevent fans finding out. The hotel staff were very used to this kind of event and ran their operation so smoothly that the star was soon ensconced in his apartment without a hitch.

As soon as Elliott Blaze walked into his hotel room he headed for the full-length mirror. Checking his looks was one of his favourite pastimes. Despite the fact that he had just flown across the Atlantic at short notice he looked terrific. His critical eyes took in the reflection of his well-built physique, the tanned skin a startling contrast next to the colour of his blond hair and steely blue eyes. His black shirt, a little too open, showed off taut muscles, absolutely no fat—in fact this guy was in peak condition, he told himself. He raised his arms and put his hands behind his head—it was one of his favourite poses. He glanced amorously at his reflection—God's gift to the movies.

Coming over to England was special to him and he was glad that he had agreed on this deal with MBC. His aides had informed him that Laban Monklaast was the kind of guy he would feel comfortable with—and they were few and far between. Even so, he felt that this extra trip to meet him before they embarked on his biggest British appearance to date, was worthwhile. Blaze loved being a star, but hated the journalists and those pesky TV presenters with their microphones forever in your face. You couldn't breathe without one of them popping up out of nowhere, pushing and shoving and yelling impertinent questions at you all day long. This was how he had built his reputation as the arrogant movie star. It wasn't that he was a pussy cat in real life—far from it—but he had always felt that his public owed him a private life. A life where he could be free to love as many women as he wanted, without the threat of their husbands seeing their faces on the front cover of a magazine the next morning. Well, if you've got it, flaunt it—isn't that what they said?

However, this visit was supposed to be low key, so there would be little or no chance for excitement this time around. Still, there was always Julie, ready to oblige—or was she just too afraid not to? A knock on the door interrupted his thoughts.

"Yeah?" he yelled impatiently. There was always someone knocking on the door or calling on the phone.

It was Julie. She looked great. She had showered and changed and was wearing a short blue skirt with a top that purposely didn't quite meet, showing her midriff tan quite deliciously.

"Hi, Elliott. Everything OK?" She had a sumptuous smile and knew that it worked on him.

"Julie, you look stunning darling," remarked Elliott throwing her a line. "When do we need to meet up with the radio guy?"

"Laban is expecting you in an hour. I've talked with his personal assistant—not your type at all, frumpy blonde—and she will make sure that we are met with the car at three." Julie glanced quickly at her watch. "Do you need to see anyone? Lincoln's busy making phone calls, he said he'll see you in thirty minutes." Lincoln Grey was Elliott's personal manager—short, loud and rather like a mother hen with her chicks. He was forever shooing and clucking people into a corner out of Elliott's way, waving his arms and yelling "OK people, that's enough! Give the guy a break, why don't cha?" He was secretly proud of the fact that he could spot talent a mile away, and Elliott Blaze was the highlight of his career.

"Nah, it's OK, babe, just give me a call a while before we go. I won't need you till then." He looked her coolly up and down"Might need you later though." He gave her a slow wink. Julie smiled and headed for the door. She wished he wouldn't do that—it made her feel so cheap. Being Elliot's secretary was a terrific thing, and she knew that sleeping with him came with the job. She secretly liked him but was well aware that she was nothing more than a convenience to him. On the other hand, she couldn't imagine any woman meaning much more than that to him. There wasn't enough room in Elliott Blaze's life for two people.

Meanwhile, Laban and Henry were working hard to put together something like a schedule for the film star's visit. They were both poring over a timetable on Henry's desk.

"If we can get our press and publicity to meet up with their people then they can put their heads together in here, while we talk with Elliott and his secretary in my office," Laban said thoughtfully. "I don't think there's any need to bring in the rest of the team at the moment. The fewer people know he's in the building the better. Oh, have you managed to reach Rachel yet?" he asked.

"Only just," replied his PA, thrashing through the files in front of her. "She said she will be here as soon as she can."

"What does that mean?" Laban looked worried. "I have to have her here to meet him! Rachel always has such a calming influence on people—I'm relying on her being here."

Henry looked up and Laban and smiled. "Don't worry Laban, she's never let you down before, has she?"

It was nearly three o'clock and the MBC team had arrived at

Henry's office. Jane Hunter, Simon Darrell and James Ledbury were pacing up and down clutching laptops, files and diaries.

"This is really not on!" remarked Jane. She had been working on her strategy for the press and did not like being caught unprepared like this.

Simon, still looking fairly relaxed, slowly shook his head.

"He's a star darling, he can do what he likes. Your job is just to make sure you obey his every command." He quite enjoyed the thought of meeting up with Elliott Blaze before the rest of the world got wind of it.

Henry looked up from the phone and said, "All systems go!" The entourage was on its way up to the eighth floor.

Laban's staff stood around in his vast office while Henry saw to the 'welcome drinks'. One never knew with Americans whether they were all going to ask for mineral water, or some obscure brand of Scotch that nobody had ever heard of—thus the extensive drinks cabinet.

Elliott, Lincoln and Julie arrived together. Laban and Lincoln immediately shook hands and spoke to each other as if they were old friends. They were both more than pleased to have pulled this deal off and felt they knew each other well already from the stream of Transatlantic phone calls. Gradually the teams were introduced to each other and small chit-chat ensued while the drinks were served.

Jane Hunter took her opportunity to study Elliott. Yes, it would definitely be a pleasurable experience working alongside him. As she stared, he looked up and caught her eye;

"Now, I know it's bad manners to forget your name," he said, giving her a long meaningful look.

"Jane," she replied, slightly annoyed that he should forget it so soon. Before she could say anything else, he interrupted.

"Ah yes, Jane. Allow me to introduce myself, I'm Tarzan," he leered at her.

It was such an old joke, one that Jane Hunter was forever hearing but she forced herself to smile, and then carried on the conversation.

"I'll be looking after the press while you are here. So please let me know what you need ..."

Elliott's face lit up and the blond charmer came into his own. "Now, there's an offer I can't refuse! Are all English girls as helpful as you?"

Even though he was making an obvious play for her, Jane couldn't help being flattered by the amount of attention she was getting from America's biggest star. To her embarrassment she found herself giggling like a schoolgirl and reacting in exactly the way he had planned. She glanced up at him through her eyelashes;

"I think we'd better keep our minds on your visit here, Mr Blaze," she replied.

"Now Jane," he cut in smoothly, and put his bronzed hand on her shoulder. "If we are to work together, you must call me Elliott—isn't that right, Julie?" He threw a backward glance at his secretary who was trying to be nice to James Ledbury, the programme controller. Julie turned round at the mention of her name, pleased to get away from this oh-so-British broadcasting man. Her eyes took in the familiar sight of Elliott Blaze charming the pants off of a girl who was acting like a rabbit caught in headlights. Really, it was pathetic the way he played one woman off against another.

Meanwhile, Lincoln, Laban and Simon were discussing the venue for the press reception.

"I think, in view of the calibre of our guest," said Simon nodding towards Elliott, "we should choose somewhere not too large and flashy. We need to keep this reception, strictly invitation only—with a very exclusive guest list."

Laban and Lincoln both nodded gravely.

"I was thinking of the Café Royal in Regent Street. They have a small ballroom that would take around two hundred comfortably. Now, if we could narrow that down to just a hundred guests, we could include national papers and magazines plus a sprinkling of A-list names." He turned to Lincoln. "Perhaps you could give me a list of the kind of personalities that Elliott would like to meet."

Lincoln Grey studied the marketing manager. Simon was winning him over bit by bit. He looked the part and had that great assurance in his attitude. If he thought this Café Royal was the place to be, then it was OK by him.

"Small reception, you say," Lincoln replied. "Hmm ... it could work. In America we would put out all the flags and have Elliott call the shots, but you could be right about this. Keep it exclusive. Yeah, have people falling over themselves to get an invite ... people begging for interviews and photos ... Hmmm."

Simon's ego was getting a great boost. "Well, I thought that as Elliott is not a fan of clamouring journalists, we would be able to keep it under control this way."

"What about an escort, Laban?" asked Elliott's manager. "Didn't you mention something about someone to show Elliott around?"

Laban Monklaast nodded. "I did indeed. My own daughter Rachel will be doing the honours. I know I can trust her to keep Elliott's whereabouts to herself she's a very reliable and conscientious young lady. The press can hound her all they like, she won't tell them a thing."

"Sounds just right," remarked Lincoln. "When do we meet her? I thought you said she would be here?"

Laban's palms started to sweat. He rubbed his hands together nervously; "Oh, she'll be here any minute."

As he spoke the door opened and Rachel walked in. "Ah! My daughter." Laban announced proudly.

As she came into the room she smiled lovingly at her father rushed over and gave him a quick hug.

"I'm sorry Daddy, this was the best I could do at such short notice." Rachel looked stunning. Her glorious hair was a shining mass of long curls, her eyes dark and luminous, with a dash of mascara accentuating her long lashes. She was wearing black and white with flashes of bright red. Her soft, flowing blouse, showed off her perfect figure with a slim, black, knee-length skirt cut tight at the waist. She wore a gold chain high around her throat with red garnets dotted amongst the links. The stones matched her lipstick and when she smiled again, the garnets paled into insignificance. She was radiant.

"Lincoln, this is my daughter Rachel," said Laban proudly.

The manager took her hand and tried to stop staring quite so hard. "Hi, Rachel, it's a pleasure to meet you." He looked around the room for Elliott who was now busy talking to Simon about the reception. "Hang on babe," he muttered, "I need you to meet my star." He dashed across the room and grabbed Elliott.

Blaze looked annoyed. "Hey! What's this? I'm talking here to the marketing guy . . .!"

"Save it!" interrupted Lincoln. "I need you to meet your escort." He walked him back to where Laban was talking to his daughter. Rachel had her back to them.

"Hey, Rachel baby!" yelled Lincoln in his loud American way. "Come and meet my boy! Rachel, this is Elliott Blaze ... Elliott, this is Rachel."

CHAPTER

5

E lliott Blaze was used to good looking women. Models, fans and gorgeous hangers-on were part of his life, they gazed at him with undisguised devotion and most times—lust. He knew how to take advantage of women, he could melt them with a couple of words or swat them like flies when he'd had enough. But he had never met anyone like this woman in front of him now. She met him eye for eye, coolly intrigued but by no means infatuated. Her head was held high and her long neck was strong as she took in this 'show biz personality'. This girl was no pushover. She was proud and beautiful and everything he had ever wanted and she was his escort. This was a time to play it very cool. Laban's daughter was not going to fall for one of his lines quite as easily as the rest.

He held his hand out and smiled lazily. "Hi Rachel. Your father has mentioned you to us. I gather you are going to show me around town when we come back."

Her hand was strong in his and much to his joy, she smiled back at him. If he thought she was beautiful before, now he was quite devastated. Her sapphire eyes flashed and her hair fell slightly away from her face revealing a smile that men would kill for.

"I'm sure London will seem very small after America, but we do have some sights worth seeing," she answered engagingly.

"And you are obviously one of them." He couldn't stop himself saying it. He knew it was a terrible cliché but it fell off of his lips before he could stop it.

Rachel looked down at the floor—she always found this type of compliment hard to take.

"I hope you have enough time on your schedule to see some of our history, as well as the nightlife," she remarked, choosing to ignore his pass.

"Do you live in London?" he asked, trying to keep her attention.

"We live outside, actually, but at the moment I'm staying in our apartment, which is quite near the Dorchester where you're staying, I believe." Rachel could have instantly bitten off her tongue! Fancy letting the guy know that!

"Hey, that's great!" grinned Elliott. "How about we do something tonight? I'm in town until tomorrow."

Rachel faltered—this wasn't quite what she had in mind. "Well, I ..." she began.

Elliott put his hand up to stop her. His mind was racing. "Better idea, babe," he said. "Write your phone number on the back of this card, and I'll call you this evening."

He produced one of his own photos from his jacket and handed it to her.

This was the nearest to a way out without upsetting him that Rachel could think of, so she wrote on the card and gave it back to him. "I'm not absolutely sure ... it's such short notice." Already a plan was forming in Rachel's mind. She would phone Leah and make sure that they were both at the apartment tonight.

Elliott's secretary Julie appeared in front of them, tapping her watch.

"C'mon Elliott, time to go." She hung on to his arm and let her eyes move up and down Rachel. "Lincoln is winding things up and then we are going to lunch at some quaint English pub. Sorry, honey," she remarked, looking at Rachel again.

Laban's daughter smiled, only too relieved to let Elliott Blaze go.

"Call you," grinned the star, touching his head with his fingers in a mock salute.

And then they were gone.

The MBC team breathed a unified sigh of relief and flopped into the waiting comfy chairs.

"Any problems, anyone?" asked Laban.

They sat around for another thirty minutes ironing out the details that had been discussed between the Americans and themselves, and decided that a good job had been done by all. Then they gradually drifted out of the main office for a well-earned late lunch.

Laban Monklaast caught up with his daughter as she was chatting and laughing with Henry outside.

"Darling, thank you so much!" He reached out and hugged her. "He obviously took a shine to you, so just make sure you look after him when he comes back and keep him at arm's length at the same time!" He wagged his finger at her in mock severity.

Rachel laughed and decided not to mention tonight. No point in stirring things up, when he might not even call.

"While you're here," said her father, "I'd like you to come and meet Aaron, our new boy. He could do with a few friends. You know what it's like here, everyone knows everyone else and the new guy can feel somewhat left out."

Rachel nodded. She had seen it happen quite a few times. The fact that you might be new talent or incredibly famous never stopped you feeling lonely in a large corporation. She had seen many a famous personality sitting by themselves drinking coffee in the large canteen. Most times it was because people were never sure if they should take a chance and sit with them, or whether they were sitting on their own for the sake of privacy. But nine times out of ten, they just didn't know anyone else.

"I'd like to meet him," she replied. "I hear you have mountains of faith in this DJ. What was his name again?"

"Aaron. Aaron Holloway. He's going to go far, darling, this one." Laban nodded sagely. He didn't become head of this massive corporation without some intuition.

They walked back down the stairs, choosing to miss the lift. Sometimes Laban said it was the only exercise he got, which was perfectly untrue as his figure and stamina showed.

They stopped on the next floor down and walked into 7001, the office frequented by David Wills and his staff. Aaron wasn't there, but a typist told them she thought he was having a break in the canteen. Rachel smiled to herself, remembering her thoughts of a few minutes ago. Her father looked at his watch, and Rachel knew that he didn't really have time to go with her.

She leaned on Laban's arm. "It's all right Daddy. I'm sure I can find him by myself."

Laban gave his daughter a rueful smile. "I take you away from your own office duties, and then can't find time for you myself. Forgive me Rachel, I'll keep in touch. Send my love to Leah," he added.

"Oh," started Rachel. "I was thinking of asking her to come and stay at the apartment with me for a few days. She could do with a bit of cheering up I think."

Laban raised his eyebrows. "Why is that? Is everything OK?" He always wanted time to be concerned for them both—even if his elder daughter was harder work.

"Oh, I'm sure she'll be fine," Rachel reassured him. "I just think that she often gets a little bit lonely."

The answer seemed to satisfy Laban and he headed back to the eighth floor.

Meanwhile Rachel carried on down the stairs and pushed open the doors of the MBC canteen. It was still fairly noisy, the canteen staff laughing and calling to one another over the sound of meals being dished up and cleared away. The cooks and waitresses knew just about everybody and were always wonderfully unimpressed with big stars. It wasn't that they didn't like them—they were just used to seeing them and treated them like everyone else. This was why you would hear them shouting to David Wills."Here David, I brought you in some of that cough linctus I was telling you about!" or to Michael, "Here Michael, d'ya want your eggs turned over or just splashed?" No one took offence in fact it was all very homely and made the stars feel less conspicuous.

Rachel ordered a cup of coffee and a Danish pastry from Arthur and started walking around with her tray.

In the corner sat a young man. Well, he looked fairly young from that distance. He was holding a magazine in one hand and pushing his hair out of his eyes with the other. His lunch was by his side. He tried to pick up his coffee cup without taking his eyes off the article he was reading, and missed by miles.

"I think it's gone cold," remarked Rachel as she took the seat opposite him.

His head jerked up in surprise, and Rachel saw what a wonderful face he had. Extremely youthful, with a puzzled expression in his eyes.

"Oh, sorry. I'm Rachel Monklaast?" The expression stayed blank.

"You know, my dad owns the company." She laughed at her own one-liner.

The penny dropped. Aaron put his magazine down and grinned hugely at her.

"Oh, right!" He said. "I'm sorry, I'm new here and it's taking me some time to sort out who's who!" He was terrific, totally unaffected either by Rachel's announcement of who she was, or by her looks.

"Is it OK if I sit with you? Daddy said I'd probably find you here and that you might need someone to say hello to."

Aaron waved his magazine in her general direction. "Yes please, sit with me! So your dad is Laban then," he commented. "He's a nice bloke, made me feel right at home. My own parents were a bit worried when I landed this job you know, big city, bright lights and stuff. I think they thought I would turn into a drug addict overnight!"

Rachel laughed at him. He was very easy company. "Oh no," she replied. "It takes a little longer than that!

But I know what you mean, show business in general hasn't got a great reputation, but MBC are really good to work for."

"So what do you do here?" Aaron asked, hoping she was working on the chart channel. He could do with a friend like her.

"Oh, I don't actually work here. I'm employed by a small entertainment agency in Byron Street, down the road," she informed him.

"Didn't fancy having Dad as your boss then?" he joked. She really was rather nice. He wondered how old she was. "Mind you, I wouldn't want to work for my old man—he's a tax inspector! He still thinks what I'm doing is a doddle. 'When are you going to get a proper job?' You know how it is."

Rachel nodded vigorously, enjoying talking to someone who didn't just stare at her all the time and make stupid comments. She put her elbows on the table and cupped her chin in her hands.

"I'm sure they will love you when you're a star. 'That's my son up there!' they'll say. Wait and see." She smiled encouragingly at him. He really was very nice. She looked over at his magazine.

"What's so interesting that you let your dinner go cold for?" She asked.

Aaron looked down at his chicken curry and rice in surprise.

"Aw, no! I'm always doing that." He pulled a face. "I was looking at some outrageous stories. I collect them and use them in between playing records. Look at this one!"

They continued to pore over the paper and laugh and joke for another half an hour before Rachel gasped at the time, and said she must be going. The eyes that were soon going to grace every teenage bedroom wall, looked down in disappointment.

"Ah well. It was great to meet you, Rache. I hope you get time to pop in and say hello again."

Rachel was surprised how nice the name 'Rache' sounded when he said it. He was so cute you could almost stroke him.

"Oh you'll be seeing me a lot, soon. My father has hired me for the two weeks that Elliott Blaze is in town. I have to escort him around and make sure he's comfortable," she replied.

"Great! I have to do an interview with him for my show, so maybe we could meet up for a ... curry?" he asked, looking dejectedly down at the congealed mess on his plate.

"Fine," said Rachel. "And don't forget, I'm only down the road, so we could meet for lunch anytime, really." It was wonderful not to feel threatened. Aaron would become a firm friend she was sure they already seemed to have a lot in common. It would be nice to have someone else to go to lunch with now and again.

"Brilliant! How do I contact you?" he asked simply.

And for the second time that day, Rachel gave out her phone number, only this time it was her office number, not the apartment.

She left soon after, with Aaron Holloway watching her go.

He ran his hands through his hair ... she was nice, Rachel. Even though he was younger than she was, he already felt a protectiveness towards her and wondered how she would cope with the likes of Elliott Blaze. He frowned as he ran the thought through his mind again. He would keep an eye on her. Make sure she was all right. After all, it was just a brotherly type of thing he felt for her. Wasn't it?

CHAPTER

6

Rachel dashed to Landers Agency just long enough to check the appointments book and make a few phone calls. Among them was a call to Leah. The plan she was formulating would need careful consideration, but she was sure that her sister would be game. She waited anxiously for someone to answer the phone.

"Monks Lodge, Leah speaking," announced the bored voice.

Rachel breathed a sigh of relief.

"Oh great! You're in!" she said. "Leah, listen this is really important could you give me enough time to get back to Park Lane and then ring the apartment?"

There was a small silence on the other end of the line. "I might be busy Rachel, what is this all about?" Leah sounded impatient.

"I'm sorry, I can't discuss it at the moment. Just start packing a few things to stay overnight. Please Leah, this really is important." Rachel's fingers were tapping the desk top in front of her. She silently prayed that her sister wouldn't start getting awkward.

"Oh all right. This has to be important you know, I have other things to do besides look after you." Leah was secretly pleased that Rachel needed her help. It gave her a small amount of satisfaction.

"Oh thank you Leah, you are a darling. You won't regret it!"

"I already do," said her sister dryly, and hung up.

Sarah swung round in her typist's chair, and looked smugly at Rachel.

"Mmm, that sounded mysterious." She raised her eyebrows in anticipation.

"Sorry Sarah, strictly sisters' business!" Rachel remarked.

Sarah shrugged. "OK, change of subject. How did you get on at MBC? What was the big panic?"

"Oh nothing much," said Rachel evasively. "Oh, but I did meet the new DJ for Chart MBC," she offered temptingly. "And all I can say, Sarah, is that if you are extremely nice to me and type these letters I've left on my desk by this evening, I might introduce you to him." She gave her friend a knowing look.

Sarah was all ears. She crossed over to Rachel's desk. "So what's he like then? How old is he? I've already heard a little bit about him."

Rachel took out a nail file and pretended to look pre-occupied. Sarah snatched the file away.

"Oh come on! Give! Give!" urged the secretary.

"All right," smiled Rachel. "He's about twenty years old he could be younger actually. He is going to knock the spots off anyone in his league. He's extra good-looking, great smile, brilliant personality and just your type!" She was enjoying herself now. "But right now, I have to go and phone my sister, somewhere away from prying ears!"

After Rachel left the building, Sarah got up from her chair and made her way over to the mirror. She took a good long look at herself. Nearly nineteen, blonde, pretty in a cute way, she had laughing eyes and an open attitude to life.

"Yes, Sarah, it's about time you had a bit of romance in your life, and it's a nice name Aaron."

*   *   *

The doorman for the apartment block greeted Rachel enthusiastically. She was such a charming girl—he was always telling his wife how nice it was to look after people like her.

"Here for a few days then, Miss Monklaast?" he enquired respectfully. Harry looked very posh in his uniform and liked to act the part as much as possible—opening doors, enquiring about the health of the people in his care. Of course, not everyone was as nice as Miss Monklaast —he had his fair share of obnoxious characters who thought that doormen were actually doormats. He stroked his neat moustache as he thought of the story his friend at the Dorchester was telling him, of some film star and the dreadful way he pushed past him as if he wasn't there. No manners, some of these Americans.

"Just a couple of days," Rachel was saying. "My sister will be down later tonight, so look out for her will you Harry?"

Arriving at her apartment door, she searched for her keys and let herself in. It always felt strange; it wasn't like coming home—there was something impersonal about it. She supposed part of the problem was, that there were very few personal items around. The flat was beautifully furnished, but there were no telltale signs that gave it the 'lived-in' look.

She shivered, even though it wasn't cold. Passing through into the kitchen, she busied herself with some fresh filter coffee and soon the aroma was filling the flat. She felt better already, curled herself up in one of the enormous armchairs and sat looking at the phone, willing it to ring.

There had been no calls—she had checked with reception on the way up. Well, at least that meant that he hadn't phoned either! She almost dozed for a few minutes and was aroused by the coffee percolating in the kitchen. She stretched, pulled herself out of the armchair, strolled into the kitchen and poured herself a huge round cup. Coming back into the room, she turned some music on softly and began to unwind.

Her mind wandered to Leah. If this plan worked, it could be great for her sister. It would be so nice to be able to help her ... to give her something she wanted. Somehow, she never seemed to hit the right chord with her, and she could see that Leah was hurting. How lovely if she could put things right.

The phone still made her jump when it rang, even though she was expecting it.

"Hello?" she answered cautiously.

"It's me," said Leah flatly.

This had to be played right, thought Rachel.

"Leah, great," she replied lamely, then pursed her lips trying to think of the best way of approaching the subject.

"Well?" asked her sister. "What's this urgent mess you're in?"

"Oh dear, is it that obvious?" Rachel half-laughed down the phone.

"It must be, if you need my help," her sister replied.

"Right. Now Leah, I need you to listen to me and not make any judgements until I've finished, please."

"I'm listening."

Rachel cleared her throat. "Well, I've got myself in a slight predicament with someone I don't really like and he's said that he's going to call tonight and take me out, and I thought if he called and I said that you were with me and I couldn't go ... he might just come round ... and ..."

"Honestly Rachel, I can't believe you're making such a fuss!" Her sister cut in. "Just tell the creep to go ... what's the matter with you?"

"No, please Leah, listen," her sister said anxiously. "You see, I know that you will like him, and he's the kind of man I don't really want to offend. So I thought perhaps we could arrange for you to be here when he arrives. Bring something gorgeous to wear and I'll do your hair the way you like it and I'll make some kind of excuse to leave or get out of the way ..."

"Has this been a particularly bad day at the office?" asked Leah sarcastically.

"No, Leah really ..."

"Rachel, you are making no sense whatsoever," her sister complained crossly. "You want me to doll myself up and chase halfway across London, just to save your face?"

This was not going well. Rachel was more than a little reluctant to use Elliott's name on the phone, as he wasn't even supposed to be in the country. She knew that her sister would never be able to keep such a secret to herself and it would be all over the grapevine if she told her the whole truth. By tomorrow it wouldn't matter as Elliott would be safely on a plane and out of the country, but if the news got out tonight and reporters started to hound him ... that would be the end of MBC's scoop.

"Leah, please believe me, you will like this guy. I've even mentioned that you might be coming over ... Oh please Leah, you will really like him!"

At Monks Lodge, Leah was lying on her bed with the phone trying to work out what this was all about. Why would Rachel be so anxious to be rid of some hunk—and why was she so sure he was her type? At the end of the day, Leah had nothing better to do, and dressing up for a night out was something she loved doing ...

"All right, Rachel. Just this once."

"You will never regret this, darling sister. You might even thank me for it one day!" answered Rachel mysteriously. "Can you get here as soon as possible?"

She put the phone back on the receiver and sent up a silent prayer of thanks. As a child, she had always been taught by her father to respect God, and she loved the way Laban would pray about important decisions. When she and Leah were small, both her mother and her father prayed with them every night and taught them stories from the Bible. Now that she was older,

Rachel remembered these teachings; she saw that it worked for Laban and tried to pray when she could. Of course, she didn't really think God was the remotest bit interested in her love life, only in important things like the future of MBC—but maybe one day she would pray for a prince to whisk her away.

She sighed and sank back into the armchair. Leah was coming, it was going to be all right. She wasn't normally a coward, but Elliott Blaze gave her a kind of creepy feeling, the feeling of being undressed, and she didn't like it. Perhaps it wasn't such a good idea to get Leah involved after all, she thought guiltily.

The phone rang once again and Rachel picked it up, thinking it was Leah ringing back to ask more questions.

"You'll never get here if you keep phoning!" she said into the phone.

"My! We are impatient, aren't we?" drawled the lazy American voice.

Rachel shot up in her seat and smoothed her hair as if she'd been caught untidy.

"Uh ... oh, I'm so sorry, I thought you were my sister," she finished lamely.

Elliot chuckled. "Well, I've been called a lot of things in my time, but 'sister'—never. So hey, how's our date? Still on for tonight?"

Rachel thought the phone might snap in her hand, she was holding it so tightly.

"Um ... well as I said, my sister Leah is on her way over. I can't really go out and leave her. But if you would like to, you could come over. I could order a meal ..." She faltered.

"Hmm, seems I have no choice. So, two gorgeous ladies for the price of one, not the kind of offer I turn down lightly." Elliott's voice still sounded jovial, and Rachel was relieved he took it so well. "I'll come around at eight."

It was a statement rather than a question, so after she

had finished giving him directions, she put the phone down.

In the Dorchester Hotel, Elliott slammed down the receiver.

"Damn!" he swore. The handsome face wore a look of twited annoyance. He knew that when he came back over to England next time, he would have Rachel eating out of his hand, but he really had hoped to have a foretaste of things to come, tonight. Now he had landed himself with two women, and who was to know what her sister was like? Ah well, this is where the acting experience would come to the fore.

*   *   *

Leah arrived just before seven to find Rachel waiting impatiently for her. She waltzed into the apartment and sat herself down opposite Rachel.

"Right! I'm here," she said stating the obvious. "What's this world-shattering news then?"

Rachel gave her sister a wide smile and leaned forward. "Remember when we were just in our teens and we used to share secrets and get up to all sorts of mischief? We'd cover for each other and everything?"

Leah remembered those times well. They were just starting to notice boys, and experimenting with make-up and clothes. They would dare each other to wear the most outrageous things and sneak out to the local disco. It was only a year or so later that Leah began to realise how attractive Rachel was to anyone of the male species. From that moment on, Leah always took second best.

"Do you remember," Rachel continued, "that boy Mark from the village? He was such a rebel, always in trouble ... and I had to tell mother that you were round at Beth's house?"

Leah smiled to herself. Mark had been her way of kicking out.

"We did get into some scrapes, didn't we?" she offered.

"Well, tonight is going to be all of those escapades rolled into one!" exclaimed Rachel.

Leah waited patiently for the explanation.

"I know this will be a bit of a shock for you ... but Elliott Blaze will be coming round in just less than an hour ..."

Leah's reaction was everything her sister had prayed for and more. Her face paled, and her eyes were opened as wide as they could.

"Here? In London? I thought he wasn't due for a few weeks!"

"That's what everybody thinks. Anyway, he's only here overnight—he came to have a sort of preview chat with Daddy. And somehow I ended up telling him that this apartment was just down the road from his hotel, and the next thing I knew, he was arranging to meet me," explained Rachel.

Leah's mind was everywhere. "And you don't like him?" she asked incredulously.

"No, he's really not for me. But I remember you saying you thought he was rather wonderful, so I thought it would be terrific if we could make this a real 'girls night', and set him up!"

"And just how do you plan to do that?" Leah was beginning to relax. This could be fun and maybe her sister was trying to make it up to her.

Rachel clapped her hands in excitement. "I thought that we could spend some time making you up, and as I said we could do your hair and make you look fantastic. Then, when Elliott arrives you can answer the door, looking stunning, and I will be in the bedroom. Then, when he asks where I am, you can look panic stricken and say that I'm still getting ready ... and I'll wander out of the bedroom with my hair half-dried and an old jumper and a pair of leggings or something ... and he'll be all yours!"

Leah chewed her lip. "It does sound a good plan. But what if he doesn't like me?"

"Oh come on, Leah! This is your big chance—the guy just

loves women, full stop!" She looked at her watch. "And we've only got forty minutes before he arrives!"

And for once, Rachel and Leah were the sisters of old, giggling and laughing, tossing mountains of clothes into the middle of the room and posing in front of the full length mirror. Finally they settled on a long, slinky black dress. It was virtually backless and had a halter neck which cascaded into fine strings of tiny black beads to the bodice. It suited Leah's figure, showing off creamy shoulders and emphasising her neck. She was slim and her slight figure gave the whole thing a slightly impish look. Rachel's handiwork on her hair had worked miracles, with the aid of mousse and curling tongs, it was pulled up on the crown with just a few whispy curls kissing her cheeks. In fact, she looked sensational! Rachel had never seen her look so good and was frustrated at the thought that if she took more time to be herself and stopped trying to look like her sister, Leah could look good all the time.

"Wonderful!" Rachel exclaimed. "He will absolutely love you! Now, stay here in case he's early. I've ordered a meal for three, but if he wants to take you out—just go, OK?"

She turned and headed for her bedroom. "And now it's my turn!" she announced.

In her room, Rachel quickly undressed, showered and threw on the jumper that she kept for times when she had a day to herself, a day when she could just lounge around and curl up with a fat paperback. The sweater was cherry-coloured, the neck was wide and loose, and the body was long and misshapen. It came almost to her knees and the only thing she had to wear with it was her black leggings. She kicked her shoes off and decided to go barefoot. All that was left was to dry her hair in a haphazard way. Not difficult, she thought to herself—her hair had a mind of its own, long and naturally curled, and it didn't behave itself at the best of times.

She was halfway through loosely drying her hair when she

heard the doorbell ring. Leah thumped on the bedroom door.

"He's here!" she hissed. "Harry just rang to announce him!"

"Well don't just stand there ... let him in!" whispered Rachel. "I'll keep the dryer going."

Leah took one more glance in the gilded mirror, licked her lips, and put their plan into action. She opened the door firmly and looked up into the steely blue eyes of Elliott Blaze. He was everything she'd ever dreamed he would be, and to have him standing in front of her was almost unreal. He was dressed for the evening, and his suit, though incredibly well cut, gave him the look of a relaxed, comfortable man who knew where he was going. With one hand resting on the side of the door, the other ran nonchalantly through his hair. His eyes appraised Leah and at once gave her the same feeling that Rachel felt. The feeling of being undressed. But Leah was going to brazen this out, so she looked straight back at him with the same attitude.

"Hello, Elliott, please come in. I'm afraid we are running a little late ..."

He admired her stance. A totally different type to her sister.

"And you must be Leah, Rachel's sister." Habit made him glance at her with flirtatious eyes.

Her hand flew to her neck. "Yes. Umm ... Rachel isn't quite ready, but I'm sure you could do with a drink. Bourbon?" This time it was Leah who looked flirtatiously at him. She managed to glide over to the tray and hold up a crystal glass. It caught the light and flashed in his direction.

"Bourbon would be great, honey." He moved in and followed her across the room. When she handed him the glass, she let her fingers stay just a little too long. Sassy, he thought, still, it's a game I'm good at.

"So, where have you been hiding? I didn't see you at MBC did I? No of course not, I think I would have remembered." He chinked his glass lightly against hers. It was all so natural to him. Women wanted him to flirt with them and this one was giving out all sorts of vibrations.

"So, where's Rachel?" he asked glancing around the room.

Leah nodded towards the bedroom. "Under the hair-dryer by sound of it." She pulled at one of the loose pieces of her hair. "It takes some people ages to get ready, doesn't it?"

It was time for Rachel to make her entrance. She unplugged the dryer and tossed her long hair back. She looked at herself brieflythis was so embarrassing, she wasn't even wearing any make-up. Still, if it got Leah the man of her dreams ...

She opened the door and stopped suddenly, feigning surprise at the sight of Elliott. She put her hands quickly to her hair and then pulled at the jumper.

"Oh gosh! I'm so sorry, I didn't hear you arrive! It must have been the noise from the hair-dryer ..." She tried to look shocked. "Gosh, I'm a mess! Look, Leah, thank you for looking after our guest ... oh dear, I feel a complete idiot ... perhaps ..." Whatever she was going to say got cut very short by Elliott. He'd been gazing at her ever since she came into the room. The dishevelled hair tousled and free, the sweater just balancing on her shoulders, the incredible legs defined in those slinky tights—he thought he'd never seen anything so exciting in his life.

"It doesn't matter, Rachel. It looks so natural and I like it."

If looks could kill, Leah's eyes would have murdered Rachel there and then. Rachel looked across to her in despair. The plan was going terribly wrong. she moved towards the film star.

"Oh no Elliott, thanks for trying but I know I look a mess. But you two, standing together, look as if you could be going somewhere special." Her mouth was dry—come on, think!

Leah came to the rescue. She turned to Elliott mustering up every ounce of charm in her body. "I think she could be right. I know some very secluded restaurants where I can guarantee you won't be pestered by anyone else." She threw a glance towards her sister. "And Rachel was just saying what a tough day it's been at work, isn't that right?"

Rachel nodded furiously. She stretched and yawned prettily. "I certainly wouldn't mind if you wanted to escort Eliott, Leah. To be honest, I'm too tired to think straight."

Elliott looked annoyed. He put his drink down. "Hey now," he said smiling a smile that he didn't feel. "We wouldn't dream of leaving you alone, would we Leah?" The ball was now firmly in her court. "I'm sure an intimate evening with two lovely ladies would be sheer delight."

Rachel went to return to her room, but he stopped her.

"Hey no! Don't change, you look great. Come and sit down, Leah will pour you a glass of wine and then we can all relax."

The evening went from bad to worse. They were the oddest trio. Leah in her magnificent evening dress, Rachel in her leggings and Elliott tieless and open-shirted from the effects of too much Scotch. They sat around the meticulously laid mahogany table, complete with candles and champagne bucket. The mood was strained. Every time Leah tried to flirt with Elliott, he turned the conversation to Rachel and every time Rachel steered the topic to Leah, he turned the theme to himself.

Rachel could see that Leah had had enough and was starting to worry about how it was going to end. If Leah got too upset she might leave and then she would have to deal with Elliott by herself. But Leah had no intention of leaving Elliott alone with Rachel and was working on a rather pathetic plan to make sure that he left before she did.

"Why don't we take our drinks into the lounge and make ourselves comfortable there?" She smiled and pushed her seat back.

Elliott stood up abruptly to assist her and caught the full force of the glass of ruby-red wine that Leah was holding at a rather odd angle. Elliott had unwittingly made it look even more of an 'accident' than she'd planned.

There were gasps followed by an embarrassed silence. Rachel was horrified. This could turn everything terribly wrong but she was transfixed, not knowing what to do for the best.

Leah rushed into the kitchen, returning with a soft cloth and proceeded to try and rub the red stain out of Elliott's shirt. It was all quite ridiculous and he caught hold of her hand:

"Please. Leave it," he said, his voice low and controlled. "I think ladies, perhaps I should call it a day. This evening was obviously not meant to be, so if you'll excuse me I'll go back to my hotel and clean up."

Rachel rushed over to him and put her hand on his arm. "Elliott, I'm most awfully sorry about this! I feel terrible!" she murmured. "Perhaps ..."

He turned and smiled at her. Even when she was upset she still looked like a million dollars to him.

"It's OK babe. Maybe we can try again next time. In better circumstances, who knows?"

She breathed a slow sigh of relief. "Then you will still be coming back?" She asked.

"Naturally. It'll take more than a soaking with a glass of wine to keep me away from you!" he grinned, his sense of humour returning. He turned to Leah. "At least it didn't go all over that pretty dress." The remark was almost cryptic, and yet it was hard to know whether to take offence.

Elliott gave his usual mock salute and slipped out of the door.

As soon as he'd gone, Leah whirled round angrily to Rachel.

" 'Oh, Elliott I'm terribly sorry! Oh, Elliott will you come back?!' " she mimicked, the fury in her eyes was frightening. This was Leah on the warpath, and her sister knew better than to try and stop her.

"Why did you do it Rachel? You knew he preferred the way you looked to the way I looked, and I let you doll me up like some Christmas tree and all the time you knew he would like you better! she yelled. "You are always doing this to me! Always! Well, no more ..." She stopped for breath, seething, her face white with rage. She felt so humiliated, standing there in that evening dress realising that Rachel could still snap her fingers and take any man she wanted—any man Leah wanted.

Rachel was at a loss. She knew there was no point in trying to explain when her sister was like this. Leah would never believe that Rachel's plan was for her sister's happiness.

Leah unzipped her dress and stepped out of it. She held it in both hands:

"This! This is what I think of your dress, your ideas, your stupid film star!" She proceeded to tear at the gown with her bare hands. The flimsy material came away easily and black beads cascaded to the floor.

At this point Rachel knew she had to do something. She held her hands up to try and silence her sister.

"Leah! Listen to me! Listen!" she pleaded. "I'm not going to try and explain—you're much too upset—but I know that I can't let you drive home like this. Love me or hate me, please just go to the other bedroom and sleep it off. Maybe we can talk about it in the morning."

Leah was exhausted and realised that her sister was right about driving home. Well, it's my apartment just as much as hers —why shouldn't I stay, she thought. She kicked the remnants of silk aside and walked to the bedroom door. Then she turned and pointed at Rachel.

"Just wait. One day, there will be someone you really care for, and I will be there Rachel ... I will be there and I promise you I will do everything I can to ruin it for you, they way you are always ruining it for me. Just wait, Rachel—just you wait."

CHAPTER

7

Rebekkah was sitting in one of her favourite places, looking out from the cool, spacious room across the wide verandah over miles and miles of parched hazy grass. She often sat here to plan her day—and there was always plenty to organise on a huge sheep-farming station like theirs, thousands upon thousands of acres of the Australian outback. She looked serene enough, but today she was wondering if her sons would ever stop arguing. They were so different. Whoever coined the phrase 'opposites attract' had not met Jacob and Esau. Today, like every other day, she could hear them at each other's throats again—it was almost as natural a sound as the kookaburras—but this time it was different.

Esau, a red-haired rough-looking man, loved the land. He was so comfortable here. He had no thoughts of ever straying from the homestead and spent every waking moment out in the open, checking on the herds, setting traps for any stray dingoes, and generally following in his father, Isaac's, footsteps. Esau was very like his father.

Isaac Lindstein was stern, intense, with an almost aggressive attitude to life, and he would flatten anything that got in his way. He was already over forty years old when he married Rebekkah and he had loved and protected her with the same violent passion. They had long despaired of having any children, but prayed and prayed for a miracle. His attitude to prayer showed the same characteristic—an almost arrogant faith that God would never let him down—and He didn't.

Jacob and Esau were twins—Miracle twins—but so different in looks and temperament. As Esau was like his father, so Jacob was like Rebekkah. His mother had an ethereal beauty, even as a mature woman, and exuded a wonderful aura of peace about her. This certainly didn't make her a weak person—if anything it just added to her strength of character. She was a shrewd, wise businesswoman, and if it was Isaac who had the know-how about land and animals, it was his wife who kept the whole business running. She had an in-built ability to organise and make money.

Her son Jacob took most of his endearing qualities from her and then added some charm of his own. Seriously handsome, with dark hair and dark eyes, his face often bore the signs of someone who was looking into the far distance and dreaming about his future. He loathed the work here. He loved animals but hated the way they were treated and loathed the work on the sheep-station—he was not a 'country boy'. His heart belonged to big cities, fame and fortune, and he could never understand his brother's attitude to life.

"How can you take such good care of all these sheep, only to see them slaughtered at the end of the day?" he would argue. His face contorted with self-righteous pain.

"What would you know? When have you ever got your hands dirty or even tried to see our side of things?" Esau used the word 'our' knowing that it rankled with Jacob to think that Esau was his father's favourite.

It was this very same argument that Rebekkah was hearing now, and she knew that one day it would get out of hand. She had to sort something out soon—she could feel the tension mounting every time they challenged each other and it frightened her. When they were children they often fought and then ran to their respective favourite parent for support, but now they were in their twenties it could not go on. Rebekkah had gone to Isaac on numerous occasions to try and make him see how the situation was worsening. His shining grey hair would wave as he tossed his head, then, as he laughed, his smile would make creases around his eyes.

"Darling, don't worry. They are both men, they can handle themselves."

But Rebekkah did worry. How long would it be before it was out of control? Esau was a fiery man and Jacob a stubborn, calculating type—how long before they killed each other?

Outside the verandah, the war continued. Jacob's arms flew out to his side and the handsome chin jutted out. "What's the point? You can't see further than the end of your nose! There's a whole world out there, and you've never even been to Brisbane!! I have no desire to spend the rest of my life in the wild!"

It was Esau's turn to use the cutting remark now.

"So why not go, Jacob? Why not spread your wings and fly? I'll take care of the business, if you know what I mean." He spoke softly, but the threat was there. "I'm sure I could persuade Dad to let you go. He wouldn't want you hanging around where you didn't wanna be, would he?"

The argument was going the same way as it always went. Esau was dangling the family estate over Jacob's head. He knew that he could persuade his father to hand the estate over to him if he could just prove that Jacob wasn't interested. And Jacob had no intention of letting it go. His dark eyes narrowed.

"You know it has nothing to do with that! I could manage this place with one hand tied behind my back—whereas you would be bankrupt within a year if you were left on your own!" Jacob jeered at him. "You might be able to handle sheep and grass," he added scathingly, "but your mind is useless!"

Esau made a grab at his brother and gripped his shirt. He pulled him roughly towards him until their faces were level.

"That was a very stupid thing to say." His face was sweating and his clothes were stained with the heat of the day. Jacob found him repulsive. The pungent smell of days of sweat, combined with the sensation of his brother's hairy muscular arms were nothing short of revolting to him. He went to pull himself away but Esau was hanging on tight.

"What are you going to do now? Would you like me to call your mother for you?" Again, the reference to family favourites was playing its part in this war.

Esau was bigger and heavier, but Jacob was much fitter and it was that factor that came to his aid now as he swung his fist in the direction of Esau's face.

It connected.

Rebekkah heard the cry as Esau hit the ground, followed by more sounds of fists hitting bodies. She could stand it no longer. Rushing from her chair and out into the yard, her hands flew to her face as she saw the state of her sons.

"Jacob! Esau!" she cried out. They were both on the ground and looked up in surprise. Esau's already dirty checked shirt was torn from the shoulder down and the vivid red hairs on his chest were blazing through. His right eye was already swelling nicely and as he slowly sat up, blood from his nose dripped onto his jeans. He wiped his face with his forearm and growled across at Jacob, who was shaking his head as if to bring himself round. Rebekkah saw that Jacob had a cut on his cheek and it hurt her deeply to see his beautiful face marred in this way. She looked from one to the other and then held her hand out.

"Esau, get back to work. Jacob, come with me." It was an order, which they both obeyed instinctively.

Once inside the sun lounge, Rebekkah sat opposite her favourite son and looked at him for a long time. He deserved better than this. She understood his feelings—his discomfort in the farming community, large though it was, bringing in hundreds of thousands of dollars every month. She pressed her lips together and pondered the best move.

"What shall I do with you, Jacob?" she asked almost to herself.

Her son lifted his hands helplessly, and the fabric of his shirt rippled across his body. Every move he made was poetiche had a grace his brother could never match in a million years. Even his hands, in themselves, could move artistically. It was this grace that had closed many a deal for them. When Jacob stood in a boardroom and pleaded his case for their company, his arms would open majestically and the expression in his eyes, his mouth and the proud movement of his head would put a stop to any further argument. It was almost a theatrical performance—only in Jacob's case it was totally natural.

"Maybe you should go away ..." These words sounded foreign on his mother's lips. He lowered his eyes.

"Jacob, you are worth more than this. You have a talent for business that cannot even begin to be tapped out here." Rebekkah explained. "I know you hate it and I know that you're staying here mainly to please me—but it's not enough. It's not enough for you, and it's not enough for me."

Jacob looked puzzled. What was she saying?

In her heart, Rebekkah had known that this moment would come. She was going to send her son away—the boy she loved more than any other.

"I have a relative named Laban. You may have heard me talk about him."

"Doesn't he live in England?" asked Jacob. He leant forward and his hands lay clenched together on his knees.

"That's right" she replied. "Laban owns the largest broadcasting company in Europe. In fact, it could be the largest in the world by now. He will give you a job, Jacob. You will do well for him—I've often told him about you and he always used to say, 'when you finished with him on the farm, send him to me.' " She smiled as she thought of her cousin. He would love Jacob, she was sure. It was the kind of company her son would fit in with and Laban would benefit from her handsome Jacob.

"But mother, I can't just go to England! What would you say to father? What about our own company? Esau would ruin it!" Jacob ran his hands through his black hair. This was the most desperate, the most harrowing, the most exciting proposition he could imagine.

"Father would cut me off without a penny—Esau would see to that! And how could I leave you? What would happen if...?"

Rebekkah silenced her son. "Don't worry, I have been planning this for a long time. I shall tell Isaac that you need to spread your wings, that your talents are being wasted here. I will explain about the opportunities ... and then I shall explain about your need to find a suitable wife." She looked calmly at him.

He rose abruptly from his seat and looked at his mother in astonishment. "A wife? When did this happen?" he exclaimed.

She laughed at her son's face.

"Oh Jacob, come on. You are always joking that the sheep are more attractive than the women around here—and it's possibly true! Now, if there is one way to get around your father, it will be by telling him you think it's time you found a wife, settled down and raised a family!"

Jacob started to object, but she continued. "That way, your father will make doubly sure that your inheritance stays intact. If there is one word that is guaranteed to set Isaac's heart on fire—it's 'grandchildren'!" She clapped her hands in delight.

Jacob's face lit up in sheer amusement. He threw his head back and laughed aloud. His arms spanned the sofa he was lazing on and his body lounged gloriously along it.

"Mother, you are the living end!" His voice was warm and full of love for her. He pointed a slender finger at her. "And if I ever find this wife, she is going to be exactly like you. Kind, wise and absolutely beautiful."

He came over to Rebekkah, bent down and kissed her still-soft cheek. She looked up at him lovingly and said, "It's going to be all right Jacob. It's going to be all right."

*   *   *

"Laban? It's Rebekkah!" She held the phone tightly, as her excitement grew.

"Well, this is very nice!" the familiar voice came back to her. "I have been thinking about you just recently."

"Thinking and praying, Laban?" she asked shrewdly.

There was a gruff laugh on the other end of the line. "You know me so well, my dear," he replied. "Anyway, to what do I owe this pleasure? I trust the family are all well?" There was a slight edge to Laban's voice as he wondered if this was bad news.

"Oh, everyone's fine Laban!" she answered. "I am ringing about my son Jacob."

"The business tycoon," he affirmed.

Rebekkah laughed. "Yes, that's the one. Laban, I wonder if the offer of a job still stands? He is such a beautiful boy and outstanding in business matters. He would do wonders for you and your company—already he outclasses people twice his age. Oh, and Laban you should see him! Such a catch! How are your daughters, by the way?"

Laban roared with laughter and Rebekkah quickly held the phone away from her ear.

"You are priceless, my darling Rebekkah, absolutely priceless! And yes! Yes, of course I have room in my company for Jacob— how can I resist such an offer? In fact, you were right when you said I'd been praying. I have a very special event coming up soon and I could do with someone to liaise with all my departments—

mind you, I would need him here almost immediately."

Rebekkah was thrilled. "It's a deal Laban! He will be with you before the end of the week. Now, give me all the details."

* * *

The next two days in Jacob's life were chaotic. The family reaction to his sudden departure was thoroughly mixed—a delighted mother, a proud father and a very very annoyed brother. Jacob was leaving for England the next day and there was almost no time to discuss it. Esau would continue to work the land, and Rebekkah was all ready to interview a new man for the day-by-day management.

Things were changing dramatically for Jacob. He had no time for nostalgia. He would work on overcoming the home-sickness later, when he had time to think. Right now, he was going over the last minute checks—passport, money—Australian and English—maps, flight tickets, cheque books and cashcards, personal effects: photos, books, clothes and after-shave! The thought of dressing in British designer clothes, catching taxis everywhere and eating in classy restaurants—not to mention the ladies he might escort on the arm of his Armani suit—gave him much pleasure. He hardly had time to think of what he was leaving behind.

When the car came the next day to take him on the first part of his journey to England, the family, staff and friends from other farms came to see him off. It was a strange farewell, because they were still coming to terms with the thought of Jacob not being there.

Jacob dutifully shook hands with his staff and hugged his friends. Then Isaac put his hand on his son's shoulder. "You make us proud, boy." It was an order, not a statement.

Then to Jacob's surprise, his father put his arms around him and gave him a huge bear-hug.

Rebekkah could hardly stand to be there. It was all her doing, yet she knew it was for the best ... but it still didn't make it any easier. Jacob, her wonderful, handsome, glorious son, was leaving her. She had said her goodbyes to him the night before, knowing that in the morning she would find it unbearable. He understood, and now came and put an arm gently around her waist and walked to the car with her. Neither of them spoke.

He did not expect a 'goodbye' from his brother, but as he went to get into the car, Esau pulled him abruptly to one side, away from everyone else. He stuck out his hand as if to shake hands with Jacob, but as the hands met, Esau's grip tightened and he looked straight into Jacob's eyes.

"If you ever, ever, get the notion to come home, think again little brother. I shall be here waiting for you and I'll kill you. Do you hear me? I don't know how you swung this—how you managed to keep your part of the company—but you don't belong Jacob, you never will. So as far as coming home again goes, don't even think about it. Have you got that?" Esau's eyes were nearly as red as his hair. He was in a terrible rage and his whole body was trembling. He let go of Jacob's hand and walked away.

Jacob watched him go. He almost felt sorry for him. Esau had nothing, and Jacob was just about to grab everything with both hands. He looked back for the last time at his mother. She was standing tall and proud with her skirt billowing around her legs— so majestic, so beautiful.

Where in the world would he find another woman like that?

CHAPTER

8

First class is the only way to travel, especially on a journey as long and exhausting as Australia to London. Jacob found he had plenty of time to examine the consequences of his actions. Leaving the family and friends that he loved and embarking on a totally new career was both exciting and frightening. What if it didn't work out? Where would he go? What would he do next? But in his heart of hearts, he knew he was born for this moment. Everything was waiting for him at his uncle's organisation, almost handed to him on a plate—all he had to do was to be himself and he would sail it, he knew it.

As he lounged sleepily in his seat, he wondered about Laban. Rebekkah had told him wonderful stories about this man who had started off with nothing and built up an entire network of radio stations worldwide. It would suit Jacob to work closely with the media—he felt comfortable with it already. He had taken the opportunity to buy stacks of magazines at the airport and was trying to fill himself in on any details of radio, TV and films that he could. As soon as they touched down in England, he would spend the entire evening glossing over every possible magazine he could buy in Oxford Street.

Buying, selling and promoting was something Jacob knew all about. It didn't really matter what the product was, whether it was sheep, farming stations, estates or broadcasting—as long as you looked good and told the people what they wanted to hear, there was really nothing to it, and judging by the admiring glances of the stewardesses, he certainly looked good. He hoped that he and Laban would hit it off instantly and that there would be no barrier of suspicion to overcome. Sitting in the plane, Jacob amused himself over long periods of time by enacting in his head the moment he would meet his Uncle Laban.

There were daughters as well, two of them. He wondered how they would react to having this unknown cousin thrust upon them, knowing he wouldn't be too pleased if it happened to him. Oh well, the Lindstein charm would doubtless come to the rescue if they were put out.

After an uneventful stop at Singapore, the Jumbo landed smoothly at Gatwick. Jacob felt the tension mounting—he had never set foot in Britain before and now he was about to make it his home. There would be no one to meet him—he had insisted that he preferred to go straight to an hotel and freshen up before meeting anyone at all. The last thing he wanted was to find he was dressed inappropriately, or to make some huge *faux pas* with English customs (*Crocodile Dundee* was popular in Australia too!) So he found himself hiring a quaint little English black taxi and being whisked off to the middle of London by himself.

The journey gave him time to look around. England was basically green, he thought to himself, as he was driven around Surrey, and pretty in parts, too. Once on the motorway, he immediately experienced his first traffic jam and his first talkative taxi driver—both of which he found amusing. The driver spoke in what he assumed was a Cockney accent. Finding the gossip and jokes very earthy, he was tempted to sit in the front so that he could catch more of this humour, until he realised there was only the driver's seat.

He found the taxis progress, weaving in and out of the traffic, quite alarming until he realised that London taxis rule the road and everyone else gets out of the way!

"First time in The Smoke, is it mate?" asked the driver cheerfully.

Jacob guessed the 'Smoke' must be a reference either to Britain or London, so he replied, "Yep, this is it. I'm an Aussie. Used to wide open spaces y'know."

The taxi driver nodded. "My mum's sister went out there. Loved it, she did. Keeps sending us pictures of them bears...."

"Koalas," Jacob filled in for him. "Cute fellas, but they bite."

"That's what she said. So, what are you doing over here—holiday?" asked the driver.

"No, I'm working here. Place called MBC, a radio corporation, have you heard of it?" Jacob asked.

"Is the Pope Catholic?" he replied, laughing. "You've gotta be living on another planet not to have heard of the MBC!"

His answer pleased Jacob. It was more than satisfying to know that the company you were representing was already a household name.

By now they were approaching the hotel; naturally, it was the Dorchester—MBC's second home. Jacob would be moving in with the family the following night, so he was going to make the most of staying in one of London's most prestigious hotels.

Park Lane and Hyde Park were exactly the same as the pictures he had seen, and it seemed strange to actually be there. It was quite a relief to get out and stretch his legs. He looked around while the driver and doorman dealt with his bags. It seemed that every other car driving down Park Lane was either a Rolls Royce or a Jaguar, and everyone walking along was impressively dressed and looked as if they knew exactly where they were going. It gave him a great feeling. Jacob desperately wanted to join this army of rich, handsome people and didn't realise that the others were already wondering who this tall, striking, dark-haired figure was, as he removed a pair of expensive shades and blinked at his new home.

As he passed through the intimidating entrance of the Dorchester, he was conscious of the silence of thick carpet and low spoken voices. It was so British—the reserve of the people, the respect for the guests. There was no one charging up to reception yelling, "G'day mate, where's my room?" Everything was so smooth and respectable, and the attendants guided him to his room with a sophistication he had never experienced before. It was hard to accept that these people worked here and were not actually guests themselves.

Jacob was unpacked and ready for action in a very short time. The adrenalin was racing through his veins. He looked out of his window at the glorious view of Hyde Park and knew that he would have to take a walk down this road and settle his curiosity before he could fully relax. So within minutes of actually being ensconced in his room, he was out again, walking briskly towards Marble Arch and Oxford Street. He passed by some magnificent car showrooms where he stopped and lusted after some very expensive and élite sports cars. The day was bright and everything looked exciting to him. On the corner of Marble Arch was a newspaper stand, selling every magazine you could think of, plus newspapers from all over the world. Next to the stand was another, covered in Union Jacks and miniature Beefeaters, and as he looked down Oxford Street, he found the assortment of nationalities was quite overwhelming. Americans you could spot a mile away, with their camcorders and loud raucous voices, and there were Japanese snapping photos from every conceivable angle, but the people who most caught his attention were Arabs (at least that's what he assumed they were) in beautiful long flowing robes and headgear—what a city! He took a deep breath and caught the smell of hot dogs, pizzas, petrol fumes and every now and then the smell of new leather from the stalls selling bags and belts. The whole place was so alive! This was where he wanted to be; this was what life was all about! He couldn't wait to get started and hurried back to the newspaper stand to buy one of everything English—much to the surprise of the vendor.

Back at the hotel he steeped himself in the papers and turned on the radio. He would listen to MBC whilst immersing himself in the media.

Five minutes later, he was sound asleep. His black hair flopping over the arm where his forehead was resting.

* * *

The Monklaasts were having a rare family Sunday at home. Laban tried hard to find time for his girls and now he had the added pressure of telling them about Jacob's arrival. It was a moment he had been putting off since Rebekkah's phone call. In one way he was sure they would not object to meeting a new relation, but on the other hand it was yet another invasion of their privacy—people were always staying at the house.

Rachel was home specifically to make peace with Leah who was still smarting from the Elliott Blaze incident. At least they were talking again. Neither of them had discussed the event with their father, so for the moment the subject was buried—although Leah would never forget it.

All three were sitting in the sun lounge at the back of the house. It was a favourite place of theirs, large and airy with patio doors that opened onto landscaped gardens, a place of peace and contentment. Laban was resting his feet on a stool which matched the beautifully upholstered wicker chairs.

"Ahh! If only I could work from home," he sighed, smiling at his daughters.

Rachel laughed. "Oh come on Daddy, you wouldn't last a week away from the office, and I don't think Leah and I could stand you pacing up and down waiting for the phone to ring!"

"It's a lovely home, even so," he replied. "You are happy here, aren't you?"

Both girls looked up in surprise at this remark, and Leah put her hand to her forehead. "That sounds suspiciously like the prelude to something you want to tell us, Father," she said.

Laban looked guiltily at his feet as he tried to think how to tell them.

"I think you are right, Leah," remarked Rachel, with a quizzical expression. "What are you planning Daddy?"

"I know," he started, "that I should have told you about this sooner ..."

There was a groan from both of them, and Rachel waved her hand to interrupt him. "Don't tell me—you are having the house re-decorated and we've got to move out," she suggested.

"No," put in Leah, "MBC are moving its main offices to ... Australia!" They both laughed at the thought.

"Very close!" Laban waved his finger at his eldest daughter.

They both stopped laughing and stared at him. Well, at least they were now thinking the worst, so maybe the news of their cousin wouldn't be quite so bad. He stretched out on his lounger and prepared to tell all.

"Now, you know that we have many important deals coming up soon—not the least this personal appearance of Elliott Blaze...."

The sisters froze. Please God, he wasn't thinking of letting Elliott stay here.

"I need," he continued, "a very special person to come into the company and liaise with all my departments. It's a specialised job and one I can't give to just anybody." He looked over to the girls. "I have prayed a great deal about this. It could alter the face of MBC if the right man is employed. And then I had a call from your Aunt Rebekkah ..."

"The one that lives in Australia!" put in Leah, catching up on the clues.

"Yes, that's right. Now, she has a son, Jacob. He's very bright and talented and has a wonderful head for business ..."

"...and you've never met him." Rachel said in a small voice. This was a little worrying.

"That is true. I have never met him, but I know his mother very, very well, and if she is anything to go by, then Jacob will be exactly the man I need."

Rachel glanced sideways at Laban. "You've already asked him, haven't you?" She countered.

Her father sighed. "Yes. I wanted to tell you sooner, but ..."

The girls stared at each other, wondering what to say next. Laban's judgement of people was almost foolproof, but to offer a responsible job with a huge salary to someone you've never met...

"What does he do in Australia?" asked Leah trying to get a grasp on the situation.

"He ran a sheep station," said Laban flatly.

Both Leah and Rachel raised their voices together. How could a sheep station have any bearing on a radio station? What would this Jacob know about the media? And what did Laban mean when he said he ran a sheep station? What was he doing now?

"I imagine he's sitting in the lounge of his Dorchester suite wondering if Laban Monklaast's daughters are going to give him a hard time," he replied.

"He's already here?!" yelled Leah, jumping out of her seat. "The guy is already in the country and you haven't even told us about him? No, let me guess ..." She held both her hands up in protest. "He's staying here isn't he? This jerk from Australia is going to be our 'live-in' cousin from the outback. Great!" She threw herself back into the cushions.

Rachel, always the peacemaker, came to her father's rescue.

"Hold on Leah, we know nothing about him. We can't go making judgements till we've at least met him."

"Well, that didn't seem to bother Daddy, did it?" She replied crossly.

Now it was Laban's turn to cut in. "You are quite right, darling." He said looking at Leah. "But please give him a chance. I know, I just know this is the right move. If I'm wrong ... I'll do what's necessary to sort it out. Hmm?"

It grew quiet in the sun lounge as Rachel and Leah sat and thought over this latest event in their lives.

"When do we meet MBC's new hero?" asked Leah sarcastically.

"He will be in the office tomorrow, and I will bring him home tomorrow night," He replied simply.

The silence resumed.

*   *   *

Monday lunchtime found Rachel sitting opposite Aaron in a sandwich bar. He had phoned her that morning and she was more than pleased to take a break from work and snatch a bite to eat with him. Aaron didn't really know his way around, so she had suggested meeting by Oxford Street Station, then they ducked down a few side streets until they found this fairly quiet cafe. Rachel realised that pretty soon this kind of place would be awkward for Aaron as his face would be too familiar to everyone—but right now it was just fine.

"So, are you finding your feet now?" asked Rachel, as she picked the cucumber out of her sandwich. This was one of her traits—she didn't realise it herself but when she was distracted she picked at things, like fluff on jumpers, corners of serviettes and salad from sandwiches.

"Don't you like cucumber?" Aaron asked abruptly.

Rachel came back to earth and shook her head. "Huh? What? Sorry, I was miles away." She smiled at him.

He grinned back and shrugged his shoulders. "It's OK, I'm used to being ignored."

Rachel automatically reached out and touched his hand. "Don't be silly Aaron. You are a great tonic to me, and I love having lunch with you—it's just that things are a bit strange at home at the moment." Her eyes looked far away again.

"Anything you want to tell me?" he asked?

To his surprise, she nodded. "You know this Elliott Blaze visit?" she asked.

Aaron felt the hackles go up on the back of his neck, but tried to look calm. "Of course. I'm having him on my show remember?"

"Well, Daddy's bringing in someone to liaise with each department—which is a really good idea—but it's just that he's never actually met the person."

Aaron frowned. "How d'you mean?"

And before she knew it, Rachel was telling him the whole story and then as much as she knew about Jacob. This was something she would never normally do, but somehow she trusted Aaron. It was good to have him for a friend and she valued his company.

"Phew Rache, you do jump in the deep end, don't you? Still, at least this Jacob character might come in handy if Blaze gets up to his tricks again. If you can't find me, you could always go to him." Already that was beginning to sound like a bad idea—he wanted to look after Rachel himself, but if this Aussie was a relation, it couldn't really do much harm.

"When do you get to meet him?" he asked.

"Apparently, he's coming in today, but I shall be busy all afternoon with auditions and it looks as if it's going to be a late night as well. I probably won't see him until tomorrow, at home. You'll see him before me I think. Daddy's bound to introduce you as soon as possible" She added.

At that moment Jacob was just leaving his hotel room for his first appointment with Laban.

Also at the same moment, Leah was thinking that maybe the trip she was making to her father's office would be good this afternoon. Somehow it might make her feel better to meet this cousin before Rachel. Who knows? He might actually be nice!

CHAPTER

9

Jacob looked impressive. Standing at the front of the hotel while the doorman organised a taxi, he was an imposing figure. Tall, straight, handsome, the expensive dark suit accentuating his dark eyes, and an elegant hand holding a brief-case—this was a guy obviously going somewhere. He slid into the cab with the practised ease of one accustomed to having doors opened for him, and enjoyed his first 'official' ride to an engagement.

His outward appearance belied the fact that Jacob was quite nervous about meeting his new boss. He knew that he had to make an impression as a businessman as well as a relation and wanted to succeed at both. The taxi moved slowly down Oxford Street and it seemed to take forever to get to the MBC building. When they finally made it, Jacob strode over to the reception desk with the air of someone who had worked there all his life.

He smiled at the receptionist and asked for Laban. He was so enchanting that it took her a few seconds to realise that she hadn't asked him for his name.

"Jacob Lindstein," he stated, still smiling as he looked her straight in the eyes. It never failed to work, and the normally efficient woman became flustered. Eventually, she looked up at him again.

"Ah yes," she smiled. "Mr Monklaast is expecting you. If you would like to take a seat, his personal assistant will be down to escort you to his office in just a moment." Her eyes followed Jacob as he walked over to the seating area. Things were looking up at MBC.

Henrietta arrived almost immediately. She had no intention of keeping Laban's relation hanging around downstairs, and like everyone else, she was curious to meet him. He had his head in a magazine and Henry had to repeat his name before he paid attention to her.

"Mr Lindstein?" she asked again.

"Oh sorry!" The engaging smile again. "You must be my uncle's PA.?"

"Henrietta, but most people call me Henry," She confided.

He liked her instantly. She was warm and friendly without being too familiar and he felt she could be relied on. Henry held her hand out and they acknowledged each other. He followed her to the lift and they made polite conversation on the way up. She was more than pleased with what she saw and felt that Laban had made a wise choice—this man was going to charm the pants off everyone—she almost chuckled aloud at the thought.

"This will be quite a family reunion," she remarked. "One of Mr Monklaast's daughters works close by, so I'm sure she will pop over to meet you this afternoon."

"I'm looking forward to it." He nodded. "I've never actually met them, and my mothers photos are way out of date!"

His Australian accent was soft and laid-back and gave the impression that everything was under control and nothing was going to be a problem. Well, if he could convey that feeling to the heads of department—he would be on to a winner, she thought.

The lift door opened and Henry ushered Jacob into her office. She immediately went to the phone and buzzed Laban. "Jacob Lindstein is here for you," she said officially.

The door to his office flew open almost before the phone was put down.

Laban stood with his arms outstretched and looked in proud admiration at this boy who was everything he could have hoped for. Yes, he had Rebekkah's features, and so handsome! Confidence oozed from him and Laban was already making mental notes of ways to bring out his character.

"Jacob! This is a wonderful moment!" he cried, and took the boy in his arms and hugged him. Jacob was elated, he couldn't have begged for a better reception. Laban kept one arm around him and waved his other arm towards his sumptuous office.

"Come in, come in! Make yourself at home, Henry will pour you a drink and we can spend some time talking of the family—and then we will get down to business!" He led the way through to the lounge area and pulled up some leather armchairs. Jacob briefed Laban on the family history and the events at the station, and in turn Laban told him of the family waiting for him here.

"The house at Monks Lodge is large and there's plenty of room for you to have your own space," he said. "My staff have made a small apartment up in of one of the wings, I'm sure you will be comfortable there. My daughters Leah and Rachel can't wait to meet you and I'm sure you will get on very well with them."

"I'm sure I shall ... er ... uncle ..."

"I think it will be best if you call me Laban—or Mr Monklaast at the office," he advised.

Jacob smiled and nodded in agreement. "Thank you, Laban. I can't wait to meet my new family and to get started on whatever project you have for me. Mother told me that you are somewhat of a workaholic—and I'm afraid I am too, so don't be afraid of pushing me too hard."

Laban clapped his hands. "I'm sure we will get along fine. And as you are so keen, let me tell you what I have in mind and I'd appreciate any input you have too."

Neither of the two men noticed how the next few hours flew past as they pored over papers and documents together. It was going to work out just fine.

*   *   *

David Lander's talent scout, Dean, wasn't having such a good day. He had spent most of it in an empty theatre watching second-rate acts trying to convince him that they were the answer to an entertainments agency's prayer. He was just thinking of a new career move when Rachel walked in to join him. "How's it going?"

As she leant across to him he could smell her perfume, she even managed to get that right. To Dean it was a heady scent and made him want to close his eyes and dream of fields and poppies and sunshine ... and Rachel.

With his usual brand of humour, he replied, "How's what going?" Then started in surprise as he turned towards the stage. "How long have they been there?" he said in mock astonishment, pointing at two men pointlessly strumming guitars.

Rachel dissolved into giggles and punched him playfully. "Really Dean, you're terrible! These poor people are in great earnest and all you can do is make fun of them!"

"Well I wish 'great Earnest' would come and take them back again," He muttered. And Rachel laughed again.

"So, nothing exciting then?" she asked. Days like this were so long. The 'conveyor-belt' system of watching new acts was soul-destroying, usually for both parties. The only thing that kept Dean going perhaps was knowing that one in every hundred acts would reveal some new sparkling talent—and the thought of letting some other talent scout find it was pressure enough for him.

"What I'm really looking for today," he told her, "is someone with an excellent singing voice for the new musical that Edward Barnsley is promoting. He asked me to keep an eye out, and I'd love to get a foot in the door there. But unfortunately he needs someone who sings like Michael Crawford and looks like Tom Cruise!"

"No joy then?" asked Rachel impishly.

"Well, I had one who could sing like Nora Batty and looked like Edd the Duck, but that's the closest so far," he whispered back.

Rachel sunk into her seat and put her hand over her mouth. Sometimes this job was hard to take seriously.

Dean turned to her. "I thought maybe we could take it in turns. You do an hour, then I'll do another and the third hour we'll both sit in. If you come across anything exciting, get them to stay behind and I'll audition them again at the end."

Rachel nodded and looked at the list of names she had been handed on the way in.

"Where are we up to? Are they the 'Palaminos' or the Dewey Brothers?"

"Both ... I think." Dean looked down the running order. "No, these are The Palaminos. The Dewey Brothers are all yours—I'm off for coffee!"

Rachel watched Dean escaping down the aisle, sighed and settled back to spend the remainder of the day and most of the evening watching mind-numbing artists giving it their all.

*   *   *

"The Elliott Blaze promotion is one of the biggest events we've handled for a while," Laban was explaining to Jacob. "Of course, we have our normal helping of celebrities, for radio interviews, live concerts and promotional ties, but Elliott Blaze is a one-off. We have to handle this with kid gloves. He is just as likely to call the whole thing off at the last moment, if everything isn't exactly right."

"Hmm. He sounds quite a handful. How are the people immediately surrounding him? Your press guys, marketing and so on?" asked Jacob.

"Ah, well, that's where you come in. I have some very impressive people on my staff and they are all excellent at their jobs, but what I need is someone to stand in the middle and collate it all. I need to make sure that every department is aware of what everyone else is doing. What I don't want is to find that the marketing department have set up a signing session the same time as an important lunchdate or interview. It's an easy mistake to make, and although they will all handle Elliott well, he won't take kindly to being pushed about." Laban's face was serious.

"So what about escorts? Is someone looking after him after hours? Do we have someone with him most of the time? You know it's the 'off-duty' hours that cause the most heartache. If the press see him wining and dining with the wrong crowd."

Laban smiled at Jacob's grasp of the situation. "That's all taken care of. My daughter will be his companion for the week. She is utterly charming, very English and the soul of discretion. I can assure you she will not let us down—as you'll find out when you meet her. I'm hoping she might be in this afternoon. It would be good for the two of you to meet and discuss your plans. She is a most beautiful girl—I'm sure you'll like her."

Secretly, having now seen Jacob, Laban's words were particularly heartfelt.

"So, I'll actually be working with your daughter for a while," Jacob mused. People in the entertainment business have a saying, 'Never work with children or animals' and he wondered whether working so closely with another member of the family was a good idea. Obviously, the daughter would not be a child, but it made him more intent on creating a good impression on them both. If he was going to live in the same house, they just had to get on!

Outside the office, Henry was being treated to the unexpected visit from Leah. Laban's eldest had no time for niceties and for-malities—if she felt like seeing her father, she just waltzed in —convenient or not.

Henry was trying very hard to be nice to her and at the same time delay her. "Leah, what a nice surprise! Come and sit with me, I've just filtered some coffee." Henry did her utmost to make her feel comfortable.

Leah glanced over to the mirror on Henry's wall. She thought she looked good today. Before she came out she spent some time trying to put her hair up the way Rachel did it, but failed miser-ably and ended up holding some of it back with combs and leav-ing the rest loose. Her make-up was well done, but again she lacked the knack of bringing out her best features. In fact on the whole, standing there in her casual jacket and black skirt, she looked like a pale imitation of Rachel. If her sister had not existed, and there was therefore no comparison, it was possible that she would turn a few heads and maybe that would have changed her attitude, make her more approachable, more likeable. But Leah had a grudge against the world and was not about to do it any favours.

"How are you?" asked Henry smiling brightly. "We haven't seen you for a while. Such a busy social person these days I hear."

Leah's chin lifted even higher as she replied, "Ah yes. Personally I think I'd die if I sat in a little office all day, making cof-fee and phone calls. Still, I suppose it suits some people." She reached over for the cup that Henry had just poured for her. "Hmm, I think there's still lipstick on this." She handed it back to Henry.

Henry fumed inside. There wasn't the slightest mark on the cup, she knew it and Leah knew it, but the game must be played out.

"Oh dear," she said. "I don't know how that could have hap-pened. Here let me make you a fresh cup."

Leah waved her hand at Henry. "No, don't bother. I'm really just here to say a quick hello to Daddy. We are expecting a relation from Australia to arrive today—is he here yet? I think his name is Jason, or Jacob or something ..."

The situation was now out of Henry's hands. She knew there was no alternative.

"Jacob Lindstein." She nodded. "Yes, he arrived for a meeting with your father—in fact they are still talking. Would you like me to buzz through and see if I can interrupt?"

"No point. I'm his daughter, for goodness' sake! I don't need an appointment!" She brushed past Henry and headed for the door. Hastily Henry reached for the phone and managed to get to Laban.

"Your daughter is on her way in!" she announced.

"Terrific!" Laban smiled as he put the phone down. "Well, Jacob, I want you to meet one of my lovely girls."

And as they both looked towards the door, Leah made her entrance. Then everything happened at once.

"Leah!" said Laban in surprise as she walked towards him. "Ah ... umm ... yes well Jacob, as I was saying, this is my daughter Leah."

Jacob watched her as she walked across the room. She was very well groomed and obviously brought up with money. Her face wasn't exactly pretty, but not unattractive; however it was her pose he had the most difficulty with. There was something in the way she held herself that made him stand back.

He suddenly pulled himself together and realised that this was his moment to make a good impression—especially if they were to work together. So as he moved towards her he let his eyes hold her face, silently appraising her. He worked on looking solemn for a moment, so that when he finally smiled at her she would be hooked—just like the others.

Leah stood still and looked at Jacob. He was without doubt the most handsome, sensuous man she had ever seen. His whole body seemed to scream at her. As her eyes moved to his face she found she couldn't look away. He smiled at her as his hand closed on hers. He pulled her to him and kissed her cheek. His lips felt soft and warm, and the cologne he was wearing seemed to drown all her senses.

"Hello, Leah," he whispered, still a little too close. "It's great to meet a distant cousin ..."

Leah's eyes met his, and she thought she would die.

CHAPTER

10

Aaron Holloway met Jacob Lindstein almost by accident. At Laban's suggestion, Jacob was wandering around the building 'getting the feel of the place'. He had a short list of room numbers and departments, and wanted to go and introduce himself to the rest of the team. He felt happier going unannounced—that way he would meet the 'real' person, rather than the one put on for show once they found out who he was.

He had met Simon Darrell and enjoyed a conversation with this 'man after his own heart', and James Ledbury he felt he could learn to live with.

Now, he made his way down to the 'bowels' of the building, where he found a set of studios, some busy, one 'on the air' and then another where Aaron sat cataloguing his records ready for his new show. Jacob saw him sitting there and knocked on the already open door. Aaron looked up at once and waved Jacob in.

Walking into a sound studio is a strange experience, because 'sound' is the last thing you get. The intense soundproofing takes the life out of the place, and for a moment Jacob couldn't be sure if it wasn't his own hearing that was wrong.

"What can I do for you?" Aaron's young face was astonishingly open, his blue eyes frank and wide, echoing his whole attitude to life. He was sitting in a swivel chair wearing a pair of very pale blue jeans and a baggy white shirt over which he wore a plain black waistcoat.'Young male model' was how Jacob saw him, and wondered who he was.

"Ah, I'm shortly to be working here," he explained "so I thought I'd have a look round."

Aaron watched the way he moved, as if he were taking over the company. This guy with his gold watch and sharp suit was intriguing. He swivelled round on his chair again.

"Fine! That makes two of us. I'm Aaron Holloway, the 'Chart MBC' station's new DJ. I don't start my show for a while, so I spend most of my time finding empty studios to work on my repertoire. See that pile of CDs? That's just this morning's—y'know when I was a DJ at a club, I used to have to beg, borrow and steal new material all the time—but here—phew! There's no way you can use it all, or even get through hearing half of it! Amazing eh!" He flipped open the top album and put it in the CD player, turning the volume down so that they could still talk.

"Perks of the job," said Jacob, frankly. "You obviously like music—it's good to get paid for something you love doing."

"Hey! You're Australian!" said Aaron excitedly brushing hair out of his eyes. And before Jacob could answer, he carried on. "Of course, you must be Rachel's cousin ... Jacob, isn't it? She's been telling me about you." He grinned.

"Has she?" replied Jacob, somewhat taken aback. "I haven't met her yet, just her sister Leah."

"Wow! The fire dragon!" blurted the DJ before he could stop himself. He bit his lip. "I'm sorry. I shouldn't be talking about your family like that."

Jacob was interested and determined to grill this guy. "What made you call her that? Laban spent a while trying to give me the impression that she was the most beautiful girl in the world. I must admit I was slightly disappointed when I met her—but as I'm to be working with her, I'm giving it my best shot."

"Working with her?" Aaron looked puzzled, and looked

distractedly at the cover of the next CD. "She doesn't work here."

"No, I realise that. But apparently Laban said she was to escort Elliott Blaze while he's here. I don't know how much of a success that's liable to be, however ..."

Aaron suddenly caught on to the mistake, and thumped the table with his fist as he laughed.

"No, no mate! You've got this all round the wrong way! Did Laban actually say it was Leah that would be working for him?"

Jacob thought back. "Now that you mention it, I think he just referred to her as his daughter."

"Well, there you are, you see! It's not Leah who's escorting Elliott, it's Rachel, Laban's other daughter," declared Aaron.

Jacob frowned. "So, if Leah is the Fire Dragon, do I take it that Rachel is the Ice Maiden?"

Aaron's face clouded. He wanted to say 'No, she's the most beautiful person you'll ever meet and she's much too good for you, so get lost, mister!' Instead he tossed the CD cover aside and said, "No, Rachel's OK. She's a good friend." He couldn't bring himself to look at Jacob. But it was too late anyway.

Jacob read him like a book. So, this little teeny-idol had designs on his second cousin, did he? Well, if Rachel was younger than Leah, perhaps it was a good thing. He didn't particularly like his women immature. Aaron could have her.

He glanced at his watch.

"Time to go. Nice talking to you, Aaron, I'll catch up with you later." They exchanged swift goodbyes and Jacob left the studio.

Aaron sat on his own, staring at the turntables for quite a while. Elliott Blaze, and now him. He knew that Rachel didn't care for Elliott, but this other guy, Jacob, she might like him. He pursed his lips and sighed heavily at the thought.

*   *   *

At six-thirty, Rachel was back in her Byron Street office, taking a well-earned break from the auditions. Sarah was just packing her make-up away into her shoulder bag, ready to go home.

"I just don't know how Dean can stand doing that, day in, day out." Rachel was saying. "I mean, it's fun for the first few hours, but after that, it can get incredibly boring. Do you know, the last four acts I had to watch, all sang the same song? No marks for originality."

"He loves it, Rachel," remarked Sarah, checking her purse for the train fare. "And he's good at it! Talent scouts are hard to come by. I remember when Mr Landers first hired him, he was so thrilled you'd have thought he'd won first prize in a lottery! Dean's a really nice guy, very genuine and a lot of fun to be with."

Rachel looked up in surprise. "What's this? It sounds as if you're trying to sell him to me."

The secretary toyed with her bag strap. "He likes you a lot, you know," she said, tentatively.

"Oh, no! Don't you dare pull that one with me!" laughed Rachel, putting her hands up as if to stop her friend's next state-ment. "I have no designs on Dean and he knows it. Don't you dare let him pull the wool over your eyes—we've been through this one before!"

"It's such a shame though," sighed Sarah. "You ought to see the way he looks at you when he thinks you're not watching."

Rachel was about to reply, when the door of the office burst open and Leah rushed in. She looked for all the world like she'd been running (unheard of), her hair blown by the wind and a wild look in her eyes. She glanced swiftly round the room, noted Sarah and said, "Just off are we?"

The secretary's face reddened. She was used to Leah making rude comments, but this was blatant. She wanted to push her back through the door and down the stairs, but instead she took a deep breath, smiled and said, "Hello, Leah. Yes, I'm already late as usual—now where's my coat?" She turned round and picked up a waisted leather jacket. "Ah. Right, see you then."

And with that she disappeared out of the door.

"Thank goodness she's gone," said Leah ungratefully. She threw her things onto the table and stood looking at her sister.

Rachel was concerned. This wasn't Leah's usual stance, and she hardly ever came to the office, since she considered it beneath her. Also, there was something different about her—an air of something Rachel couldn't quite define.

"You're lucky to catch me here ..." Rachel started.

"Tell me about it!" her sister cut in. She walked over to the desk that Rachel was sitting at and leant over, placing her hands on the top of it. "I never expected to 'collect' quite as soon as this, but something's come up."

"Leah, stop talking in riddles." Rachel was still concerned about her. She couldn't remember seeing her quite like this before.

"I've come to collect, Rachel." Leah looked straight into Rachel's eyes with a stare so fierce that it made her sister glance nervously round the room.

"I'm sorry, I'm still not with you."

Leah began roaming round the room, like a lioness wary of her opposition. She turned quickly and focused on Rachel's face again. "The Elliott Blaze incident, Rachel. You made me look a fool and I told you that one day I would want paying for that—it's just that the day has come sooner than expected." She paused for effect. "I've just come from Father's office."

Rachel stared at her blankly.

"I've just met our distant relation. The guy from Australia who is coming to stay with us."

"You've met Jacob," said Rachel, stating the obvious and wondering what all this was about.

"Yes."

As she answered, Rachel saw her sister's face change dramatically. It softened, her hands went to her hair, her eyes moistened and her lips parted. "He's mine, Rachel. I've just met him and he's mine. We just looked at each other and knew ... I ... "

Rachel rushed out from behind her desk and took her sister's hands in hers. "Leah! This is marvellous! Tell me, tell me! What happened, what's he like?" She was so thrilled for her sister. If this cousin could make Leah act this way, and if he felt the same way about her—it was fantastic!

In a sudden change of temperament, Leah threw Rachel's hands away from her, and walked to the other side of the room.

"I don't want you anywhere near him." Her hands went to her hips and she threw out a challenge with a toss of her head. "Not that he'd be stupid enough to fall just for looks—no, he's beyond that. He's sensitive and intelligent—and you are keeping well out of his way, understand?" The flashing from Leah's eyes, in fact from her whole being, was frightening.

Rachel's heart was beating fast. She knew she had to try and calm Leah down, so that they could talk sensibly. She moved over to the filter machine and poured two cups of coffee, then placed one cup in Leah's hand.

"Please sit down, Leah," she said softly. "I don't want your man, I would never do anything to come between you and someone you like." She put her coffee down. "Please, Leah. Tell me about it, don't let's quarrel—I'm happy for you, really I am."

This was too much for Leah, who was dying to talk about Jacob to someone ... maybe ...

Rachel pulled Leah's hand and made her sit down. "Leah, please believe me. I have never tried to spoil things for you. The Elliott thing was dreadful, but I only wanted to please you— it just went wrong, that's all. There is no way I would try to drive any sort of wedge between you and someone you l ..." she was going to say 'loved' but somehow it didn't seem right ... "wanted," she ended lamely.

Leah looked livid. "If you really mean that, then I want you to do something for me."

"Of course," Rachel answered.

"Don't come home tonight," She said flatly.

"Oh Leah! I can't not come home! Daddy would be extremely upset if I didn't at least meet Jacob. It would look so rude!"

"Then come home late. Go straight to bed and meet him in the morning! Please, Rachel! Just give me one evening to stake my claim!"

This was crazy, thought Rachel. What do I do? "Okay," she said. "I'm going to be late anyway, we don't finish auditions till around ten. I suppose I could always eat here and arrive home in the early hours." Her mind was buzzing, she hoped this cousin was on the level and not some fortune-grabber with designs on her sister.

Leah stood up, satisfied with Rachels answer.

"Thanks." And she was out of the door, hailing a taxi and making plans.

Rachel was left alone in the office wondering what to do. She picked up the phone and dialled MBC.

"Aaron Holloway, please. It's Rachel Monklaast."

She waited, hoping he was still there, then smiled and looked relieved.

"Hi Aaron! I know this is short notice, but I'm having to work late—do you fancy that curry we always talked about? Later tonight?" She laughed at his reply and made arrangements to meet him at ten-thirty.

In Studio Two, Aaron put the phone down and stared at it with mixed feelings.

CHAPTER

11

Aaron was still sitting staring at the phone, half-an-hour after Rachel had rung. There were so many thoughts running around inside his head. Everything seemed to be happening at once. One minute he was playing records in local clubs and doing the odd stint on commercial radio, and the next he was flying high in probably the best job he would ever have.

Only a couple of days ago, he had been for a photo session. This was all new to Aaron, and he expected the whole experience to last about an hour. Instead he was there most of the day. The photographers were obviously very good and were bringing the best out in him. He had spent hours sitting cross-legged on the floor in front of a totally white screen, hugging various cuddly toys, pulling at his own clothes, looking up, looking down, looking surprised, looking as if he had just been caught doing something he shouldn't, crawling around on all fours, and standing up against the backdrop with his hands in the air as if someone was going to shoot him. It was all to make his yet-to-be-discovered fans, want to protect him.

At first they made him up heavily but then realised he didn't need it and just blackened his eyelashes and blushed his cheeks. The whole thing was very confusing for Aaron, who at this point was unable to see the end results.

Now, the first prints were on his desk and he still couldn't come to terms with what he saw. Some of the poses made him feel guilty just looking at them—it was him, and yet it was this other guy, this teenage idol he was becoming, even before anyone had heard of him. He decided he needed to talk to someone—and then Rachel rang. Here was another question mark in his life. He was doing his best to treat her as a friend (and he really needed her as one) and yet he knew that he was growing to like her more as the days went by. He glanced at the photos again—did she see him like this? He fervently hoped not, it wasn't what he wanted at all.

He rubbed his face with his hands in an effort to bring himself back down to earth. Perhaps they could talk these things over. He sat looking over his desk, his fringe tangling with his eyelashes. He pushed the hair roughly out of the way—that was another thing: they wouldn't let him cut his hair either.

* * *

The Shahi was a good Indian restaurant. Rachel used it quite a lot when eating late—it was a wonderful way to wind down. The waiters walked around so silently, and the feeling and smell of the place almost made you want to take your shoes off and stretch. She often went there with Dean and Sarah if auditions had run late. It would be nice to sit and chat with Aaron for a change. She wondered how he was coping with life at MBC. The nice thing about being with Aaron was that he was hardly likely to notice that she looked tired and that her make-up was a little the worse for wear. She sat nursing a glass of wine, as she waited.

He arrived in his usual style, white shirt tails flying out behind him, hands in jeans pockets and grin a mile wide. For the second time that evening, people turned to stare. They had done the same when Rachel walked in earlier. There were some low whisperings as he took his seat opposite Rachel. The Indian waiter presented them with a menu each and walked away smiling to himself.

"Hi Rache, you look great!"

Rachel couldn't help laughing. "No I don't! I look disastrous! I've been working since nine this morning and I'm shattered." She picked up the menu.

Aaron looked at her quizzically and shrugged his shoulders. "You look fine to me. Man, I'm starving—did you eat anything earlier?"

It was so refreshing to be with this guy. In all probability she could turn up for lunch wearing overalls and a balaclava, and it wouldn't worry him in the slightest.

"So how's it going for you at MBC?" she asked.

"There's a lot of things I want to ask you," he replied. "There's more to this game than I first thought. I really would value your opinion on a few things." He looked up at her through his hair, blue eyes pleading to be taken seriously.

"OK. Let's order and then talk. I've a few things to tell you as well." She said discreetly.

He raised one eyebrow and she laughed at him.

"What shall we eat?"

They spent a few minutes choosing too much food, because Aaron thought he could eat everything on the menu. Finally, they settled down to chat while they waited for the food to arrive.

"So, what was it you wanted to discuss?" Rachel asked.

Aaron frowned and sat back in his seat. He put his hands behind his head. "It's this whole 'teenage idol' bit." He sat forward quickly and asked, "Rachel, when you look at me, what do you see?"

Taken aback by the abruptness of the question, she laughed and asked, "What do you mean?"

"I don't know ... first impressions—that sort of thing."

She tried to take in the picture of the young man sitting in front of her. "I don't know ... young ... good-looking ... funny—yes definitely funny ... confident ... enthusiastic. Why? What do you want to know for?"

"I had to go for a photo session the other day. It really freaked me out," he confided.

Rachel nodded. Photo sessions were certainly an ordeal and even gruelling if you were not used to it. She had seen plenty of stars suffer the pains of these sessions.

Aaron produced an envelope and passed it over to her.

"Look at these. Tell me what you think."

She undid the brown packet and put the pile of photographs on the table.

"Wow!" She sat up in surprise. "They really went to town, didn't they!" She sifted through the colour prints and stopped to gasp now and again. She held up the photo of Aaron looking guilty with a finger in his mouth, and looked at him quizzically. "How did they get this one?" She joked.

"That's just what I mean!" replied Aaron. "They're experts at getting you to pose just how they want. I don't know how they do it—they just egg you on ... I don't know ... " He was lost for words.

Rachel put the prints down. "Do they worry you?" She asked him seriously.

"I don't know if 'worry' is the right word. They frighten me a bit ... I mean ... I'm not that guy in these photos. That's not me ... not the real me. Am I going to have to get used to seeing myself as someone else?" His eyes were quite piercing.

"Is that why you asked me what I thought of you?" Rachel asked quietly.

The food arrived, and they helped themselves from a series of dishes in the middle of the candlelit table.

Aaron pointed his fork at her.

"If this is going to be the 'new me', I'd like to think that at least one person knows me as I really am."

It was difficult not to run round the table and hug Aaron when he was like this. She could understand both points of view. The publicity people would think he was God's gift to every teenage girl, but Aaron was expecting to be a DJ—someone who is heard but not seen very often.

She took a deep breath. "You know, you and I are very alike, Aaron. I have spent most of my life wondering if people like me for myself. Good looks can be a blessing, but they can also cause a lot of heartache. My father always says I should count my blessings, that God gave me good looks—but it certainly makes you wary of why people are nice to you."

Aaron's knife and fork clattered to the table. "You don't think that I like you just because you look great, do you?" It hadn't occurred to him that this thing could work both ways.

"Present company excepted!" she smiled. "No, I'm just saying that I know how it feels. Look, my father will make sure that you get a group of people around you who will always accept you for what you are. Henrietta is a great person to lean on when the going gets tough. She'll never ever treat you like a star. She will certainly respect you, but she will always see you as the nervous young man who walked into her office on his first day. She still buys me jelly babies!"

"What's with you and jelly babies, then?" asked Aaron enjoying this banter.

She waved her hand at him. "Oh, the first time I went to her office, when she first worked there, she had a jar of sweets on the desk and I absent-mindedly ate most of them while I was talking to her. You know how terrible I am for picking at things!"

Aaron's face lit up as he laughed at her. "You know, we should make a pact. If you ever get conceited about your looks, I'll remind you of the jelly babies, and if I ever become a mean and moody pop star, you can remind me that my mum will tell me off if I don't behave myself!"

"It's a deal!" Rachel held out her hand and Aaron grasped it firmly.

"Here's to us, then," he said softly, not letting go.

The spell of the moment was broken by the waiter enquiring after their meal.

"Everything's fine," Rachel nodded at him. Aaron let go of her hand self-consciously.

"Wasn't there something you wanted to talk to me about?" he asked. "All this talk about me is getting a bit boring. What's happening in your neck of the woods then, Rache?"

Rachel was thankful for Aaron's tactful change of subject.

"Ah yes," she replied thoughtfully. "I don't even know if I should be telling you this, but I haven't really got anyone else to talk it over with ..."

"Fire away" he was always so down to earth. She trusted him implicitly.

"Leah came round to the office earlier," she started.

"Wow! Is that the same Leah that wouldn't be seen dead anywhere near your place of work?" he asked in surprise.

"The very same," she joined in. "Apparently, she has met our new cousin. You know, Jacob the Australian?"

Bells started to ring inside Aaron's head and he subconsciously gripped the side of his chair. He nodded for her to go on.

"I'm a little worried Aaron. She seems to think that it's love at first sight. He looked at her, she looked at him—you know the kind of thing?"

He swallowed hard not daring to speak.

"Anyway, she wanted me out of the way tonight so that she and Jacob could have some time to get to know each other. I promised to stay out of the way and sneak in late tonight and not meet him until the morning ... which is why I wanted you to have a late meal with me," she explained.

Throwing cold water on Aaron could not have done a better job than those words. He hated the thought of being 'an excuse'.

Rachel saw a shadow cross Aaron's beautiful face. "Oh, no! I'm sorry—that sounded as if I was using you! Aaron, I love meeting you, our talks and things are very important to me, and as I said before, there's no one else ..."

"It's all right Rachel, I know what you meant." His heart lifted a little. She was worried—he shouldn't expect so much of her. "So, Leah fancies Jacob, eh?"

Rachel shook her curls. "No, no. I think it's more than that. She's got it into her head that he's the only man in the world for her. Intelligent, sensitive—those were her words. But what if he's just after the MBC money? Its happened before, you know."

"You're joking!" said Aaron, incredulously. "You mean, people really do go after each other for money? I thought that only happened in books!"

"It's happened to Leah on numerous occasions. That's why I'm worried. I haven't met Jacob yet, but I'm already wary of him." She sighed. "That's not a very good attitude. Judging someone before you've even met them."

There was silence and Aaron played with one of the candles.

"I've met him," he said simply.

Rachel looked amazed and then puzzled. "You've met him? Why didn't you tell me? When? What is he like?"

Aaron pursed his lips. "Well, to answer in order: yes, I have met him, I didn't tell you because I haven't had a chance, I met him today and he was all right."

Rachel looked at Aaron closely. What wasn't he telling her? His head was down—she was getting used to his way—he always looked down if he wasn't sure of something. His hair covered his eyes so you couldn't see what he was thinking and his hand invariably went to his mouth and covered up any other expression.

"Aaron?"

He glanced over to her.

"Tell me about him, please," she asked.

He let out a long sigh and his over-large long white shirt spanned the chairs as he stretched out his arms. "I don't know

Rache. I really did only just meet him for about ten minutes."

"First impressions?" She reminded him.

"Umm ... Good suit, very good suit. Gold jewellery, watch and stuff. Air of confidence. Dark hair, handsome—tall, dark and handsome in fact. Oh yes, and he had an Australian accent!" He finished, trying to smile.

Rachel leant across the table and pushed him playfully. "Australian accent, huh? You're very quick, aren't you? Oh well, he sounds OK. Not my type, so I don't think I'll cause much of a threat."

"What makes you think he's not your type?" asked Aaron quickly.

"You've heard the expression 'Medallion Man', haven't you?"

Handsome guy, gold jewellery and although you saw it as 'confidence' I would guess he loves himself. Definitely not for me," she stated flatly.

Aarons' heart started to soar. Maybe it would be all right.

"What am I thinking of?" he thought. "She's my friend, nothing more." Aloud he said, "Come on, give the bloke a chance. And anyway, what do you think this is?" He drew a delicate silver chain from inside his shirt.

Rachel moved to take the chain in her hand—it was warm from his body. There was a small silver cross attached to the links.

"Means a lot to me," was all he said.

"It's beautiful," she replied.

There was a comfortable spell, where they just sat and enjoyed each other's company. The conversation became mellow and the time rushed by. They both asked the waiter for the bill and had a mock battle over whose turn it was to pay. The evening ended peacefully and they both emerged from the restaurant looking happy but tired.

Aaron stopped a taxi and insisted that she took it—he would

wait for the next. They were going in opposite directions. He gave Rachel a quick hug.

"Night, Rache. Go home—meet the Aussie and tell me all about it soon."

"I'll phone," she replied and turned and kissed his cheek.

The taxi whisked her away before he could say anything else.

CHAPTER

12

Laban took Jacob out to Monks Lodge in his chauffeur-driven car. They got on well together and the journey took no time as they mixed talking business with pleasure. Laban pointed out places of interest and Jacob enjoyed watching the Buckinghamshire countryside roll by. Everything was so different to Australia—it was just so very British! All the things he had imagined about England were unfolding before his eyes. He thought the British were very polite—even on the roads—and he was looking forward to seeing a real English village.

When the car finally rolled into High Montley, he was taken aback. It was like a scene from a picture postcard. They had negotiated some incredibly small country lanes, but now the road spanned out to meet the little village nestled in a valley—tiny thatched cottages, little rural shops and people walking along at a leisurely pace, nodding and talking to each other.

"It's like an Agatha Christie novel!" he mused. "Are you sure Miss Marple doesn't live here?"

Laban laughed to himself. It was good to show off some English countryside to an Aussie ... even if he was family. The car swung along another small lane and suddenly they were moving down a long winding drive flanked on either side by tall poplar trees. A pheasant ran across the road in front of them, and in the distance Jacob could see Monks Lodge. It wasn't a 'flashy' place—more a rich man's quiet residence, which was exactly what Laban wanted it to be.

"Phew, that's quite a place," Jacob said. "Seems strange not to have the grounds covered in sheep, though!"

Laban laughed and looked forward to showing Jacob around.

Inside, Leah was as prepared as she would ever be, for what she hoped would be one of the great moments of her life. She'd been very busy, chasing the staff, making sure things were as perfect as possible for Jacob's arrival. The evening meal was exactly to her specifications and nothing was going to go wrong. The front lounge was re-arranged, so that when dinner was over, they could relax in comfort. She had spent ages making sure the lighting was subtle and kind to her looks, positioning chairs and low tables so that when she sat opposite Jacob he would not fail to fall for her.

Leah was looking and feeling good. The thought of this man was revealing a countenance that was usually hidden. There was a glow on her face that helped her eyes to sparkle just a little, and she had used less make-up in an effort to look a little more the way Rachel did—natural and unspoilt. Unfortunately, it didn't work quite as well on Leah—she still couldn't come to terms with the fact that she and her sister were different.

In an effort to look casual, she chose to wear a little black dress (Rachel swore by them). It was pretty in its simplicity—tiny straps with a slinky silk bodice which called for no underwear, and a slight A-line skirt that ended just above her knees. For once she had chosen right and coupled with a fine chain necklace and a strappy pair of heels, she looked carefree. She left her hair down and was now toying with it anxiously, waiting for her father and Jacob to arrive.

She heard the crunching noise of tyres on gravel and ran to the window and peered through the heavy curtains. It took iron-will not to rush to the front door to greet them both, but Leah knew she had to play it cool.

"Blanche! Get that will you?" she commanded the maid.

Before they arrived she had rehearsed over and over, where she would stand and how she would look when they came into the reception room. She knew they would come here first—her father always did. He would throw his coat on the small telephone table in the hall, pick up any mail and then make his way through to the reception room and head for the small drinks cabinet. Laban wasn't much of a drinker, but he appreciated a small port after a hard day at the office.

Today was no exception, apart from the fact that Jacob was with him. They entered the room laughing and joking with each other.

"The British thing to do is have a small glass of sherry, but as it's your first real day here, how about a small Scotch? ... Oh hello, darling! Home already!" Laban held his arms out to Leah.

She twirled round in an effort to look surprised.

"Daddy! I didn't hear you come in. Shall I get that drink for you?" She couldn't stop her hand going to her throat as she continued, "And Jacob, nice to see you again. You must be very tired—it's been a long few days."

Jacob surveyed Leah. She had certainly made an effort. His eyes roamed over the skimpy dress—she had a decent figure, slight, but everything in the right place, and her eyes told him she was ready to play if he was. The thought caught him unaware—it really wouldn't do to chase his cousin round the room on his first evening at home! Still, he could file that thought away for another day.

"Hi there, Leah," he said smoothly. "Great to see you again. I was telling Laban how much I admired the house—and its surroundings." The pass was noted, and she flushed with pleasure.

"I'll enjoy showing you around," she said, looking straight at him. Touché, my friend, she thought.

Jacob merely smiled and joined Laban at the cabinet.

Leah took this moment to breathe slowly and hold herself in check. He was dynamic. How could anyone look that good after a journey from the other side of the world and one night's sleep?

Slow down girl. She said to herself. He's here to stay.

She strolled over to Laban and purposely put her arm around his shoulder. "Enjoy your drink Father. I shall go and check on dinner."

Laban looked vaguely surprised, but patted her cheek and replied, "Thank you Leah. You're a good girl."

Then he turned to Jacob. "Well now, perhaps I could show you around the house, we can take the drinks with us. I'd like you to feel at home, so the sooner you know where everything is, the sooner you can start treating the place as your own."

Jacob was finally shown to his 'quarters' and unpacked a few pieces of hand-luggage—the rest would be following on afterwards. He sat on the fine double bed and surveyed his rooms. Care had been taken to make them into a suite fit for a male. The richly polished dark wooden furniture smelled only of beeswax and was complimented by maroon velvet curtains, sofa, and darker velvet at the head of the four poster. He walked across the room and pushed open a connecting door. This room would serve as a sitting room and an office—pale carpet with thick pile, and more deep maroons and very pale greens, antique furniture with the same highly polished dark wood as in the bedroom. In one corner, a desk was arranged, with phone, fax machine and word processor. The 'office' faced a huge bay window and Jacob found himself looking out over the lawns to the countryside beyond—he was to find this a comfort on busy light evenings.

Leah had informed him, with a seductive smile, that dinner would be in about an hour. That meant he had time to change from his day clothes into something relaxing for the evening. He wondered how his first evening would be, as he carelessly stripped off his shirt and left it lying on the bed. Soon he was wandering around his new room totally naked, the way he always did at home. He heard a noise outside the room and suddenly realised he was no longer in the Australian outback—people were liable to drop in at any time. He hastily grabbed a bathrobe and wrapped it around himself. He tried the other connecting door in the hope it was a bathroom, and it was. There was a tentative knock on the main door, so he quickly turned on the bath-taps and left to answer it.

It was Beth, the young housemaid. She was eighteen years old and working for Laban as part of her training for hotel work. Her huge round eyes took in Jacob's muscular form as he towered over her at the door. There had been several people to stay at Monks Lodge since she had been there, but no one quite like this. He stood half smiling at her while she stared at him; this gorgeous man with unbelievably thick black hair and dark—almost black— eyes. He was wearing only a dark blue robe tied very roughly at his waist. Her eyes fell to the belt and she hastily looked away.

"Hi," Jacob's voice held amusement as he realised the effect he was having on this young girl.

She blushed to the roots of her light brown hair. "Umm ... I was sent up to see if you have everything ... er ... everything you need—is there anything?" It all sounded wrong and Jacob wasn't helping her at all. He just stood there waiting for her to finish.

"And who are you?" he said.

"I'm the maid," she explained.

"I know that ... don't they let you use your name?" he smiled

"Oh ... er ... yes ... It's Beth," she replied uncomfortably. Then looked past him. "Oh! Is that the bath?"

He turned round quickly and ran to the bathroom, his robe getting looser by the minute. He grinned at her as he came back. "Thank you Beth, you saved my life. Let me know if I can return the favour, anytime."

With that he gave her a slow wink, and she ran back down the corridor towards the stairs.

After she had gone, Jacob sank into a huge bathtub of soapy water. He fell back into it until his head went under, then rose forward and gradually lay back again, letting the back of his head rest against the top of the rim. He let out a huge sigh and laughed to himself. There were times when all you needed was a shower, and there were other times when you really needed to lie back and enjoy the feeling of warm water rippling over your skin.

It was good to be in England, away from his annoying brother Esau and close to this new family with his rich uncle, flirty cousin and innocent maid! He closed his eyes and lost himself in his thoughts.

The next thing he knew, a gong was sounding through the house. He sat up quickly and looked down in distaste at the water that had now gone cold. Leaping from the bath he towelled himself dry.

Rummaging around the wardrobe, he pulled out some dark casual trousers and a light blue silk shirt. He thought about a tie, but decided against it, preferring to keep the shirt open at the neck. He glanced at himself quickly in the mirror. His hair was still wet, but looked great, and the pale blue shirt made his dark eyes look even deeper. He smiled at his image, and the smile creased his face, showing even white teeth and a strong jawline. Even the small scar that was a legacy from Esau, suited him.

The gong sounded again, as he made his way to the dining room.

The meal was a success—the food excellent and the company even better. Laban had 'small talk' down to a fine art, and soon had Jacob feeling relaxed and welcome.

Leah was trying her best not to get flustered, but it was so hard as just the mere sight of him turned her to jelly. He listened to Laban with his head to one side, and gradually let his eyes wander to where Leah sat. For him, it was a delicious game, but for her it was pure love. At that moment, there was nothing Leah wouldn't have done to make this man her own. She was trying so hard to look cool and collected, but her heart was racing whilst her thoughts were making her blush.

He liked her—she was so sure of it. This really was it.

"Wonderful meal darling," said her father. "God has blessed me with two wonderful daughters, Jacob."

Jacob nodded. "I'm sure I will agree. If this daughter is anything to go by." The undercurrents of his conversation were knocking Leah's emotions sideways.

"Well, children." said Laban rising from his seat. "I have a few urgent phone calls to make, so why don't you make yourselves comfortable next door?"

Leah rose a little too quickly. "Always working, that's my father," she stated. "Come on Jacob, let's get comfortable."

He followed her through and she sat down as she had planned and looked across at him. Now that they were here, she wasn't so sure what her next move should be, but she didn't need to worry—he took over.

"I hope you're not looking at my hair. I'm afraid I didn't have time to dry it." He moved his hand seductively through his black locks.

"Not at all. Wet hair can look very attractive," she replied. "Did you find everything you needed? I sent a maid up to make sure you were all right."

"Ah yes, Beth." He used her name effortlessly, and Leah didn't like it.

"Silly little girl, but Daddy will take on these protégés," she said, trying to make light of it.

"I hope that doesn't include me." Jacob's reply was swift and his face suspicious.

Leah realised her mistake and put her hand to her mouth. "Oh no, of course not! We've been looking forward to meeting you. Tell me about Australia."

Back on an even keel, they sat and talked.

"You have a brother?" She asked.

Jacob frowned. "Yes I do. He's not my favourite person—a bit ham-fisted. He likes sheep and grass, and I like big cities and fast cars—that's about it." He was giving nothing else away.

Leah laughed. "Sounds like he'd get on well with my sister Rachel. Her idea of heaven is working in some tiny back-street office. I prefer to have a good time, but at least if I did work I'd be like you and go for the big time."

Jacob raised his eyebrows. "Really? So how is it that Rachel is working with me on this Elliot Blaze thing, and not you?"

Leah's mind raced. "Oh well, I don't suppose it matters if you know—but actually Rachel is crazy about Elliot. Can you imagine? Not my type at all ..." she waved her hand nonchalantly. "So she begged Father to let her help out. I just hope she doesn't mess it up—she's only used to working for that little two-bit agency."

"So, we are very alike, Leah. I have a brother who looks no further than his nose and you have a sister who doesn't dare to put her foot outside into the big wide world. We must have plenty of stories to swap—I wonder just how compatible we are?"

Leah bent over gently to the coffee table she'd put between them. She picked up a coffee cup and let her eyes rise to meet his. "You're here now Jacob. I'm sure we will have a lot of fun finding out."

Jacob had to bite back a million suggestive retorts to her comment. This girl was crazy for him, and if he played his cards right, he could do very well for himself here. Very well indeed.

CHAPTER

13

Rachel was on her way down to breakfast. Still yawning, she'd come home late and crept upstairs as planned. Her evening with Aaron had been pleasant and she smiled as she thought of the way he talked to her. He was so warm and human, no airs and graces, and she appreciated that. Soon she would introduce him to Sarah—she was convinced they would make a wonderful couple.

Right now, she walked downstairs with her hand lightly touching the bannisters. Although she was dressed and made up, she carried that 'still sleepy' air with her. She crossed over to the breakfast room and began helping herself to scrambled eggs and toast. Breakfast was always laid out on hotplates at the side of the room, so that the family could help themselves as they arrived.

Rachel put her plate down and stretched her arms wide to try and wake herself up. Her arm connected with the coffee pot and Jacob who had just walked into the room. He swiftly ducked out of her way and caught hold of her hand before she did any more damage.

"Whoa there!" he cried and looked up to see who was attacking him. He found himself staring into the sleepy blue eyes of a girl so astoundingly beautiful that he was at a loss for words. It had to be Rachel, but she was nothing like the girl that Leah described to him. This girl was everything he desired—but how could he feel like that? They had not even spoken.

Rachel was in the same situation. She stood, rooted to the spot looking into the face of the man she knew she was going to love for the rest of her life.

They both came to at the same time, and started to talk to cover up the embarrassment of the blatant signals that had flashed back and forth as their eyes met.

"You first." Rachel smiled shyly at him, and all he wanted to do was to take her hand and run away with her—anywhere.

He swallowed hard and tried to appear normal. "Ah, um ... Rachel. You must be Rachel." It sounded pathetic. It was so unlike Jacob to lose his cool, especially with women, but then this wasn't just any woman.

"Which has to make you Jacob," she said simply. They could not take their eyes off of each other. She looked down at her hand that Jacob was still holding. He followed her glance and quickly let go.

"Ah! I see you have met my pride and joy!" The sound of Laban's voice brought them to their senses.

Laban walked over to his daughter and kissed her cheek. "Where did you get to darling? Leah said it was auditions and a late meal with someone. I was surprised not to see you for Jacob's first night here." The disapproval in his voice dissolved as he smiled at her.

"I'm so sorry Daddy, you know it was unavoidable. I would never let you down intentionally." Obviously her father knew nothing of Leah's little plan.

Jacob smiled at her. This was a girl who kept her word— she was honest and straightforward ... and as sexy as hell.

"Are you joining us for breakfast, Jacob?" Laban cut into his thoughts.

"Of course," Jacob replied, and began piling food haphazardly onto his plate.

He followed them to the table and found himself seated

opposite Rachel. Laban talked on about MBC and the busy day ahead, while the two of them tried to get their breath back and avoid looking up at the same time. Jacob couldn't understand his feelings. It was as if he was a schoolboy again, all fingers and thumbs, looking at a girl for the first time.

"Good morning everyone!" Leah waltzed into the room as if it was the first day of spring. She quickly helped herself to a small piece of lightly buttered toast—this was no time to put on weight!

Laban glanced up in surprise at his eldest daughter—this was so unlike her.

Leah sat down next to Jacob. "What a beautiful morning! Are you looking forward to your first real day at work Jacob?" She looked up at him through dark eyelashes.

"Hi, Leah. You're looking good." Jacob felt he should try and act as normally as possible. Meanwhile, Leah looked over to her sister and slipped her a wink that said, "Isn't he fantastic? Didn't I tell you how good we were together?" Rachel found herself nodding back at her sister. This was insane! She'd never been in such a predicament! How could this possibly be the man that Leah had told her about—the man whom Leah thought was made in heaven for her!

"You must have come in really late last night, Rachel," remarked Leah candidly. "Jacob and I were talking until the early hours." She touched his shirt sleeve with a show of familiarity. "What on earth we found to talk about I just don't know. The time just seemed to vanish, didn't it, Jacob?"

Jacob was in a total flummox. Certainly last night he had led Leah on, but that was before ...

"I had some auditions and by the time I'd finished it was so late, and I'd not eaten ..." Rachel was explaining.

"Oh yes, that's right." Leah cut in. "You had a meal with that new little DJ—what was his name? Adam?"

"Aaron," Rachel corrected, feeling uncomfortable.

"I met him." Jacob joined in.

"Yes, he told me," Rachel answered, remembering Aaron's description of Jacob, and how she had laughed and called him 'Medallion Man'.

"Nice guy. Enthusiastic," he said.

"I'm glad you like him, Jacob." Laban commented. "You'll be working very closely with him and of course with Rachel, on the Elliott Blaze promotion. It's hard to believe it's such a short time away."

The conversation carried on with Leah flirting outrageously with Jacob, and Jacob trying hard not to look at Rachel.

"Yes, another few days and Elliot Blaze will be all yours," remarked Leah looking pointedly at her sister. "Bet you can't wait.'

"Well, he's certainly a challenge," Rachel answered. "I just wonder how many people will be in his team this time."

She went on to explain to Jacob about the entourage of the 'low-key' visit. He grinned engagingly at her and hardly heard a word she said—she could speak Russian for all he cared, just as long as he could sit here and look at her.

"Rachel handled him extremely well," remarked Laban. And Leah coughed politely behind her hand—the suggestion was not missed by either Jacob or Rachel.

Her father continued. "He has a reputation for being very awkward, and when he first arrived with his band of assistants we wondered if he would stay. But Rachel was marvellous. She put him totally at ease, and the roaring lion became a pussy cat!"

"Daddy!" Rachel looked flustered.

"It's a natural charm—she gets it from her mother. Actually, when I think about it Jacob, she's quite like Rebekkah too."

Jacob was stunned. He had travelled halfway round the world and found himself falling for someone likened to his mother. Had he unconsciously noticed that? He couldn't be sure. He nodded politely at Laban and made busy with his breakfast.

"Do you know," continued Laban, "this girl has a wonderful talent—but will she work for me?" He shook his head. "Believe me Jacob, I've had to beat her into submission on this one! How someone can prefer the small time to the big time is beyond me."

"Where do you work, Rachel?" Jacob asked. He was interested in what made her the person that she was. He gazed at her intently as if seeing through her would help.

"Oh, it's a small entertainment agency in Soho," she replied, and laughed as she caught the reaction on his face.

"Now, now! There are a few more things other than strip joints in Old Compton Street! We deal mainly with small acts, the kind of thing that would go second billing at a variety show or musical— and just now and then we discover a star," she added proudly, and pushed her father away playfully as he raised his eyes to the ceiling.

"And when they discover a star, what do they do?" he asked Jacob. "They sell him to the highest bidder! That way they make sure there will always be Landers Entertainment Agency of Byron Street, and never Landers International. Crazy!"

"I guess their priorities are slightly different to that of MBC," remarked Jacob. "And although I prefer to be a high-flier, I can understand that it must be fun to be involved in such a small firm."

Rachel smiled at him gratefully.

Leah had had enough of this talk and decided it was time to turn the subject back to herself. "Well, I for one would not like to work for a living," she sighed. "I believe that a lady should be pampered and loved and never have to see the sordid side of life. Rachel might be happy being known as a working girl, but I prefer to be known as MBC's Heiress."

Laban decided to indulge his daughter. He often felt that she lived a lonely life for all the 'trimmings' that wealth brought her. "Leah's idea of fun, Jacob," he said "is to find herself on the society page of any respectable national newspaper—preferably with a photo of herself with some glamourous film star—walking out of a restaurant.'

They all laughed politely and Leah pretended to look put out. "Father, honestly!"

It intrigued Jacob to compare the two sisters. He noticed that usually Leah would refer to Laban as 'Father', while Rachel nearly always called him 'Daddy'. Such was the difference between them.

"Time to go," said Laban looking at his watch. Jacob got up immediately and followed him, eager to get to work.

"Are you coming with us Rachel?" Her father asked.

Leah threw a venomous look at her sister, and she remembered their conversation of the day before.

"No, no, it's OK. I worked late last night, so they won't expect me in till the middle of the day."

It was Jacob's turn to throw a look at Rachel. One that said "Why?" But she had no way of answering him. No way at all. She just leaned on the breakfast table, shrugged her shoulders and cupped her chin in her hand.

"Don't make it too late tonight, Jacob." Leah called after him. He turned around.

"Tonight?" he asked.

"The video." She turned to Rachel. "Would you believe it? Jacob and I have the same taste in films and neither of us have managed to get the time to watch Dangerous Liaisons." Can you imagine? So, Jacob suggested that I hire it for tonight, so that when he comes in after a hard day at Father's office, he can relax ... with me. It's a shame it's not your kind of film Rachel, but I'm sure you will have lots of other things to do anyway, knowing you."

"I'll get him back for you, darling," shouted Laban from the front door. This was good. Jacob and Leah obviously got on well —his wife would have liked that.

Leah ran to the door to wave them off.

"Bye! See you tonight!" she said happily.

Rachel stood in the hallway. Jacob looked back to wave and caught her eye. Would time always stand still when they looked at each other?

The two sisters walked back into the breakfast room where Rachel immediately started to pile up empty plates.

"Rachel, please!" Leah remarked. "We have servants for that! Anyway, come into the other room and let's talk about my Jacob!" To Rachel's surprise, her sister grabbed her hand and ran through to the early-morning sunshine of the lounge.

Throwing herself down on the sofa, she gazed at her sister intently. "Well? What do you think? Did you see the way he looked at me? Isn't he fabulous? And how about us liking the same films—I could hardly believe it! I hope you didn't mind me getting rid of you—but no, you wouldn't would you? Come on Rachel, tell me what you think!"

What could she say? The truth would be horrendous—"I've never met anyone I could love, as I could love him" . . .

"He seems very nice," she replied lamely.

"Nice? "yelled Leah. "Honestly Rachel, I will never understand you! How can you possibly call someone who has the body of Superman and the face of a dark Adonis, nice!"

"You seem to get on well together," she tried again. "I'm very pleas d for you." This was probably the hardest moment of Rachel's life. What was she supposed to do? Had she read the signs wrong? Maybe Jacob really did like Leah or maybe he was the money-grabbing opportunist she had first idealised. Maybe he was playing them off against each other. She just couldn't think straight.

"You should have been here last night, Rachel." Leah continued. "I wore that black dress—the one you told me always makes me look good. And Jacob spent the whole evening telling me how lovely I was. It was like a glorious game of seduction—two step forwards, one step back."

Leah was almost beside herself with joy. He was everything she had ever wanted and he was hers, all hers.

"You don't think you may be going at this a little fast do you?" Rachel asked cautiously. She knew her sister well and had a terrible feeling that Leah would try to snare him, hook, line and sinker before he had time to breathe. What if he fell for it?

"Well, you heard the man Rachel. Live fast and dangerously— and I think that includes his women! We will fly high together and demand that the world stops and watches us—just see if we don't!" Leah hugged herself. "Oh Rachel, it's going to be fantastic!"

Rachel sat and looked at her sister. The happiness on her face, the excitement running through her—how could she destroy that? How could she let her down so badly? Leah's happiness was important to her—it was so rare to see her smiling and laughing. She couldn't destroy it, she just couldn't.

I'll just have to hide my feelings and ride this one out, she thought to herself. Other people have done it before. But everything within her body screamed, Jacob, I love you!

CHAPTER

14

"Elliott Blaze will not want a high public profile." This was Jane Hunter giving Jacob her considered opinion on the promotional visit. Her violently red hair was swinging from side to side as she became more animated. Jacob Lindstein found her mildly amusing. This was his first 'proper' working day at MBC and he was trying to collate some kind of system for making sure that everything ran like clockwork from one department to another. Jane was fiercely possessive of her position in the company and became the same way with anyone she was called to work with—hence the confidence with which she spoke about Elliott Blaze.

Jacob's lips curled. He knew that there was no way Jane knew this film star as well as she was making out.

"So then, Jane," He answered. "How do you intend to keep the public away from him?" He turned and looked at the press photos on the wall while he waited for her answer.

"Well, we have to itinerate his schedule down to the minutest detail. If he does venture out into the big wide world, he will always have someone with him—notably Rachel Monklaast. She will be his constant companion and she's very good at her job. If he wants to go out and eat—she'll go with him; if he wants to see the sights—she will take him out, discreetly. But unfortunately for Elliott, I'm afraid he will spend most of his stay locked up in his hotel room. That's the price of fame," She added, shrugging her shoulders.

Jacob was studying her. He hadn't heard a word she had said after the mention of Rachel's name.

"Jacob? Mr Lindstein?" Jane frowned at him.

"Oh ... er ... yes. Well, that seems fine, Jane. You are doing a good job, I can understand why Laban put you in such a position of responsibility. We'll meet up later when I have seen the others, OK?" And with that, he turned and walked out the door, leaving Jane to wonder about the good-looking stranger.

Jacob wandered down the corridor in pursuit of Simon Darrell, the marketing man, but his mind was wandering even further afield—Rachel. He didn't know anything about her, apart from their brief meeting at breakfast this morning. She seemed to him to be the most wonderful woman he had ever met, so very feminine and shy and yet strikingly sensual and very much alive. He couldn't imagine her with someone like Elliott Blaze—no, he didn't want to imagine her with him. He needed to see her, to talk to her again.

"Hey, Jacob! I'm just on my way!"

Jacob spun round and saw Simon coming towards him, looking, as usual, as if he'd just walked out of a designer's shop window. He held out his hand as he reached Jacob, the Rolex watch gleaming on his wrist. They shook hands. Jacob liked this guy.

"So, has Jane been giving you the low-down on our star?" He smiled.

"She's very thorough," replied Jacob with a mockish grin.

"Hmm. I hope she wasn't putting on the pressure, too much. I would like the guy to put in a few appearances at some prestigeous places while he's here, but if Jane has her way she'll lock him up and throw away the key!" he said, throwing his hands in the air.

"I think that's why Laban asked me to pull this thing together.

Tell me what you need Simon, and I'll start working on it. I need
to make sure that you and the press office are not working against
each other," said, Jacob instinctively.

Simon nodded. "We need to get Rachel in on this when we
have a schedule sorted. She needs to know his movements exactly."

"Rachel," stated Jacob.

Simon's eyebrows rose. "Ahh, so you've met." A knowing look
appeared on his face. He put his arm on Jacob's shoulder and
gave him a friendly pat on the back. "The queue begins about four
streets away, my friend. And unless you're Superman, I have to
tell you that the success rate is nil!"

Jacob forced himself to smile and act normally. "That's the
way, is it is?" he replied. "So Elliott Blaze is in for a big let-down."
It sounded bad, and he didn't want to talk about Rachel in this
way.

Simon rubbed his designer-stubbled chin.

"W ... e ... l ... l—I don't know. They say the guy has such a
charismatic effect on women, that they fall like nine pins every
time. In fact, looking at his face when he met Rachel at the pre-
promotional visit, I'd say she's in for a rough time if she refuses
his advances."

Inside, Jacob shook with anger. The thought of this arrogant
blond hero making up to his Rachel was boiling his blood. He swallowed hard and tried to dismiss what he had heard.

"So, what do you have in mind for Elliott? I see we only have
four days to fit everything in, and the press reception is just a few
days away ..."

They went on to map and plan things—trying to piece together an itinerary that would suit all departments and be best for
the station. This included the on-air interview with Aaron, a visit
to an exclusive nightclub and the obligatory press call at a children's hospital.

It would to take a lot of fine tuning, but in the end MBC were going to come up smelling of roses.

* * *

Rachel was sitting, staring at her office keyboard. She looked from screen to keys and back again. She could see her own reflection in the computer screen and was surprised by the hugeness of her eyes against the rest of her face. She looked wistful; the curls that kissed her cheeks almost seemed to be sympathising with her.

She played absently with her hair as she tried to make sense of her feelings.

How can you fall in love with someone you have only met for twenty minutes? How does that happen? How can you feel so wound up about someone you don't know? If I could just hold his hand for a moment, just put my arms around his neck and ask him if he feels the same way ...

She shook her head vigorously. This was outrageous! She was Rachel Monklaast, Laban's quiet daughter, the one who had learnt over the years how to deal with handsome men and their advances. Who could spurn them easily with the turn of her head. She could talk to them and laugh with them, without sending out the wrong message—and they loved her all the more for it. She could handle them. She was in control! But now ... If he walked into the office this moment and came towards me, I would be helpless, She thought. This just isn't me! I sound more like Leah.

Leah. The shocking thought brought her back to earth with a resounding bump. Leah, her sister, was in love with Jacob, her Jacob ... What a mess.

Tonight Jacob would be watching a video with Leah and she had to keep out of the way again. How did Jacob feel about that? She really wished she knew. She glanced at the phone ... no it would be stupid to call him, and anyway, what would she say?

'Hello Jacob, I wondered how you felt about me?'

She reached over and turned the computer off, there was really no point in trying to work.

Sarah arrived back from a late lunch and sensed something was wrong as she walked in. "Hi Rachel. Mr Landers in a bad mood?" She knew he wasn't because he wasn't the type, but she felt as if she should try and break the atmosphere.

Rachel looked up and sighed. "No, it's me. Well, I'm not in a bad mood exactly—I just have a few things to sort out."

Sarah smiled and sat down at the desk opposite her.

"Oh well, let's change the subject. How was the meal with Aaron, and when do I get to meet him? You know I saw the first publicity shot in the *Evening Mail* last night—phew! He's going to break a few hearts! But remember, you said you would keep him for me!!" She laughed happily as she opened the file on her desk and started to check audition dates for Dean.

"Oh, Aaron's fine," murmured Rachel almost to herself.

Sarah gave her a quizzical look. "You're not falling for him yourself, are you?" She looked concerned.

Rachel shook her head.

"If only life were that simple," she answered. "Of course, he's younger than me, but we get along great. No, no Sarah, don't worry, I won't go stealing your man."

There was something in the way she stated that last fact that made her worry. She left her chair and came over to Rachel's desk, perching on the corner

"What's happened, Rachel?" she asked.

"I don't know," she said simply. "I just don't know."

Sarah's frown deepened. "This isn't like you."

Laban Monklaast's younger daughter got up from her seat and moved over to the small reception area. She took her soft leather coat from a hanger and put it on. With her fingers on the door handle, she turned to Sarah.

"Cover for me. I have to go out for a while. I need to think."

Sarah nodded and waved.

Outside, Rachel had no idea where she was going. She just knew that she had to sort this out in her own mind and soon, before it got the better of her. There was Leah to think of. Leah's happiness. The happiness that Rachel had promised not to destroy—before she had stood face to face with Jacob.

* * *

At home in the Lodge that evening, Leah was making her own plans. It wouldn't do to be waiting for Jacob as he walked in tonight, so she had decided to wait until it was nearly time for him to arrive and then drive out to find the desired video. Then she could arrive back at the house, after he was there, and the film would be the excuse for her absence. She would dress with the utmost care and her make-up would be fresh, her perfume nearly overwhelming—she was determined he wouldn't see a minute of the film. She knew that playing it cool was the way to get this right, but it went against her nature to do things that way. And for once, Rachel was not in the picture. This man was hers—he only had eyes for her and she only had eyes for him. It was perfect, the most perfect thing she could imagine. But just in case, she was ready to do anything he asked. His fate had to be sealed quickly, and for Leah that meant doing whatever it took. If sleeping with Jacob would keep him securely by her side, it was no problem to her—he would hardly be the first. She was determined to make him love her at any cost—and tonight they would be alone.

'Let the battle commence!' She laughed to herself, then glancing at her watch, walked nonchalantly out to her Mercedes Sports, whirling the keys around her finger.

Jacob Lindstein saw the car going in the other direction as he drove his company car into the village. He was sure it was Leah in the driving seat, and he wondered where she was going. He had remembered his promise to stay in with her as he was driving home, and was trying to think of a way out. However, he realised that if he was not to appear extremely rude and bad-mannered in his uncle's house, he should really take a deep breath and go ahead with the evening. After all, he could be polite and have a nice time, Leah was OK and he felt he could manage to get through it without too much hassle. He just hoped that her flirtatious way was normal, and not put on especially for him.

He breezed through the front door and winked at Beth as she made her way down the stairs in front of him. "Hi honey, I'm home!" he joked to her, and was pleased to see how easily she blushed. Jacob enjoyed the pursuit of women, but rarely thought about them after the conquest was over, which was why this thing with Rachel felt so different. He made his way upstairs and laid his jacket on the bed. He stretched and then put his hands across his face. He felt tired after his first full day but knew he had coped well and Laban was pleased with the results. He'd told Jacob to go home and relax, and that he wouldn't be back until much later. Maybe it was just Jacob's imagination, but he had the feeling that Laban was more than a little pleased at the thought of him spending an evening alone with Leah.

He should change his clothes, he thought to himself. He stripped off his shirt and trousers, fell back onto the bed and relaxed ... perhaps just a few minutes with his eyes closed ...

When Leah tapped on the door half an hour later, Jacob was dead to the world. She tried knocking quietly a few times, convinced he must be in there, but wondering why he hadn't put in an appearance downstairs. There was still no answer, so she tried the door. It opened at her touch and she took a deep breath before stepping lightly into his room. What she saw made her heart stop.

It was just getting dark and the shadows playing on Jacob's body made him look unreal—the abandonment of his arms, thrown away from his naked chest, the line of muscles from his neck to his toes, merging with the dark sheet he lay on, the black hair falling away from the strong jawline, deep dark lashes caressing his cheeks. His handsome well-formed body wrapped in nothing more than Calvin Kleins ... he slept like a baby.

Leah couldn't move. She had never seen anyone look so lovely. She wanted to run from the room in despair, run to him in love—she desperately needed to lie down beside him. In the end she heard herself call his name, very softly as if afraid of disturbing his dream.

"Jacob."

He stirred. His eyes willing themselves to open, his body moving sensuously as he tried to come around. He slowly pushed himself up onto his elbows, and as he did he saw Leah looking down on him. Her face left nothing to his imagination. Thoughts came rushing through his mind ... Leah ... Rachel ... MBC ... Beth ... Monks Lodge ... He was at home in his room and he should be watching a video—that was it.

"Leah!" He rubbed his eyes. "I'm sorry, I must have fallen asleep ..." He had to get rid of her—this was ludicrous. But Leah was heading towards him, lips parted and cheeks flushed.

"Jacob, it's OK," She was saying. "We don't have to watch the film ... we can stay here ... it's all right ..." Her hands were reaching towards the top of her dress.

Jacob sat up abruptly and broke the spell.

"No! Leah ... hold on ..." He began to rise from the four-poster and grabbed at a pair of jeans.

She looked surprised and upset.

His mind began to race. This was going terribly wrong and it was partly his fault. Yesterday Leah was giving him all the signs of a good time and he was responding to it—but that was before Rachel. He had to get out of this. He put the jeans on roughly, and came over to her. He took her hand.

"Hey, what's the hurry? We have plenty of time. It's probably not such a good idea to start something the day after I move in." He tried to give her a disappointed smile, as if he would love to do this—but not yet.

To his surprise, she put her hands around his neck and gave him a small kiss. "You're right Jacob. We have all the time in the world. Today—the same house. Tomorrow—the same bed. See you downstairs in five minutes." And she was gone.

Jacob breathed a sigh of relief, walked over to the bathroom and ran a very cold shower ...

Leah's night in with Jacob was a strange mixture of excitement and disappointment. She realised immediately that she had come on to him too quickly, but the sight of him lying outstretched on his bed had been overwhelming. She had to have this man!

After leaving his room, she had gone downstairs and set up the video, wondering how to play the rest of the evening. She felt fairly secure in the fact that he liked her a lot, and the way he'd given that little disappointed smile only fuelled her expectations of him. The thing that excited her most of all was the thought of Rachel's attitude towards Jacob. Her sister was not the remotest bit interested in him and had given Leah her blessing—in fact was encouraging and helping her in her plans to snare him. It was all too fantastic for words.

The door opened and Jacob walked in. His relaxed smile masked his true feelings. He was trying to look casual and in control, his hands thrust into the pockets of the light blue jeans. He sat on the sofa opposite Leah.

"Hi. I'm sorry I was so late. I think that first day at MBC took it out of me more than I imagined".

Leah nodded at him and tried to look into his eyes. He glanced away.

"So, did you get the film? It would be the perfect way to end the day—I don't think I could do another thing."

The message was clear and Leah, already creating her own plans for future days, smiled affectionately at him.

"Of course Jacob. You must be exhausted." She got up and walked over to the sofa curling herself up beside him, she picked up the remote and pressed 'play'. The video sprung into action —and so did Leah, lightly putting her head on Jacob's shoulder and snuggling down beside him.

There wasn't an awful lot Jacob could do about this situation without upsetting her, and he sensed that getting on the wrong side of Leah would be hell. So he decided to brazen it out. He stretched his legs out onto the coffee table, and his arm around Leah. At least this way he would get to see the film.

Leah was totally content, and when the video ended and Jacob said he really needed to go to his room, she didn't try to stop him. She just stood up with him and found his mouth with her lips. Kissing him just a little bit too long, she felt a response, but then his arms put her lightly away from him.

"Goodnight Leah. Thanks." He walked out of the room, leaving Leah to wonder what the 'thanks' were for.

She sat back on the couch and thought for a long time.

Eventually she grew tired and made her way to the empty kitchen to make herself some coffee. Normally she would have rung for a maid, regardless of the time of night, but this time she wanted to be alone with her thoughts, so she didn't hear Rachel come in behind her, and jumped as she spoke.

"Hi, Leah. OK?"

Leah turned around and saw her sister looking as weary as she did. She was still very beautiful, but in a more delicate way. Her eyes were smudged and tired, her hair tousled and loose. She looked towards the coffee pot.

"Is there enough for two?" Rachel had to find out how the evening with Jacob had gone—it was tearing her apart. She wasn't used to putting on a facade—all this pretence was hurting her.

For once, Leah had a big smile for her sister. She came over to her and actually put her arms around her. "Rachel, I can't thank you enough for keeping yourself scarce these last few days! You just wouldn't believe how well it's going with Jacob. We had such a night!" She leaned towards Rachel as if to stop anyone else hearing.

"You know, I had to go and wake him, he was so tired after a day at MBC. I walked into his room and he was just lying on the bed. He'd obviously thought of taking a shower and then lay down instead ... and when he woke up and saw me standing there, we had such hard time leaving that room!!" Leah was so taken up with her 'story' that she didn't notice her sister's white face.

"And then, I said to him. 'Jacob, we are staying in the same house—we have all the time in the world!'" She sighed. "In the end he agreed with me that there was no hurry and we should take our time. What was it he said? 'Today the same house—tomorrow the same bed' Oh Rachel! I can hardly believe it's happening to me!" She hugged her sister again.

Rachel drew herself away and with the greatest effort, managed to say, "Leah, darling, I'm so pleased. You deserve some happiness, you really do. Take care though, won't you?" And she turned to leave.

Leah held up a china coffee cup. "Hey, what about your drink?" She smiled.

"It's OK, I'm more tired than I thought—I think I'll just go to bed." She didn't turn round again, so Leah never saw the tears streaming down her face.

CHAPTER

15

It was official—Elliott Blaze was in Britain. Chaos just about reigned everywhere, as Jane Hunter and Simon Darrell tried to protect their star from the photographers and hard-hitting journalists that surrounded the MBC building.

Getting him into the place had been hell. His own entourage of minders and PR were really not helping the situation. They were so American, shouting and waving their arms around as if they were protecting the President of the United States. The MBC team were working in a totally different style. The first press release was being given out by Jane Hunter, with reporters stopping *en masse* to make sure they received their copy, while a hundred mobile phones went into action calling their offices with the first pieces of news.

Elliott was more concerned that he looked good for these photo-guys, and was constantly checking his hair and calling for Julie Redwing who fussed around him like a hen.

The reception area had been cleared and only the door commissioners remained. The entourage swept through and into the waiting lifts, like a swarm of bees, while upstairs Laban and Jacob were waiting to greet them.

The idea was for Elliott to have a few hours to relax before being taken on to the Café Royal for the reception. Some of the team had wanted Elliott to go straight to his hotel, but the general feeling was that the press would hound him more there, than if he was safely ensconced in Laban's office or apartment.

Julie Redwing, Jane Hunter and Simon Darrell entered the room with Elliott Blaze. They were smiling and confident that it was going well. The paparazzi were safely outside the building and most of them were making their way to the Café Royal to get the best shots of Elliott when he arrived.

Jacob and Elliott were introduced and shook hands. They looked intently at each other, sizing each other up without meaning to. It wasn't often that Elliott Blaze had to deal with someone who matched his good looks, and he found himself feeling slightly threatened by the thought.

To an outsider looking in, it was quite a unique event. The contrast of the blond American with his chiselled features and groomed film-star looks, to the dark Australian with naturally handsome features that owed nothing to plastic surgery was almost like a negative and positive of the same photo.

Elliott looked closely at Jacob and tried to fathom out what it was that felt so threatening. This guy was here to smooth things out for the reception, almost acting as his right-hand man, so he shouldn't feel like this. What was it?

Meanwhile Jacob was staring at Elliott and trying to understand why Rachel was so attracted to this man. Leah had told him how much her sister was looking forward to working with the star, and yet he could see nothing in him that the Rachel he knew would like.

"So Jacob. That's a fine accent you have. I hear you were a sheep farmer before Laban took you on." The glossy star was talking down to Jacob in a way that made his hackles rise, but he was determined not to rise to the bait.

"Yeah, too true, but management is fairly much the same whether you're dealing with people or sheep. You can either head them in the right direction—or you can't."

To his surprise, Elliott laughed. He didn't often hear people talking straight from the hip and he found it refreshing. Maybe this Jacob guy could become an ally after all. He decided to test the water.

"This press reception in Regent Street, I'm quite looking forward to it. Have you met my 'chaperone' yet? Rachel?" Then he clicked his fingers. "What am I saying, of course you have—you're related aren't you?"

"Distantly," replied Jacob stiffly.

Elliott sensed the tension returning—so that was the way the cookie was crumbling. "Beautiful girl, and her apartment by the hotel is great—still you would probably know that. When I came over on a flying visit, we spent an evening at her place." He laughed almost to himself. "You know, she'd forgotten our date so when I turned up she was just wearing a beautiful long sweater and wet hair—wow! She's something else, isn't she?"

Jacob's jaw stiffened and he found it increasingly hard to be nice to this guy. Changing the subject was his only way out. He glanced at his watch.

"Nearly time to go." He waved his hand at the rest of the team in order to assemble them together and sort out who was arriving with who, and which cars were being used.

The atmosphere at the Café Royal was already electric. There were as many people outside as inside. Most magazines and newspapers had sent at least two people to cover the event, and so the press were posted at both stations. The invitations were in the form of gold cards with an indelible mark, to make sure that only the right people were allowed into the building, but even so there was a crowd of people—notably women—trying to convince the doormen that they had 'mislaid their invite', 'were relations of Elliott' or 'their card was still in the post'.

The amount of noise made by everyone talking was quite remarkable and made the sudden silence even more noticeable. A

line of smooth black cars swept up to the entrance. After a few
seconds the hubbub started again, but this time much louder as
people fought for a better position. Cameramen jostled with
reporters, bulbs flashed and a host of mini-recorders and TV cameras pressed forward. The first car held some of the more minor
members of the entourage, but still the cameras flashed, afraid of
missing something. The second car was a strange mixture of PR
and personalities, including programme controller James
Ledbury, and DJs David Wills and Aaron Holloway. The press
shouted to David—he was always a favourite with them. His
show was just about the most popular on radio, and he was
always pleasant to the media, therefore he had little trouble with
them. He took his time and posed for the cameras. Then they spotted Aaron. He was trying his best just to get inside, away from the
crowd—this was his first experience and he wasn't sure what
was expected of him.

"Aaron!" Some photographers recognised him from the official
photo in the evening paper. They realised immediately that he had
incredibly photogenic good looks and whatever else, they could
always use some good copy for their files.

Aaron found himself surrounded and quickly decided that the
easiest option was to do the same as David Wills, and smile at the
cameras. As soon as he obliged, it was like a strobe effect at a
nightclub—the bulbs flashed non-stop. He felt someone grab hold
of his sleeve and pull him inside. It was David.

Outside the third and last car was drawing up and the crowd
realised this contained the man they were waiting for. There were
many cries of "Elliott! Elliott!" as everyone but the film star
stepped out of the limo. The crowd surged forward and a line of
policemen joined arms to form a barrier to let the élite through.
Elliott's press and PR people headed up the small procession, with
Jacob and Laban following on. Finally Elliott appeared. At first
they just saw his shock of blond hair, as he ducked out of the car.

It was enough to set them off. Jacob and Laban stepped back a few paces and flanked Elliott. It was a great photo opportunity, and the media loved it. The famous MBC owner with two of the best looking guys in the business—everybody wanted that shot.

Elliott Blaze looked great. He was everything the fans wanted him to be and they screamed their appreciation at him as he attempted to enter the Café Royal, in one piece. Once inside, his entourage did a superb job of keeping the media out of the way until the interviews started. The drinks were flowing, courtesy of MBC, and all around the heavily mirrored walls stood elegant tables laden with smoked salmon, fresh strawberries and other delights.

Laban Monklaast looked around anxiously. He knew that Rachel should already be here and he needed to check out some details with her. He didn't particularly want her seen on Elliott's arm, but he needed to know that she was ready if they left in a hurry. He gave a sigh of relief as he saw her unmistakable figure walk in from the cloakroom area.

She looked radiant. Laban's heart swelled with pride as he looked towards her—the dark luxurious hair wafting behind her, her eyes huge and bright blue that seemed to sparkle with fun.

Her dress was a deep shade of cerise, and made of lycra. It clung to her figure, making many men in the room wish they could do the same. It was dramatically cut at the shoulders to give the impression of thin straps at the top and long sleeves further down her slender arms while the whole ensemble fitted like a kid glove. It made her look vulnerable, as if she needed protecting, and men were standing in line to do just that.

She stood still and looked around the ballroom, trying to take in who was there, and as she searched, her eyes met Elliotts'. Handing his glass quickly to the person he was talking to, he made his way over to her.

"Hi, honey! You're looking even more gorgeous than I

remembered!" He surveyed her coolly, taking in every curve, the swell of her breasts, the shape of her hips.

Rachel blushed at his blatant stare. She hoped he wasn't going to be difficult.

"Hello, Elliott. Nice to have you back. I don't suppose you've had time to breathe yet." She gave him a wide welcoming smile, and before she could stop him, his arms went around her as he greeted her American style. The hug and kiss were totally over the top and he knew it. He laughed down at her surprised face and hugged her again.

As Rachel leaned her head on his shoulder, she looked over and saw Jacob staring right at her, his eyes black with anger. He turned and walked away.

She re-composed herself quickly and carried on chatting as lightly as she could with Elliott—after all—she was responsible for him, and her father was relying on her.

The time came for the press call, and Jane Hunter's system worked perfectly. Everyone had their questions answered, got the photos they wanted and then when they had finished, Jane was ready with a few special interviewees for major TV programmes.

Things had gone without a hitch and the media were now happy to eat, drink and socialise until they were thrown out. Rachel freed herself from the 'in crowd' and managed to find a glass of wine. She began to sip it and relax.

"We really need to talk."

The voice by her side was unmistakably Jacob's. She whirled round at the sound of the Australian accent and looked at him in despair.

"Jacob, I ..." she began, nervously fingering the crystal glass and looking down at the white wine.

"No, Rachel, listen, to me." Jacob hunched his shoulders. "I'm completely at a loss to know what's going on here, but I know that you and I have to talk."

Rachel looked wildly around her, as if seeking help from somewhere.

"I think maybe we should do this some other time Jacob. I'm in the middle of helping my father."

"What do you think I'm doing here?" He hissed, trying to keep his voice down. "Come on Rachel, you know what I mean! When can I see you?" His hand automatically caught hold of hers and she moved back instinctively. She could not let him touch her for a moment—already the feel of him was playing with her emotions.

"Please Jacob! Let's get this reception out of the way. I'm too caught up ... I can't think straight ... " She moved her hand to her forehead and brushed away some straying curls. Even that movement was nearly too much for Jacob.

"When? Rachel, When? I have to see you!"

Neither of them noticed Elliott looming up behind them. He put his hand on Rachel's shoulder.

"Say! There you are, sweetheart! Julie has a list of places I'd like to see while I'm here, and she also has the schedule. So, if you would like to make yourself available, we'll start tonight." He steered her back to where Julie Redwing was standing, and left Jacob on his own.

Jacob swore under his breath and helped himself to champagne.

Aaron Holloway saw Jacob by himself and went over to him, pleased to find someone he knew. "Hi Jacob! This is some kind of do! I've been asked the same six questions by every journalist here! Do you think it's always like this?" As usual, Aaron was just being himself, naïve, wide-eyed and cheerful.

"I'm the wrong person to ask. I've been in the business less time than you," Jacob replied dryly.

The young DJ didn't see this as a re-buff, and carried on talking.

"Don't quite know what to make of that Blaze character

though. I've got to interview him on Monday, and as much as I've worked on getting to know his background, I still don't think I've quite nailed him down," he mused.

"I can give you a few words to describe him—try 'pretentious womaniser'," retorted Jacob.

"Oh, you noticed that too then," replied Aaron looking down at his shoes. "He's coming on a bit strong with Rachel, isn't he?"

Jacob looked at him suspiciously, and Aaron quickly added, "She's my friend!" His face was so honest and open, that all Jacob could say was, "Good. I think she's going to need you."

Without realising it, they had joined forces—Aaron who would defend his friend Rachel to the bitter end, and Jacob who loved her more than he could bear.

CHAPTER

16

Entering the MBC building the following morning, Rachel's head was still buzzing. Yesterday had been one hectic day, it seemed to have a whole week crammed into it or so it felt. After the Café Royal reception, Rachel had found herself with a huge list of things Elliot wanted to do. The evening started with a meal at the hotel—happily this meant that others were involved and she wasn't alone with him—but afterwards he wanted to try out a new nightclub called 'Babes' in Wardour Street. Its reputation was hot, and only the élite of the élite actually got through the front door. However, once inside, the whole thing nose-dived. Secure in their little nest, the 'flavours of the month' drank too much and passed the cocaine around. This was not Rachel's scene and she kept a watchful eye on Elliott. When he saw her face, he laughed.

"Don't worry, honey, that stuff is for creeps. I've got too much style and I want to keep it that way. I've seen what it's done to too many of my friends. It's OK, relax, I'm only here to sight-see."

She twirled the stem of her glass around in her fingers. She had not touched a drop—afraid of what else might be in it. Rachel was well practised at holding the same drink all night and making it look as if she was enjoying herself. She smiled nervously at Elliott and continued to twist her glass.

Elliott himself looked fantastic. He was cool and casual in an open black silk shirt, black trousers with a heavy silver chain hanging around his neck. Blond and tanned, he looked ready for the film set.

The evening passed without incident and Rachel was relieved when he eventually suggested that they leave. It was getting late and as they climbed into their waiting car, she was pleased the night was ending. He tried without success to get her back to his hotel for a]nightcap'. She gracefully declined, suggesting that they both needed to be fresh and ready for the next day.

"You drive a hard bargain darling—but you're so beautiful, we'll play it your way." He grinned lecherously at her. "For now."

Rachel spent the night at the London apartment along with Laban who was staying there for the duration of Elliott's visit.

But now, going up in MBC's lift, Rachel could still feel the strain of the day before—or was it? Visions of Jacob kept popping up in her mind. Life was confusing—perhaps a chat with Aaron might help her get things into perspective. At the very least, he would cheer her up and make her laugh. She stopped the lift and went in search of Studio Three.

Unknown to Rachel, her sister was already in her father's office. She was sitting in a soft-backed swivel chair, swinging from side to side and waiting for Laban to finish his phone call.

Laban was winking at her. He was a very happy man. The American visit was the talk of Britain, and he had both his lovely daughters in London with him. Leah's visit was a surprise, and his PA Henry had raised her eyebrows at the sight of Leah Monklaast at MBC twice in one week. She wondered what was going on—there must be something on the cards for Laban's eldest daughter to waltz in like this.

Leah was glad that her father's phone call was long and involved, because it gave her a chance to rehearse what she wanted to say to him. This was a good moment to talk—Laban was in a very receptive mood.

"Well my dear," said Laban, putting the phone down and smiling. "You are looking wonderful, and to what do I owe this pleasure?"

Leah smiled back and bit her lip, wondering how to begin. She got up from her chair and walked over to his huge desk.

"Daddy darling ... it's about Jacob."

Laban knew they were in for a serious talk—Leah never called him "Daddy". He looked faintly amused.

"Jacob?"

Leah leaned over and put her hands on the desk. Her lips felt dry and she licked them. "Well, I don't know if you've noticed, but we have become quite attached to each other." She put her hand up to stop him interrupting. She knew she had to keep going before she lost her nerve. "I know he's only been in England five minutes—but honestly father, it just happened. My feelings for Jacob are ... well ... I've never felt like this about anybody before. And I know he feels the same way about me."

As she faltered for the next sentence, Laban cut in.

"Leah, you know more than anything that I want to see you happy. Your mother especially wanted you to find the right man and settle down. If you feel Jacob is this man, then you have my blessing."

Leah was quiet for a moment. Then, taking a deep breath she said, "I may need your help. I know we are right for each other, but so many times things have gone wrong for me. I want this time to be perfect. I don't want anything to get in the way ..."

Laban knew she was talking about Rachel. It had always been such a difficult situation, with Rachel being so beautiful—Leah never stood a chance. He could understand how his eldest daughter felt, and if Leah's heart was set on Jacob, then he would do all he could to make sure it worked out for her. His wife Elizabeth would have been so proud to see her eldest daughter marry first. It had always been important to her. 'Right and proper' she used to say. He smiled fondly at her memory.

"Don't worry darling. I'm on your side. I'll do what I can." He suddenly had a thought. "And we can start right now!"

Leah looked up at him, startled. "What do you mean?"

"Jacob has an interview this lunchtime with a columnist from *This Week* magazine. It's a profile on his job here. You know the kind of thing: 'Handsome new face takes executive position at leading broadcasting corporation'. Anyway, I thought maybe Rachel should accompany him, but I'm sure she'll be worn out after last night—so why don't you go instead? All I need is for him to have an attractive girl in tow, to help build up the image. What do you say?" He asked.

Leah's face lit up. It was a marvellous idea. Not only would she have Jacob to herself once more—but there would be a journalist watching their every move!

"Father, you're wonderful!" She clapped her hands like a little girl.

Laban laughed aloud.

"Alright my love," he waved his hands to quieten her down. "Now listen. Let me handle this, please. I would suggest that you pop into town and do a little shopping or something, while I sort Jacob out. Get back here for one o clock. I will do the rest. Off you go!"

Leah left on a cloud and her father picked up his phone once again.

"Henry, let me know when Jacob's in the building will you?" he asked.

*   *   *

Jacob Lindstein was already in the building and just opening the door to Studio Three. As he pushed, he heard the strains of infectious laughter and saw Aaron and Rachel engrossed in a magazine.

". . . and he actually smeared it all over his face, thinking it would get rid of his acne!!" Aaron was thumping the table with his fist. "I just have to use that story on Monday! Just think, my first show—they're gonna love me or hate me aren't they Rache?"

Rachel's head was bent very near his as she replied, "They'll love you, Aaron. How could they not?"

Jacob tried to ignore his feelings and made them both jump by standing behind them and saying, "You'll be a star in no time, Mr Holloway."

The two heads twisted round almost guiltily at the sound of the voice. "Oh, Hi Jacob! It's you." Aaron's infectious smile and friendly way made Jacob relax. But then, that's why Aaron was going to make such a special DJ.

Jacob smiled graciously, and looked over to Rachel. "I hope you don't mind my butting in before your first day, but I really need to talk to Rachel for a moment."

It was so smoothly done that Aaron just nodded his head innocently, making his hair fall straight into his eyes. "No, of course not. Take her away, she stops me working anyway!"

Rachel tapped him lightly on the head with the rolled up magazine. "I'll get you back for that later!" she laughed.

Jacob opened the studio door for her, and they left. They walked down the corridor not looking at each other and not saying a word. When they got to the end, Jacob turned right and Rachel followed him.

She looked at him quizzically. "Where are we going?"

"The back way," he replied and opened an exit door. They found themselves outside in the car park.

Rachel's blue eyes blinked in the light and she looked up at him. She really was quite beautiful.

Jacob shuffled his feet and looked around him, as if scared of being caught "out of school". "Rachel. We have to meet and talk. I really can't go on like this any more." The seriously handsome face looked troubled and Rachel longed to touch it.

"I'm not seeing Elliott until later this evening. Perhaps we could meet up after work?" she suggested, blushing slightly.

Jacob was so relieved. "Where?"

She pursed her lips and frowned. "It is probably better if we are not seen in a restaurant or anything. How about the river? The London Embankment is beautiful in the early evening. We could walk ... and talk ..."

They both stood looking into each other's eyes. The silence was almost palpable. They were so attracted to each other it made talking very difficult. If they stood here much longer ... Jacob cut in.

"Right. Meet me by that bridge—the one they've just painted blue ..."

Rachel smiled to herself. Jacob hadn't been here long enough to know the names of the various bridges that spanned the Thames.

"OK. The blue one at seven?" Her eyes sparkled as she drank in Jacob's face.

After a while, he turned away. "I'd better go." He started to walk across the car park.

"Where are you going?" She called.

"I'll go in round the front way—you can use that exit, it's still open." He pointed behind her.

Rachel stood for a few more moments, watching him go. What was she getting herself into? Meeting in parks? She turned and walked back through the fire door, trying not to think of the other issues clouding her mind. Looking at her watch, she saw it was time to go up to her father's office. She had promised to report in. He would be anxious to know that Elliott was still in one piece.

* * *

Rachel left the building at lunchtime, satisfied that she was doing her job well. Her father was so pleased with her that he had given her time off for good behaviour! This was good news for her. It meant that she could spend the afternoon getting ready for her date with Jacob. She hailed a cab and sat down thankfully in the back seat, letting her mind wander. A terrible feeling of excitement and despair ran through her. What was she doing? How could she be seeing Jacob behind Leah's back? Was her sister really involved with him—or was it just words? Then she could see Leah's face shining as she said, 'Oh Rachel! I can hardly believe this is happening to me!'

She closed her eyes and laid her head on the back of the car seat. This couldn't be happening. Life could not get to be that much of a mess.

* * *

At a small and intimate restaurant just by Curzon Street, Jacob sat facing Leah. She was gazing dreamily into his eyes, and he was frantically thinking of his next move.

Leah stretched her arms lazily and tossed back her hair.

"Oh Jacob, isn't this wonderful? I did not think for one minute that I would see you today! Don't you just love the way things keep working out?" Leah was trying hard to be the perfect partner. She knew this was officially a "working date" and wanted Jacob to be proud of her. Unfortunately, her idea of power dressing didn't quite work. Her hair was clipped up at the front and didn't suit her face, and the tailored two piece jacket and skirt with it's pencil-thin lines did nothing for her at all. In fact, the whole outfit looked rather 'school-marmish'.

Jacob looked around the room. It certainly was a fine eating place, the soft carpet creating extra hush as the waiters tiptoed around their valued customers. Soft lights and even softer music added to the effect. They had a table in a corner, so that when they did the interview, they would not disturb anyone else—and wouldn't be disturbed themselves. As he looked around, Jacob saw the waiter talking to a young woman and nodding towards their table.

Leah let out a moan. "Oh great!" she whispered sarcastically. "They have sent us Myra Fletcher."

"You know her?" asked Jacob.

"One of the biggest bitches in the business. Be careful darling, she'll eat you alive." With that, Leah reached across and laid her hand on Jacob's. "Just as well you have me here," she murmured, giving him a secret smile.

Myra Fletcher wasted no time. She was watching them as she walked up to the table, and had already formulated her own ideas on the couple she saw in front of her. Ms Monklaast was no doubt wearing this handsome guy out in bed every night—nothing much changed in this business. Usually Myra would accept this as 'routine', but as she got closer to Jacob, she realised he was better than that. She hugged her mini-recorder closer to her—this could be quite a story.

She extended her hand as she reached them. Her dyed red hair made her look older than her thirty years, and the long beige cashmere sweater gave her that 'I've been there darling' look. Certainly, over the years, Myra's interviews had become legendary and people accepted the way she looked as part of the production. This lady bowed to no one.

"You must be Jacob, MBC's new wonderboy." Her voice had a marvellously low throaty sound that came from chain-smoking and spending her life shouting over crowds.

Jacob couldn't help but look amused. He had not met anyone like her outside his ranch in Australia. He imagined her out on the land in a pair of suede trousers, riding bareback and yelling out the farm hands. They'd love her! He pulled himself back to reality and stood up from his seat.

"Myra, a pleasure to meet you." He smiled.

The journalist started to take in what she saw. Fabulously dark, rugged and handsome—she could do a lot with him. Her photographer would be along later—this piece would be short on copy but very heavy on pictures. She turned to greet Leah and was delighted to see that she looked a mess. 'Beauty and the Beast', she thought to herself, this was going to be good.

The lunch was pleasant enough and it was soon time for Myra to place her recorder discreetly on the table and conduct the interview, as only she could. She leaned back casually and looked at the couple who had been placed side by side so that the microphone would pick them up properly. The journalist had a very clever way of extracting things out of people. She started by putting them at ease and beginning with small talk, before she went for the jugular.

"So, Jacob. I can see you are every inch an Australian—how do you find our little island?" And so it went on until the direction changed just slightly.

"You are actually related to Laban Monklaast, aren't you?" Myra asked casually.

"That's true." Agreed Jacob. "My mother and he are cousins. They were always close, even though we lived so far away. When I first met Laban, it was as though I'd known him all my life."

Myra gave him a companionable smile and carried on. "It must have been very pleasant to find that you also had female relations nearer your own age ... "

She left the statement open, hoping that he would take the bait and finish it for her. He did.

"It was great." He agreed. "At home, I had a brother whom I didn't really get on with, but I get on fine with Leah and Rachel." He made a point of looking over to Leah when he said this, and she squirmed with delight.

"Well, you two certainly seem to hit it off." Myra clicked the record button on the machine and waved to the photographer who had just arrived.

"Let's pop outside and get a few shots, shall we?" she suggested, and left before either of them could argue.

Jacob was surprised that the interview was over so quickly and looked at Leah. He shrugged his shoulders. "Is that it?"

Leah was smoothing down her skirt and trying to make sure she looked good—she was determined to get into one of the shots. "She obviously got what she wanted. Let's go outside—we don't want to keep them waiting, they can be so fickle."

The photo session seemed to go on longer than the actual interview. There were shots of Jacob by himself, standing casually by the wall looking into the distance; close-ups showing his sensuous dark eyes to their best advantage; and then they wanted a few of Jacob and Leah leaving the restaurant. Leah immediately hooked her hand around Jacob's arm and smiled at him.

"OK. That's wonderful!" Myra Fletcher was packing up fast. "I'll make sure MBC receive plenty of copies. It will be out in two days. Bye!"

It was over. She was gone.

Jacob ran his fingers through his hair. "Phew! That wasn't as bad as I imagined."

Leah gave a short laugh. "She went easy on you. She doesn't want to offend my father, what with you being a relation, and all that. You wait till she wants to interview that new little DJ at MBCs. She'll give him a hard time—she'll dig out every bit of dirt she can, and she'll have him sleeping with every good-looking female and male in the country!"

Jacob looked genuinely offended. "Really?"

"You've got a lot to learn yet, Jacob," replied Leah, laughing softly.

Meanwhile as they walked away, Myra was already giving her

photographer instructions. "I want the best ones coming out of the restaurant. Get me one of that stupid woman gazing up at him— oh, and go through the files, dig out what you can on Leah Monklaast and her other dates. And we had better have a good head and shoulders of the smouldering eyes, too. Got that?"

The cameraman nodded. There was no way he wouldn't get it.

CHAPTER

17

Rachel Monklaast paced up and down the apartment. It was just gone six o'clock and she was still wearing her 'work' clothes. Her conscience was driving her crazy. One part of her wanted to dress up and look her best for the man she knew she loved more than anything, and the other part told her she was a cheat, she couldn't be trusted and was ruining her sister's chance of happiness. How could she dress up for this?

The thing that bothered her most, was that she had never considered not meeting Jacob. That of course, would be the brave thing to do, the sisterly thing. But no, she needed to find out the truth. Was there anything going on between Leah and Jacob—and if so, why on earth was he pursuing her? He could not possibly believe that Rachel was the two-timing type—had she given him that impression?

She shook her head furiously. No. She would not dress up. She made her way to the bedroom and picked some faded jeans from the wardrobe. As she pulled them on, the mirror told her that they fitted her like a glove and looked far from unattractive. She sighed, and reached for a long silk shirt. It was a mid-blue and shot through with darker navy threads. She tucked the shirt in and added a soft black leather belt with a large silver buckle. The mirror shouted 'gorgeous' at her, and she wondered why.

She stepped closer and looked at her reflection. The vision that gazed back at her, had pink flushed cheeks and bright blue eyes that glittered with expectation, pale pink lips slightly parted and startled. This is what Jacob had done to her already.

"It's ridiculous," she said to the mirror.

Out in the hallway, she put on a deep blue wool jacket and pulled the belt tightly round her waist, as if to protect herself. She thrust her hands deep in the pockets and cuddled up to the soft warmth of the material—she couldn't stop thinking of him for a second.

*   *   *

Jacob had to make do with wearing his 'interview clothes'. He looked smart and professional and slightly over-dressed for a walk by the water, but it hardly mattered to him. He was meeting Rachel. At last, he was going to be with this woman, this woman who affected him like no one had ever done before. He felt his stomach churn as he freshened up in the cloakroom on the top floor of MBC. At least the men's room was equipped for guests to use and was fully stocked with towels and decent aftershave.

He inspected himself in the huge lighted mirror.

He was attractive, he knew that, he had been told it often enough by women who made their feelings pretty obvious. But he knew that wouldn't be enough for Rachel. True, they didn't know each other very well, and they only had appearances to go on at this stage—and yet, it was more than that. When he looked at her, it was as if he was seeing into her soul—as if he knew her already. He was sure she felt like that too, and could almost feel her looking back with the same emotions.

Then of course, there was this mess with Leah. But surely he could explain that. It wouldn't be easy, but it had to be done. His mouth was dry.

'I'm nervous!' He surprised himself with the thought. He ran the taps into the sink and threw handfuls of water into his face. He looked up and saw the rivulets raining down, catching on his eyelashes like tears, running down his cheeks like sweat and landing on his lips like ...

"She's got to like me!" He said aloud to the reflection in the mirror.

*   *   *

London is a strange place—such a mixture of intoxicating sounds and smells. Along the Embankment, people were rushing for trains, taxis and buses. The noise was confusing and most of it came from angry drivers trying to manoeuvre their vehicles in and out of suicidal pedestrians. Jacob, without noticing, walked past it all. He had his sights set on the 'blue bridge'. It was quieter down this end and eventually he found a barrier to lean on and looked down into the muddy brown Thames. He was early, he knew he would be. At least he could watch for her and have the joy of seeing her walk towards him. He looked up from the river, and—as if by magic—there she was. Walking slowly in his direction, almost hesitantly. He smiled to himself as he noted the jeans—she could be eighteen, he thought. There was a short moment where he wasn't sure what to do. Should he walk towards her, or wait here for her, at their meeting place?

She looked up and saw him. He made his way towards her as if being pulled by a magnet. It was an overwhelming moment for them both—neither was sure how to react, what to say, so when they came face to face they both automatically looked at the ground and then up into each other's eyes.

"Hello." It was Jacob who broke the silence. He looked at her and smiled with obvious relief.

She smiled shyly back at him. "Hello."

He looked round and tried to see a space where they could be on their own. Further along, it was emptier still. "Let's walk down there." He pointed ahead .

They strolled along beside the river in companionable silence. It was as if neither of them wanted to destroy the moment. They came to a busy road. Jacob looked up and down and grinned. "I think we'll have to take a chance!" He grabbed Rachel's hand and ran across the road. They both laughed as they dodged the traffic and found themselves on the other side. It was the most natural thing in the world to carry on with their hands firmly linked together. Once again they lapsed into silence—only this time it wasn't the friendly quietness of before—it was the silence of lovers who don't want to be disturbed. As they walked, Jacob pulled Rachel's hand so that they moved closer together. Finally, they stopped. Jacob turned to face Rachel and lowered his head towards hers.

They stood still, their faces a breath away from each other and suddenly it was all too much. They were in each other's arms. Jacob's lips quickly found hers and he kissed her softly. His breath was swept away as she readily returned his kiss. Her mouth was soft and trembled under the pressure of his lips. He held her tighter and the kisses grew stronger and stronger until she gasped and pulled away. He still had his hand in her hair and her arms lovingly clasped his neck.

"Jacob! We are in the middle of London!" she cried. "What are we thinking of!?"

Jacob pulled her to him roughly and a quiet laugh came from his throat. "You tell me!" He kissed her again. She pulled away and placed her hands on his chest.

"We can't do this! It's ridiculous! What if.....?"

Jacob gave a rough sigh. "You're right, of course—so what do we do now?"

"Can we walk again?" Rachel asked. "I think we have a fair amount of things to sort out."

He caught her hand again and started to move away.

"I suppose you mean Leah," he said flatly.

"There's a lot I don't understand, Jay." She used this shortened version of his name quite naturally, as naturally as everything they did seemed to be.

They walked for a while, and then Jacob stopped abruptly. "I can't do this! I need to be somewhere with you! I want to see your face while I explain everything."

He dashed to the side of the busy street.

"What are you doing?" she shouted to him.

"Getting a cab!" he yelled back.

"To where?" she joined him at the kerb.

"Nowhere! Anywhere! Taxi!!" He flagged one down and opened the door for her—Rachel looked bewildered but got in.

Jacob spoke to the taxi driver who laughed and saluted.

"It's your money, mate!" And drove off towards Trafalgar Square.

Once safely inside the cab, Jacob put his arm around Rachel and she automatically laid her head on his shoulder.

"What did you say to him?" she asked, smiling dreamily.

"I said we wanted to see London the long way round, and to get stuck in as many traffic jams as he could!" Jacob's face was animated, his smile a beautiful curve that ended in a crease by his cheek. Rachel wanted to kiss it, but was afraid that her feelings had been too much on show already. He looked down at this beautiful girl in his arms and wondered for the millionth time what was happening to him.

Rachel's eyes turned serious and she looked up at him. "Talk to me, Jay."

He bent his head over to hers and whispered, "Oh, Rachel." She touched his hair lightly—it was so black and shiny. He caught her hand and put it to his lips. "What can I say?" He told her of his first meeting with Laban, and how her father had been insistent that he would like his daughter. When he was introduced to Leah, he felt honour-bound to be nice to her, but it was pretty obvious that she was taking it all very seriously.

"The stupid thing was..." he continued, "that I didn't find out until I met Aaron that the daughter Laban was talking about was you and not Leah!"

Rachel's blues eyes looked even more puzzled. "So ..."

"So, darling, by then Leah had decided she was going to have me for breakfast—and I was put into one of the most embarrassing positions of my life!"

Rachel hadn't heard a word past the moment he called her 'darling' and just smiled at him, waiting for him to continue.

"Well, I could hardly turn round and tell her to go and find someone else. By the next evening she was planning the cosy night in with the video ..."

Rachel sat up a little straighter so that she could look at him. "But Leah told me that you and she are made for each other—in fact, she told me that she had to fight you off the other night, and you nearly didn't make the film anyway!"

Jacob laughed. "Er ... read that round the other way will you? I've been jumped on by a fair number of females, but at least I've been awake most of the time!" He went on to explain how Leah had found him practically naked on his bed.

Rachel blushed and put her hands to her cheeks. "Maybe I should mention here, that my sister and I are very different characters ..."

Jacob threw his head back and laughed. "Rachel, you are so sweet, and I would be very disappointed if you behaved anything like Leah!" He pulled her over to him and held her very tightly. When she looked up, his rugged face was serious. "Don't you ever be anything other than the girl who nearly knocked a pot of coffee over me the first time we met."

"Jay ..." Anything else Rachel was about to say was lost in a torrent of kisses as Jacob took charge of her lips, her eyes, her body, her soul. Rachel was lost. Jacob's body was so firm, so protective next to hers, she wanted him to stay there forever.

Trafalgar Square, Piccadilly Circus, Marble Arch, Madame Tussauds—they all drifted past the window. The taxi driver even shouted out "That's where the Queen lives!" as they drove past Buckingham Palace, but he was talking to himself. Jacob and Rachel were in another world, they were flying round a planet with no desire ever to come back to earth, completely wrapped up in each other.

When the taxi finally came to a halt, they were still locked in a passionate embrace and the driver had to hit the horn very hard to gain their attention.

They both looked up in surprise, and began to laugh sheepishly.

"Pay the man!" giggled Rachel. They had stopped outside the Park Lane apartment.

"No, I think perhaps you should get out here and I'll go carry on to MBC, pick up a few things and make my way back to Monks Lodge." They sat looking at each other, not wanting to part.

"You are right, of course." Rachel's lovely face looked forlorn as she thought of the night ahead, dealing with Elliot Blaze. "I have a busy weekend ..."

"You know the last thing I want is for you to be alone with Blaze. Rachel, you look after yourself." He played with her hands.

"You know the last thing I want, is for you to be at home with my sister!" she replied, pretending to be cross.

He stroked her hair lovingly. "Rachel ... my Rachel ... I won't even know she's there. Won't you be at home at all this weekend?" He asked.

She shook her tousled hair. "Not very much, but at least Elliott goes home on Monday after his interview with Aaron."

"Then I get you all to myself!" Jacob said happily.

Rachel managed to extricate herself from Jacob and stepped outside the cab.

Jacob opened the window and called her back. "By the way— no one but my mother has ever called me 'Jay'."

Rachel kissed him softly on the lips and whispered impishly, "I like her already."

CHAPTER

18

Another late night out with Elliott Blaze was the last thing Rachel needed. Saturday night had been a riot of 'A List' parties and as she came in from her shopping expedition in Kensington, there was already a message on her ansaphone.

"Hi baby!" the American accent coming over loud and clear. "My car will pick you up at ten, OK? We can eat and then go on somewhere special—put on your glad rags, honey, it's gonna be a long, long night!"

And it was. Elliott had had a day of hanging around in the hotel and was ready to party. By the time they got back into the limo, it was five o'clock in the morning. Rachel was shattered, but happily so was Elliot. He looked over to her and smiled lazily, "Had a good time baby?" His jacket was flung onto the seat and his shirt was open almost to the waist. For most of his fans, the thought of sitting opposite Elliott Blaze in this situation would be dynamite—but Rachel casually glanced at her watch and then at him. "You have an interview at MBC just after eleven tomorrow morning ... sorry, this morning. I think perhaps you should be thinking of sleeping some of this off."

They had been to club after club, making sure they missed out nothing he could tell the guys back home about. Then they drifted in and out of various other night haunts, mainly to see who was in. The advantage of the night club scene was that there were little or no fans around to bother the celebrities. Of course, the staunch groupies were always around, but they were no trouble once they were given the word to keep out of the way. It was the hords of screaming women that always caused the problems—those who generally ran amok anywhere they thought their 'idol' might be. Sometimes the police had to be called in if the minders were outnumbered. But in the early hours of the morning, only the regular clubbers were around, and anyway, the kind of places they were going to had a priority members' list so high that even some famous names couldn'tget in.

So, by the time they were in the limousine, Elliott had been introduced to film stars, pop stars, TV stars and royalty! He was a happy man.

"Ever thought of working in the States, honey?" he was asking her, as he slouched half-asleep.

Rachel shook her head. "I don't really think it's me, Elliott. Believe it or not, I prefer the quiet life!" She laughed at his surprised face.

Somewhere along the line, Rachel had managed to give him all the right signs indicating that however hard he tried, she was not 'bedroom fodder'. He had finally taken the hint and their relationship became relaxed. He liked that—to him he had the best of both worlds. When he was outside, the public saw him with this gorgeous girl on his arm, and when he went back to the hotel, he could rely on Julie Redwing to be waiting in his bed for him. The system actually kept everyone happy, especially Julie, who felt she would lose Elliott's attention even more once he set eyes on Rachel.

The car stopped outside the Dorchester. (It was more important to make sure that Elliott was delivered to his door first.) Then it carried on and took Rachel back to the apartment. She stepped out and watched the Park Lane traffic which was already organising itself for the rush hour. The sun was up, and in another five hours she would need to escort Elliott to MBC and up to Studio Three where Aaron would be waiting nervously for their arrival.

* * *

Aaron was in the studio at eight that morning. It wasn't just that
he wanted to make sure he had everything covered—it was his
usual routine. He sat with a massive pile of early morning newspapers, scanning through them quickly, circling any newsy items
he could use with a red felt pen, and then tearing them roughly
out of the paper, writing the name of the journal on the top of the
caption. Reading through funny stories of bizarre situations subconsciously helped him to relax. By his side was a roughly script-
ed programme, and now and again he would pencil in a reminder
to use one of the clips.

The next paper in the pile was a copy of *This Week* magazine.
He liked this, as it often had plenty of content for him. He flicked
through it casually, and a picture caught his eye. He turned back
a few pages and the magazine fell open on a two page spread.

The headline screamed—Heiress and the Poor Relation.

Aaron gradually focused his eyes on the display of photos in
front of him. In the top left hand corner was a quarter-page of
Jacob looking steamy and romantic, his dark brown eyes piercing
through. On the opposite corner was a photo of Jacob and Leah
looking terribly cosy, obviously leaving some swank restaurant.
Leah was gazing up at Jacob lovingly and he had his head thrown
back in laughter. No doubt about it, it was a great shot. Aaron's
mind was racing—had he read everything wrong? He was sure
that Jacob had his eyes firmly fixed on Rachel—so what was this
all about?

He started to read the article.

MBC Heiress Leah Monklaast is seeing new boy Jacob
Lindstein. Apparently the pair are related—but not too
closely, as our exclusive picture shows! We talked to
MBC's handsome new executive Jacob Lindstein, and

found out a little more ... Giving us the benefit of that rugged Australian smile, Jacob told us he was "delighted to find himself in the company of new relations ... especially one so young and female!" Well, *This Week* knows plenty about the haphazard lovelife of Miss Monklaast ... and in case you've forgotten, we have printed a string of photos of men she has 'loved and lost'.

Aaron glanced at the bottom and was shocked to see similar photos of Leah with other famous personalities. The captions underneath yelled, 'Has she got it right this time?'

The article went on to make sarcastic and cutting remarks about Leah's looks and money, intimating that Jacob was set on inheriting MBC through her.

Aaron slowly put the magazine down. What should he do? Was this true? And more to the point did Rachel know? His heart raced and burned within him—he had to warn her! He grabbed the phone by the CD files and rang her apartment. He let it ring for ages, realising that Elliott had probably kept her out half the night and she would be in a deep sleep by now. It rang and rang. Finally he gave up and put it back down again. He sat for a moment with his head in his hands, wondering what to do for the best. This had to be the worst day for things to go wrong. Professionally, his mind told him to concentrate on the programme and to put this dilemma behind him, at least until afterwards. But Rachel would be coming in with Elliot ...

He picked the phone up again.

*   *   *

It was actually a waste of time ringing Rachel. She was walking by the Serpentine in London's Hyde Park. She had tried to sleep, but by six-thirty it became obvious that sleep was not going to come.

For one thing, she was too awake after such an active night, and for another, there was Jacob. So, here she was, hands thrust deep in her warmest coat, strolling along by the water. She was trying hard to put things into perspective. Was she wrong to love Jacob so much when Leah liked him too? But then, Jacob had explained that—it was all a mistake. But it still didn't make her feel any better. She didn't like betraying people and she felt in her heart that she had let Leah down—even though Jacob had no feelings for her.

Some ducks came racing over to her, looking up expectantly waiting to be fed. She took her hands out of her pockets and waved them at the birds. "I'm sorry—I haven't got anything." They looked at her disbelievingly.

She shivered a little, and decided it was time to go back. But first she dodged the traffic and went to the newspaper stand on the corner. If she wasn't going to sleep anymore, she might as well buy a *Daily Mail* and a copy of *This Week* and go back to the flat. It was only a short walk back, and so she strolled slowly, opening the magazine as she went.

An involuntary gasp burst from her as she stopped dead, staring at the photos in front of her. Through glazed eyes the tears sprung up and spilled over, splashing the page as she tried to read Myra Fletcher's outrageous report.

Still clutching the paper firmly, she ran blindly down Park Lane and back into the safety of her room, where she collapsed, weeping on the bed. The sobbing didn't stop for sometime, and only then because the phone rang. She sat up and stared at it, wiping her face with the back of her hand. It could just be one of Elliott's entourage checking up on arrangements, or it could be someone who'd read about Jacob and Leah—Jacob and Leah!! How could he do this? How could she have been so stupid? Played for a fool—and all the time he was conning her! She bit her lip as she thought how close she had come to giving in to Jacob. On Friday by the river, she had been so besotted with him that it was almost she who had fought to hold back! Her head started to swim and the tears began again.

The phone continued to ring, and with enormous effort, Rachel picked it up. "Hello?" she whispered.

"Oh Rachel! Thank God!" It was Aaron's voice. Probably the only person she could cope with at the moment.

"Aaron."

"Rache, are you OK? Have you seen ...? Do you want me to come over?" Aaron's voice sounded thick with worry. He was probably as stunned as she was.

There was silence on the other end, but he could hear her breathing. Then she spoke. "Oh Aaron—what am I supposed to do? Have you spoken to anyone? Does ... does anyone else know?" Her voice was faltering.

"Listen Rache, I haven't seen anyone. I'm in the studio sorting my show out." He paused not quite knowing what to say, but at the same time he realised she needed to talk.

"The timing couldn't have been worse could it? Are you still bringing Elliott in?" Stupid question he thought to himself.

"Yes, yes of course ... Aaron ... did you know ... about this?" she could hardly bring herself to ask.

"Did I? Rachel, I thought Jacob fancied—sorry—really liked you! I had no idea, no idea at all! What is going on?"

"I don't know Aaron. I thought he liked me too." She sounded so small and hurt that Aaron was beside himself. How dare Jacob treat her like that! This was his Rachel!

He started to talk to her, and then heard her crying softly in the background.

"Oh please don't, Rache. It'll be all right. Perhaps the papers got it wrong." It was all he could say.

"I'm sorry Aaron. Don't worry, I'll be OK—it was just a shock, that was all. I'll see you at eleven-thirty with Elliott—it's going to be a great show. Good luck Aaron—and I really do mean that."

The line went dead.

Rachel sat on the end of her bed trembling and tearing a paper handkerchief into shreds. She had to put this behind her—postpone it for a few hours while she prepared to go to MBC. With a tremendous effort, she rose and walked into the bathroom. Stripping herself completely, hoping a shower would help. She stepped in and let the warm water cascade through her long black hair and over her body, like fingers caressing and caring for her. She put her hands forward onto the bathroom wall, her palms pressed hard against the ivory tiles ... and then she cried, really cried—loud and long until the shower and the tears were indistinguishable from each other.

*   *   *

On the eighth floor at just after ten o'clock, Laban Monklaast was perusing the article in front of him. Good shot of Jacob, wonderful shot of the couple. The headline? Well, they have to hang it on something. He chuckled to himself when he thought of his eldest daughter. She had obviously not seen the article yet, or the phone would be red hot from her call. He leaned back in his office chair and put his hands behind his head, and looked at the copy again. The 'MBC heiress' thing had been done more than once, and sometimes it had been quite threatening. But this time, he knew that his daughter really liked Jacob, and if someone had to inherit his money, why not keep it in the family? In many ways, it couldn't be better.

The intercom buzzed. "Yes, Henry?"

"Jacob is here, shall I send him in?" said, Henry, ever businesslike, but ever friendly.

"Of course! Of course!" Laban beamed at the machine and looked up expectantly at the door.

Jacob Lindstein walked in innocently, looking terrific in an expensive leather coat, a pale pinstripe collarless shirt held at the throat with a gold pin, and black trousers with small darts at the waist. He had his hands in the trouser pockets with the coat thrown back away from him. His dark features and physique made him look as though had walked off the front page of a fashion mag. He nodded at Laban and grinned.

"So it's the big day today," he stated.

Laban frowned and looked confused.

"Oh come on, Laban!" Aaron starts his show! Elliotts' interview? What time is the press reception afterwards?" Jacob was walking round the room, absently reading faxes from the machine in the corner.

"Oh that! Yes of course." Laban interjected. "The press will come down to the studio after the show—we thought shots of Aaron 'on the air', so to speak with our American film star would work well."

"You seem somewhat distracted?" Jacob looked at his boss.

Laban put his hands on the desk and gave the impression of a cat who'd just had the cream.

"Well, it's pretty obvious that you haven't been through the papers this morning," he stated.

"Oh, sorry! Yes, of course I have. Those shots of Elliott are outstanding! They'll do the company no end of good—we can run with those for quite a while."

Laban sighed and shook his head. "*This Week*." He said. "You definitely haven't seen *This Week*, have you?"

"No, no I haven't," he said, and then hit his head with his hand. "Of course! The interview! I'm sorry Laban I've been so wound up making sure everything is set for Aaron's big day, I'd totally forgotten it. Have you got a copy?"

Laban laughed again and went over to the pile of *This Weeks* sent in by Myra. He placed his hand on the top. "Everybody's got a copy!" He said, and threw one over to him. "Pages eight and nine."

Jacob opened the magazine and his blood froze in his veins. He could feel his face turning white as he stared and stared at the horrific sight in front of him.

"Thought you'd be pleased!" said Laban thumping him on the back. "Speechless eh? Well, it's your first big story. How do you like seeing yourself in print? I can't tell you how pleased I am to see you and my daughter getting on so well!"

There was no response at all from Jacob. He couldn't move as he thought of all the implications. He had been set up! He wasn't sure who by ... Myra? Leah? Laban even?

The phone rang and Laban waved Jacob away. "Back to work, my boy! Plenty of things to do if you want to inherit the company!!" He picked the phone up. "Hello? Yes. Hey—great to hear from you!"

Jacob's feet felt like lead as he walked out of the office. With hindsight, he should have stayed and put Laban in the picture— that would have been the best thing to do. 'Nipped in the bud' the English said. He should have stayed and explained everything, but he didn't. He was too shocked. Stunned by it all. Him and Leah? Did Laban say everyone had a copy of this?

He stopped and closed his eyes as he realised that this meant that Rachel was almost bound to have seen it.

Time was rushing on—it was now nearly eleven and Aaron would be going on the air shortly. He should be there, in the control room to watch and listen. He should be there to greet their guest Elliott Blaze when he arrived—with Rachel. His stomach sank so hard he almost heard it. Would he be able to explain beforehand, and would she ever believe him, even if he did?

CHAPTER

19

Aaron Holloway's hands felt clammy as he picked up a CD and pushed it into the player. Inside the studio it was quiet. Out in the control room it was bedlam. Jane Hunter was doing her best to keep the press upstairs in the hospitality suite until after the show, but they kept creeping down the stairs, cameras at the ready, hoping to get a sneaky shot of Aaron looking nervous before he started. The studio engineers and the programme producer were getting fed up with the commotion and decided that anyone not directly involved with the programme should leave straight away. This was definitely the way forward, and Jane managed to shunt journalists, PAs and hangers-on out of the studio.

The producer Graeme Harding pressed a button on the mixing desk and spoke through to Aaron, who received him on a pair of small headphones. "Everything ready there, Aaron?"

"Just brilliant!" Aaron yelled back. "I can't wait to start!" The adrenalin was flowing fast as the countdown began. He could hear the end of the news in his 'phones and then an engineer's voice counting him in.

Suddenly the theme tune hit the airwaves and they were off.

Aaron was shouting and waving his arms at an audience he couldn't see, but knew was there. He loved it. "Hello, you look nice today ... my name's Aaron ... what's yours?" The music cut in and then he started again. "Actually, we should really get to know each other better if we're gonna start meeting like this everyday at eleven ... why don't you give me a call? Introduce yourself ... let's be friendly ... tell me your likes and dislikes ... let's hear a bit about you!" The music came back up again, and Aaron faded it as he said, "I'm on 0181 637 7272 and this is East 17." The band's record came thrashing through the speakers and Aaron was away. He quickly moved his chair over to the script and pile of magazine clippings, grabbed a few and pushed his chair back to the mike. He faded the song ending.

"East 17, the band from Walthamstow ... I'm sure you knew that—but did you know this? According to this morning's copy of the *Mirror*, we are all going to die by the year 2010! 87-year-old Victor Matthers has been counting the rings inside a rather large beetroot he grew this year, and is convinced that he can tell, just by looking at the inside of this beetroot, that the weather is going to be bad for the next few years, and then England will gradually freeze over and that will be the end of us!

Any comments? 0181 637 7272 is the number to ring." The next CD started to play.

"Oh and by the way ... if the name Elliott Blaze means anything to you ... hold on to your seats . . . he'll be with us in just over half-an-hour ... yes thirty minutes ... and I've just given you his phone number ... think on!"

The engineers were cheering him through the glass partition and signalling at the amazing number of calls flooding through to the control room. The switchboard was jammed already, and Aaron was pre-recording phone calls in between records. (You could never be too careful—you had no idea what a listener was going to say, so most calls were recorded about five minutes before the listeners at home heard them.)

The show continued at a really fast pace, and Aaron's infectious laugh soon had callers phoning in with the most outrageous stories. He was loving every minute of it and his listening audience knew it. The programme was going to be an unqualified success!

Upstairs, Rachel was just arriving with Elliott. Normally for a radio interview there is no great need to dress up and guests had been known to come in unshaven and almost in slippers, but Elliott was well aware that this was a good profile for him to end on, and that the press would be just as interested in him as they would be in Aaron and the show. So, dressed with care, he made his entrance. There were already huge crowds outside MBC. Some had found out earlier in the week, and the rumours had spread like wild fire, and then, suprisingly, there were hundreds of people who had arrived even since Aaron had announced the interview on the air, only moments ago.

Rachel took Elliott to a quiet comfortable room. She didn't want the press hounding him before the show, and Julie Redwing who was with them on this occasion, was more than concerned that Elliott was relaxed. (She knew more than most, that he could be absolutely evil to interview if he wasn't happy with his surroundings.)

A young girl came into the room and asked them to follow her to the studio. Julie checked her watch and nodded. The small entourage moved down the corridor and were joined by Laban and Jacob. Laban put his arm around the star and walked ahead chatting amiably to him.

This left Rachel and Jacob to walk together, as Julie was busily shouting at someone on a mobile phone.

"Rachel ... " began Jacob, but she cut him off.

"Please," she said, holding up her hand. "I really have enough to cope with. This is crucial for Aaron's programme and I'm not going to spoil it by listening to ... your ... " She couldn't finish. The words 'excuses' and 'lies' were on the tip of her tongue, but she knew that once she gave into them, she would crumble. She focused her eyes ahead of her and carried on walking as if he wasn't there.

Jacob was devastated. He was at a loss to know what to do next, but realised that professionally she was right—this really did have to wait. He glanced over to her.

"Afterwards," he said.

She didn't reply.

The young assistant opened the studio door and ushered them through. They could hear the show from the room and it was buzzing! A young boy brought over a tray of tea and coffee and the team grabbed a mug each and tried to sit somewhere out of the way. Julie propped herself up by a vacant tape machine, and Jacob stood by the door. Rachel was very intent on knowing what was happening and stood behind one of the engineer's chairs, so that she could see through to the other room.

She sighed with relief when she saw Aaron. He was talking animatedly to a caller and charming the listeners out of the trees at the same time. He leaned over the turntables and brushed his hair out of the way as he continued to talk. He was wearing an oversized jumper that almost came to his knees with the sleeves pulled up around his elbows. His jeans were light blue, baggy and in a terrible state—he looked as if he had been climbing trees in them. But the overall picture was fantastic.

Elliott Blaze came and stood by Rachel. He automatically put his arm around her waist and leaned towards her.

"Hey, he's OK, isn't he? Very different from a presenter in New York." He was smiling his approval, and everyone in the room beamed with satisfaction.

Graeme Harding spoke to Aaron again. "After this record, Aaron. We'll bring in Elliott and then you've got one phone call and another single and that's it. Everything OK?" he asked.

Aaron looked through the window and waved his thumbs in the air. It was no problem to him—this was where he belonged.

As the record played out, Rachel took Elliott through and stayed with him. Aaron took his call, made a few announcements and then put the next CD on.

He swung round and put his hand out to Elliott.

"Hi! This is great! I can't tell you how chuffed I am to have you on my show. Is there any subject you want me to keep away from? Would you mind if I asked you some trivial things?" His smile was wide and his eyes shining.

Elliott shook his head. "No no, you're the DJ and you look as if you know your job!"

"Great!" enthused Aaron. Then he turned to Rachel. "Hi, Rache." He pulled her arm towards him and kissed her cheek. "OK?" he whispered looking terribly concerned.

"I'm fine. Don't worry about me—worry about him!" She hissed back.

Elliott looked from one to the other, but decided there couldn't be anything in it. They were miles apart.

The music faded and Aaron motioned with his hands for quiet in the studio.

"Well, if there are any more calls as nutty as Mandy out there—I don't want to know! Mandy—sort yourself out, get a perm or a new outfit! Call me again after the world ends—what time was that going to be, Mand? Two o'clock—fine. In that case I'd better get on and interview my guest—Mr Elliott Blaze!" He clapped his hands.

"OK, maybe there was only me clapping just then, but I know you were all sitting there next to your radios cheering and screaming, so Elliott, consider yourself well and truly welcomed to the show."

Elliot leaned forward to the mike by his seat. "Thanks very much Aaron."

"Tell me, Elliott. We've been chatting to some listeners who think the world will end soon. In fact Mandy from Ipswich doesn't think you've got time to get back to your hotel! Does the end of the world bother you?"

It was a startling question for someone who is used to answering things about his movie career, but happily Elliott laughed aloud, "The end of the world? Well, let me see, I don't really want it to end before I do, although having said that, it would be interesting to see just how it's done." He mused.

"Do you believe in God?" Aaron's question shot through before the Elliott had time to take a breath.

"Ah ... um ... I would have to say yes to that. I can't imagine a world without some kind of a ruler. Even though I have to say, I'm not very good at keeping the rules."

Aaron nodded thoughtfully. "In the old days of epic movies and stuff, the Charlton Hestons of the world all wanted to play Moses or someone. But what about now? Is there someone you would love to portray?" Aaron was good. He looked straight at Elliott all the time, never looking down at his notes or cuing things up. He looked totally absorbed with his guest.

Elliott was finding the experience somewhat novel, but enjoyable.

"Who would I like to portray?" he repeated. "Maybe royalty or an eminent politician—of course I'd have to dye my hair for those parts. It's so blond and I can't think of any famous blond men. Can you?"

"Robert Redford?" joked Aaron.

Elliott laughed again, joining in the fun. "Hey, but no, can't you see me made up to look like Saddam Hussein or someone? Now that would be a part to play!"

They went on chatting like old friends and then Aaron invited Elliott to stay and take a few phone calls. This was not planned, and the PR department were thrown into panic.

Julie looked nervously at Jacob and they both raised their eyebrows at Graeme Harding.

Graeme was a friendly natural sort, in his mid-thirties, with greying brown hair and a small moustache. It smiled when he did, and right now it was doing just that.

"The guy's a natural. If he thinks Elliott can manage this, then we have nothing to fear. And don't forget, it will be taped first, so if it doesn't work, we have an escape route."

But of course it was a marvellous piece of forward planning on Aarons part. The listeners asked him all the usual questions that journalists do: 'Is your hair naturally so blond?' 'Who is the love of your life at the moment?' and 'What is your next film going to be about?'

So everyone got what they wanted. And both Elliott and Aaron were winners.

When the show eventually finished and the theme tune was playing out, they let the press in. Both rooms of the studio became the reception area for around thirty hand-picked journalists and cameramen. The flashbulbs were doing overtime and everyone was congratulating everyone else. Nobody really noticed the looks that were flying across the room. Jacob desperately trying to catch Rachel's eye, Aaron cheerfully wanting to throttle Jacob, Rachel just wanting to go home, and Elliott—who had not seen the magazine—wondering what was going on. Champagne corks popped, and the music got louder and louder.

*   *   *

Back at Monks Lodge, Leah was having a lazy day. She knew that MBC would be chaotic and she decided to stay out of the way and listen to Aaron's first show in comfort and luxury. She was very surprised to find herself getting quite wrapped up in the programme. At one point she was tempted to phone-in and put her point of view!

When the show ended, she fancied some coffee, and rang for

Blanche. There was really no need, the kitchen was just a walk away, and Blanche was busy preparing a special meal for Laban, Jacob and Rachel. She knew that they would be tired, because not only was it the first day of Aaron's show, but also the last day in Britain for Elliott Blaze. They would want to relax, and (hopefully) bask in their success. But Leah wanted coffee, so everything had to stop while it was freshly made, and of course, she would also expect home-cooked biscuits to go with it. It was so frustrating working for Leah. It wasn't that Blanche resented her position. She loved doing things for Mr Monklaast and Rachel—it was just Leah who abused her role in the house—always bossing and shouting, usually for no reason.

"Make sure that it's full cream, Blanche? Don't give me that slimming alternative, it's disgusting," She called from the sofa.

It had been a beautiful day for Leah. She rose very late, showered, washed her hair, ate a very late breakfast and now stretched herself and thought about getting dressed, rather than lounging around in her satin house coat. But it was so cosy lying here with her toes stuck into flimsy mules—all she really wanted was some fresh coffee and a magazine, and she could stay here for ever.

Blanche came through with a small tray. She laid it on the coffee table and glanced over to Leah. "Would you like anything else? I've found some shortbread that the cook made yesterday."

Leah kicked her slipper off and sat up. "No, that will be fine Blanche. Oh, could you bring today's papers through before you go?" Already she was pouring herself a drink and ignoring the maid's presence completely.

Blanche quietly left the room, brought back a pile of papers and left before her temper got the better of her.

The smell of the coffee was almost better than the taste, and Leah put her cup down and fell back onto the cushions with a copy of *This Week*. It only occurred to her as she opened it, that Myra had said she would be using their interview in this issue.

'Hmm ... well, how did it look?' she smiled to herself and turned the pages slowly.

The two page spread excelled anything she had in her mind. The large photo of her and Jacob was utterly wonderful! She sat up slowly and reached for the internal phone.

"Blanche ... there's a box of Belgian chocolates by my bed. Bring them here, will you? I feel like celebrating ... "

CHAPTER

20

Jacob left the house early the next morning without having to face anyone. Leah stayed up until her eyes wouldn't keep open, but went to bed happy, knowing she was bound to see him in the morning. But by six-thirty Jacob had gone. He felt pretty bad, having only had around four hours' sleep, but he just couldn't face anyone at that time. The only safe thing to do was drive out into the country and sit alone and think.

The Buckinghamshire countryside was beautiful. Autumn was setting in and the reds and golds in the early sun were something to behold. His mind wandered back to his home in Australia—his mother would love this place. He remembered how she would get up early some mornings and walk in the cool of the day. She said it was her favourite time—she would walk and pray. Rebekkah cared deeply for her family and made it quite clear that she prayed for them too—even if they didn't pray for themselves.

'I wish she could pray for me now,' thought Jacob as he brought the car to a halt beside a group of trees. He had almost phoned her at about three this morning—but the situation was so complicated he couldn't think where to begin. He still hadn't spoken to Rachel, which was the priority, but at the moment she wouldn't even answer the phone. No, the only other thing to do was to wait until Laban was at work and then sit down and have a serious heart-to-heart with him.

He sat and examined his feelings for Rachel. She was so

beautiful, so full of charm—he couldn't find fault with her. But it wasn't just that. He'd been out with plenty of beautiful girls in Australia but Rachel was different. She was a part of everything he did now. It was natural for him to think, 'I wonder if Rachel would like this?' 'Rachel would laugh at that', 'I wish Rachel had been here'. She shared his life, even though at this moment his life was being torn apart because of her. The more he thought about it, the more he came to one conclusion—He loved Rachel more than anything on earth.

He laid his arms on the steering wheel and rested his head. Within minutes he fell into an exhausted sleep and was woken when the morning traffic started to build up. He yawned and stretched and looked blearily out of the window. Winding it down, he took in some fresh air and looked at his watch. He couldn't put it off any longer—he was going to face Laban.

* * *

Henry couldn't remember a day when she had put so many phone calls through to her boss. They just kept coming and coming, and he kept taking them! Normally, Henry would vet his calls for him and be selective, but Laban was on a high—things could not be going better for him. He appeared to have pulled off three of the most newsworthy stories of the year—all in the course of a couple of weeks! Henrietta set a tray for two and walked into Laban's office.

He smiled as she appeared. "Wonderful! "

She shook her head in disbelief and laughed back at him "Really Laban. I've told the switchboard to hold your calls for fifteen minutes while you have a break!"

"I'm glad you joined me, Henry." He was always appreciative of her, and from time to time they set aside a few minutes to discuss the events at MBC.

"Can you believe it?" He asked. "I've spent the best part of the morning answering the same three questions, from our press office, from the national papers, from other radio stations and from the TV. They all need direct quotes from me."

"And the three questions are ... ?" demanded Henry.

"One: Will Elliott Blaze be coming back and do I now consider myself to be a close friend? Two: How much will it cost us to use Aaron for our TV show, radio show, centrespread? etc. And Three: How do I feel about having Jacob for a son-in-law?" He chuckled to himself.

His PA looked concerned. "It's early days for the son-in-law routine, isn't it?"

"Ah Henry, how little you remember of young love!" He moved forward helping himself to biscuits. "My Leah is besotted with young Jacob, and I think he will be extremely good for her. From what I've seen they are very happy, and I've already given Leah my blessing. If it's what they want, I won't stand in their way."

Henry frowned. "Are you sure about this Laban? You know ..."

He knew what she was going to say. She was going to remind him of all the disastrous love affairs that she had had in the past. But it was no use, he had already made up his mind about this one.

"Henry, they are in love—what can I do?" He raise his hands up and shrugged his shoulders.

There was a tentative knock at the door and Henry got up to answer it.

The subject of their conversation walked in. He looked slightly dishevelled and intense.

"Come on in, Jacob!" Laban turned to Henry. "Another cup and some more biscuits, I think?"

She walked from the room, nodding absently at Jacob—her mind trying to keep one jump ahead of Laban.

"I can't really blame you for looking a bit rough this morning, it's been quite a week, hasn't it?" Laban was looking fondly at Jacob.

Jacob moved forward and sat down. Then he immediately got up again and began pacing up and down the office. "Laban, we have to talk.!"

"No, it's all right, Jacob. I've seen the magazine article, I've talked to Leah, and you really have nothing to explain. I am happy for you both, believe me! The photos were stunning and the papers have been calling all morning. I've given them a rough statement saying how thrilled I am that you and Leah are ... what is it they say? ... 'an item'?"

"Laban ... " Jacob tried again.

But the MBC chief carried on quickly, making sure that Jacob had no chance to cut in. Laban's shrewd eyes were taking in his behaviour, however, something wasn't quite right.

"It's excellent, Jacob! To have you here as a relation and working for me in an executive position, is marvellous, but if the relationship gets closer, then the prospects for you could reach the top." Laban held Jacob's eyes with his own. The hidden message was becoming clearer.

Jacob's heart thumped inside him. What was going on here? "Laban ... I don't think you ... "

Monklaast came around the desk and put his arm affectionately around Jacob's shoulders. He walked him towards the door. "I think that before you say anything else son, you should think over your prospects and your future. Have you phoned your mother lately? I'm sure she would want to know how successful you've been—so far." He patted Jacob on the back and opened the office door.

Henry was pouring coffee, and looked up, confused. She caught Laban's eye and he winked at her. Then they both stood and watched Jacob leave the room and head for the lift.

"Laban, what are you up to?" asked Henry in a serious voice.

"Just taking care of business, Henry, that's all." And he went back into the safety of his large office and closed the door.

*   *   *

At Landers Entertainment Agency, Rachel worked hard all day. She arrived soon after nine and threw herself into her work. The sight raised the eyebrows of Sarah and Dean, who came in at around ten.

"Wow! What a hive of industry!" exclaimed Dean in his usual jovial manner. Rachel carried on typing furiously at the word processor.

"We didn't expect you back today!" remarked Sarah. "Elliott only left yesterday afternoon, you can't have had time to breathe."

The phone by Rachel's hand rang. She lifted it off the receiver and put it back down again.

"Hey! What was that all about?" said Dean looking mystified.

Rachel shrugged. "I don't know. Some kind of obscene phone call or something—won't stop ringing, so I've given up answering it."

Sarah grinned mischievously. "Ooh! Can I have a go next? I've never actually heard an obscene phone call!"

Dean slapped her wrist and wagged his finger at her mockingly.

"Now, now! I shall answer it personally. You never know, he might just have the right tone for the voice-over part I'm looking for at the moment. Rachel, how would he sound saying, 'A piece of our pizza won't leave you in pieces'?"

Rachel shot a glance at them and went to reply.

The phone rang again.

Both Sarah and Dean made a dive for it before Rachel could move. They giggled and wrestled it out of each other's hand.

"Hello?" Sarah waved at them to be quiet. "Shh! Sorry,

Lander's Agency here. Who's speaking?" She put her hand over her mouth to stop herself giggling again, and then whispered, "Rachel! It's for you! It's Jacob—your brother-in-law to be!!"

Dean and Sarah fell into each other's arms laughing at the mistake, and were too busy explaining the situation to each other to notice Rachel's white face.

"Hello?" Her voice was very small and quiet.

"Rachel please, please, don't put the phone down again!" Jacob sounded desperate.

"I'm very busy," she said softly. "I've been away from the office for so long, I have a lot of catching up to do."

"So have we! Rachel, please! Listen to me ... "

"Umm ... can this wait until after work? I really do have a lot to do ... "

"Meet me! Anywhere! Name it! I don't care! Rachel, darling, please!" There was a sob in his voice that was real. He just didn't know what else to do.

Rachel put her hand to her forehead. "I have to be at Trafalgar Square at seven." It was a stupid, clumsy coded message but she couldn't think of anything else to say." She heard the sigh of relief on the other end of the phone.

"Thank you darling. I will wait there until you arrive. if you don't show, I will wait there everyday until you do ... I love you, Rachel."

The line went dead and she stared at the computer screen.

Sarah's voice broke into her thoughts. "Well, it's all happening in your neck of the woods, isn't it?" she remarked happily. "What with Leah and Jacob—and of course, we all know you're pining for Elliot don't we?"

She gave Dean a quick dig in the ribs and winked knowingly at him.

Rachel pulled a piece of paper out of the printer and screwed it into a ball.

"Look. Yes, it has been hard work for me. Yes, I've been seen around with Elliott a lot and Yes, Leah has been seen with Jacob—but please don't read anything into it as much as the press are." She threw the paper into the bin.

Sarah looked puzzled, and signalled to Dean to get lost. He clicked his tongue and made for David's office to sort through some tapes. Sarah came over.

"You haven't been happy for weeks now. Before all this Elliott stuff started. What is it?"

Rachel looked up, her blue eyes filled with tears. "It's so complicated Sarah. It's not that I don't want to tell you ... it's just that I don't know where to start."

Sarah kept quiet for a few minutes and then spoke tentatively.

"I know what it is Rachel. And I know why you don't want to tell me—but it's OK, really it is."

Rachel stared hard at Sarah, her long black eyelashes wet and spiky.

But Sarah continued. "Look, I know that you said you would reserve Aaron for me ... but it was just a joke between friends. I know you've been meeting him, having meals together and people say that he never stops talking about you."

"Aaron? ... " Rachel's mind was confused.

"He sounds fantastic, and maybe he is a little younger than you, but once you find the guy you really like—then go for it! I've always had that philosophy." Sarah passed her a tissue.

She wiped her eyes and smiled up at her friend as the tears started again.

"Thanks Sarah, you're a good friend—but this time you've got it all wrong." Her face was earnest.

"Don't worry." Sarah gave her a look that said 'your secret's safe with me', and went back to her own desk.

Rachel continued her work for the rest of the day, ploughing through unanswered letters as if her life depended on it, but in her heart she was just trying hard not to think. Not to think at all.

At seven o'clock however she found herself standing in Trafalgar Square holding Jacob as tightly as she possibly could, terrified to let go of him in case it all happened again. They must have clung to each other for quite a while, neither of them wanting to say anything or even move from the spot. They kissed, oblivious to everyone. While they were in their own world, no one could break in and spoil it.

"Darling, from now on, you listen to no one but me, OK?" Jacob's voice was heavy and serious. There was no way he was going to lose Rachel again.

"I don't understand. What about the photos in the magazine? What about Leah?"

Jacob gripped her arms and put his head to hers. "I love you Rachel. I will always love you. I will never love anyone else. Does that make any sense to you?" His lips smiled and she touched his face. "I love you too, Jay. Please help me understand." Her wide-eyed-innocence was almost too much for him to bear. His mind went back to the strange unspoken warnings from Laban.

"I don't think I can at the moment, my love. You're going to have to trust me." He pressed her to him and knew he wanted her. Her body was warm and yielding. This had to be right. Nothing that felt this good could possibly be wrong.

"Jay..." She whispered his name and he was lost. He kissed her longingly, parting her lips, caressing her with his tongue. She was his! He was never going to lose her—never!

CHAPTER

21

Family nights at Monks Lodge were rare, so Blanche always made the most of them. Although she kept a discreet distance, she kept her ear to the ground and usually knew roughly what was going on. She knew they were at the end of a very heavy promotion at the broadcasting corporation, and that Laban, Jacob, Rachel and Leah had all been heavily involved. Now that it was over they needed a night to relax and enjoy the triumphs of the past few weeks. Blanche knew that some people thought working in the media industry was easy—easy work and easy money—but they couldn't be more wrong. Working with personalities was a trial in itself. Over the years, many famous people had stayed at Monks Lodge and Blanche was aware how difficult they could be to cater for. Americans with their allergies to everything; pop stars with their sunflower seeds; TV presenters who couldn't walk past a mirror without declaring they had put on pounds.

But tonight, she had just the family. All day Blanche had been assisting Mrs Hamilton, the cook, in baking and preparing food, trying to get everyone's favourite into one big meal. Laban's tastes were simple, so they decided on his favourite roast beef (rare in the middle), well-done roast potatoes and of course Yorkshire pudding. Rachel had a penchant for cauliflower cheese, so that was easily arranged. Leah had a sweet tooth, so Mrs Hamilton was making her favourite lemon torte and a fresh raspberry pavlova. Young Jacob, being a new addition to the family, was proving more difficult. They didn't really know what he liked but Blanche had noticed that he seemed to go for liqueurs, so she arranged for pears soaked in red wine to be placed by the centre piece on the dining table.

The family arrived intermittently. First was Leah, who had been shopping for most of the afternoon. She whisked herself straight upstairs, dying to try out a new outfit she thought Jacob would like. Then Laban and Jacob came in still talking 'shop'. They both stopped as they reached the drawing room and caught the aroma of the roast beef wafting in the air.

"Oh, my!" exclaimed Laban "I think I just died and went to heaven!"

Jacob nodded appreciatively. "This is an aroma that will always remind me of England!"

"Talking of England, have you spoken to Rebekkah recently?" asked Laban.

"No, I haven't," Jacob answered. "I did think of ringing her later tonight. Would you like me to pass the call over to you afterwards?" As he spoke, he suddenly remembered the meeting in the office earlier that day, and was relieved when Laban, who had been talking generally, replied, "No, no! You have a good talk with your mother. I'll catch up with her later. Just send her my regards, will you?"

"Of course," said Jacob and quickly changed the subject. "What time do we get to eat this deliciously smelling food?"

Blanche walked in to greet them, took their coats and handed over fax and phone messages left that day. She smiled pleasantly at them. "I'm glad it smells so good. Rachel should be here in about half-an-hour, so we'll give her time to change and eat ... say at eight?"

"Marvellous!" Laban rubbed his hands together. "That gives me chance to go through these ... (he held up the messages) and make a few calls."

Jacob laughed softly. "Laban, don't you ever rest?"

"Got to keep the wheels turning, my boy!" He retorted as he left the room.

Jacob picked up a daily paper and made his way to the lounge, where he sat down by the fireside. It was good to relax in this beautiful home, listening to the sounds coming from the kitchen and the quiet flow of music from the CD player in the corner. He was warm and content.

Rachel arrived at seven-thirty. She too felt the warmth and comfort as she quietly took off her coat and hung it on the hat stand. Glancing in the mirror, she saw that she looked weary from her day at work. Frowning slightly, she decided to go straight upstairs and freshen up before she faced the evening. She ran lightly up the stairs and almost bumped into Leah. The two sisters held on to each other to steady themselves.

"Oh Leah, that looks lovely!" Rachel admired the new dress that her sister was wearing. It was a soft peach, very plain but with an A-line. The colour added warmth to Leah's cheeks and brought out the chestnut lights in her dark hair.

"Well, thanks!" replied Leah. She faltered just for a moment and then asked. "Do you think he'll like it?"

The words hit Rachel like a brick. Obviously, Jacob had not had the chance to talk to Leah yet. She bit her lip and tried to answer the question. "I ... ah ... yes, yes of course. Anyone would. You look great." It hurt Rachel very much to see the look of sheer delight on her sister's face.

"It cost the earth, you know," Leah confided, "but he's worth every penny—and I really have to keep up appearances now. You know, the press just seem to pop up any time we're together!"

Rachel looked away from her sister hastily.

"Well, I suppose I'd better change out of my working clothes ... " She went to pass Leah, but her sister held her arm. The look in her eyes was pathetic.

"Please, Rachel—don't look too good tonight." The rest went unspoken, but they both knew what it meant.

Rachel nodded briefly and ran up the remaining stairs to her room.

She was still shaking as she came out of the shower, wrapped in a huge soft towel. She had tried to keep her hair out of the water spray by catching it up in a hairband, but the ends still got wet, and as she undid the band her hair fell into long silky tendrils down her back. She shivered again and began to rub herself dry. Throwing a bathrobe around her she set about searching for something to wear.

As she pushed through the clothes in her vast wardrobe, she felt slightly ridiculous, actually searching for something that didn't look too nice! The thought passed through her mind that perhaps she should feign some kind of headache and stay upstairs—just not go down at all. But that would leave Jacob with Leah ... alone. She carried on looking, and finally settled on a short blue shift. It was nice material, but cheap. She remembered buying it in Kensington Street Market. (Leah would never do that!) Thin straps held the short dress together, with a scooping neck that just edged the swell of her breasts. It had no shape, being a straight fall of material, but because Rachel had so much shape, she didn't realise quite how it looked on her.

When she looked in the mirror, she saw an unremarkable sapphire blue dress, sheer stockings and flat black pumps. She wore no jewellery and just a hint of lipstick.

When she came downstairs, Jacob thought he was seeing a vision—an angel with black hair cascading down the back of a sheaf of material, which inside held the most stunning body he had ever seen in his life. From her face to her feet, she was the picture of elegance, her bare shoulders pulling back from her perfectly rounded breasts, slim waist and shapely thighs and legs that went on forever. No gold or silver marred the perfection. Deep,

deep blue eyes shone through long black lashes, her skin was clear and slightly flushed with lips brushed lightly pink.

He wanted to run to her, he wanted take her in his arms there and then and just run, run away ... to anywhere ... anywhere they could be alone ... and then . . .

"Hello, Jacob." As she spoke to him, breaking the moment, her eyes beseeched him not to look at her that way.

Leah was also in the room, but had been busy sorting through the music selection, trying to find something soft and romantic to put on. She looked up as she heard Rachel's voice.

"Oh." It was a nonchalant comment that sounded like 'oh it's you ... I thought it was something exciting.' She continued, "Hey, Jacob, how about this one?" She threw a CD into his lap and he caught it in surprise.

"Yeah, that's OK," he replied and tossed it back over to her. She caught it playfully and laughed towards her sister.

"You just wouldn't believe how much Jacob and I have in common! I can even pick his style of music! Can't I, Jay?"

Rachel stiffened on hearing his 'pet name' being used by someone else.

"Jacob," He said flatly. "My name's Jacob—I don't like being called Jay." There was a moment's embarrassed silence while Leah recovered from this slight.

Rachel came to the rescue, not quite knowing why.

"Do you remember how you hated people calling you 'Lee' at school?" She smiled, trying to lift the atmosphere. "Still, it was better that being called 'Ray'." She made a funny face.

Jacob laughed involuntarily. "I can't imagine anyone calling you Ray!" he said.

Leah's head jerked up as she watched them talking together. Her eyes glittered. "Oh, I forgot to tell you Rachel. Mrs Hamilton wanted you to check over something in the kitchen—something to do with the menu, I think."

Rachel turned towards the door. "OK," she said lightly. As she walked away she knew she wasn't wanted in the kitchen—but Leah didn't want her in the lounge either.

* * *

The meal was fabulous. Considering the situation surrounding it, it went very well indeed. Leah had looked after the seating arrangements, making sure that she sat next to Jacob, and that Rachel was diagonally across from him, making it awkward for him to look at her without making it obvious. The conversation was general, for which at least two, if not three, people were thankful. It was only when they retired to sit in the comfort of the lounge that the trouble really started.

The two sisters had gone on ahead of the men, and now sat either side of the room—Leah on the neat two-seated sofa and Rachel on the sprawling leather four-seater. As Jacob and Laban walked in, Leah immediately patted the seat next to her and motioned to Jacob. He looked around anxiously, but before he could do anything about it, Laban came up behind him saying, "That's right, Jacob, go and keep your lady company. I'm sure we won't mind—not now that the world's press know about it. It's hardly a secret any more!"

Jacob really had no option, so he went and sat next to Leah. This seemed to cause Laban an enormous amount of pleasure, and he beamed at them both.

"Your mother would love to see you so happy, Leah. Sitting there with such a handsome man—and a distant relation too! Who knows, we may keep this company in the family yet!"

The statement was so blatant—the wedding bells were almost audible. Jacob got up from the sofa.

"Thanks for reminding me, Laban ... when you mentioned their mother just now—I promised to ring home. Would you excuse me for a minute? It shouldn't take long." He left the room hastily.

Leah looked at the clock on the wall. "What time is it in Australia?" she asked anyone.

"Well, it's ten in the evening here, so it must be about eight in the morning there," Laban guessed.

Leah pouted. "Fancy phoning now. I thought we were supposed to be having a relaxing family evening."

Laban smiled shrewdly at her. "Well who knows my dear. Perhaps he has something important to tell her."

Leah blushed. "Excuse me, I think may be I'll take this opportunity to powder my nose." She ran excitedly from the room.

This left just Laban and his youngest daughter to keep each other company.

"Are you all right darling?" Laban asked her. "You seem quiet this evening. I usually rely on you for a funny story about work or something." He was staring at her intently.

Rachel pulled herself together and smiled lovingly at her father. "I'm sorry. I think the last few weeks took it out of me more than I thought. I know, let me tell you about Dean and the magic rabbit." She went on to describe, animatedly, the audition of a few weeks ago. It actually helped, taking her mind completely away from the man she loved who was upstairs making a private phone call to Australia. Or so he thought.

*   *   *

Leah sat in her father's office and quietly picked up the receiver. It was an extension of the one in Jacob's room. She put a handkerchief over the mouthpiece to cut out any sound or breathing he might hear. Jacob had been on the phone for a few minutes. She listened intently.

"It sounds as if everything is going wonderfully, darling!" his mother was saying. "I'm so pleased for you. You know, Esau is better-tempered now that he hasn't got you to fight with!"

Leah heard Jacob laugh. "Is that so? I have to say I'm surprised! You can give him my regards, if you like—although I doubt if he'll be thrilled."

"So Jay, tell me what it is. I can hear in your voice you have something to tell me. I know you so well." Rebekkah's voice was full of caring, for her son.

"What is it with you, mother? Do you have a sixth sense or something?" he answered.

"More than that," she replied. "I've just been for my morning 'walk and pray'. I felt for you. Almost burdened for you. I couldn't quite decide what I should be praying for. Is everything alright?"

"It will be. Quite soon," He said. "Mum ... I've fallen in love ... "

Leah's heart leapt as she heard his voice. She was almost overcome.

"She's the most ... oh, I can't describe it. How I feel ... how we are when we're together ... "Jacob's tone was emotional in the extreme. He ran his hand through his hair as he tried to think of the words.

His mother's voice cut in. "Tell me, Jay."

"I have never felt this way. I know it sounds weak and trite. But honestly mother, it was as though I had found the other half of me," he explained.

"That's how it should be, son. Don't go for anything less. I don't care if she's a princess or a pauper—as long as you know it's right, Jacob, you have my blessing."

It was everything Jacob wanted his mother to say and he felt so satisfied to hear her voice. It was like a confirmation to him.

On the party-line Leah was trying to stop the tears of joy from running down her face. She stifled a sob.

Rebekkah carried on. "Well, I need photos and lots and lots of information, but tell me just a little more about her, Jacob."

He took a deep breath. "Mum. She's Laban's daughter ... " He paused, waiting for her reaction.

"Laban's!" His mother caught her breath. "But that's perfect, darling!"

"Thank you for saying that. I'm very relieved!" He laughed.

"You will love her, mum, you really will."

"Which one is it darling?" Rebekkah asked with enthusiasm.

"Rachel, mother, I'm in love with Rachel."

In Laban's office, Leah reached for the chair. She was shocked beyond belief. She could not think—she was speechless. She put the phone back on the set and sank into the seat.

The tears of happiness that had been trickling down her face were now tears of agonising disappointment—but then quickly turned into tears of emotional fury as Leah took hold of herself and the situation she found herself in.

She stood up and took a deep breath. She moved over to the door and waited until she heard Jacob join the others in the front room. Then she ran up to her room and quickly tidied herself up. Looking in the mirror, she saw her determined face. She was angry—very angry—but resolute. This was not going to happen. She would destroy anything that stood in her path. Leah was beyond reasoning now. She was going to have Jacob and she didn't care how she did it. There was no depth she wouldn't stoop to.

But right now, she was going to mask her feelings and go back downstairs and sit with Jacob and act as if nothing had happened. She would smile up at him, curl beside him, flirt outrageously— and stoke up as many fires as she could.

She would *not* give Rachel the benefit of knowing that she knew that Jacob was in love with her. There was no point anyway. Rachel wasn't going to have Jacob.

That was final.

CHAPTER

22

Laban Monklaast also had an office at home. He sometimes referred to it as his 'sitting room' because it had been fashioned to encompass both functions. He hardly ever used it for 'sitting' in, but it was his little safe house if he wanted to get away from everyone.

This Thursday morning found him sorting through the morning papers and making notes on a large writing pad. Working from home was a luxury Laban treated himself to now and again, and as the recent promotion had been tied up and put to rest, he could relax.

The radio was playing in the background as he worked. He constantly had an ear open to whatever the current presenter or DJ was saying.

In the MBC building, every office had a sound system that could be tuned to any of the MBC stations. It was vital that if anything went wrong—a warped record, a DJ swearing without realising, a joke that might offend—as many people as possible would be on hand to sort it out, immediately. The press office would swing into action and prepare statements etc., thus nipping any bad publicity in the bud.

Laban wanted to hear Aaron's show that morning. He was getting great reviews in all the papers and his first set of pubicity shots were currently spread over the middle pages of just about every teenage mag in the country. Aaron was a great notch in Laban's belt.

He also wanted time to think through this romance of his eldest daughter and Jacob. There was something not quite right, and he couldn't quite put his finger on it. Certainly, Leah was blooming. Laban thought he had not seen her look so good and excited for a long time. But Jacob? Maybe things were moving too fast for him.

His thoughts were interrupted by a slight knock on the door.

He was mildly surprised at the intrusion. This was his domain and the household generally kept out of the way. "Yes?" he called.

A muffled voice outside answered, "Father, it's me, Leah."

"Come in, my love!" Laban shouted.

The door opened and Leah walked in. She stood still and her father stared at her. She looked awful. Her eyes were red and sore, her lips swollen and her hair falling uncombed into her face. She was still in her dressing gown and wore nothing on her feet. Laban went to her immediately and put his arms around her. Drawing her to the leather suite, he made her sit down and then stroked her hair.

"Darling, what on earth is the matter? Do you need me to fetch Rachel? Shall I get you some tea?"

Leah shook her head furiously. "Oh Daddy, I'm so dreadfully unhappy, I don't know what to do!" She sobbed as if her heart was breaking.

Laban continued to cuddle his daughter. "Come on, Leah! It can't be that bad! Only last night you were so radiant! What can have gone wrong between last night and this morning?" He fervently wished that his wife were here now. Elisabeth would know what to do.

Leah raised her head as she explained between tearful sobs. "Oh Daddy! It's all gone terribly wrong! I really thought Jacob loved me—loved me as much as I loved him. We were so good

together! Everyone said so—what can I do? I won't let him go!"
She added fiercely, screwing up her fists.

Laban was bewildered. Panic buttons began to press inside his
mind as he thought of his statements to the press and the photos
in the papers. He gently lifted Leah up until she was sitting
straight opposite him. "Leah," he said gently. "I think you'd better
tell me what this is all about."

So Leah sat and went through the whole mess, making sure
that Rachel got the worst of it. It was Leah who saw Jacob first
and they hit it off immediately. It was on the cards—they were
made for each other. Jacob had made it very obvious that he
found her attractive. Then she added few pieces about Jacob trying to get her to stay in his bedroom rather than watch the video.
A few suggestive remarks that Jacob had made in fun, were now
twisted . . . 'couldn't wait to be shown around' . . . 'was looking
forward to getting to know her better.' She painted a picture for
her father that made him see red. She was now firing on all cy-
linders.

". . . and now he has the audacity to try the same thing with
Rachel! I'll confront him! He's not getting away with this!" She
looked up pleadingly at her father, and changed the tone in her
voice from violent anger to pitiful helplessness. "Please help me. I
love him and I want to have him, but I will need your help Daddy."

Laban was still reeling from the shock of what he had heard,
but his mind was working overtime. This was disastrous, it would
make him look a complete fool if there was no romance, no wedding, no joining of Monklaast and Lindstein in the MBC corporation. It was also a catastrophe for his daughter, and he didn't know
how to handle it. She was falling apart in front of his eyes and it
hurt him deeply to see her so broken. But he also knew that Leah
was strong inside and if there was a battle to be fought, she would
fight it.

So, at that moment on a Thursday morning . . . two of the most important things in his life met at a crossroads: the wellbeing of his eldest daughter and the reputation of his empire.

He looked over at his daughter and held her eyes with his own. They both knew in their hearts that they were about to do wrong. But he was her father, and she was his daughter.

"Tell me what you want," he said.

CHAPTER

23

Jacob and Rachel met at lunchtime the following day. He managed to see her the night before on her own just long enough to make arrangements to meet by their 'blue bridge'. Rachel was excited. It was always a thrill to meet him, but somehow meeting like this, almost in secret, made him even more precious to her.

Today she was wearing red. Her long heavy curls balanced on the shoulders of her warm red jacket and tumbled down her back, in a cascade of bouncing shiny curls, which looked the way she felt. The plain black 'office' skirt was well fitted and looked good with the sheer dark tights she wore. Because it was a working day, she had her hair clipped back away from her face, making her eyes seem twice as large and accentuating the red lips that matched her coat so well. Rachel never failed to look beautiful.

Jacob was late. He came running down the road, his beautifully tailored suit flying in all directions. He had been caught up in a departmental meeting at MBC and was going on to meet with some TV executives this afternoon—hence the smart suit. As always, he was immaculate.

A wide smile came to his face as he saw his Rachel waiting for him. He didn't stop running but caught her in his arms as he went, lifting her off her feet. She giggled delightedly and thumped her hands on his chest.

"Jacob! For goodness' sake, put me down!" She landed lightly on the pavement.

They kissed automatically—long and hard. Jacob seriously wondered how much longer he could wait for her.

"Serious face," she mocked him lovingly.

"Hmm. I think it's time we made some kind of plans before I make a dishonest woman of you!" He tried to make the comment sound offhand, but Rachel held him closer still and laid her head against his neck.

"You're not the only one with problems, you know," she whispered.

Her words sent him soaring. He knew her well enough already to know that it wasn't easy for her to say that. He tried to move her away from him so that he could look at her face, but she clung on to him, burying her face even deeper into him.

"Rachel, come here!" he laughed.

"No!" came the muffled, giggling reply.

"Why not?" he spoke into her hair, kissing it as he did.

"I'm blushing," she said, and squeezed him again.

So he teased and tickled her until she begged him to stop. They carried on clowning around until it was time for them both to head back to work. Jacob was going across the bridge to a TV station, so he hailed a cab to take Rachel back to Byron Street. Before she got in, he held both of her hands and said, "I'll see you back at Monks Lodge tonight, and we'll sort it out and tell them, OK?"

Rachel nodded. It sounded so easy when he said it like that, but she had seen the delighted look on her father's face when he saw Jacob with Leah. She knew there would be a price to pay.

"Jacob, be careful, won't you?" she asked, looking worried. "Mind how you handle Father. You saw how he was last night."

The cab driver butted in to ask if they still wanted him.

"Sorry, yes," replied Jacob. "Byron Street please. And be very careful with this lady. She means a lot to me."

The driver shook his head and laughed.

"Don't worry mate. She's as safe as 'ouses with me!" He looked back at his passenger. "Young love, eh?" And drove on.

Jacob stood on the side of the road for quite a while. He was trying to figure out the best way to deal with this very delicate situation. Laban would be home tonight. He would come home early himself and thrash this out with Laban until they were both in no doubt of the truth.

Jacob wanted to marry Rachel. And the sooner the better.

*   *   *

When Rachel got back to the office, she was surprised to find a message from her father on her desk.

"When did my father ring?" she asked Sarah, as she read the message again.

"Must have been about two minutes after you left," replied the secretary. "You know, you really must get a mobile! Dean swears by his ..."

The talent-scout joined in the conversation. "Actually, it's more like 'swear at it', than by it." he remarked. "They are very convenient, it's true—but anyone can get hold of you at any time. You can't skive off once you've got one of these." He waved the small mobile phone at Rachel.

She laughed at his stupid humour, and shook her head. "I just can't see me with one of those things. It's not my style at all."

"Do you want me to get Laban for you?" asked Sarah.

"No, no, it's OK, I'll do it." Rachel picked up the phone and dialled MBC, wondering what he wanted. She finally got through.

"Hi, Daddy! It's me. Are you OK?" Rachel's first thought was always for her father's health, not that there was anything wrong with him—she just thought he worked too hard.

"I'm fine, darling. No, I just need you to do me a favour. Well, it's not so much a favour—more something you'll enjoy," he answered.

"And what's that?" she smiled to herself.

"I'm having a meal with Aaron tonight. It's fairly general, but we have to talk through a few deals that are coming up. Now, I know he would love it if you came along—and let's face it, you're much nearer his age group than mine. Your small talk would help me considerably."

Rachel's mind flew to Jacob who would be waiting at home for her later. "Umm ... " She was playing for time.

"Oh dear, have I done something wrong?" This was Laban's persuasive tone. "I'm afraid I have virtually told him you will be there. As you can imagine, he'll be very disappointed if you aren't there, darling."

"No! No, it's fine, Daddy. Of course I'll be there. Where are you eating?"

She went on to find out the necessary details and put the phone down with a sigh. Now it was Jacob who needed a mobile phone! She had forgotten he wasn't in his office and she had no way of contacting him until he got back to Monks Lodge. And of course, by the time he was home, she would be in a restaurant with Laban and Aaron, and would have no excuse to phone him.

Which was exactly the way Laban and Leah had planned it.

*   *   *

Jacob was surprised that he was home before Laban. It was already past seven. All the way home in the car, Jacob had been practising what he was going to say to him. He had to be careful. He knew that Laban was dangling a directorship of the company at him. And yet, surely it didn't matter to Laban whether Jacob fell for Leah or Rachel, as long as he fell for one of them. He put his hand to his eyes. That sounded crude. It wasn't what he meant at all. He was going to have to be a bit more subtle than that!

He thought in the end that it would be better for him to be honest and say how he felt about Rachel, wait for the reaction, and take it from there.

Now he was home, things felt different. He walked into the lounge and could almost see last night's scenes being played out before him. At least there was no one else here yet, and he could freshen up and be ready when the time came for him to make his move. He slowly made his way upstairs.

After an invigorating shower, he pulled on a pair of tight-fitting black jeans and walked around looking for a suitable shirt. He laughed to himself as he thought of how quickly he got dressed these days, taking no chances on Leah walking in on him. However, had she walked in just then and seen the picture that he made in just a pair of jeans—tight stomach muscles, just the right amount of black hair covering his powerful chest—she would have reacted exactly the same, anyway! He found a clean white shirt and put it on leaving the tails to fall over his jeans. He felt rested and relaxed and ready to take on Laban.

He turned round quickly thinking he heard someone at his door—then laughed to himself. He must be getting paranoid!

Downstairs, he told Blanche that he had already eaten, but she brought him a fresh pot of coffee anyway.

His hand went to the remote and he hit the TV button. After a quick search he found some late news, and settled down on the soft sofa. He spread his arms across the leather and laid his head back on it.

He had been watching the screen for half an hour or so, when he felt a presence in the room. He looked up to see Leah standing by the door. She wore a floral print dress, buttoned down the front. It was pretty and fairly short. She'd coupled it with pale stockings and her hair was brushed to one side coquettishly. It gave the impression of naïve innocence. She stood with her finger in her mouth, looking at him strangely.

"Am I disturbing you?" The double-meaning was all to clear.

"Leah," he replied with a great effort. "No, of course not."

She slowly walked towards him and sat down opposite in a huge armchair that swallowed her as she curled up, tucking her legs under her.

"I mean, I don't want to be in your way ... if you have better, more important things to do." Her fingers were still playing with her lips.

He felt uncomfortable. What was she playing at? He tried to diffuse the situation. "Is anyone else home? I thought Laban would be here by now." He flicked through the channels with the remote control, trying to find something, anything to occupy him.

"He's been caught up at work. Didn't you know?" She replied slowly. Her body moving around on the armchair.

"Er ... no. I didn't." Jacob kept his eyes on the television.

"It doesn't disturb you, does it? Being here with just me? After all, everyone knows we're good friends, don't they?"

Her hands kept travelling to the neck of her dress, circling the top button with her finger.

"Leah ... !" Jacob began, but she got up from the chair and walked away. As she reached the door, she turned around, letting her hair cover one side of her face. "Back in a while." And she was gone.

Jacob was mystified. What was going on? Where was Laban? Why wasn't Rachel here? He rang for Blanche.

"Yes, Jacob?" she smiled politely at him.

"Blanche, do you know where Laban is? I thought he was due back here earlier."

"No. He phoned to say he had a meeting at a restaurant, so he wouldn't be home until later. I don't think he'll be too late," she replied.

Jacob swallowed hard. "And what about Rachel?"

"Oh, she's with him. I suppose they'll arrive together. Would you like some more coffee, sir?" The 'sir' came naturally to Blanche, even though the family told her there was no need.

Jacob's mind was in confusion.

"Er ... coffee ... er ... yes, yes, that would be fine, thank you Blanche."

Once he was on his own again, Jacob tried to work out the events of the evening. As he did, certain things fell into place. Rachel couldn't contact him, because he had been out all afternoon. But she knew this was imperative! But there again, if Laban had asked her to go with him, she would realise that Jacob could not talk to him anyway.

The TV was showing the captions for a thriller, so Jacob decided he could do no better than sit there and enjoy the film.

He heard the film ending as he gradually woke up. He looked at his watch—it was nearly eleven. He stretched and shook his head.

She was sitting opposite him. "You look beautiful when you're asleep," she mumbled, sitting in the same position as before. "Except, last time you didn't have quite so much on." Her eyes roved over his body quite openly.

Jacob sat up. There was something about her voice. He looked at the occasional table in front of her. On it were two crystal glasses and a half empty bottle of wine.

He sat up further as she offered him a glass.

"Come on, Jacob, let's drink to us! She held the bottle and started to pour. Some fell into the glass, some on the carpet.

Jacob reached over to her. "Here, give me that." He took the bottle from her and continued to pour the wine. He thought he should humour her for a moment—and besides, he really needed that glass of wine!

"You're such a ... such a gentleman, darling." She held out her glass to him.

"I think maybe you've had enough, Leah." He said gently.

"Oh I've had enough, alright! I've had enough of just about everything!" There was anger in her tone as she waved her arms.

"And do you know what the stupid thing is Jacob? Hmm? The stupid thing is, I still love you." She held both her hands up to stop him answering, and left the armchair to kneel beside him at the sofa. "Don't say it! It's not worth the argument. You only think you love someone else, but you don't."

She made her fingers crawl to the top of her dress and this time she very slowly started to unbutton it. Jacob was transfixed.

"I can make you love me, Jacob. It's so easy!" Her voice was drawling now—the top half of the dress falling off her shoulders. She wore nothing underneath and her flesh was almost transparent against the curls of her long dark brown hair. She held her arms out to Jacob, and her full breasts beckoned to him. She took his hand and brought it to herself.

Jacob felt her nipple in the palm of his hand and an electric shock ran through him.

'Move, you idiot, move!' his mind cried out but his body did nothing. This was unreal—she was climbing on to the sofa and wresting his shirt from him.

"We're made for each other, Jacob! You might hate me, you might love someone else (she still couldn't bring herself to mention her sister by name) but we're good for each other." Her hands were everywhere.

In the back of his mind, Jacob heard a car door slam. It was a sound he would never forget as long as he lived. Before he could move, the door opened and Laban walked in laughing at some little tale Rachel was telling him. "Rachel, you are such good company! I can't ... "

It was just like a freeze frame. Everything stopped—a drama frozen in time.

Laban stood stock still, his face like thunder.

Leah had moved away from Jacob and was facing them, bare-breasted and proud.

Jacob was lying horrified across the settee, his shirt torn and sweat trickling down his chest.

And Rachel.

Rachel's heart turned to stone, her hands fell listlessly at her side. The look of agony and betrayal in her eyes would stay with Jacob forever.

CHAPTER

24

"This is my house." Laban's voice was controlled. "When I come home, I don't expect to find it used as ... " Words failed him as he looked from Jacob to Leah and back again.

"Jacob, would you leave us please. I want a word with you in my office, and then I would like to speak with my daughter." His voice was lower than normal, expressing his profound disappointment in both his daughter and Jacob. He stood straight and commanding, and (almost) in control.

The silence in the room was deafening.

Jacob slid along the settee and stood up, buttoning his shirt as he did so. His dark eyes shone with a mixture of guilt and sadness, and as he passed Rachel he stopped. He put a hand up to her arm. She didn't move. She just stood like a statue, staring blindly at the wall in front of her. He dropped his hand and closed the door quietly as he left.

"Get dressed and wait for me here." Laban was looking at the carpet but directing his words at Leah. She threw herself onto the sofa and thumped the cushions with her fists. Then buried her head in her arms.

It was almost as if Rachel didn't exist. Nobody spoke to her. But then they wouldn't. Nobody knew how much she loved Jacob. Nobody knew that she was hurting so bad inside that she couldn't move for fear of falling apart. Nobody had the faintest idea that her world had just come crashing down, that her spirit had just died, and her feelings obsolete.

She couldn't remember leaving the room, or even reaching her own bedroom. She made it to the sink, just in time, and threw up. She drank some water quickly and lay down on her bed. She was cold. Freezing cold. She would never be warm again ... and it would be a long, long time before she allowed herself the luxury of tears.

In Laban's office, the atmosphere was tense. Neither men really knew what their next move was. Jacob was just about to say 'I can explain', and realised how futile it all sounded. He had been caught in the world's most famous trap. Seduction.

In the end it was Laban who spoke first. He stood with his back to Jacob. "There are only two solutions in this situation." He paused and turned round to face him. "Either you get out of my house, or you marry my daughter." It was a flat statement, a matter of fact.

Jacob started to exclaim, but Laban cut in. "I don't want to hear it Jacob. I don't seriously think you want to try and explain away what I have just seen with my own eyes."

Jacob looked wildly at him. He couldn't believe this was actually happening.

"What do you mean?" His mouth was dry.

Laban walked over to the window and looked out over his estate. "I am a rich man. A powerful man. I do not appreciate being made to look a fool in my own house. What I have just witnessed was particularly degrading, regardless of your feelings for my daughter." He turned once again and this time he was in total control. "You, Jacob. You could become one of the most powerful men in the broadcasting industry. Over the next seven years I intend to introduce MBC's sister TV company. I had you earmarked to manage that. The plans are laid Jacob, the offer is there. You have made your bed—are you going to lie in it? Or go home with your tail well and truly between your legs?" Laban's voice was menacing. "Maybe you need time to think about this. I suggest you go to your quarters and think clearly about your future. And by the morning, I want an answer."

Jacob was fuming. Never in his entire life had he been treated this way. He felt like some naughty schoolboy caught playing a prank. Only this was no prank and he was no schoolboy.

Upstairs he marched along the hallway, his face scarlet with anger and shame. He stopped in front of a door and banged his fist on it. He knew it was locked—he didn't even try to open it—he just stood there beating his fist against the oak panel and began to shout. "Rachel! Please! Please! You have to listen to me! ... Rachel! ... darling ... " He knew it was pointless and his voice petered out as he let his fist fall against the door towards the floor, where he collapsed in a heap. He sat there shaking, his arms on his knees, leaning forward, seeing nothing and trying to think. His shirt sleeve was torn where Leah had tried to pull him to her ... what had he been thinking of? He bent his head down and closed his eyes. The open cuffs of his shirt fell to his elbows as he lifted his hands to his head. The handsome, broken man, sat and wept.

She could hear him outside the door. She heard him slide down and hit the floor, but she was powerless. Every time she tried to move, the horrendous picture of Leah in that dress ... Jacob in that shirt ... the smell of the room ... wine ... perfume ... passion, came flooding back to her. She quickly banished it to the furthest recesses of her mind and lay staring at the ceiling.

She heard him sob. The fragments of her heart broke into more pieces, but it was too late. She vaguely thought how good it would be to weep. She could almost envy Jacob that. Maybe if he cried for long enough, he would have the strength to pick himself up and go back to his own room and stop bothering her. A knife twisted in her stomach ... 'you don't mean that!'.

They broke their hearts either side of the door.

*   *   *

Leah was waiting for her father to come back into the room. She sat perfectly still in the middle of the sofa.Straight backed, hands together, clothes buttoned.

He walked in and stopped. He shook his head and looked over to where she was. "I don't know, Leah," he said, walking towards her.

She gave him an enquiring look.

He continued, "That was a very convincing performance, probably a bit too convincing!" He eyed her shrewdly. "Anyway, it's over now—let's just hope he has the decency to marry you!"

Leah leapt from her seat and hugged her father.

Blanche walked past the door outside and wondered what they were laughing at.

PART TWO

LEAH

And Jacob said to Laban. "What is this you have done to me?"
(Genesis 29:25)

CHAPTER

25

The Daniels can make it, and the Forsythes—oh, Kevin and Maria can't come, ah well. Who on earth invited Jeremy Smithboro? Oh, Daddy of course."

And so it went on. Leah sat in the midst of a heap of letters and cards, sifting through them and talking to anyone who would listen. It didn't bother her that normally this was the kind of thing one would happily do with one's husband-to-be—she would orchestrate the whole darn wedding alone, if she had to!

The only people in the room were Beth and Blanche who were dusting around her, and Rachel who sat trance-like, looking out of the window, a magazine on her lap. Occasionally, she flicked a page over.

It had been a momentous decision for Rachel to stay and help Leah with the wedding arrangements. Her hands were automatically tied. Her romance with Jacob was not public knowledge and she had no wish for it to become so by her absence at the church. Also, her father naturally leaned on her, in place of his wife on such an occasion as this. She was the obvious choice to take charge of the whole affair, and Laban told her at least once a day how indispensable she was. She felt like a small fly caught in a huge spider's web.

"Hey, Rachel!" Leah was waving a letter at her.

"Aaron's just replied, isn't that nice? Perhaps he can escort you to the wedding!"

Rachel gave a small smile and nodded. She was surprised that Aaron had accepted, but then once she had thought about it, he really had no choice. 'He's like the rest of us' she thought. 'Laban Monklaast says "jump" and we all jump'.

It was now two months since Rachel's world collapsed. She was living more or less in London at the Monklaast apartment these days, and that was where Aaron had finally found her two weeks after the event. She had cried and cried. He held her for an hour, until she stopped, and then just sat with her, holding her in his arms for another two. He said nothing to her, knowing that whatever had caused her to be so broken could not be mended by anything he was going to say. They sat huddled together for most of the night. He put the TV on low to fill the huge silences that were only interrupted by Rachel catching her breath now and again. She fell asleep in his arms and when they awoke, it was five in the morning.

She opened her eyes and was at first startled to see him looking gently at her, pale blue eyes full of concern.

"Oh Aaron!" she whispered. "I'm so sorry." She sat up and shook her tumbled tresses.

He sat where he was and said, "Don't worry, it's all right," giving her a sad smile as he helped her untangle the curls.

She looked around the room. The TV was playing to itself in the corner. "I'll make some coffee." She made to get up and Aaron caught hold of her hand.

"Don't be so silly. I think I can manage to work a filter machine! Will you just sit still please?" He got up and placed her firmly back on the cushion.

The aroma of continental coffee made them both feel more human, and they were soon sitting cross-legged facing each other on either end of the large settee, mugs in hand.

Rachel looked at Aaron for a long time. He was so nice. She could imagine that when he was young, he was forever bringing home birds with broken wings. He was so pretty, so open, so friendly—why on earth couldn't she have fallen for him?

"You're not going to ask me, are you?" she said.

"Ask you what?" The eyes looked through the hair.

She laughed softly, for the first time in weeks.

"You're not going to ask me what's wrong."

"Oh, that," he answered. "No. That's for you to tell me when you're ready."

She put the mug down and came over and hugged him. "Aaron, you are so good. I wish."

"What?" He gazed at her.

She sighed. "Nothing . . . and I do want to tell you, but I think I need a least two more mugs of coffee first."

As they relaxed in each other's company she finally told him the whole terrible story. There were tears of anger in his eyes, when she had finished.

"I can't believe it, Rache, I just can't believe he'd do that!"

She agreed and sighed again. "My guess is, there's more to it—but I don't know what exactly. I keep going over and over it. Why? "

"Don't do that Rache. It won't help, not at the moment anyway. Give it a bit of time."

* * *

And now here she was, two months further on and feeling as empty as ever. At least Leah was right, Aaron was bound to take her to the wedding. That would really help a lot. She made a mental note to phone him later.

"Just imagine!!" Leah was carrying on. "In one more week I will be Mrs Jacob Lindstein!" She looked over to Rachel.

"Oh come on now, Rachel! Be happy for me! I know we always thought you'd be the first to marry, but I'm sure Mr Right is only just around the corner. In fact, haven't I heard a some gossip about you and this little DJ?"

Rachel tried to smile. After all, her sister was not to know that she loved Jacob herself. But the more she thought about it, the less she could convince herself that Leah loved him too. What she'd seen on that fateful night had looked an awful lot more like 'lust' than 'love'. It wasn't just the nakedness—it was the whole feel of the situation. Love had not been in the room that night.

In fact, Rachel had been slightly wrong in her estimation. Leah loved Jacob as much as she had loved anyone so far, but there was one major feature that turned the whole thing sour— that love was not reciprocated. As much as Leah tried and tried, she could not get a loving response from her husband-to-be. She was determined that this was not going to spoil things and that as soon as she got Jacob into bed, she could change his whole life. She was certain it would work. After all, it was sex that had got them into this situation in the first place!

"Where is Jacob?" Rachel asked. It still hurt to use his name, but it was unavoidable.

"Oh working away, earning lots of money! He knows I have expensive tastes, but then, he keeps me happy with what I like . . . and I'll make sure I keep him happy with what he likes!" Her bawdy sense of humour made Rachel wince.

Leah put down the cards for a moment and looked at Rachel seriously.

"The only thing I can't understand, is why his family are not making the effort to come to the wedding."

"Leah, they live on the other side of the world!" Rachel stated. "You can't just drop looking after a sheep station and head for Britain!"

"Hmm. You have much more patience and understanding than me, but I suppose you're right."

In actual fact, Jacob had not wanted his family at this sham of a wedding. He spent days sorting it out with himself before he phoned Rebekkah. It was an incredibly expensive phone call, lasting over an hour. The only thing he could think of doing was to start at the beginning and explain the whole mess to her, hoping she would have some kind of sympathy with him. He knew that it was partly his fault and the fact that he chose to marry Leah and not go back to Australia showed that the pull of MBC was a strong one.

But then, there was nothing for him at home, and when she heard the whole story, Rebekkah was inclined to agree that he was making the best of a bad job. His brother Esau was making a real go of the station, and his father Issaac was very proud of him. Neither of them would particularly want Jacob back—and they certainly wouldn't be overjoyed to travel to England just for Jacob's wedding. So, the only person it affected was Rebekkah.

"Mother, I don't want you to witness this!" Jacob was telling her. "One day, if I get myself out of it, maybe Rachel will. . . " He couldn't finish the sentence. He knew how stupid and futile even the thought was.

On the other end of the line, his mother bit her lip. She'd had such high hopes for this son of hers. It was painful for her to hear him speaking like this.

"Jay, I will pray for you every day, darling. Please don't give up. I know it will be hard for you to honour Leah, but she will be your wife. Please be careful."

Jacob hung his head. How was he supposed to even look at Leah, let alone be nice to her?

"Mother—if you could only see Rachel. If you could only see her for a second, you would understand."

Rebekkah understood. Her son was deeply in love with someone who would never be his. He had made a stupid mistake with the wrong person and now he was going to pay for it, dearly.

"I love you, Jacob. Write and call me as often as you can. I'm always here."

They said their goodbyes and Jacob put the phone down with a mixture of relief and sadness. The biggest day of his life was going to be the worst day of his life. Well, his body might be at that altar, but his soul would never be hers. From that moment, he vowed to throw himself into his work, making MBC the most prosperous corporation of all time. He washed his hands of the wedding arrangements—she could do that herself.

Which, of course, was exactly what she was doing, and everything was going her way. Without Jacob to consult, Leah just went ahead and arranged it all to her liking.

One of the worst moments had come when Rachel realised that Leah expected her to be a bridesmaid. She was horrified. Leah had milked this one for all it was worth, knowing that at the end of the day, she didn't actually want Rachel as a bridesmaid anyway. (What bride would be happy with someone as stunning as Rachel, arrayed in a flowing dress looking like a goddess, holding her train?) But she put her through it until she had wrung her dry. She made her sit through piles and piles of dress designs—choosing colours and materials, talking for hours about the role her sister would play, plunging the knife in deeper and deeper. She was beginning to hate Rachel—this younger sister who had everything and nearly stole Jacob from under her nose. How dare she? She wanted Rachel to pay for every unhappy moment in her life, and she was enjoying watching her face paling until she thought Rachel would faint.

Then, with great satisfaction, she announced, "You know, thinking about it, maybe it would be more of a focal point if Jacob and I had no bridesmaids at all. Just think— everyone would be watching us. Nobody else involved. Just the happy couple—the bride and groom!" She turned to face Rachel earnestly, but with mocking eyes.

"Rachel, darling . . . do you think it would be too awful for me to do that at this late stage? I know that you would love to stand behind me and Jacob . . . but would you mind if you didn't?"

Rachel's eyes were racked with confusion. Why was she doing this? "No . . . no, of course not Leah. It's your wedding. Just tell me what you want and I'll help you arrange it."

Leah looked down and sorted through the invitations again. A glow of enormous satisfaction surrounded her. It was going to be fun, this married life of hers. She wondered how long it would be, before Rachel finally found out the truth?—that Leah knew all about her little clandestine affair with Jacob.

She hugged the question to herself with great delight.

CHAPTER

26

Everyone was there. The small parish church in High Montley was full to overflowing. The late November weather had held good, and autumn leaves gave a gold carpet from the wedding car to the church door. Photographers waited anxiously outside, and relatives, just as anxiously inside. The front pews held the immediate Monklaast family and their respective partners. Laban was missing of course—he would arrive with Leah—but Henrietta would be by his side in the church. She could always be relied on to be the perfect partner for any important occasion, and was terribly flattered to be asked to accompany her boss to the wedding. They looked good together earlier that day, Laban in his grey suit, holding the top hat in his hand, and Henry in a very festive navy blue and pink.

Laban had two sons, both of whom had made their own way in life, preferring not to be directly involved with their father's business. Hugh was in Cairo and sent his love and apologies, but Edward had just come home after spending three years in Africa. He had a large company over there which was involved in an environmentally controversial rain forest dispute. So Edward, his wife Antonia and their two children were in the second row, all very excited at the prospect of seeing the family again.

Rachel was particularly overjoyed to see them and had made

promises to go and stay with them at the earliest possible convenience. Teddy was her favourite brother, and seeing him here made her realise how much she had missed him.

She whispered to Aaron standing next to her, the Who's Who of the Monklaast family. He made her giggle as usual and she squeezed his hand tightly.

"Shh! This is supposed to be serious!" she said.

Rachel was looking wonderful. Her hair was swept back and hung down at the nape of her neck. A few stray curls played on her cheeks. Her suit was severe, but extremely well-tailored. It was blue/black with a straight skirt and she was wearing it with a beautiful white silk blouse. The skirt made her legs look even longer than usual, and she wore black patent shoes with a short stiletto heel.

Aaron was so proud to be with her. He knew that her heart was elsewhere, but he just wanted to support her in any way he could. Outside the church, a group of fans had screamed ecstatically as he got out of the car with Rachel. There were lots of murmurs as the girls tried to figure out if Rachel was in fact his girlfriend. Aaron grinned and waved and hurried inside, trying not to cause a scene. Following were the MBC crowd complete with their top presenter David Wills. Other faces included most well-known celebrities, top sports personalities and some of Europe's aristocracy.

Inside, it was growing quiet and the minister asked Jacob and his best man to stand. Simon Darrel had been surprised and delighted to be asked to play this part, although he acknowledged that he probably knew the groom as well as anyone else in this country.

Jacob, who had been staring in front of him since he got there, left his seat and joined Simon in the aisle.

It was customary at this point for the groom to stand slightly to the side and watch his bride as she came down the aisle, but Jacob had no intention of doing anything remotely like that. So, as the small orchestra started to play, he stood stone-faced, his eyes glued to an ornate gold cross on the table behind Rev Martyn.

There were several gasps as Laban escorted Leah down the aisle. The papers, the following day, all agreed that the make-up artist had done a stunning job on Leah. She looked every inch the bride and her dress was magnificent. The white satin was beaded with thousands of crystals on a bodice which gave her figure a heart-shape. The skirt flowed out for miles, Cinderella-style, and took up most of the small walkway. She held a bouquet of which the only colours were pink and white, and it trailed to the hem of her dress. Tiny crystals hung from the tiara she wore, holding on a glorious veil, sheer and plentiful. And her face shone in antici-pation.

She went through the service without once noticing Jacob's feelings. As far as she was concerned, he was nervous and she kept giving him a small smile and even a sly wink on one occasion to try and calm him down. When they exchanged vows, her voice was small and excited. His was resonant, but dull.

As they walked back down the aisle together, he concentrated on picking out people he knew and nodding at them, as if he were at one of the many press receptions at work ... and then after waiting patiently for all the photos to be taken, they found them-selves alone in the back of a huge white Rolls Royce. It was to take them back to Monks Lodge where a very private and extremely expensive reception was being held.

The car purred along, and Leah unceremoniously put her satin-clad feet on the seat opposite.

"Well, Jacob, we did it!" she cried joyfully. "Did you see that dreadful suit Henry was wearing? Did you think Father was ner-vous? I wondered actually, he kept looking at you as if you were going to run away!!" She laughed to herself.

Jacob didn't answer straight away, and she looked over to him, curling her arm around his. He took hold of her hand and firmly unhooked it from his sleeve.

"I will never love you, Leah," he said slowly. "There will never be a day in my life where I will give you the benefit of any feelings at all. You are low and evil, the most devious person I have ever met, and I will never, ever love you—are you listening to me?" His voice was low and trembling with fury, his eyes dark with hate.

To his enormous shock, Leah went into peals of laughter, almost screaming with mirth. She wiped the tears from her eyes. "Oh Jacob! You're marvellous! You sounded just like one of those virgins in a Charles Dickens novel! I know! Why don't I pull down the window for you, and you can shout out 'Rape!' out to everyone." She leant over him to catch the lever on his window, and as she did so she pressed her body against him and looked up into his eyes. "Don't lie to me, Jay." She hissed venomously. "You want me as much as I want you! That little speech won't wash with me—and if you don't believe me, tell me again in the morning!"

He threw her aside and she leant up against the seat, still mocking him. "You don't stand a chance," she said simply.

*   *   *

By the time everyone arrived at Monks Lodge, Rachel was feeling decidedly claustrophobic. She was desperate to get away from this mockery of a wedding. On all sides people were congratulating either Jacob, Leah or Laban. The wine was flowing, the band, set up in the sun lounge, was entertaining those who wanted to dance, and the constant chatter, on top of it all, was too much for her.

Two people noticed Rachel's dilemma at the same time. They both rushed over and said, "Are you OK?" But one called her Rachel and the other one called her Rache. The girl was Sarah and the guy was Aaron. They looked up at each other and laughed automatically at the coincidence.

"Well, it's nice to know I'm not the only one who cares about you!" Aaron glanced at Rachel and back at Sarah.

Rachel smiled at them both and then put her hand to her lips. "Oh ... I'm sorry, you don't know each other do you? Aaron, this is Sarah—she works with me. Sarah, this is Aaron, he works with my father.!"

They shook hands, which gave Aaron a chance to look more closely at this pretty little blonde girl. She had a cheeky smile, and her eyes sparkled as she spoke. She was nice.

Naturally, Sarah was taking her time sizing up Aaron too. She could immediately see why Rachel spent so much time with him. He was very warm and friendly—and had a kind of caring attitude that was very rare in this business.

"So," Sarah went on, "shall we quarrel over who is the most concerned about her? Take off your jacket—I'll give you a fight!"

Aaron laughed aloud and pretended to remove his coat. She was really quite sweet.

"Perhaps I should find us all some champagne and then we can settle this like gentlemen!" Rachel joined in the fun. It was a relief to be with her friends. She sauntered off to a heavily laden table and prepared a small tray.

"It's nice to know Rache has someone at work she can talk to." Aaron was studying this girl in front of him. He wondered how much she knew of Rachel's dilemma.

"She's been very quiet lately," confirmed Sarah. "I don't really know what the trouble is—actually, I thought it might have been you for a time."

"Me?" The surprised blue eyes widened and the fair hair fell straight into them. He flicked back the offending strands and continued, "How do you mean?"

Sarah found herself fascinated with his face, he was more than handsome, he was beautiful. "Well, she seemed to be forever dashing out to meet someone, and then later she would say that you'd had a meal together or something ... so ... " She shrugged her shoulders and looked at him quizzically.

Aaron shook his head. "Rachel is the most beautiful woman on earth—but unfortunately, she's not mine. We get on incredibly well, but it's definitely more a 'brother and sister' thing." He wondered why he was explaining all this to her.

She was nodding in agreement with him. "You know, Aaron," (it was the first time she had used his name, and he liked the way she said it) "if I had a pound for every guy that had fallen for Rachel, I would be extremely rich!"

He grinned at her. He liked the way she talked.

Then Sarah was serious. "Aaron, I think there is someone in Rachel's life. I don't know who, but I think there's a problem. I think maybe he's married or something—when we were at work the other day, someone kept phoning and she was picking the phone up and putting it down." It was a great relief for Sarah to confide in someone like this. "She's been such a good friend to me, I hate the thought that after all this time she's maybe managed to find a guy she really likes—and for some reason she can't have him."

Aaron would dearly have loved to tell Sarah the whole story, but under no circumstances would he betray Rachel's trust in him. Instead he said, "I think we'll have to join forces and keep watch." He winked in a conspiratorial way and turned to see Rachel coming back with the drinks.

"Sarah, I'm so glad you made it today. You know, Aaron has been fighting off aunties who want to smother him and young girls who want autographs, all afternoon!" It was an offhand comment, but Sarah and Aaron found themselves looking at each other.

Suddenly, there was a commotion, and everyone turned to see Jacob and Leah coming through the door, dressed in their 'going away' outfits. Jacob was tall, dark and rugged even in his hand-made suit. But Rachel gave an involuntary gasp as she looked at Leah. She'd chosen to wear the button-through flowered dress—the same one she was wearing when Rachel and her father walked in on them. Rachel bit her lip and left the room. Fortunately, there was so much noise and cheering going on that nobody noticed her leave. Except of course, Aaron and Sarah. Her friend immediately started after her, but Aaron stopped her with his hand. He gave her a pleading look, and went after Rachel.

There was pandemonium as the crowd followed the bride and groom to the door. Sarah turned to find her friends but they were nowhere to be seen. She tentatively stepped out of the room and into the drawing room but still there was no sign. She opened a door and walked along the hallway. The door to the library was slightly open and she thought she heard a noise. She pushed the door lightly with her fingers.

Aaron was in the room. He had his arms round Rachel as if he would never let her go. His head was buried deep into her hair. Sarah held her breath, but couldn't turn away from the scene. Rachel's hands were circled around Aaron's neck and she was holding his hair. She saw the hands tighten and then as Aaron pulled her closer still ... she heard Rachel cry—deep heartfelt cries, muffled as her head sank deeper on his neck. Gradually, as Rachel cried and cried, the sound turned into heaving sobs..

Aaron rocked her in his arms and said, "Don't worry darling ... it'll be all right ... I promise you it'll be all right ... Rachel please stop crying ... "

Sarah turned and walked back down the hallway, trying to figure out exactly what it was she had just witnessed.

CHAPTER

27

This is an absolute joke!" shouted Jacob as he slammed the car door shut and walked towards the hotel.

"Temper, temper!" laughed Leah, catching up with him. She shook her hair and giggled as confetti fluttered to the ground. "Whoops! What a giveaway! Now everyone in the hotel will understand when we don't come down for breakfast!"

They went through the heavy oak doors of The Excelsior and were immediately met by the manager. He waved over two porters who took the car keys and set about sorting out the luggage.

"I can't tell you how proud we are that you have chosen our hotel, Mr Lindstein—Mrs Lindstein," he said, acknowledging them both. Leah felt the thrill of being called 'Mrs'.

Jacob checked his watch and looked unimpressed . "Do you have facilities for a fax machine in our rooms?" he asked.

The manager smirked a little, at the thought of the young couple wanting to bother with such a dull thing on their honeymoon. "Yes, of course, it has already been arranged. We received all your instructions, and I hope we have followed them exactly. If you would like to come to the desk and sign in, you will be shown straight to your suite." In fact, Rowland Streeter had received so many instructions that his staff were very confused. There were faxes from Jacob, requiring his office facilities ... faxes from Leah making sure it was a four-poster bed ... faxes from Laban, ordering champagne and flowers for every room.

"This way." The manager took them personally to their suite. He was most anxious that everything was absolutely as they wanted it. He knew that MBC would use them again if they liked the service, and it would be a wonderful feather in his cap.

"I hope you enjoy your stay here. Please do not hesitate to ring if there is anything, anything at all that you need." He was gone. Nobody ever wanted to stay around honeymooners—most of the staff had tales to tell about couples who couldn't wait until the door was shut!

They both stood in silence. The suite was vast. The huge sitting room overflowed with gigantic flower arrangements. The highly polished floor was covered in beautiful Persian carpets, and on one side, the long dome-shaped windows virtually took up the whole wall.

"We'd better make sure we keep the lights off in here!" commented Leah, throwing her cashmere jacket onto the couch. There were several doors leading away from the main sitting room. She walked through and tried one of the them—it led into a well-equipped office. Another door led into another lounge, and the third led into a bedroom that was the same size as the sitting room. It was a glorious room, especially designed for this honeymoon suite. The enormous four-poster bed was covered in white satin sheets. The carpet was thick and luxurious and Leah could not resist kicking off her shoes and snuggling her toes into its deep rich pile.

"Ooh, Jacob! You should come in here and feel this carpet. Mmm ... I do believe it's even softer than the bed." As there was no response, she put her head around the door and said, "What do you think? Mmm?"

"I'm going down to the bar," he stated flatly. Leah ran out of the bedroom and caught his arm.

"Oh please Jacob, don't do that! Just think what it would look like! The gossip the journalists will get hold of!" She pulled him further into the sitting room. "If you insist on getting drunk, at least do it here!" She led him to the well-stocked bar. It was flanked either side by buckets of vintage champagne, courtesy of Laban. Delving into the stock, she came back to him holding a bottle of malt whisky.

"Scotch for you—champagne for me!" She remarked triumphantly. "Now, where are the glasses?"

All this time, Jacob was standing staring through the huge glass panes. They had both decided on a short local honeymoon, so it was the Sussex countryside which rolled out before his eyes. The Excelsior was an old English castle, but when the proprietors took it over, it became an exclusive hideaway for the super rich.

Jacob stood there, his mind wandering back to London and Rachel. How could this have happened? Why wasn't he in this room with Rachel? She probably hated him now, and who could blame her? What kind of explanation was there for Leah's seduction and Jacob's weakness? Nobody got to turn back the clock. Nobody got a second chance.

Leah came over to him and put a large glass of whisky in his hand. She faced him and searched his eyes for some kind of confirmation. "I love you Jacob. I know you find that hard to believe at the moment, but I do. I will do anything to please you ... "

He turned round sharply, and sarcastically replied, "You mean I get a divorce so soon?"

Leah sipped her champagne and watched him. Her spirits had been so high when they first arrived and she felt she had everything sewn up. As soon as he saw how romantic this place was, she was sure he would come round, and if he didn't, she still felt she could gradually coax him. But he was being more difficult than she imagined. She had to be careful, so that she didn't push him further away.

"Darling, don't be too hard on me. I will make you a wonderful wife—wait and see. You will learn to love me Jay—I know you will." She spoke softly.

He tossed the whisky into his mouth, and it burnt the back of his throat. His eyes blazed. "I have told you before. I don't like being called 'Jay'."

He could hear Rachel's gentle voice whispering it to him and it hurt him so much.

"Oh, but I thought your ... " Leah was just about to say that she heard his mother calling him 'Jay', when she realised that he didn't know about her listening in on that phone call.

"What?" he asked.

"Nothing." She smiled ruefully at him. "Am I forgiven?"

He walked away from her and threw himself into the corner of one of the large sofas.

She hastily joined him, taking her chances whenever she could. It was already starting to get dark, and the room was looking cosy even though it was so big. Jacob closed his eyes to blot out the scene, and Leah was left alone with her thoughts: 'If only he loved me. I have to make this work!' She looked over to him. The shadows on his face in the half light were magnificent. How could anyone fail not to fall for him? She cast her mind back to the look on her sister's face when Rachel saw Jacob with her. At the time, it gave her a feeling of great triumph because Jacob had fallen hook, line and sinker for the seduction routine she was so good at. He had wanted her—she was sure of that. She had seen the lust in his eyes, his lips, his body—another few minutes. But, that had been the idea. Rachel was to walk in exactly when she did. Looking back, she wished Rachel had been late, just a few moments longer and there would have been no turning back. Jacob would have been completely hers and this honeymoon would be almost a formality.

Whereas now, it was going to be hard work, and it was Leah

who would be doing everything. She knew she had to wait until he calmed down. To even attempt to touch him at the moment would be the wrong move. She glanced at the whisky glass on the side, and fervently hoped she wouldn't have to get him drunk later. No, he was going to be fully aware of what was happening the first time she made love to him! She was positive that she could get this to work. Maybe at the moment it was a one way love, but she had enough love for both of them—so what did it matter? He would love her eventually, she was sure of that. She was going to make him forget all about her sister. She looked at him again. His body was taut against his clothes, and the outline was clear from the muscles in his neck through to his restless legs. She desperately wanted this man.

She took a deep breath and poured herself some more champagne. Patience was not one of Leah's strong points but she knew that he was worth waiting for. She picked up the phone and quietly ordered a meal to be brought up to the room. She had always laughed at people who said 'the way to a man's heart is through his stomach', but right now she needed him relaxed. She let him sleep while she went into the bedroom and unpacked her clothes. Everything was flimsy, everything was lacy, everything had been bought with Jacob in mind. She held a soft satin slip to her face and caressed it as if it were him. What could she do? How would he react?

Looking at her clothes, she decided to change. The button-through dress was probably pushing it a little too much, and anyway it was done to annoy Rachel—and she wasn't here now! Trying to keep aware of her plan to 'slow down' a little, she picked up a cherry red dress that flared out from the waist and ended just above her knees. She put an ornate black belt around her waist to accentuate its slimness. She looked pretty, now that Rachel wasn't around for comparison—and as she looked in the full-length mirror she thought that the dress was good but not threatening—just the way she wanted it. Her natural self would have chosen something low-necked and strappy by now, but she knew she must stick to her plan.

Half an hour later, there was a tentative knock on the door. Leah let in the waiter with the food and then sent him away quickly. Jacob stirred as he heard the sound and looked around in surprise at the table Leah was setting. She surrounded the beautiful candlesticks with the large silver dishes from the trolley.

"Come on, Jay—Jacob, this looks great! It's been a long day, aren't you famished?"

The aroma of the food gradually wafting towards him was tempting. He realised, with surprise, that he was actually hungry. Moving over to the table he stopped suddenly and gave an involuntary laugh. He had been expecting some fancy high-class menu, but instead he was looking at huge rare steaks, salad and French fries!

"One point to you," he said as he sat down. Leah felt the most wonderful satisfaction and tried hard to just keep calm as she picked up the salad. Maybe the 'old wives tale' was right after all!

They ate in virtual silence with only a few words spoken as they passed the food back and forth. "I didn't know what you liked for a sweet, so I just ordered fresh fruit salad," she said. She bit her bottom lip and waited for a reaction.

"Fine," he replied, and helped himself.

It was becoming unnerving for her. He only spoke in response to something she said.

After the meal she tried again. "How about coffee somewhere more comfortable? Sit over there and I'll bring it to you."

He picked up a serviette and put it to his mouth, watching her all the time. "I think I'll take a shower." It was a statement. He tossed the napkin onto the table and left the room.

Leah was left standing holding the coffee pot. Her mind was in a turmoil. Could it be that he was playing his own game with her?

She poured coffee for herself, sauntered over to an armchair, sank into it and sighed. What next?

As she sat there, listening to the shower she tried not to let her feelings run away with her. It would be so easy to go into the bedroom and wait for him to come out of the bathroom—it crossed her mind that maybe that was what he was hoping she'd do, so that he could play her at her own game, and then walk away. It was almost torture waiting to see what would happen next. She needed to be in control.

Jacob, however, needed the shower to try and wash away the pain and trial of this awful day. He stood under the heavy cascade and waited for it to take away the dullness in his heart. He knew it was useless—the water hit his face, his body, but of course it couldn't touch his soul. He grabbed the towel and went to leave the room—he hesitated and put on a bathrobe instead. He wandered around the bedroom and threw one of his cases onto the bed. The vibration made the underwear that Leah had left there slide onto the floor. The white satin of the sheets making a slippery path for the black silk. He automatically bent down to retrieve it. As he did so, Leah entered the room. She had brought some coffee through for him, hoping it would make her look like a thoughtful wife. She held her breath as she saw the silk in his hand. She put down the coffee and took the nightie from him—slowly, very slowly.

"It fell," he said, eyes still dark and brooding.

"Yes," she replied. She sat on the bed and slowly undid her belt, unable to wrench her eyes from the robe that Jacob wore, loosely now, around his body.

He didn't move. He was almost like a snake fascinated by the sound of the pipe—an animal caught in headlights.

Her dress slipped off easily and fell to the floor. Leah lay back on the bed, lacy suspenders holding sheer black stockings. Jacob felt his heart beating faster as she smiled at him lazily. He'd been in this place before, his mind was flashing back to the last time. And now this woman, this slut, was doing it again. Only this time she was his wife, this time he could legally take her. Pictures moved faster in his mind—images of Rachel looking like stone, mingled with this picture of Leah calling him to her bed. He could hear, physically hear Rachel crying, sobbing, behind that door— and now Leah was pulling him towards her, taking off his robe, revealing the body that was hers for the taking, smiling delightedly as she saw he was ready for her. Something snapped in Jacob's head and his anger hit fever pitch. He took Leah with all his wrath. His forceful arms pinning her to the bed. He thought he heard her cry but didn't know if it was in pleasure or pain. He only knew he hated her.

He finally rolled away from her and lay exhausted, his head sinking into the pillow. He felt Leah move away and slide off the sheets. He vaguely saw her naked body go past him to the bathroom. Then he fell into a deep, troubled sleep.

Leah stood by the mirror next to the shower. She looked at her reflection as the bruises appeared on her body. Her swollen lips trembled.

It wasn't supposed to be like that.

CHAPTER

28

Laban's wedding present was the four-bedroomed house they had just moved into. When Leah found out about the gift, just before the wedding, she was thrilled to bits. She gushed out the news to Jacob but didn't notice when he just nodded absently and continued reading from the file on his lap. She whirled around the room and made plans aloud.

"We have to give it a name," she said, throwing her arms wide with excitement. "What do you think?" This was a question she had asked with increasing persistency as the wedding drew nearer. 'What do you think?' Jacob always nodded and she took this for a 'yes'.

That was why they were now living in a sprawling lodge in its own grounds with the unlikely name of 'Seventh Heaven'. The letters were carved into a huge piece of oak that lay at the entrance to the long drive. The house itself nestled amongst various types of pine trees, and gave the impression of luxurious privacy. It was a fairly new house, but had been built to look old. White external walls, black beams, and a loft with wide and airy windows gave it the look of a Swiss chalet.

Leah dreamed of how it would look in the snow. Winter was nearly here, and she pictured a roaring fire in the wide inglenook, and pine trees bending under the weight of a thick fall ... and

Jacob sitting beside her. Her heart felt heavy as she thought of her
husband. The honeymoon had been an assault, not only on her
body, but also on her mind and emotions. The misty dream of
Jacob carrying her over to the four-poster bed had died amid a
nightmare. It wasn't even the violence that had hurt her—no, she
felt that being taken forcefully in love wasn't so unappealing—it
was his face: the rage and hatred in those beautiful dark eyes, the
tight lips—it occurred to her the next morning that Jacob had
never kissed her. All the time at Monks Lodge, at the hotel, even
at the church, he had never kissed her properly. She had kissed
him a number of times and been received without warmth. Would
it always be like that between them?

They had been married now for a month. He still came to her
bed. He still made love to her without emotion, sometimes almost
mechanically, sometimes brutally. But for the rest of the time, he
worked. He left early in the morning and came home late in the
evening. MBC was his life and he was becoming very, very good
at his job.

In theory, Leah now had everything she wanted, and yet she
still felt so empty. The satisfaction of taking Jacob away from
Rachel had been shortlived, mainly because her sister lived in
London most of the time, making it impossible for her to 'pop in'
and do the 'busy wife' routine. She had been looking forward to
flouting her success in Rachel's face. The husband, the house, the
wedding. But in truth, the husband was always at work, the house
was empty and the wedding only brought with it memories of the
honeymoon.

Leah roamed listlessly around the lodge, wandering from room
to room. Everything in 'Seventh Heaven' was decorated and furnished to her own specifications. It was comfortable and lavish.
Downstairs the colour scheme was warm and cosy, where she
visualised Jacob relaxing with her after a long hard day at MBC.
Upstairs it was stark, with polished floorboards and fine white

painted walls. It gave the impression of space and sunlight, with large pastel paintings hung from every wall. Their bedroom was enormous, and the huge picture window threw rays of light onto the king-size bed. Leah was aware that this room needed to be masculine too, so the drapes and sheets were an array of dark maroons and deep blues. Jacob looked wonderful when he was asleep in the Swedish four-poster, but as she looked at it now— vacant, duvet cast to one side, the way he had left it early that morning—she wondered what she could do to make him stay longer, and more often.

In the pit of her stomach she knew there was one way, but it was something she didn't really want, just yet. She walked out of the bedroom and down the stairs again. Her days seemed so long now. She had resisted the temptation to turn up at MBC, knowing that Jacob would either ignore her or be furious at her for inter-rupting his work.

Sitting by the log fire, she stared at the phone. Perhaps a visit to Rachel would do her good. She had hardly seen her since the wedding, and she desperately needed to flaunt her marriage in front of someone. The locals were boring and not her type, and Monks Lodge was the only other place to go. Blanche and the other maids were quite sick of Leah prancing in and out, flashing her wedding ring and telling them how busy she was. They knew there was something wrong, even though they didn't know what it was. They felt uncomfortable in her presence, and she in theirs. So that really did only leave Rachel.

* * *

In the London apartment, Rachel was just finishing a phone call. She put the receiver down, and blinked back the tears. Her bro-ther Edward was so good to her. At the wedding, when he told her to come and stay with them, he really meant it. Now his wife

Antonia had just called to press her into the visit. They wanted Rachel to spend some time with the children—they had grown so quickly since she last saw them. Three years was a long time to be out of the country, and now they were back they wanted to make up for lost time. The idea was appealing to Rachel as she wanted to get as far away from everyone as possible, in order to clear her mind.

She made plans in her head to phone David Landers and ask for some holiday leave—she had never had any before. She had never wanted any, since she loved working at the agency.

When the phone rang again, Rachel thought it was Antonia phoning back with some detail she had forgotten. She smiled to herself as she picked it up.

"Hello?" she said, brightly.

"Well, well!" Leah's voice was as sarcastic as ever. "I must admit I didn't expect you to sound quite so enthusiastic! Got a man with you?" As she delivered this line, Leah felt a short stab as the thought flashed through her mind that Jacob was there. She composed herself quickly, realising that even he wasn't that much of a fool.

She heard Rachel gasp and then reply; "Leah! I thought it was ... oh, never mind. How are you?" Her heart was beating fast. She was desperate for news of Jacob.

"Thinking of paying you a visit, darling." Leah replied. "I haven't seen you for a while, there must be so much we can catch up on." Her words carrying different layers of meaning.

"Good idea," she said. "When would you like to arrive?"

They made their plans and both rang off wondering what the other one wanted.

Rachel sat and thought for a while. Maybe if she got out of the way, then not only could she sort her own life out, but Jacob and Leah would be able to get theirs sorted out too. She knew things were not going too well. Her father had talked to her on several occasions about it. Rachel tried to keep away—in fact the only time she had visited the new house had been just after they got back from the honeymoon. It had been awful—she felt uncomfortable the entire time she was there, not daring to speak to Jacob, trying to avoid eye contact at all times; feeling the dreadful atmosphere, as Leah enthused and ran around the place and Jacob stood staring out of the window. She left as soon as she could, and vowed not to go back unless it was absolutely necessary.

So now, at least whatever Leah threw at her when she came to the flat to visit, Rachel would counterbalance with her news of leaving. It wasn't much, but she knew that underneath it all, Leah still needed her.

*   *   *

Leah arrived at the apartment as planned and Rachel was quite shocked at the change in her. It was hard to pin-point, but her whole persona was different. Her clothes were the same, but not the attitude she wore them with. She was brash, invading the room as if she owned it. Looking around with a critical eye at the furniture. Her face had altered, she looked older somehow and maybe more headstrong. As Rachel looked closer, she saw the circles under her sister's eyes, and a certain look of despair behind the mask. It worried her.

"Coffee's on." She waved Leah to an armchair, and tried to smile.

"This place is looking a tad tired," Leah commented. "You're letting it go a little. Maybe I should recommend the company who decorated for Jacob and me."

Suddenly it came to Rachel—Leah was on the defensive! How strange! She had expected her sister to lord it over her, and yet here she was trying to prove something. Why?

"How is the house looking?" Rachel asked, trying to get back on an even keel.

"Oh, it's wonderful! It's so warm and comfortable, and Jacob adores coming home to it. Sometimes I wonder if he does any work at all in that office of his. He seems to spend all his time phoning me and making plans for the evening." Leah sank further into the chair. "Mmm ... I love being married."

Rachel handed her sister a mug of coffee and tried hard not to let her feelings show.

"I'm glad it's all working out for you," she murmured.

"And why shouldn't it?" Leah retorted. "We were made for each other—we knew it straight away. You may be able to turn people's heads, Rachel, but you're not so good at holding on to anyone."

The comeback was so harsh that Rachel looked up at her sister in surprise. "What was that for?" she said.

"Do you need to ask?" replied Leah, casually. "Did you really think that I didn't know what was going on?"

Rachel's heart thumped inside her. Surely Jacob hadn't told her about the two of them? She tried to look puzzled.

"Don't give me that look, Rachel. You know, I always thought you were the innocent one. Butter wouldn't melt in your mouth, huh? I thought that you cared for me, even though we had our differences."

Rachel started to protest, but Leah needed to do this. She needed to do it for her own sake. Things had to work out for her and Jacob. Her frustration continued. "I know, Rachel. I know about you and Jacob. But you tell me this—if he really wanted you, why is he with me?"

Rachel opened her mouth to speak, but Leah continued. "I'll tell you why. Because I love him, and he knows that. My need of him was greater than yours—I showed him that. He came to me, Rachel, me! If he loved you so much, he would never have let you walk in on us, like you did. Maybe he liked how you looked—but I gave him what he needed. He's mine, Rachel. Mine. Never forget that." Leah was standing now, pacing up and down, pointing an accusing finger at her sister.

Rachel was mortified. "How ... how did you know? ... Did he tell you?" She whispered.

Leah threw back her head and laughed. "Oh, no. I heard him talking about you, to his mother on the phone." She clapped her hands. "Isn't it great, darling? He doesn't know that I know! Can you imagine the kind of power that gives me? My trump card!"

In spite of everything, Rachel could only think of Jacob and how terribly unhappy he must be. She tried not to picture him living in the same house as Leah ... being with her ...

"Leah, please listen to me!" her sister pleaded. She left her seat and took hold of Leah's hands. Leah looked back at her with contempt.

"Listen to you? What could you possibly say that would interest me? Ah! But I have something that will be of tremendous interest to you!" She shook her hands free and looked at Rachel with glittering eyes. "I think that very shortly, I shall have to start checking the calendar—if you see what I mean."

Rachel's eyes darted to her sister's'. "Leah ... "

"I wonder if it will look like him or me?" Leah mused. "Well, whatever. When I have Jacob's baby, he will love me. He will love me very much." She stared at her sister. "Oh, I'm sorry, you said you had some news for me. What was it?"

Rachel's voice was void of all emotion as she said, "I'm going away."

CHAPTER

29

The day-to-day routine at MBC was a complete refuge for Jacob. He couldn't wait to get there in the mornings and face the challenge of the day. MBC gave him two very important things. It gave him a way of escape out of the clutches of Leah, and it also gave him a career with sky-high prospects.

Jacob found that he fitted well into the media business with the greatest of ease. He loved everything about it and was enthusiastic to learn more and more. Because his role of liaison manager brought him in contact with every department, he began working on a routine of staying in one department for the most part of a week and picking up on how that department worked. So, as time went by, he could talk with confidence about Sales, Promotion, Press and Broadcasting. He learnt quickly and Laban became more and more impressed with him. Jacob had most people in the palm of his hand. The heads of department loved him and found him good to work with—as long as they worked as hard as he did. The presenters admired the way he admitted that he had little knowledge about broadcasting, and happily showed him what he needed to know. David Wills even let him try his hand at cueing-up records and playing jingles. 'Hands On' was always the best way to master things.

As a professional, he worked alongside Aaron. But personally, he tried to have little to do with him, knowing that the young DJ was bitterly disappointed at the way he had treated Rachel. In fact, Jacob found it hard to face him. The young man had such a trusting attitude, and he hoped it would be a long time before he lost it.

Laban had given Jacob a new office. They spoke in depth about the up-and-coming TV station that MBC was to own, and Laban needed to mould Jacob into director material as quickly as possible. The vision of his future gave Jacob much to think about, but each time he sat in his spacious office and toyed with ideals, he hit a blank when he thought of his personal life. Since marrying Leah, he had heard many stories of people who married for gain—men who wed the boss's daughter and substituted their private lives for a glittering career; women who married rich old men so that they could further their modelling prospects.

Had he done that? He didn't feel that his situation was entirely the same, but to outsiders, it was no different. The whispering and gossip had stopped fairly quickly, but left its mark. The guys at the station saw him as a bit of a 'Jack the Lad', all be it a very smooth one, and the girls saw him as 'fair game'. Deep inside himself, Jacob knew that neither was a fair description. He was a fool, a complete idiot who had been seduced away from the girl he loved, bewitched by a temptress from Hell. He was caught in a trap from which he saw no way out. He had loved and lost, and now he was paying for it.

This never stopped him thinking about Rachel. Maybe physically he couldn't be hers, but emotionally and spiritually he would never, ever belong to anyone else.

For the millionth time he put his hand on the phone. He wanted to talk to her so urgently—it was burning a hole in his heart. She had only come to their house once, he could hardly blame her for that—but even then she wouldn't speak to him, wouldn't even look at him. He needed to explain, even though there was no explanation. Perhaps if he could see her face-to-face and at least lay it to rest, they could both walk away from each other and start again somewhere else. It was all nonsense of course, but he was doing a good job of convincing himself.

He picked up the phone and dialled her number. He knew it off by heart.

She answered straight away, and it completely threw him.

"Hello?" Her voice was soft and vulnerable.

"Rachel, please don't put the phone down." He tried to sound controlled. He could hear her breathing on the other end of the line.

"Rachel? Are you still there?" He knew she was holding the phone, but didn't know what to do next.

"Darling, say something to me ... please." He recognised that he was putting her in a dilemma.

" ... Jay ... "

The relief went flooding through him and he almost wept. "I ... I've been wanting to hear you ... speak to you ... " he faltered. "I know it's wrong ... please forgive me darling ... but I have to see you ... even if it's for the very last time ... you must give me a chance to tell you ... " He paused, not quite knowing his next move.

She spoke again. "Jacob. I've been thinking a lot too ... I have things to tell you ... "

His hopes soared out of all proportion. "Oh sweetheart, I have so much to say to you!"

Her voice cut in, still softly, but troubled this time. "No, Jay, listen. I want to talk to you. Tell you my plans. I don't want you to think anything else ... "

It was too late. He didn't care what she told him. She was agreeing to meet him! He was going to see his Rachel again!

He spoke hastily, before she changed her mind, "Can you drive out of London, on the Bath Road? You know there's a lay-by where they sell flowers?"

She almost laughed at him. "Yes, I know the one."

"I'm sorry," he said, sensing her puzzled amusement. "I can't think of anywhere else where we won't be interrupted or recognised."

"It's all right, Jay. I understand. I think it's right that we talk things through." Her voice was firmer now. "I'll be there at seven." She said.

Jacob could hardly trust himself to say anything else—he was so overjoyed. "Thanks." He put the phone down, and covered his eyes with his hands.

* * *

She owed it to him. That was Rachel's way of thinking. If she was going away, she should at least tell him to his face. That way it would be over. It was only right.

There were butterflies in her stomach but she knew she had to be strong and if she swayed from her original idea, she would be lost. She was going to see Jacob to finalise things—that was all. She picked up the car keys and played with them nervously. Now was the time either to back out, or to go through with it.

Rachel didn't often drive. She relied on taxis when she was in town, and took the train back to Monks Lodge. Her car, a two-seater Mercedes sports, was kept in the underground resident's car park in Park Lane. It suited her well, the dark metallic blue body and the pale grey leather seats. It had been a special gift from Laban. He liked to spoil his daughters now and again. The car had been given a name of course: she called it Bullet—it was sleek and fast. Stepping in, she spoke to it, as she always did. "OK, Bullet. Let's go and get this sorted out."

As she made her way across the city, she wished the weather

was warm enough to take the top down. There was something
about driving along in an open-top car that cleared your head—
and she needed to clear hers fast. The main roads were becoming
less busy as she drove out of town, and coming down the Bath
Road she could see Jacob's car already parked at the far end of
the lay-by. Her heart pounded as she drew up behind his BMW.

She got out of her car and walked towards his, slightly surprised that he was not already standing there waiting to meet her.
She looked in the window shading her eyes with her hand.

"Excuse me, Madam. What exactly do you think you're
doing?" The serious official voice made her whirl round guiltily.
Her astonished face looked straight into Jacob's. He was holding
a huge bouquet of flowers from the stall, and smiling at her. The
shock made her laugh back at him and she hit his shoulder with
her fist. The laughter and the slight physical contact threw them
both off-balance, and they were in each other's arms immediately—flowers thrown to the ground. They stayed locked together for
much too long, both of them knowing that this could be the last
time.

They finally drew apart and gazed at each other. "I think we'd
better get in my car," Jacob suggested. "It's a bit open around
here." It was a sensible suggestion, but one of which Rachel was
wary. Out here, she could check herself, keep things in order. In
the car would be more intimate—He took her hand.

Once inside, they both sat and looked ahead of them, talking
to the windscreen.

"I think we needed to do this. Clear the air ... talk it over." This
was Jacob's opening line. It sounded weak, but words were hard
to find.

"Yes," she replied. "I made a decision on the way here, to listen to you. I promise I won't interrupt, but afterwards I have to tell
you something too."

He took a deep breath. "OK. I have been a complete idiot.

When Leah came on to me, it flattered my ego and I responded to her. She made a lot of suggestive remarks and I was stupid enough to think that there was nothing more behind them than a one night stand."

Rachel said nothing, but her eyes started to sting.

Jacob continued, "She said things that made me think she wanted some fun. I led her on ... and then the next morning, I met you for the first time. I don't want you to think for a minute that I dropped Leah in place of you. It was nothing like that. If I am honest, I have had many girls like Leah. They are easy to come by, and normally easy to drop. If that makes me sound cheap—well, that's the way it was. But it has always been because I never ever thought I would find someone I wanted to keep." His hand went through his hair. He wasn't making a very good job of this. "What I felt that morning when I looked at you, was different from anything I've ever known. I loved you immediately Rachel. I knew it, and I am positive you knew it too—I was completely out of my depth."

Rachel carried on looking ahead through her tears.

Jacob didn't see her. He didn't want to know how she was taking this. "I then had the task of letting Leah down as gently as I could. I'm not stupid—I could see you were close—but she wouldn't have any of it, Rachel! She wouldn't let go! In fact, she tried all the harder: the nights in with the video—do you know she even came to my room?" His voice was raised now, and he took a moment to control himself.

"I suppose she thought we were two of a kind, and in a way she was right." He put his hands on the steering wheel and carried on talking, slowly. "That night. The night you came home with Laban ... "

Rachel couldn't see any more; her entire vision was blocked with a steady stream of tears. She could only hear his voice.

"I don't know what happened. She ... she was sitting behaving

normally. Talking about everyday things—and the next minute ...
" His hands slammed hard on the wheel. "She was all over me,
Rachel. She didn't give me a chance—No! That's not true! I could
have got out ... I should have pushed her away and left the room
... but she was so strong, so beguiling, like some kind of sorceress
... I don't know ... "

He heard Rachel speaking in hushed tones. "It wasn't all your
fault."

"How can you say that?" Jacob stared fixedly at his hands.

Rachel turned and looked at him for the first time. Her black
hair moistened to her face. "She knew," she said simply.

Jacob's face drained of colour as he searched her eyes.

"She knew?"

Rachel just nodded and tried not to see the hurt and misery in
him. He held her shoulders and almost shook her.

"How could she know? About us? How?!"

Her watery blue eyes were cast down as she replied, "Leah
came to see me the other day. She came to flaunt her ring, but I
knew it was more than that. And eventually, she told me that she
heard you talking to your mother on the phone. Apparently, you
told her about me ... "

One shock wave after another hit Jacob. "I was set up!" he
muttered, unbelievingly.

"No, Jacob. We were both set up," she said. "According to
Leah, she saw you first and claimed you for herself. After that, it
was just a case of working out the strategy. Cold, calculating
tactics."

Jacob was speechless. He was trying to get this straight in his
mind. Leah had cold-heartedly ruined his life. Thoughts were
telling him that Laban must have been involved, but it was all too
ridiculous to contemplate. Besides, how could he tell Rachel. She
had lost her sister, lost him, how could he suggest she had lost her
father too?

He cleared his throat but still spoke huskily. "So what happens now?"

It was the moment Rachel had been dreading. "I'm going away for a while, Jacob." She said.

"Going? Going where? What do you mean?" He asked panicking.

"It doesn't matter. Just please let me go. I'll come back, eventually, but I have to get away. You need to get on with your life." It was a statement more than a plea.

"Rachel! I won't let you go!" He held on to her but she pushed him away.

"I have to!" She cried.

"No! That's not true! Don't go! Please don't go!" He was shouting now, pulling her firmly towards him. "I can't let you go Rachel, please don't make me do that!" His lips found hers and their passion was released. She thought she would drown in his kisses. The voices in her head told her to leave, but the voice in her heart just cried out for more. Their bodies melted into one and with a certainty that they should be together. When they were with each other they were as one, whole, complete.

But it was too late. With an immense effort, Rachel tore herself away from Jacob. Neither of them could catch their breath . They sat breathless, staring at each other. Rachel reached for the door.

"I am so sorry. I am so so sorry. Please don't hate me, Jay, but we have to live with this."

He stretched out his hand and stroked her cheek. "No we don't, Rachel."

She kissed the palm of his hand and drew further away. "Jacob ... I think she might be pregnant."

*   *   *

He had no idea how long he sat there. He vaguely heard Rachel's car, as the tyres crossed the gravel of the lay-by.

She was gone. She had left him and he didn't know where she was going. All he could hear were her last words echoing in his mind.

Leah was going to have his baby.

Leah had risen at the crack of dawn to prepare breakfast making sure that when Jacob came downstairs, everything would be perfect. The oak kitchen was subtly lit with hidden lighting—the effect was warm and cosy. The round breakfast table was laden with Jacob's favourite things ... even the morning's newspaper by his plate. She stood back and surveyed her handiwork and pursed her lips. This had to work—Jacob's fate must be delivered smoothly. A shiver ran through her and she hugged herself—this morning her husband was about to fall madly in love with her!

Leah turned her head as she heard his footsteps in the hallway. She quickly busied herself and tried to look surprised as he entered the room.

"Oh Jacob! I didn't expect you down so soon!" She remarked playfully.

He ignored her, but sat down and reached for the newspaper.

Leah took a deep breath and carried on, "I don't know why you bother to read the paper, it seems to be full of gloom and doom. Don't you sometimes wish you could hear some news you really wanted to know?" She was bursting with pride and finding it hard to keep the excitement out of her voice.

"I have to keep up with current affairs, it's part of my job,"

Jacob murmured. He shook the paper and carried on reading.

Leah waltzed lightly towards him with her hands behind her back. "I have some news, Jay. Would you like to hear it?" She tried to make her voice sound demure, but it only sounded childish and irritated him all the more.

"Is there any coffee?" He totally ignored her question and recoiled from the fact that she called him 'Jay'.

Leah bit her lip and poured him a cup of strong coffee. She placed it beside him, touching his hand as she did so.

His only response was to nod and drink the coffee. He still had not looked at her.

She paced up and down the kitchen, this wasn't going the way she planned, so she changed tactics. She walked over to the table and took the chair opposite him. Arranging herself as prettily as she could, she clasped her hands under her chin and whispered, "Jacob."

His dark eyes glanced up from the paper. They met hers fiercely, he didn't like the intrusion, but she carried on. "Just now I asked you if you would like some good news?" Her eyes sparkled as she looked at him.

"Not now Leah, I have a lot on today." He glanced efficiently at his watch. "I'm running late as it is."

She reached over and held his wrist, covering the watch with her hand. "Be late for once, darling. This is important." The look in her eyes turned to one of light seduction—she had to keep him here.

Jacob looked through her impatiently.

She held her hands up. "Jay darling, listen just for a moment, and I promise you won't want to think about work ever again!" She spoke softly, imploring him to seek her face, and the minute she had his attention, she told him. "I'm pregnant, Jacob. We are going to have a baby ... "

She sat still, silent, waiting for him to react. She knew it would be a shock, a wonderful, glorious shock, and he would need a few moments to let this sink in.

She waited, her heart pounding so hard it seemed to hurt.

Jacob very slowly folded his newspaper, got up from his chair and walked out of the room. He never said a word.

Leah sat like a statue facing the empty chair. But Jacob was gone. She could hear him starting the car.

Why? Why was he going without a word? Maybe, she thought anxiously, it was too much for him to take in, she should have told him that evening—not the start of the day. She could not move—frozen to the chair. Thoughts started to haunt her mind ...

She loved him. Gave him everything. Even a baby—maybe their first son.

He didn't love her. The truth screamed at her. Her fists flew at the table top and smashed everything before her.

She had given him everything, and he still didn't love her.

Why? Why? Why?

She laid her head in her arms amongst the broken crockery, and wept. Why wasn't her love enough for both of them?

*   *   *

It was becoming obvious that Jacob's home life was having an adverse effect on his work. Mistakes were made and vital broadcasting events overlooked. The MBC staff were beginning to make noises and the noises were reaching Laban's ears. For a time he let it be and gave Jacob the benefit of the doubt, but now he needed to sort it out.

Laban sat in his office waiting for Jacob's arrival. He had been thinking over the events of the last few days.

Complaints were coming in from all departments. Even Simon the marketing manager had made remarks about the whereabouts of Jacob's brain just lately.

Jacob breezed into Laban's office unannounced, as he had taken to doing lately on Laban's agreement. As he walked in he was already talking to Laban. "I know, I know what you are going to say!" "I have no right to let my personal life interfere with the company. I think I'm on top of it now." He came and sat by Laban's desk.

Monklaast surveyed the young man he knew could bring MBC to the forefront of everything broadcastable.

"I can't understand you, Jacob. Most husbands, on being told they were going to be fathers, would be working even harder to feather their nest."

Jacob had not been looking forward to this conversation. He still had a suspicion that Laban Monklaast knew more than he was letting on. How involved had he been in the management of his marriage to Leah? He decided to test the water.

"You must know I'm not happy about that," he stated frankly.

The two men eyed each other.

Laban toyed with a Parker pen as he spoke. "I have given you an open door into my company. In a few years you could be running your own TV station—don't throw it all away."

"I don't love her, your 'open door'. I doubt if I ever will, whether I work for you for another year, or another fifty." Jacob spoke openly now.

Laban sat back in his seat and sighed. "She thinks the world of you, you know. She was so excited with her news, and so was I—a grandfather for the first time!" He paused and looked at Jacob in earnest. "Is it so hard to be with her?"

Jacob looked away, aware that he could feel the passion in him coming to the surface.

"Maybe if I didn't love someone else—I could live with it."

They both knew who Jacob meant, but neither of them wanted to mention her by name.

Then Laban uttered the words that Jacob would never forget.

"Leah is a reasonable girl. She only wants to be a wife and a mother. What she doesn't find out won't hurt her. As long as you keep her in her rightful place, I think you will find that it's all she wants."

The words stung as they hit Jacob. He got to his feet and leaned over the desk. "What exactly are you saying?"

Laban stood up and faced him over the table. "I'm saying, that what you do outside of my house and my business, is your concern."

Fire flared into Jacob's eyes. "Marry one and sleep with the other—is that really what you're saying?" He half-laughed, his face contorted as he tried to make out his father-in-law.

Laban was angry with Jacob's blatant outburst. "Can't you see how much you have to lose here? So you don't love your wife—OK—but in six or seven years you will have the world at your feet. Stay with her until then! Build up my company with me, and once we are there ... " His voice became low and defeated. "You can do what you like."

Jacob was shaken to the core. Laban had two sides, but the second side had been well and truly hidden, until now. Jacob had always seen him as a moral, upright man, indeed he could remember him talking of prayer and 'doing the right thing'. He cast his mind back to his arrival at Monks Lodge, where he and Laban had talked briefly of Elizabeth, Laban's wife. The subject of her wish for her eldest daughter to be happy, and Laban had lovingly referred to it as 'his duty'. Maybe Laban Monklaast felt he was only doing the right thing by marrying Leah off to him, even though all the other reasons were wrong. This whole affair might have been orchestrated for the love of Laban's wife!

But surely if Laban loved his wife so deeply, he would understand how desperate Jacob felt to be married to the wrong girl? And what of Laban's love for MBC? 'Work for me for seven years—and then do what you like'?

All the time he was thinking, he had been searching Laban's face. "I don't think I like you, Laban Monklaast."

His boss faced him with sorrow. "I suppose I deserve that. But we work well together. Your mother was right, you are an outstanding businessman and I need your help. Maybe later we can put things right."

Jacob looked at the man who had ruined his life, and knew he would stay.

CHAPTER

31

Aaron Holloway was fast becoming the most popular DJ ever. His beautiful face adorned the front page of every teenage magazine and two secretaries were employed just to deal with his fan mail. Laban Monklaast turned out to be the shrewdest adviser he could have wished for, and as promised, had shielded him with a small team of professional and management people. Unfortunately, all of this spelled 'loneliness' for Aaron, who suddenly found dining in his usual haunts a thing of the past —unless he wanted an audience watching him.

He missed Rachel more than he thought possible, but didn't quite know what to do about it. He tried phoning the apartment, but all he got was the answerphone. He had left so many messages that it was pretty obvious that she wasn't around.

It was evening, and Aaron was in his own flat. He rented a place in the West End, complete with doormen and security system. It was a beautiful place, with spacious rooms overlooking sophisticated busy streets. He wondered if Rachel was at work. He didn't think she could be, because surely she would phone? In desperation he picked up the phone and dialled the Landers Entertainment Agency.

"Hi! Landers. How can I help you?" The friendly voice belonged to Sarah.

"Um ... I was wondering if Rachel Monklaast was in today?"

Aaron's voice trailed off, knowing it was a lost cause.

"I'm afraid she's not at the moment—oh! Aaron, is that you?" Sarah sounded concerned.

He was confused for a moment. Many fans recognised his radio tones and he really didn't want this right now. He played for time. "She's not there? Do you know where I can reach her?" He asked vaguely.

"Aaron? It's me, Sarah. We met at the wedding"

Relief flowed through him. Of course! Little blonde Sarah! "Oh, hi! I'm so sorry, I couldn't think who ... " This didn't sound very complimentary. "I mean, I do remember you ... "

He heard her tinkling laugh. "It's OK, you must meet thousands of people these days."

"So you don't know where she is then?" He continued single-mindedly.

There was a short silence at the other end of the line, and then Sarah spoke. "Well, um ... I sort of know. Aaron, I'm very worried about her."

He could hear in her voice that she meant it and had no hesitation in cutting in ... "Meet me."

Sarah felt her cheeks flush and tried to brush aside all sorts of confusing thoughts. He was concerned for Rachel, not her. "Where?" she asked.

"Do you like people watching you eat?" he replied.

Sarah made a funny face at the telephone. "No! Do you?"

Aaron laughed. "No, I don't—which is why the meal will have to be at my place, or nowhere."

Sarah became a little serious. "I understand." The entertainment business taught you the difference between a chat-up line, and plain common sense.

He gave her the address of his apartment and they arranged to meet later that evening. They were both concerned for Rachel.

*   *   *

Later that year, Reuben Lindstein was born. The Monklaast household was in uproar and Leah was the happiest woman on the
planet Earth. Reuben was born at Monks Lodge, with the best
possible nursing care money could buy. Leah had a fairly easy time
giving birth to her first son, and within minutes was joined by
Jacob and Laban.

"I have a grandson!!" exclaimed Laban, carefully picking up
the baby and rocking him backwards and forwards. He turned and
offered the bundle to Jacob.

It was a magical moment for Jacob, because although he had
few feelings for Leah, this small innocent boy in his arms had a
profound effect on him. He looked down and saw a likeness, just
slight, but there all the same.

"Reuben," he breathed. "My little son. You are a beautiful boy."
Tears welled in his eyes and reluctantly he handed the baby back
to his mother.

Leah was astounded at her husband's face. All through this
pregnancy, he had shown little or no interest. She admitted to herself that he had treated her with greater respect—but no more
than anyone would for an expectant mother. But now, he smiled
at her.

"Well done, Leah. We will look after him well." He spoke
gravely without really knowing what he meant.

"Oh, Jacob!" Leah trembled as she smiled back. This had to be
the happiest day of her life. Deep inside, she was rejoicing
because she had won. He would love her now, just like she
planned. This child had won him over to her side. At last!

Visitors came and went over the next month. The birth of a
baby boy brought relatives they hardly knew, and friends not seen
since the wedding. Amongst these were her brother Edward, his
wife Antonia and their house guest, Rachel. Reuben's birth had

coincided with Rachel's return to London, and Edward had insisted on bringing her home. Naturally, when the family heard of Leah's great news, they automatically stopped on the way.

If the last visit was difficult for Rachel, then this one was ten times more so. Her brother had no idea of the love between Rachel and Jacob, and knew only that his sister had been pleased to get away from London to nurse a broken heart—who had broken it was unknown to him. Edward and Antonia had gone along with the story that Rachel had been unwell and needed a break in the country.

Certainly, anyone who saw her at Monks Lodge would have been taken in by the tale. She was pale and waiflike. The blackness of her hair accentuated the pallor of her fine skin and there were still signs of dark shadows under her eyes.

Jacob was visibly shaken when he saw her, but she turned away and made herself scarce any time he came into the room. As soon as it was feasibly polite, she asked Edward to take her home. She could not bear to see Jacob.

Later the same day, Edward and Antonia dropped Rachel at the entrance to the Park Lane suite.

"You are sure this is what you want, sweetheart?" Her brother looked doubtful—he loved his little sister and was still slightly worried by her demeanour.

She gave him a faint smile and then a large hug. "You're the best. Look after your gorgeous family and I promise I'll phone often. I'll be fine, honestly."

Reluctantly, he let her go, and she waved them off down towards Hyde Park. Afterwards, she stood for a few minutes and looked at the massive building which encased her small home. Yes, this was her home now. She could not go back and live at Monks Lodge—the memories were too painful. She took a deep breath and pushed open the door. Walking into the lounge, she felt so empty, alone and insignificant. She put her case down in the middle of the floor and said aloud, "And now, I have to start again."

There was a huge pile of letters and messages and her own personal answerphone was flashing fit to burst. She pulled off her shoes and wandered into the kitchen.

By the time she had made coffee, found her comfortable old sweater and curled up in the large armchair, she felt more in control. She eyed the letters and made a start, opening them carefully as if they would bite her. Rachel was sure that Jacob would not be so careless as to write to her, so reading the mail was probably safest. It was the messages and the answerphone that she wasn't looking forward to.

As it happened, most of the letters were from relatives, saying how lovely the wedding was. She glanced at these quickly and put them aside, knowing she could read them later when she was ready. There was a beautiful card from her boss David, telling her to take her time and that she was only useful to him in tip-top condition! She smiled at this, knowing he was trying to make things easier for her.

The receptionist messages were a relay of the same half a dozen notes. 'Aaron rang' ... 'Mr Lindstein rang' ... 'Sarah rang' ... 'Aaron rang' ... and so on. She toyed with the strands of her hair.

So, Jacob was still ringing. He had to stop—it was over, finished with, somehow he had to understand that. She looked again at the pieces of paper. Poor Aaron, what must he think? And Sarah too, she hadn't given either of them much of an explanation. Hesitantly, she pushed the 'play' button on her answer machine.

'Rachel! Where are you?' It was Aaron's worried voice. 'I will keep phoning every day till you get back. Your machine is going to get really sick of me ... I have my own apartment now ... please, please call me.' He went on to leave the details of his address and number.

'Rachel? Sarah here. It would really help me if I knew where you were—or at least if you're OK. Phone me.'

Then there were several beeps, with no messages and then the worried tones of her friends again. It made her feel really bad to know she had just run off and left them. Well, she was back now and determined to put the past behind her and 'get on with her life'. She would start tomorrow, she resolved. Today was just for recovering and sleeping—which she did until well into the next day.

Rachel ate breakfast at three in the afternoon. She sat at the breakfast bar, reading a magazine and munching cereals with icy cold milk. She had managed to wash her hair and put on her make-up, but was still favouring her 'comfy jumper' and tight black leggings. MBC Radio played softly in the background. The music was interrupted by a trailer for Aaron's show. His voice came brimming over the airwaves, young, innocent, and very friendly.

"Hey! Where are you? I can't do the show without you ... make sure you meet me at eleven ... just you and me ... hmm?" The music behind his vocal was bright and welcoming, the message slightly seductive now—but that was bound to happen as the marketing department made use of his personal magnetism. Somehow, it felt to Rachel as if he were talking just to her, but then, that's exactly what the listener was meant to feel.

She was dying to phone him, see him again and tell him everything that had happened, but she felt so guilty about the way she had just run off and left everyone. She knew Aaron would understand, but he was a big star now—the chances were he didn't have much time to listen to whingeing friends. In her heart she knew that was not true, but it helped her to put off the phone call for just a little longer. She should really get back to work. She pondered on the idea of just turning up, and decided maybe that would be best. If people were expecting her at the office, then forewarned would make them wary of her and she didn't want them to treat her any differently. She jumped off the breakfast stool, walked over to the full length mirror in the hallway and surveyed the sight.

"Yes, Rachel Monklaast. It's time you put on some decent clothes and went out and earned an honest wage!"

But first, she had to deal with Aaron. He would be free from late afternoon, if he didn't have interviews and specials to do. She decided to phone him at the programme office at MBC.

She waited impatiently for the direct number to connect, and then found herself talking to a possessive secretary who was doing an excellent job of protecting Aaron. Once Rachel explained who she was, the girl dropped her guard slightly (only slightly) and asked her to hang on. Eventually Aaron's breathless voice came on the line.

"Rache!! Is it you? I can't believe it! I thought you'd left the country! Where are you? Are you OK?" He could hardly bear to stop.

She laughed at him. "Yes. Believe it. I haven't left the country. I'm in the flat ... mmmm ... I'm not sure about the last question ..."

"Are you OK?" He repeated slowly.

"I know what the question was ... I'm just not sure of the answer, that's all," she replied.

Aaron's heart sank. He had very high hopes of Rachel coming home full of confidence and raring to go, especially as he had something to tell her.

"Still bad, huh?" He looked at the floor, still a habit when his feelings were touched.

"Oh, I'm sorry Aaron. That wasn't a very good start was it? Listen, I'm a lot better than I was, but basically I'm back to the beginning and it feels a little strange. Have you got time to see an old friend in your busy schedule?" She was teasing him a little now.

His reply surprised her. "Do you mind if I come round?"

"Of course not!" She said suspiciously. "You haven't forgotten the address, have you?"

"I don't think I'll do that in a hurry, Rache. I'm leaving here in about half-an-hour—can I come round straight after?"

"I'll put the coffee on." She smiled to herself as she rang off. A small bell rang inside her head, a warning bell? There was just something in the way he spoke …

When he finally arrived, Aaron nearly hugged Rachel to death. "Oh, I am, so so glad to see you again! I've missed my best friend —hey, you've lost weight." His pale blue eyes looked worried and his lips took on a small pout. "What's been happening to you?"

Rachel took his hand and guided him into the lounge.

"Plenty of time for that! I want to know how you've been getting on! Now, excuse me if I've got this wrong, but you seemed a little cautious about coming round to see me?" She put her head on one side and looked at him quizzically, but smiling too.

To her amazement, Aaron blushed. The fair hair fell softly onto his face and he brushed it protectively out of the way. He looked over to her, the long dark lashes almost shielding his sapphire eyes from view.

"Things have changed for me," He went on hastily. "I know I've only been in this business for a short while, but if you've seen just about any magazine lately, you will understand what I mean."

Rachel looked awkward. "I … er … I've been out of touch Aaron. Purposely. I haven't read anything or listened to anything. I had to get away from it all."

It was Aaron's turn to be dismayed. He reached out and took her hands in his. "I'm sorry Rachel, of course you did." He blew a sigh and sent his hair floating round his cheeks. "This is difficult. Can I just tell it like it is, without you thinking any different of me?"

"Of course! This is me, remember?" They sat together on the settee and faced each other. Rachel thought back to the last time they had done this—when she told him all about ...

"Life has changed considerably for me Rache." Aaron was saying. "Remember the Shahi where we used to pig out on Indian food?" He nodded as she laughed. "Well, I can't go there anymore. I can't go anywhere, any more. Fans have defaced the walls outside the restaurant and the owners were not too pleased. Girls still hang around outside, in case I go back there." Rachel gasped in surprise. He carried on. "I have my own place, but it's just there for my protection. There's a minder on the door, a security system like Star Wars ..." he shrugged his shoulders. "The girls don't mean any harm, but it has rendered me helpless! That's why I had to come here. I couldn't meet you anywhere—I'd get my clothes ripped, you'd probably get beaten up and the whole thing would be in the papers the next day!"

Rachel was stunned into silence. Aaron grinned and hugged her again. "Welcome home."

His silly remark broke the mood and they both dissolved into waves of giggles. The talk became general, with Aaron bringing Rachel up to date on the MBC gossip and Rachel vaguely mentioning her brother and sister-in-law and their wonderful place in the country. As time passed, the conversation grew heavier. There were now two half-empty bottles of wine on the low table, and two very sleepy people on the sofa. Rachel laid her head across her arms and looked up at her friend. "It's good to be back here, seeing you again."

"It's been rough for you, I know." replied Aaron. "But here's to new places and different faces." He chinked his glass next to hers. "He's out of your life now, and it's time you found someone to appreciate you properly."

Rachel put her glass down. "What did I ever do to deserve you?" She leaned over to him and suddenly caught a look of panic in his eyes. She straightened up. "What's wrong? Aaron?" Her hand strayed to stroke his hair.

He was still holding the drink, and he chewed his lip as he thought over the best way to tell her. He put the glass down slowly and clasped his hands between his knees.

"Aaron?" Rachel's heart was beating fast. "What is it?"

He didn't look up, but began to speak. "While you were away, I was very worried about you. In the end I phoned the agency and your secretary said you'd gone away and she was very upset. At first we just met to decide what to do for you ... then to console each other ... and it just went from there." His eyes bore through hers as he said, "Rachel. I'm in love with Sarah."

CHAPTER

32

Within four years, Leah had borne four sons. She was a radiant mother and doted on her children. They were her life now. More and more they became a substitute for the husband who lived, ate and breathed MBC. Jacob loved his boys and had taken great care to bless them with strong names: Reuben, Simon, Levi and Jude. He could picture them all being characters in their own right, although he fervently hoped one or two of them would follow in his footsteps.

His life had changed so much over the years. People who worked with him and knew him well admired his stubborn ambition to succeed. He had his sights firmly set towards his own TV company and thought nothing of beating down the opposition in his ruthless desire to succeed. Nothing stood in his way—people said he was a man with no feelings, just a headstrong go-getter.

They were wrong of course. The only reason Jacob behaved this way was to hold back the flood of passion he still felt for Rachel. She was still the love of his life and nothing would ever change that. While she was alive, he would never put another woman above her. Unfortunately, there were only two ways to live out this kind of existence: you either gave up everything and lived in a monastery, or you became a womaniser.

Jacob hit the second category with the same force that he put into his career.

He tried to be some kind of husband to Leah, but the memory of her deceit still twisted like a knife in his stomach. He could never forgive her for losing his beloved Rachel—the aching and longing never waned. So as much as it ruined him as a husband, it fired his ambition and his lust.

"But you still find time to come to my bed, don't you darling?" Leah said to him one night, as she taunted him and used her sexuality to keep him by her side. She loved the hold she had over him, even though he stayed only for sex.

"I am here for the sake of my sons," he replied, despising the fact that he still found her sexually attractive.

Leah crawled up the bed to where he was laying, making the most of the sensation.

"Ooh! Let's make some more!" She sighed and gradually moved her body over him.

Jacob took her with the rage and passion she had come to welcome, it hurt her badly that he never whispered 'I love you', never held her tenderly afterwards. Sometimes he would even sleep in one of the guest rooms. Jacob's 'other room' was fast becoming his refuge. In here he could be alone, away from prying eyes and questions. He had been known to spend a whole weekend there, locked away from the world. He could let down his guard—even cry if he wanted to. And he did.

It was on one of these days, while he was seated forlornly on the bed, that he was disturbed by someone entering the room. This was unusual and he frowned as he looked round to see who it was.

Priscilla, the maid stopped in her tracks. "Oh! Mr Lindstein, I'm sorry! Mrs Lindstein told me to clean in here today—I thought you were out." Her brown eyes were wide and her full shiny lips parted. Priscilla had worked in the house for just over three months and was rarely seen by Jacob. He didn't take that much notice of household staff—happily Leah loved looking after the place. Now, he looked at this maid, taking in her shapely figure and long innocent-looking legs. Her hair was auburn and dead straight—she wore it pinned up, to keep it out of the way as she worked.

"What's your name?" Jacob spoke for the first time.

The maid loved the sound of his voice. He had an accent—she had heard he was from Australia or New Zealand or somewhere. She took in the rugged dark looks, the firm jawline and the intense dark eyes. He was outstanding!

"I'm Priscilla," she said simply, with a half-smile. Her teeth were white and even, and her eyes tinted with hazel lights.

Jacob stayed seated on the bed but extended his hand to her. The crumpled white shirt sleeve fell back to reveal a strong arm. "I'm unhappy, Priscilla," he said by way of a small joke.

She took his hand and he pulled her down beside him. He looked so sad and automatically her hand reached for his face, her long slender fingers stroking his cheek. Jacob's hand touched her face in return, and he traced her cheeks with his finger. He kissed her with practised ease, pulling her to him, needing the comfort of this woman. The natural movement from the embrace to laying her on his bed was never discussed—it just happened. The maid was too flattered to think and welcomed his gentle lovemaking with affection and warmth, holding and rocking this broken man in her arms until he cried out. "Rachel!!"

Priscilla opened her eyes with astonishment. She couldn't decide what was the greater shock, the fact that he hadn't used her name—or that the name he did call out, wasn't his wife's name either. She sat up, her long heavy dark hair hiding her ample breasts. She put her hand on Jacob's shoulder. "It's OK."

Jacob sat on the edge of the bed with his head in his hands, and talked with his back to her.

"I'm sorry. I shouldn't ... have ... my life is a bit of a mess at the moment." He couldn't finish, couldn't explain.

She was touched by this handsome man. Who had hurt him so badly? Why would they do that to someone as gentle as he had just been? She made a rash decision.

"Mr Lindstein ... I know it's not me you want, but if it helps ... " She felt herself blush at her words. This wasn't the kind of situation she was used to. She had heard other maids in other households talk about it, but never imagined being in such a position herself.

She started as he turned quickly round to face her. "I think," he began with a steady look, "that if you are going to 'help me', you should at least learn to call me Jacob, while we are alone."

She nodded but said nothing. Embarrassed by her surroundings and the sheer enormity of what had just taken place, she gathered up her clothes and ran into the bathroom. She emerged a few minutes later, pinning her hair up. Shyly she glanced around the room.

"What shall I do about the cleaning?" It seemed a stupid thing to ask, but she didn't know what else to say.

"I think you can leave it for now. I'll tell Mrs Lindstein I sent you away." He touched her hand as she walked past him.

"Will you come back?" he asked.

"If you would like me to," she replied, and closed the door quietly behind her.

And so began a long-lasting affair.

* * *

When Priscilla told Jacob she was expecting his baby, he was stunned. His feelings swayed from disbelief to excitement. There was something great about having a child that had nothing to do with Leah.

Leah found out about his affair with Priscilla a few weeks after it had started. She was a shrewd person, realising that to make a scene was synonymous with driving Jacob even further away. Therefore she swallowed her pride and asked her husband to have the decency to be discreet. Leah was gradually changing. She still appreciated expensive things and loved her life of luxury, but caring for her sons had made her take on a much more sedate role. She was a proud mother, and still wrote to Rachel once a month with full details of her 'wonderfully fulfilled' married life with the world's most virile man.

She knew that Rachel would read the letters—even though she probably wouldn't want to—because she wanted to know about her beloved Jacob. Just a few times a year, Leah would receive a polite card from her sister, thanking her for the news and wishing her well.

Well, here was one piece of news Leah didn't want Rachel to know! Jacob fathering someone else's child was too much!

She decided that Priscilla should stay on the pretext of being a 'poor unmarried mother', and that Leah was the caring, doting woman who took both the mother and the child under her wing. And so, little Garth became part of the Lindstein home.

In the following years, Leah unexpectedly produced three more children of her own ... Zak, Jed, and her only little girl, Diana. Priscilla also gave Jacob another son whom they named Ashby. Inevitably, they built more rooms onto "Seventh Heaven" and the eight boys and one little girl grew up as one family.

Jacob meanwhile was gradually falling apart.

With such a large family and two women at home, he stayed at MBC more and more often. Leah and Priscilla were tearing him apart every time he set foot in the house. He recognised this was his own doing, and cursed the day he ever came to England. His career was at a pinnacle, MBC TV was about to be launched and it was his. Laban had been true to his word and given him the

unattainable. He had worked hard for seven years and the cracks
were beginning to show.

His reputation at work began to suffer. Only a few months ago
he had sacked three people for their 'inefficiency', and the rest of
the staff had been shocked by his actions. The result was that the
people who worked for him began to re-think their loyalty and
began reacting differently to his commands; but Jacob Lindstein
was so distressed himself, that he didn't see or understand the
changed behaviour of his team. He just carried on regardless
towards his goal.

MBC-TV was to be launched the next month.

CHAPTER

33

Laban Monklaast thought long and hard about the launch of MBC-TV. He wondered if it should be a huge glitzy affair at some night club, or go for a quiet but sophisticated evening such as the one MBC had given Elliott Blaze. The ideas had been tossed backwards and forwards at many a company meeting, and now Laban was sketching out the final details on a notepad on his desk.

His son-in-law's lifestyle had caused him much concern lately, and he wasn't completely sure if he would be able to cope with anything too emotional. Finally, it was Simon Darrell who had come up with the perfect presentation.

The Monklaast family and close friends would have an informal party at Monks Lodge, while at the same time there would be a huge spangled affair going on in MBC-TV's Studio One. The set in the television studio would be designed to scream 'Celebration!' as the guests arrived—the music would be loud, the food and drink plentiful, and the celebrities ... innumerable! Everyone, who was anyone, wanted to be there! Stars and agents had been lining up for over a year to get a piece of this action. Shows were up for grabs, and the solid foundation of the MBC Broadcasting Corporation made it a sure-fire hit.

The icing on the cake was Simon's idea. A cable link from the studio to Monks Lodge. Several giant video screens were to be hung around the studio, and at a crucial point in the launch, the lights would be dimmed and the screens would show a beautiful family scene of Jacob and his lovely wife Leah, Laban and his beautiful daughter Rachel, standing by a huge fireplace and wishing everyone the greatest success through their new company. It would be almost presidential in its effect and be the perfect finishing touch. Jacob Lindstein would make a short speech and then pronounce his new TV station officially open. The guests would see the family being served with the finest champagne and turning to face the camera with filled glasses chinking each other. In the studio, an orchestra would be standing by ready to play in a style befitting to the New Year's Day celebrations—and the party would really begin.

Laban read through the notes once again and then called Henrietta in to have them printed and sent out to the appropriate departments.

When Jacob received his copy the next day, he was somewhat relieved to see he wasn't expected to be the star of some massive affair. The fact that he would be seventy miles away from the hordes, was a comforting thought. But then as he read the second part of the plan, the paper crumpled in his hands.

Rachel would be here. Rachel was coming to Monks Lodge.

* * *

The phone call from Rachel's father came as a shock. She was almost running the small agency now that David Landers had gone into semi-retirement. He still came in from time to time to keep an eye on things, but Rachel, who knew the business well, was now the boss of Lander's Entertainment Agency. The staff had grown. Dean now had an assistant who went out on his 'talent spotting' expeditions with him. A young girl named Meg had joined to make the tea and act as a kind of receptionist. She was small and olive-skinned, her calm and quiet presence brought a greater sense of ease to the chaotic, sometimes crazy daily life of their agency.

The new secretary's name was Laura. Sarah had left shortly after marrying her wonderful Aaron. They had been married for four years now, and Aaron was about to host his own chat show on MBC-TV. After three years as a 'teenage idol', the company had seen fit to move him on, let him spread his wings and try other avenues. He was a natural in front of the camera and had widened his audience by being a guest on other people's talk shows. Everybody loved him. His own show was the next obvious stage.

Sarah was coping with it very well. Aaron had chosen wisely in finding a wife who understood show business. Her head wasn't easily turned by famous names and well-known faces, but at the same time she took Aaron's fans in her stride, often answering some of his mail for him.

Consequently, they began to love her too. They were becoming a well-known and well-respected media couple. They kept in touch with Rachel and were still among her best friends.

Now she had to deal with this latest crisis ... "Daddy, is it really necessary to have me there?" Rachel asked anxiously.

"Darling, of course it is!" Laban replied. "Besides, I want you by my side—it is a terribly important day for Jacob. I know it's not such a good thing for you, sweetheart, but you know how people will talk if you are missing from the family scene."

Rachel knew. This was not a time for gossip. To promote the new station with its 'family' ideals and programmes, the journalists had to be given the right impression of its owners. There was little or no choice for her. She had to be there. She sighed to herself.

"Yes, Daddy, I know you're right. Don't worry, I won't let you down—what time do you need me?"

They carried on talking for a while, discussing times, dates, dress etc. By the time Rachel put the phone down, she was exhausted. So many old feelings began welling up, nothing had ever really changed for her.

*   *   *

The day of the launch arrived all too soon for Rachel. It seemed no time at all from the day her father phoned, to this afternoon as she stood in the middle of her bedroom and tried on an outfit for the umpteenth time.

The full length mirror lied to her. She knew she was thirty-one years old, but the reflection said that she was years younger. It was as if time for her, had stood still. Her hair was still as black as before, long, luxurious, shining as it fell past her shoulders and curled around her arms. Her eyes were larger than ever, but now filled with the sorrow of those harrowing years. The effect gave her a lost, naïve and alone look—in fact the mirror was telling the truth.

Since she had 'lost' Jacob, there had never been anyone else. A couple of times, Rachel had pushed herself to go out with other men, but it was useless. They were pushy and full of their own self-importance—trying to impress her because she was the beautiful daughter of the MBC boss. None of them could ever hold a candle to the man she would always love, and she didn't want them to. For a while it appeared that she had lost everyone she loved. Jacob, Leah, even her father was distant (knowing he had wronged her), and then Aaron. Although she only ever loved Aaron as a friend, once he belonged to Sarah she felt honour-bound to stay in the background and not take up his time. So when she did see him, it was usually in Sarah's company as well, which meant no more little heart-to-heart talks at midnight—she missed that terribly.

Through the years, her mind went over and over where things had gone wrong. She knew beyond a shadow of a doubt that Jacob loved her—and maybe if she had given him a chance to explain why he was with Leah that night, things might have been different now. It hurt her to think that her father was involved in all of this, and often she spent time trying to prove to herself that he was innocent. That in itself would make it all Leah's fault, but then she still couldn't believe her sister could be capable of such an act—surely she didn't hate her that much?

Rachel looked over to the heap of clothes on her bed. Who was she dressing for tonight? Herself? Her father's company? Jacob?

She slowly picked up a delicate black dress. It was almost nothing, weightless in her hand, the material was so light. It was strapless, and the bodice had a delicate 'V' woven in silver. She had a pair of long diamond earrings that complimented the glittering sequins. Black and silver. Jacob always liked her in that. The black accentuated her eyes and hair, and the silver brought out the shine, making her glow. Jacob used to say it made her dazzle.

She smiled as she put the dress up to her and turned round to the mirror. It did add something to the stunning beauty that was already there. Suddenly, she made up her mind. Her looks were all she had left.

By the time Rachel stepped into the car which was to take her to Monks Lodge, she looked outstanding. Her figure had always been the envy of women and the hunger of every man, and the long evening dress accentuated this as it clung to her figure like a second skin. The sheer sophistication, with which she always carried herself, was magnificent next to the cascade of long, black curls. It gave the impression of the gypsy girl inside the princess and it suited her to perfection. She was ready.

When the limousine drew up outside her father's house, she felt the butterflies stirring in her stomach. This was one situation she had to brazen out. As she stepped out of the car, Blanche came running forward, laughing and clapping her hands.

"Oh, Miss Rachel! Oh!" was all she said, and moved back to let the driver take the car away.

Many lights were burning inside the house. Rachel could see through the large windows, that although this was a 'small party' the numbers were heading towards fifty. The crowd consisted mainly of close friends, and a few relations. (She was delighted to see Edward and Antonia there.) Most of the MBC team were at the studio and she was disappointed, although not surprised, to realise that Aaron was heading up the show at the other end.

She walked in and saw that Leah was playing the part of hostess and greeting everyone as they arrived. There was no way out of this situation. Leah and Rachel were facing each other. Leah looked perfectly composed, although just for a second her guard slipped and she momentarily froze at Rachel's appearance. Then she rushed over and threw her arms around Rachel as if nothing had ever happened between them.

"Darling!!" she almost screamed. "Let me look at you! Oh, you're a little thin—but then you've not had the burden of motherhood, have you?" She smoothed her matronly figure. "You look wonderful—are you with anyone?"

It took all Rachel's self-control to stay in the hallway. Breathing deeply, she returned her sister's embrace. "Leah, you look lovely." It was a lame response, but was all she could manage.

Leah hooked her arm in hers and guided her away. "Now, you must come and see the children ... " She was going to rub her face in it for all she was worth.

Suddenly Laban was by their side. "Rachel, my darling!" He hugged her tightly, waved Leah away, and started to talk in soft undertones to his favourite daughter. "Thank you, my love. Thank you so much for coming." Aloud, he said, "This way! The champagne is already flowing!"

She followed him through to the large reception area. People were laughing and talking loudly, competing with the music in the background.

Then she saw him.

He was standing looking very bored, listening to some distant relative telling him about some totally irrelevant film he had seen on another channel. Rachel kept herself out of his line of vision, in order to take in the sight.

She gasped inwardly at the streaks of silver in his glorious hair. The lines around his eyes—she knew they would look beautiful when he laughed, but they didn't look like laughter lines. The weariness, even in the way he held himself, was unbearable to her. He was still the handsome masculine figure he had always been, but the stress and fatigue were showing in the way he held his shoulders—as if something were weighing them down.

Rachel felt as if she was being pierced by a knife. Had she caused him to look like this? Was it just the tension and anxiety of running a huge company? She couldn't decide. All she knew was that she still wanted him—wanted to take care of him, soothe away the pain, the heartache....

At that moment he turned, his expression hiding boredom, and then he saw her. The relative was still talking animatedly to him, but Jacob wasn't listening. He thought for a moment that his heart had stopped, and he put his hand to his chest. With the other hand, he waved the man away and walked towards Rachel. She turned and quickly made her way out of the room. He followed her—whatever happened next, it was definitely not going to happen in front of TV cameras!

She ran down the hall into the library, the same place she ran to when Aaron found her at the wedding. There was no one in this part of the house, and she took her time to stand by the wall and catch her breath. But almost immediately Jacob was there.

He didn't speak her name, and she didn't utter his. He just held

onto her like a drowning man. Rachel clung to him and let her
tears flow onto his shoulder. How long they stayed like this, they
didn't know, they didn't care any more. His arms ached from holding her so tightly and as he put his face next to hers, it was hard
to know whose tears they were.

His husky voice broke the silence. "I've lived seven years without you, Rachel. I won't live a moment more."

She looked up at him, puzzled by the finality in his words.
"What ... what do you mean?" She whispered.

He took her hand and led her to the far side of the room, where
there was a fireplace, a Persian rug, a sofa and armchairs. It was
a place that Rachel had often used as a child. She would reach up
onto the high shelves and pick out a book, carry it carefully over
to one of the large chairs and curl up with it. She would lose herself in the book, let it carry her on a journey to some fairyland.
Sometimes it would be hours before her mother found her and
chased her down for tea. They were beautiful unspoilt days . . .

Rachel was now curled up in the same chair, in the arms of
Jacob. He was stroking her hair and talking softly to her. "I have
a lot to explain to you darling, and if—after—you still want to be
with me, then I will be the happiest man alive."

Rachel was alarmed by this strange attitude. What did he
mean?

He continued playing with her hair as he spoke. "I have been
caught in a trap. I've been selfish and bewildered at the same
time. I suppose I made my bed and had to lie in it, as the English
say."

Rachel twisted round in his arms and looked into his eyes.
"Jay, you don't have to tell me anything, you know ... "

He put his finger on her lips. "I do, believe me I won't rest until
I can be free of all of this. You see Laban, your father, made a deal
with me."

Rachel started to speak, but he hushed her again.

"Please darling, let me tell you. The day after you walked in on Leah and me, I went to see Laban in his office. I pleaded with him to drop this insane wedding." He paused for a moment. "He as good as told me that I either went through with it or went back to Australia."

"He said that?" Rachel was visibly shaken, but he just kept on holding her.

"My choice, it seemed, was that I either went home and never saw you again, or I stayed and married Leah. So I married your sister. From then on, Laban dangled career moves at me and tempted me with a glittering future. I took the bait but kept imploring him to let me leave Leah. Finally, he told me his plans for MBC-TV. He said it would take six or seven years to get it off the ground, and once it was up and running under my leadership, he would release me and let me divorce her. "

Rachel knew nothing about any of this, all she could hear were his words circling around inside her head. "I ... I can't believe this! How could my father do such a thing!"

Jacob was quick to reply. "Darling, I'm sure in Laban's mind I was just one of a whole host of men who could make you happy. He thought you would find someone else, and his concern at the time was for Leah. "

"Why are you standing up for him?" Rachel's eyes searched his.

"Because he's your father —and I know how much he means to you." He kissed her forehead, and carried on, "The main thing now darling, is that the seven years are up. MBC-TV is up and running and now it's my turn to do what I want. And I want to leave Leah, MBC, Monks Lodge and anything else that keeps me away from you."

Rachel's mind was in turmoil. She kissed him and said, "But this is everything you've worked for! I can't let you walk away from it all!" She shook her head. "No, we have to think this one through ... " She snuggled up to him, laying her head on his shoulder.

"Rachel, I have been a fool. I nearly lost you completely through stupid deals and career moves. I am not willing to do it again. Can't we just slink away somewhere, get married and live happily ever after?" His eyes sparkled as he smiled at her, picturing himself carrying her off into the sunset.

She pulled his head down to hers. "Do you really want to do this? Marry me, I mean? Are you sure?"

He didn't answer. He did not consider the question worthy of a reply. He just took her fully in his arms and kissed her. The soft kisses raining down on her turned into harder, more urgent, more passionate caresses as they lost themselves in each other. Nothing mattered any more.

Jacob and Rachel were together.

PART THREE

RACHEL

So Jacob served seven years to get Rachel, but they seemed
only a few days to him because of his love for her.
(Genesis 29:20)

CHAPTER

34

It is a well-known fact that throwing a pebble into a pool of water will cause ripples to spread outwards until the whole pond is covered in circles. When Jacob threw his huge boulder into the lives of the Monklaast's, the far-reaching effects were catastrophic.

The day Jacob told Leah he was going to divorce her, she was outraged.

"You are going to divorce me?!" She yelled. "You actually think I would give you that much satisfaction?"

Jacob had explained as calmly as he knew how, that he was going to marry Rachel as soon as possible, and he just wanted out.

Leah continued, parading around the room at 'Seventh Heaven', like a snorting horse about to charge.

"If anyone is divorcing anyone, I am getting rid of you!" She swung round at him, her face almost purple with rage.

"Yes! You can go to your beloved Rachel, but you won't be taking anything with you. I shall see to it that you haven't a penny to your name! You have nine children here ... NINE! Do you have any idea of the alimony?" She stopped for breath, her heart beating faster. "Why don't you just go, Jacob? Go now! Take your belongings and get out! Just don't come back for anything, because there won't be anything. I shall take it all, Jacob. The house, the children, the money! You will have nothing! Do you hear me?

Nothing!!" She screamed this last word and then fell to the floor and wept in sheer rage, her fists pounding the carpet .

Jacob stood for a moment and looked at her. He nearly pitied her. He pursed his lips and spoke to her very quietly. "I shall have everything, Leah. Everything I have ever wanted." He left the room.

Leah sat on the floor, catching her breath and wiping away the angry tears. She was thirty-six years old, she had seven children of her own, and two bastards. She looked around the room, so silent now the shouting had stopped. She couldn't help wondering why he had chosen this moment to leave. If he hated her that much, why had he waited so long before he left her, for her sister? How could she love someone who didn't love her? What else was there to give him? They had a beautiful home, happy children, an affluent lifestyle and a fairly decent sex life. What more? Leah got up from the floor and sat down in an armchair.

She had to face it. Jacob just didn't love her.

Suddenly, she felt a desperate need for her mother. Leah was only young when her mother died, but they sat and talked for ages. She had loved her very much and shared lots of secrets with her. There had never been any favouritism when Elizabeth was alive—she treated both her daughters the same. She brought them up to understand the strong faith she had in God, something that Leah found hard to comprehend. But as she sat here now, she remembered her mother telling her that God loved her very much, but it would never make a difference to her unless she loved Him too. Leah had always tossed this idea aside, thinking that when she needed her prayers answered, she would be good for a week and then God would see what a wonderful little girl she was, and answer her special prayer. It hadn't worked, so Leah had decided that God probably didn't exist.

But as she sat in the stillness of this empty room, she began to see the wisdom of her mother's words. God didn't hear her, because she didn't love Him. Jacob didn't take any notice of Leah, because he didn't love her. It was all one way. No one was giving anything back. 'Being good' didn't make any impact on God—He wanted her love.

Jacob gave Leah children—but she wanted his love.

"I'm sorry," She whispered. She wasn't sure who she was talking to. Maybe God, maybe Jacob, maybe even Rachel. All she knew was that her husband had never ever loved her, but she still loved him. And now he was going. She would be left with nothing. Oh, the bravado of taking him for every penny was cute, but it wasn't what she wanted. She felt crushed. Maybe, just maybe, if she went through with it and sued him, bled him dry, he might think twice about leaving and stay with her. It was really her only hope.

When Jacob left the house, he didn't feel particularly proud of himself. Leah had been within her rights to yell at him as she did, even though she had tricked him into marriage in the first place. They had been together for over seven years and she must have thought they had settled down to a life with one another. It had taken just two days after he had held Rachel, to work out the cost of what he was doing. And when he weighed it up, there was nothing he wouldn't do to be with her. They could live without riches, he could get another job . . .

Whilst driving to work he contemplated his next conversation with Laban. It wouldn't be easy. He was right of course. Strolling into Laban's office and announcing his resignation was not the easiest thing he had ever done—and if he thought Leah's reaction was over the top . . .

"Are you out of your mind?!" The gruff, aghast tones of Laban Monklaast were heard in Henrietta's office.

Jacob stood and waited for him to calm down.

"Listen, Laban. I told you I would be around until MBC-TV was up and running. If you like, I'll hang on for another few months to iron out any teething problems but after that, I'm out." He sounded more confident than he felt.

"You want to leave the company," Laban stated flatly. "You come in here and say to me, you want to leave MBC. Am I allowed to know what has brought on this brainstorm?" He tapped his fingers on the desk impatiently, biding for time.

Jacob's eyes seared into Laban's as he replied, "Let me remind you of a conversation we had many years ago. As I recall, I asked you to release me from my ridiculous marriage to Leah and you refused. Later on, you dangled MBC-TV in front of me and told me that if I spear-headed that company, you would OK my divorce."

Laban turned pale and made to reply, but Jacob stopped him.

"It's taken over seven years, but they are over, and so is my deal with you and your company and your precious elder daughter." He came nearer to Laban. "As soon as ... the very second ... my divorce is through, I will marry Rachel. I have had it with plans and deals. I now know what I want."

In his heart, Laban was deeply moved to watch this proud handsome man fighting for Rachel. Jacob was always a sight to see when battling with the everyday issues of the company, but now, as he strove to make clear his intentions for the woman he loved, his whole being was infused with passion and fire.

Laban got up from his chair, walked over to Jacob and put his arm around his shoulders. He drew him over to the drinks cabinet and poured them both a Scotch.

"Please sit down with me, Jacob. I want to try and understand what has happened. You are terribly upset, and I am very shocked. I have so many questions to ask." Laban's mind was working overtime.

The two men sat down. "Have you discussed this with Leah?" He tried to ask as gently as he could, knowing he was on dangerous ground.

Jacob gave a sarcastic laugh. "I suppose you could say we've 'discussed' it. Actually, it was more like World War Three ... "

Laban sighed, but let Jacob continue. "I have told Leah that I am divorcing her and that I am going to marry Rachel. In a way it should never have been a surprise—" He looked sharply at Laban "—to either of you. You have both known from the start, how we felt about each other. Love doesn't just go away." He felt drained and took a sip of the whisky. "We met again at the TV launch and decided there and then that we couldn't go on without each other. I have no choice, Laban, but to leave and make my life with Rachel."

Laban got up and went to his desk. He pressed the intercom.

"Henry. No calls, absolutely nothing." His voice was curt. He faced Jacob again. He looked serious and somehow a little older.

"There is a way out of all this." It was a blunt statement and it caught Jacob by surprise.

"If this is another one of your scams ... " he began.

"Hear me out, please," Laban replied, and came back over to him. He perched himself on the arm of the chair opposite. "I know—I admit—that this is partly my fault. I find myself torn between my family and my company, and in between the two— there's you. Now, I don't want to lose any of you. I can see that a divorce as sensational as the one you will go through, will leave you all but penniless—please don't interrupt—I am sure you are going to tell me it is worth it. Well, you have worked hard and well for me Jacob and I don't want to see it end like this. I am a very rich man, and as I am partly responsible for this mess, I will pay for it."

Jacob stood up, outraged, and went to leave the room.

"Don't be a fool, Jacob!" Laban yelled at him. "Listen to me! I am offering you the chance to have your cake and eat it!!"

Jacob stopped and turned around. "You can't do this Laban." He said quietly.

"You know I can," he replied. "I don't want to lose your hand in my company. There is nothing to stop you staying on as Head of MBC-TV. Think about it. Why should you lose, after all that's happened to you? We can work round it ... the press ... Simon and Jane can handle it. I can talk to Leah—she has her children ... "

Jacob was confused and suspicious. He had come in here to resign from the company and in the end he was being offered more than he could handle.

Laban walked over and patted his shoulder. "Go home Jacob. Go home—wherever that is—and think it over. Discuss it with Rachel. Take your time."

Laban was ushering him towards the door, willing him to go before he had time to think.

When he finally left, Laban poured himself another drink. A large one.

CHAPTER

35

The wedding of Jacob and Rachel was as different from Leah's as it was possible to imagine. It was a small registry office affair with just three guests—Aaron, Sarah and Jacob's mother, Rebekkah. Laban was missing for Leah's sake, and also to keep the press away. He purposely planned a press reception to coincide with the secret wedding, so that all interest would be turned towards him, and away from Jacob. So, it wasn't until after the event, that the news broke.

All Jacob and Rachel wanted was to get married, as soon as possible, with the minimum of fuss. They were both moved when they read the fax message from Australia, announcing that Rebekkah was arriving. It was a beautiful time for them—to have Jacob's mother there was very special—and the two women found an instant bond, much to Jacob's delight.

She insisted on being around for the week before the wedding, helping Rachel as if she were her own mother, and Rachel loved her for it. She had accepted the fact that her wedding day would not be the one of her childhood dreams, no church, (although they had a small service arranged for a blessing, later in the month,) no huge wedding list and no invitations. But Rebekkah had been so wonderful. She had taken Rachel out for a 'girls' night', just the two of them—they went to an exclusive restaurant and talked until it was light. They went shopping, and Rebekkah insisted on paying for everything. They chose new furnishings for the apartment that Laban had handed over to Rachel and Jacob as a wedding present. So by the time the big day arrived, Rachel felt every inch a bride. They would never be able to thank his mother enough, and she insisted on leaving England straight after the wedding, announcing that the business would be 'a wreck' if she didn't get back to Australia.

The parting was tearful, with promises to visit again and invitations to Australia. They had waved her taxi off from the Registry Office and then driven home in Jacob's BMW.

*   *   *

The day after their wedding, they were in bed having an afternoon breakfast. It was two o'clock and Jacob was lying under the silk sheet of Rachel's double bed. They had spent all day, laughing, making love, laughing some more, making love again, just totally immersing themselves in each other. And now he was teasing her.

"You know, darling, I never thought of you as the kind of girl who would drop crumbs in the bed." His dark eyes looked up at her as she sat half-undressed, eating toast. He thought he had never seen anything so lovely as his wife.

She looked at him, her hair tumbling over her bare shoulders, and his eyes wandered to her perfect breasts and long, long legs. She smiled at him. "Well," she sighed and stretched her arms, waving the toast all over him. "It's just one of the many things you are going to have to get used to!"

Pieces of the toast fell onto his chest and he brushed them away, grinning and scolding her as he did. She caught hold of his hands and pushed them away. "Hey! That's my job!!" She bent her head and began to lick the crumbs off his body. When she was with him, everything was so natural, they became so close that it seemed as if they had always been together.

He rolled over and caught her in his arms and their lovemaking began again.

Much later, they laid in each other's arms and talked quietly about their plans. Jacob rested his head on her hair. "Are you sure you're happy with your father's plans?" It was a question he had asked her many times.

She moved her head against his. "Jay, I would have been devastated if you'd lost all you'd worked for—just to be with me. I'm much happier knowing that you are keeping your dreams and ambitions. It's important, you know." Her sparkling blue eyes looked up at him.

He hugged her tightly and smiled to himself. How did he deserve this woman?

"What about you? What do you want to do? Carry on working at Landers, or become a 'lady of leisure'?" He laughed aloud at the thought of Rachel as a housewife.

She punched him playfully. "I don't think so, somehow ... well, not just yet ... " Her thoughts went ahead of her.

"What do you mean, 'not just yet'?" He asked.

She caught the corner of the sheet and put it to her lips, chewing it gently. Shyly she said, "I know you already have a large family, Jay ... but ... "

Jacob could hardly believe his ears. When he married Rachel, he decided that he would bow to whatever she wanted, but the idea of children—he somehow thought it would remind her too much of Leah. Yet here she was, hinting that she wanted a child. Their child! He gazed at her in astonishment. "Do you really mean that, Rachel? You want us to have a baby? Honestly?"

Rachel stroked his cheek—she loved him so much. "Well, I'm not getting any younger ... " her look becoming mischievous. "How do you feel about that? Will it look like you or me?"

"I want what you want, darling." He said.

*   *   *

A week later, both of them were back at work, and in the following months Jacob made a huge success of MBC-TV. Rachel kept a low profile, enjoying her days back in Byron Street and making sure she was always home for Jacob, when he returned exhausted from the station. It was a lifestyle that suited them both and they were extremely happy and contented. They heard little from Leah, although she did phone when she knew Rachel would be alone. Her tactics were icy and Rachel wasn't sure whether Leah was trying to make friends, or 'muscle in'. She made a few stabbing remarks about 'her children' and how Jacob had probably had enough of the 'family' life. However, she always tried to be nice to Leah, even though it would never be the same again.

*   *   *

Time passed and Rachel waited patiently to become pregnant. It was approaching their first anniversary and she had fervently hoped she would be expecting by now. Today, her hand went to her empty stomach and a feeling of concern overcame her. Sometimes she found herself wandering around the department stores in Oxford Street during her lunchtime, looking at baby clothes and maternity outfits. She had even secretly bought a few items, and stowed them away in a drawer at home.

Of course, it was early days, and maybe because she was a little older, it might take a bit longer for the miracle to happen. She tried hard not to worry about it—she didn't want Jacob to think there was anything wrong, which of course there wasn't. Was there?

As it happened, Jacob did notice a slight change in his wife. He would be in the middle of telling her something and then notice a faraway look in her eyes.

"Darling? Rachel? I was telling you about Aaron's new show ... " He looked slightly perturbed.

Rachel shook her head and her long curls danced around her face. "Oh! Jay, I'm sorry, darling. Tell me again?" She reached for him as he sat by her.

Jacob looked down at the small hand in his, and stroked her fingers. "Where were you?" He smiled, but felt slightly uneasy.

Her hand tightened on his. "I'm sorry, busy day at the office and all that." She tried to sound cheerful and carefree, but it didn't quite work.

"Rachel, are you OK?" Jacob sounded concerned.

"Of course! What were you telling me about Aaron?" She tried hard to change the subject, but her husband wouldn't have it.

"You've been looking pale, just lately. Are you sure everything's all right? You're not being given a hard time at work or anything? Nobody hassling you?"

She put her arms around his neck and kissed him.

"You have an overactive imagination! What could be wrong?"

Jacob wasn't convinced. And over the next six months, he realised he was right to worry.

He came home one day and found her standing amongst a pile of clothes in the bedroom. She didn't hear him come in, and continued to throw the clothes onto the bed.

"Rachel! What on earth are you doing?"

His voice made her jump, but she looked cross and said, "What am I supposed to wear for the MBC party on Friday? Nothing looks good!" She held up a Chanel original. "Do you know, I only bought this dress last week, and it looks dreadful!"

Jacob was more than worried about her mood. He watched as she threw even more dresses onto the heap, becoming angrier with every item. He had never seen her like this. He went over to her and held her.

"Darling, calm down! Come and sit down for a moment."

She wrenched herself free. "How can I? I've got much too much to do ... I haven't even sorted out a meal for tonight yet ... "Her tone was becoming pathetic and Jacob couldn't understand. He pulled her away from the bedroom and physically put her onto their favourite couch.

"Now," he said, holding onto her gently but firmly. "What is all this about?"

Tears welled up in Rachel's eyes and she bent her head. Jacob felt the tears land on the back of his hand. He was beside himself with worry. He caught her as she fell into his arms, and cradled her like a baby until she stopped crying. Then he spoke. "I don't care what it is Rachel. I really don't care what has happened, I will take anything you throw at me—just tell me, darling, please tell me!" He was whispering into her hair—she could feel his hot breath.

She lifted her hair out of her eyes and tried to look at him. "Oh Jay ... "

Jacob was past caring. The thoughts rushing through his mind were driving him crazy. "Tell me ... Rachel!"

Then in a very small voice she murmured, "Jacob, I think there might be something wrong with me."

It was as if his life had ended. Rachel was ill, seriously ill—how did she know? What did she mean, 'there was something wrong with her'? He carried on rocking her in his arms and talking into her hair, he couldn't bear to see her face. "What? What do you mean, darling?"

She untangled herself from his embrace and sat forlornly on the couch. She didn't glance up, but started to speak. "I ... um ... I don't seem to be able ... ah ... I don't know if I ... it's not your fault ... it's me ... " She faltered so much and then took a deep breach. "I can't get pregnant Jacob! Why am I not pregnant? What's wrong with me?" She broke down into convulsive sobs.

Jacob was so relieved he could hardly speak. "That's all? You're not pregnant? That's what this is all about?" His breath was coming back.

Rachel gazed at him in despair. "What do you mean 'Is that all?' I want to give you our baby, and it's not happening ... !"

"Rachel, you scared the hell out of me! I thought you were dying!!" Jacob's voice was loud and thick with emotion.

They stopped and stared at each other, the relief flowing out of them both.

"I'm not dying ... " Rachel said softly.

"You're just not pregnant." Jacob answered with a smile.

"You don't mind?" she said anxiously.

"I've married an idiot," he replied, raising his eyes.

Rachel responded to his warmth and love. She moved back over to him and laid her head on his shoulder. "Are you sure you don't mind?" she asked again.

"How could I mind, sweetheart? All it means is, we'll have to try harder! He laughed at the thought.

Rachel joined in, but said soberly, "But what if I really can't have a baby?"

"Then we won't have one," he said simply.

Rachel's very small voice beside him murmured, "I've never had one."

His arms were round her in an instant. He hadn't understood how she felt, he thought that she was just worried in case he was upset, but now he could see she was taking this personally, as some kind of retribution, a punishment—for what?

"Talk to me, Rachel." His voice was firm now, and it was an attitude that she felt safe with. When they had their moments of sharing secrets, he would talk to her this way.

She held onto his arm and poured her heart out to him. "I've never had any reason to doubt that getting pregnant wouldn't be easy for me. Look at Leah, she had seven babies in as many years.

I just assumed that it would be easy, that the moment we decided we wanted a child—that I would just ... have one! I know there's nothing wrong with you, that much is obvious, so it must be me. There's something wrong with me!"

"Rachel," he replied, "there's nothing wrong with you. You are just over anxious. If you really are that worried, we'll call in Dr Mortimer and he can check you over. But I'm sure it's a false alarm. You'll see." He was trying his best to reassure her.

"Am I worrying for nothing, Jay?" she asked him again.

"Of course you are," Jacob kissed his beautiful wife.

"It will be all right?" she asked again, biting her beautiful lips.

"Everything will be fine," he replied, but even as he said it, a small doubt began to grow in his mind.

CHAPTER

36

D r Mortimer was a wise, grey-haired, confident man. He looked after all the Monklaasts when they were in London. Harley Street specialists were expensive, but worth every penny when you hired the right one.

He finished examining Rachel and called Jacob into the bedroom. At the same time as he sorted out various instruments in his case, he said, "I am pleased to tell you there is absolutely nothing wrong with your beautiful wife."

Jacob and Rachel looked at each other with relief. The doctor continued, "I have been talking to Mrs Lindstein for quite a while, and in my opinion, she is finding this whole 'pregnancy thing' stressful. I understand she is feeling the pressure of competition from her sister, and this could be part of the problem." He turned and smiled at Rachel. "You know, my dear, it's not such an old wives' tale that you have to be relaxed to conceive. That's why so many people have tried drugs in desperation. Valium, anti-depressants, even mandrakes and rhino horn! Not that you need anything like that—but I must advise you to live your own life and not to worry about anybody else's. Getting pregnant should never be part of a competition—you don't get Brownie points for it, you know!" he warned, wagging his finger at her. "Mr Lindstein," he turned to Jacob, "please make sure that you pamper this wife of yours, and make her see that having children is a joy, not part of some university course!"

Jacob laughed. "I will do my best."

He walked the doctor to the entrance of the building, in order to have a private word with him. "What do I do if she doesn't conceive?" he asked anxiously.

"As I have already said," replied Dr Mortimer, "there is no reason why she shouldn't. But if there's no news in say, six months, then perhaps you could both get back to me and we'll take things further."

Jacob looked worried. "How? I thought you said there was nothing wrong."

"There isn't. But sometimes it happens and sometimes it doesn't. We can always run tests, to make sure we haven't missed anything. But don't worry—I'm sure she'll be fine." They shook hands and Jacob went back to the apartment.

She was in the lounge, pacing up and down. She ran to him as he walked in. "Did he say anything else?" She hung on to his shirt.

"Yes, he said I had to love you even more than ever and take you somewhere special at least once a week!" He lifted her off her feet and twirled her round.

She giggled and beat her fists on his shoulders. "Come on Jay! Did he say anything else?"

He lowered her gently to the ground.

"Only that we could call him again in six months, if ... "

He couldn't bear to watch the crestfallen face. "Rachel, he said it was OK! There's nothing wrong with you—we've just got to take it easy, that's all."

It was an easy thing to say, and a hard thing to do. Gradually their lovemaking became an 'exercise in getting pregnant' rather than an expression of love. Jacob was a very patient man when it came to his Rachel, but he could see that things were not improving.

After one particularly restless night, he spoke to her again. "Darling, this is getting silly! It's very difficult to make love to someone who is looking over her shoulder at charts and calculations ... " He leaned on his elbows and looked at her.

Rachel was shocked for a moment, until she gradually realised that he was right. Her eyes took in the beautiful man lying beside her. "I'm so sorry, Jacob." She used his full name, and he knew she was serious. "Please always tell me when I do the wrong thing."

Immediately Jacob felt contrite. What right had he to add to her worries? "No, it's my fault. I can be a bit of a bulldozer at times. I did't mean to put you down like that."

Their making-up was pure pleasure. For the first time in many weeks, they made love, rather than just had sex.

The weeks quickly ran into months, and there was still no sign of a baby. By now, Rachel had tried every remedy on the market and was worrying herself sick. Nothing was working.

The phone rang and she picked it up without thinking. "Yes?" she said abruptly.

"Rachel? My—you sound rough!" The sarcastic tones of Leah came sailing across the wires.

"Oh! Hello Leah, sorry, I was busy," she replied.

"Will it keep? I'd rather like to talk to you."

"Yes, yes of course. What is it?" This was proving difficult for Rachel, who found Leah hard to handle at the best of times.

"I've heard some rather interesting gossip lately—of course, I'm sure gossip is all it is—but a friend of mine swore she saw you in Keyes Bookshop the other day. She said you were buying all the titles to do with pregnancy and fertility ... " Leah waited for a response.

Rachel felt herself growing cold and start to shake.

"Leave me alone Leah. You've done enough damage."

She heard her sister laugh on the other end of the line. "No, no dear, don't get me wrong—it's just that if you are having trouble becoming an expectant mother, then maybe I can help ..."

This was all too much for Rachel, who was sure her sister was goading her. "I'm sorry Leah, I'm busy." She said and put the phone down.

"Are you all right Mrs Lindstein?" The voice belonged to Billie Jean, their newly-acquired maid. She was an American woman in her mid-thirties who helped with the day-to-day chores in the apartment. Jacob had insisted on some help for Rachel, who was trying to manage her job and the house. He worried so much about her, and was doing everything he could to relieve her of stress.

Billie Jean watched Rachel with a worried expression. With no one else to talk to, the maid and Rachel had become quite good friends. Billie was slightly older than her, and very homely.

"Oh, I don't know," sighed Rachel, and then took a chance. "B.J, you and your husband have four children, don't you?"

"Yes, we have," replied the maid, wondering where this was leading.

"Do you think you would have missed out on something if you hadn't had them? Or would your life just have been different?" Rachel asked.

The maid sat down on an upright chair and thought about the question. "Well, I'm sure I prefer life with them. Even though they cause a lot of heartache at times." She smiled, thinking aloud.

"Did you become pregnant very easily?" It was an impertinent question, but Billie Jean didn't seem to mind.

"Oh yes!" She gestured with her hands towards her stomach. "My husband used to say that he only had to speak the word 'baby', and there I was, having another one!" She giggled at the thought. "Do you know, I've often thought I'd make a good ... oh what do they call it? ... suffragette ... no *surrogate* mother!"

Rachel's heart leapt inside her. This was one of the subjects she had read about in manuals from the bookshop. She decided to probe further. "Don't you think you would have trouble handing the baby over, afterwards?"

The maid shook her head. "My husband would kill me if I brought another child into the house. He's always said four is enough for anyone!" Billie Jean caught the look of longing on Rachel's face. "Are you sure you're all right?"

"Yes, yes, I'm fine." Rachel replied. But the seed was sown, and the idea well and truly planted. She just had to convince Jacob.

CHAPTER

37

For two weeks Rachel worried and agonised over her plan. She knew she should confront Jacob with it, but had no idea how he would take it. It would be yet another baby fathered by Jacob and not with her—but at least it would have absolutely no ties with Leah. Was she so wrong to want something that had never belonged to her sister? Even Jacob had been Leah's first! The last few days had been stressful. Rachel knew that Jacob was worried about her, but somehow she couldn't bring herself to talk to him about it. She knew this must be hurting him, but didn't realise quite how much.

She had planned a cosy evening, soft lights, a nice meal and just the two of them relaxing together. However, when Jacob arrived, it was obvious that he had been through a hard day at the office, and his mind was elsewhere. Normally, Rachel would have seen this immediately and backed away, given him some space and gradually coaxed him round—but tonight she was too deep into her own plans to notice.

Jacob came in and flung himself on the couch. His coat went one way and he went the other. "Oh, that was a bad, bad day," he started. "Do you know ..." he shouted to Rachel who was in the other room fixing him a drink "... they are still trying to poach Aaron. Ha! After all I've said to them, I can't believe it, I really can't! And the stupid thing is—he doesn't want to go anyway! I wish they'd just get off my back. And then the set for the 'Family

Matters' programme is a disaster! You should see the colouring! It's supposed to be 'restful'—what a joke!"

He could hear Rachel in the other room, making sympathetic noises. It was good to be home, and he hoped she wasn't going to start up this 'baby' thing again tonight.

She came through, carrying a small silver tray with two sparkling crystal glasses and put it down by his side. He smiled lazily at her. "You sparkle twice as much as the crystal, and you're as beautiful as ever. Come here and tell me how your day was— it has to have been better than mine."

It was all Rachel needed to release her ideas. She sat close to him and started to chatter excitedly. "Jay ... I have this great idea. I hope you like it! I've been reading in this book—"

Jacob stopped her. His face looked tired. "Please Rachel, not tonight. Tell me anything but another recipe for baby-making! I am so tired—we have to give it a rest, my love." He tried hard not to hurt her feelings, but he could see by her expression that it was too late. Only this time, she wasn't just unhappy, she was upset.

Her eyes fired up and she turned away from him as she spoke. "If you can bring your work home and fill my evening with it, then I think I should be able to share my days with you too!" Her voice was low and troubled.

He reached for her, but she shrugged him away. "No, Jacob, this is important to me! Why won't you listen? If you don't like the idea, then fine—but at least let me tell you."

"Darling," he began firmly. "I am not God. I know you think that if we talk about it enough, it will happen, but I can't do it! I cannot manufacture you a child!" He was angry now. The conversation went round and round in circles. Dr Mortimer was still insistent that there was nothing wrong—it was just a case of waiting. The most frustrating thing was, that Jacob couldn't help in the one thing that Rachel really needed—and that hurt. He heard her voice in the distance of his thoughts.

"You can."

He leaned over to her. "What are you talking about?"

She looked up, her eyes shining with urgency. "Jacob you can manufacture a child!! I've been talking to Billie Jean. We've had a lot of time to work on this—darling, I'm sorry I did this a little behind your back, but I had to see if it was OK before I talked to you."

Jacob's handsome face looked troubled. "Rachel, you are not making a lot of sense."

She smiled and clapped her hands in delight as she explained it to him. "Darling, B.J. is willing to have the baby for me ... ". She held tightly onto her husband's hands and her glorious blue eyes pleaded with him to listen.

"She's had four children of her own, and her husband doesn't want anymore, so she will be happy to hand the baby over to us afterwards! She will be virtually living under our roof, and then nearer the time, she's agreed to come and live-in properly, so that the child can be born here with us. I'm sure Dr Mortimer would agree to help! Jacob, isn't it fantastic! Billie Jean has agreed to be our surrogate mother!!"

Jacob felt as if someone had punched him squarely in the stomach. His breath was completely taken away by his wife's suggestion. He gazed at her, trying to see inside her—was she serious about this? Or had she actually been driven crazy by the stress of her barrenness? He eventually found his voice. "Rachel, my love, what are you saying?" He was shaking, almost with fright.

Rachel was still smiling, and laughing. "Isn't it a wonderful idea? I know it sounds a bit wild, but its quite common, and we know we can trust B.J."

Jacob's mind was a state of confusion. He couldn't deny the joy on her face, but—surrogacy??

"Darling, Rachel, listen to me." He whispered low, holding her face with his hands. "The child still won't be yours. Do you understand?"

Rachel covered his hands with her own. "But it won't be Leah's or Priscilla's either. It will be the nearest thing I may ever get to a child of my own. Please don't deny me the chance, Jay, please."

The silence seemed to last forever. Rachel sat looking at Jacob, and Jacob sat looking at the floor. Finally he spoke. "We would have to look into this very carefully. Legally, it's a minefield. Physically and mentally, it could be a nightmare"

Rachel broke into his thoughts. "I would be willing to take the risk, if you would. I feel physically and mentally stressed anyway —so how bad can it get?"

Her husband shook his head. "Oh darling, I don't know ... "

"Well, can we at least talk to the doctor about it?" She pleaded.

Jacob would have given Rachel anything she desired, but he had no idea whether agreeing to this proposition would do her more harm than good.

"All right. We'll ask him to call round. But don't get to excited ... I'm not sure if it's even legal."

Rachel's body melted into Jacob's and she kissed him passionately. Her lips were soft and inviting and Jacob responded instantly. If this was his reward, then Rachel could have as many offspring as she liked.

*   *   *

Dr Mortimer sipped his black coffee while he listened to the plans Jacob and Rachel were putting forward. He could see the earnestness and the yearning on both their faces, and his heart went out to them. It was potentially dangerous, and he had seen it back-fire many times. When they had finished, he put his cup down and looked at them seriously.

"Firstly, I need to explain what you are getting into. This surrogacy thing won't actually work for you ... "

Rachel gasped and put her hands to her mouth. He hushed her and carried on.

"There is no point in inserting one of Rachel's eggs into another woman. At the moment, we know that she is finding it hard to conceive, and placing her egg into someone else won't help that situation. If Rachel were becoming pregnant and not carrying the child for the full-term, then we would be able to use this system. However, what we have here is a woman who is finding it hard to get pregnant in the first place." He took a breath and surveyed the unhappy couple in front of him. "If you seriously want to go through with this idea, then you need to consider artificial insemination. Now, we know there is nothing wrong with Jacob, so his sperm could be used to fertilise an egg with no problem. If your maid is willing and absolutely sure of her own feelings, we could impregnate one of her eggs with Jacob's sperm, whilst the egg is still inside her—" They both started to speak at once, but he held up his hand to stop them.

"Legally, the child would belong to Jacob and Billie Jean. But, if you feel that this woman is trustworthy enough to hand the baby over to Rachel at it's birth ... then it can be done."

"Is it legal?" asked Jacob seriously.

The doctor pursed his lips. "As I said. 'It can be done.' " The two men understood each other.

Jacob rose from his seat and extended his hand to Mortimer. "Thank you very much for your time, and consultation. We will be in touch."

Rachel was looking from one to the other, not sure what all this meant, and was still sitting mesmerised by what she had heard, when Jacob came back to her.

He paced around the room and blew a huge sigh. His head felt as if it was breaking in two.

Rachel still sat, waiting for someone to tell her what was happening. He came and knelt by her, his hands resting in her lap. "We have a lot of talking to do, darling. Did you understand most of what the doctor said?"

"Yes ... er ... well, no ... I'm not sure ... " Her eyes grew large and a frown creased her forehead.

"It is as I thought," Jacob explained. "If we go ahead with this scheme—if Billie Jean is willing—then the baby will still technically be hers, and she can withhold it from you at the last minute."

"No, she wouldn't do that!" Rachel retorted. "I know she wouldn't do that!"

"We can't stop her." He swallowed hard, because he knew what he had to say next would not be easy. "Rachel, do you realise that we will be 'buying' this baby? A lot—and I mean a lot—of money will change hands here. For B.J., for the doctor—and even after all that, we have no guarantee."

It was taking a while to sink in. Rachel was dumbfounded. Before, it was just words in a book, a thought in her mind, but now, it was a reality. She had a real living chance of sharing a baby with Jacob. No one need know it wasn't hers.

Jacob left her and returned holding two large brandies. "Drink this, and try and think of something else for a while."

She glanced at him quizzically as she took the glass. "Jay ..."

He spoke carefully. "I think we need time to let all this sink in. We now know what we are up against, and I think we should digest it, before we do anything else."

"And then?" she asked.

"And then we will talk to Dr Mortimer again."

Rachel let her glass fall to the floor as she rushed over to him. Her arms went around him and they held each other tightly. "I love you, Jacob." she said. "I love you so very, very much."

CHAPTER

38

Documents were duly drawn up between Rachel, Jacob, and Billie Jean. They were only pieces of paper and would not stand up in court, but they all felt happier to sign something.

"You know I'm not doing this for money?" Billie asked anxiously as she signed the contract.

"Don't worry, B.J., you deserve every penny if you make my wife happy again." Jacob spoke with more than a little feeling.

The amount of money for B.J. and the doctors fees was substantial, but as Rachel had said, 'they had money—they didn't have a baby.'

"We will take very good care of you," Rachel was advising her. "And if there is anything at all that you need you know you only have to ask."

The whole affair was quite sombre. The four of them had talked solidly for two hours before any decision was eventually reached and Dr Mortimer was witness to the signing.

"So," the doctor said as he turned to leave, "I will see you at my clinic on Monday. Take care." He left the apartment.

Billie Jean left soon after. She assured the couple once again that the baby would be theirs, and that everything was going to be fine.

After she left, Rachel and Jacob stood in the quietness of the room and held each other. It was as if they were trying to keep this agreement safe. They had to hold on now for nine months.

*   *   *

Billie Jean moved in to the apartment when she had three weeks to go.

Rachel was rosy with anticipation, and B.J. was so happy for her. They were alike in many ways. Both the women were dark-haired, and had similar features. Whereas Rachel's face was refined and regal, Billie Jean's was rounder, more homely—but the similarity was still there. Rachel fervently hoped that the baby would be the right mixture of deep brown hair and dark eyes.

They had decided that they would tell everyone that the child was 'adopted' from birth, but wherever possible they would just refer to it as 'theirs'. They had chosen names already, Daniel for a boy and Danielle for a girl. Rachel could hardly bear to wait any longer.

When the time came, Billie Jean had no problems giving birth to Daniel. Dr Mortimer was extremely pleased with the result and at once handed the baby over to Rachel.

It was an occasion graced with many tears. Rachel was totally overcome by the baby in her arms. Jacob was elated at Rachel's reaction. And Billie Jean cried for every possible reason—the birth of her son, the loss of him on the same moment, the fact that her husband wasn't there (something she had insisted upon herself) and the expressions on the faces of the two people she had grown to love.

Dr Mortimer ushered Rachel and the baby away from Billie Jean and into the small bedroom next door—"We must give the mother—'m sorry, I mean B.J.—time to rest for a while, and I need to get this little lad cleaned up."

"Can I stay and watch?" Rachel was all eyes, following every move Daniel made.

The doctor laughed. "I don't think I have any hope of getting rid of you! Although, if you could, it would be nice to go and talk to Billie Jean in a while. She might need her hand held for a time."

Jacob appeared at the door. He looked flushed and happy. "Is everything all right?"

Rachel ran over to him and hugged him. Then she pulled him over to where the baby was lying. "Look! Look! He has your eyes, Jay! Gorgeous liquid brown eyes—and hair as black as ink!" She turned to him. "He's ours, Jacob!" And buried her head in his neck.

"Well, I'm finished in here, if you would like to take over Mrs Lindstein?" The Doctor held Daniel out to her. "I shall go and have a word with my patient, and see you before I go."

Once they were by themselves, Rachel and Jacob sat on the single bed and took it in turns to nurse the little one.

"I don't know what to say to you, darling." Rachel murmured. "I have everything I have ever wanted." She looked at him anxiously. "There's never been a moment I haven't loved you, and if this baby was not to be, I would have accepted it, really. You are enough ... but ... "

Jacob threw his head back and laughed. "Honestly Rachel, you've been getting very good at talking yourself into corners lately. Don't worry, I've never doubted you for one second, but it's wonderful to give you something you've always wanted."

For the next half-an-hour their attention was totally absorbed by Daniel.

When the doctor came back through to them, they were still examining the baby's tiny fingers and exclaiming at his toes. Dr Mortimer coughed politely behind them.

"Ah! I see you agree with me that he has the right amount of everything!" He pulled a chair over and sat facing them.

"Now, I have a few things to sort out with you. First, a car will be coming for Billie Jean this evening. She will be driven back to her home, where I shall make sure she is comfortable and well looked after. I have hired the nurse you asked for, and she will see to anything else that has to be done ... and sort out the milk too."

They had all agreed that it would be much too emotional for the women, if B.J. fed the baby, and the sooner the maid and the child were separated, the better for everyone.

The doctor continued, "Your own nurse—to help you with Daniel—is on her way, and I shall leave as soon as she arrives to take over. Now, if you have any questions, please phone me. Anything at all." He concentrated on Rachel for a moment. "This will not be all plain sailing for you. You may find yourself depressed, or just not coping, although you haven't actually gone through childbirth yourself, your body will have taken an enormous strain. So take care of yourself as well as junior here."

A buzzer sounded to announce the arrival of their nurse, and Dr Mortimer said his goodbyes.

That evening, Rachel, Jacob and Daniel were alone for the first time. The Lindstein family had begun.

* * *

Rachel was more than happy to leave work. Now that Daniel was here, she wanted nothing more than to catch up on all the years she had lost. She was determined that her home would be a constant source of warmth and contentment for the two most important men in her life.

When her father had first heard about the plan for their baby, he was very sceptical. He put up many strong arguments, only to see them knocked down one by one, by an even stronger couple. Leah, of course, ridiculed the whole thing, even to the point of implying that Jacob had actually slept with B.J.—as he had with Priscilla. But both Laban and Jacob kept Leah out of Rachel's way as much as possible.

The early months flew by, as they always seem to do, and as Daniel grew into a sturdy toddler Rachel's father and sister also grew away from their initial reactions to his birth and accepted him. Then Rachel announced the hope of their second child!

The 'adoption' had been such a success, that both Rachel and Jacob saw no reason not to try and have a brother or sister for Daniel to play with.

"He's such a lovely boy, but he needs the company of another little person." This was Rachel talking to Jacob. "At his nursery school, you should see him, Jay, he plays for hours with the other children."

Jacob pulled Daniel onto his lap. "You don't have to convince me darling, I'm sure he doesn't want to be an 'only child'. Do you Dan? Hey! Let go of my hair!" The child giggled and held onto the black locks mercilessly. They both loved him immensely, and the transition had been smooth. Billie Jean only came in once a week now, and was content as long as she saw Daniel was happy. And although she was telling the truth about 'not doing it for the money', it had made a better life for her and her husband. So when they were asked if they would enter a second agreement, they decided they would.

And so Nathan was added to the family. He was very different from his brother, with red hair and a fiery spirit to match. He was a bundle of energy and spent all of his time taking things to bits. He made short work of any 'executive toys' presented to Jacob by his company, and would play for hours with the contents of Rachel's handbag, while Daniel looked on in admiration.

"I am sorry Rachel, it's my fault!" Jacob would say. "He is unbelievably like Esau, my brother! I'm just so pleased he gets on well with Daniel!" The rift between Jacob and his brother had never really healed.

*   *   *

During the next two years, MBC TV grew faster than anticipated, and acquired the huge status of Britain's most popular station. And so, after a time of living in the Park Lane apartment, they decided they should find a 'proper home'. They searched around the greenbelt areas, and finally agreed on a sprawling country-home only ten miles from Monks Lodge. This was greeted with great enthusiasm by Rachel's father, who felt that his younger daughter had come home again. Naturally, it was ideal for both the MBC executives. They could have planning meetings and lunches at each other's houses. And a certain proud grandfather always managed to find some excuse to return with a file he had absently picked up by mistake.

Rachel filled her days with her husband, her children and playing hostess to the many guests who came to their home. Aaron and Sarah (with little one Jessica) were always welcomed with open arms, and lately there had been a flying visit from Elliott Blaze whose latest film was smashing box office records everywhere. Elliott was pleased to see Rachel looking so happy, even if it wasn't with him! In fact, they were living an ideal life. But all that was just about to change.

CHAPTER

39

Monday was Rachel's 'day off'. These days she had her life well-organised, and Monday was the day she kept for herself. The children were taken care of, it was Jacob's board-meeting day, and the answerphone was on. Therefore, it was her day to be free of everything. Her ritual was to decide on a nice place to shop in, and then jump in her beloved Mercedes Sports and go!

This morning was bright and clear, and warm enough to put the top down on 'Bullet'. She decided to head for Henley-on-Thames and have lunch in a small restaurant she loved, and then maybe on to Reading for an intense shopping spree!

The warm wind rushed through her long hair as she drove through the country lanes at her leisure.

She ran her fingers through her hair as she walked, trying to straighten out some of the tangles caused by the wind. Men could not help but give her a backward glance as she strolled by. Rachel was oblivious to it all—she had what she wanted, and didn't see the need to look elsewhere.

The restaurant was pleasantly quiet, and she was shown to her favourite seat. She ordered a fruit juice with lots of ice and sat looking out of the window dreamily.

"Well, well, fancy meeting you like this!" The voice cut in on her thoughts, and she looked up to see Leah, smirking at her.

Rachel was flustered, which annoyed her, and so she said nothing.

Leah sat down opposite her. "I was just about to have lunch myself. How about we have it together? Catch up on old times?" Her tone was sarcastic but her face a complete mask of congeniality.

"Leah," Rachel found her voice. "What brings you to Henley?" Even after all this time, her sister still had an effect on her, and she could feel her pulse racing.

"Oh darling, I love it here! Now that I'm the 'rich bitch' I can afford this kind of luxury whenever I like!" She looked closely at Rachel. "Jacob let you off the lead for the day?"

Rachel decided she had to brazen this out, so she laughed as if Leah had meant to be joking. "Yes, that's right! He only trusts me in the big bad world on Mondays!" She picked up a menu and tried to study it, whilst keeping her feelings under control.

"How about you Leah? How are you these days?" She asked.

Leah took out a small mirror from her purse and brazenly started to apply lipstick. Rachel looked round quickly, wondering what people would think in such a respectable establishment.

"These days?" Echoed Leah. "What, the days since I gave Jacob to you?"

"Please, Leah!" Rachel whispered harshly.

"Oh, don't worry! I won't embarrass you in front of the notables." She glanced at the menu. "What do you recommend?"

Rachel felt as if she were beingl backed into a corner. "Oh, I'm having the salmon—their green salad is excellent. It comes with a lemon sauce." 'I'm rambling,' she thought to herself.

"Mmm." Leah was obviously not impressed. "No, I think I'll stick with steak. I suppose they do know how to cook a decent one here?"

"I'm sure they do, Leah," replied Rachel. She was finding it harder to keep her temper. She tried again.

"How are you?"

Leah threw the menu back on the table in a blasé fashion. "I am fine. The children are all growing up now. Do you know, Simon is seven!" The underlining of the number was not lost on her sister, the seven years that Jacob had been married to Leah were embedded in her soul.

"You must send me some up to date photographs." Rachel replied.

"Now wouldn't that be fun?" Leah waved impatiently at a young waiter.

"Leah," Rachel began. "I really would like to enjoy my meal ... if you are going to be ... "

"Sorry, darling! Not another word!" Her sister put her fingers to her lips. Leah's figure was much broader these days, which was to be expected as the mother of seven children. Her hair was cut fairly short—it looked good and probably cost a fortune every week—but she still didn't dress to make the most of herself. Her blouse was too flamboyant, although obviously expensive, and the skirt wasn't quite the right match.

Their meals arrived and they started to eat.

"Can I ask you something—it's quite personal, but I'm dying to know ... ?" Leah left the question dangling in mid-air.

Rachel waited for her to continue.

"The two boys—Dan and Nat, how did it feel?" She bit her lip almost in relish of the answer.

"I don't know what you mean," replied Rachel quite genuinely.

"Well, having a baby handed to you straight from someone else's womb—I can't imagine!" She at least kept her voice down while she was talking.

Rachel was dumbfounded, but Leah continued, "I mean, I know Jacob slept with my maid and we passed her brats off as part of the family ... but at least I knew he was cheating on me! But to know that he ... well!" Leah's face was glowing with interest.

Rachel was shaking inside. It wasn't so much that her sister was mocking her, as the fact that she was dishing out the dirt on Jacob.

"Jacob has never been unfaithful to me." Her eyes shone as she stared at her sister. "If he was unfaithful to you, then it could only be because ... because ... "

"OK! Sorry, dear." She passed the whole issue off as unimportant. She changed the subject slightly. "So, you're still having no success then?" She asked.

Rachel tried to eat her salmon and look nonchalant.

"No success at what? Jacob has the most successful TV company in Britain." She replied.

"No, no," said Leah. She looked around, and lowered her voice again. "I mean, with a baby. Your own, rather than the maids!"

Rachel was fighting to keep control. The panic inside her was rising.

"You know only too well that I can't have children," she spoke softly and put down her fork.

"Now, now, that's not strictly true is it?" Leah taunted. She was enjoying herself.

"I don't understand," Rachel looked at her sister in confusion.

Leah put her steak knife down and clasped her hands under her chin. "It's not that you can't have children, Rachel. It's just that you haven't had your own yet. Wasn't that the doctor's final analysis? That's what Daddy said, anyway." She lifted her shoulders in a simple gesture.

Rachel was more confused. It was a long time since she had discussed this problem with anyone, and Jacob had been more than pleased to see her lose that terrible determination to have her own child. What was Leah talking about?

"Leah, I really don't understand what business this is of yours," she said bluntly.

Surprisingly, Leah put her hand out and caught hold of her

sister. "Rachel, listen. There are ways around most things. Remedies, potions ... "

"I've tried them all, Leah!" Rachel almost shouted at her. Tears filled her eyes and she looked at the table.

"No. No you haven't, darling," Leah's eyes took on a cunning look. "You've not tried, everything."

The two sisters looked at each other, and the food was left uneaten.

"I can get hold of something for you. An aphrodisiac, an aid to fertility," Leah offered.

Rachel laughed half-heartedly. "What do I do? Put a string of bay leaves round my neck?"She had heard so many stupid ideas.

"I'm serious. If you don't want to know, then fine. I just thought ... " She led her on.

"What is it?" Rachel asked.

"Rhino horn. Powdered Rhino horn." She smirked, as she said it.

"Leah! That's illegal! The rhinoceros is an endangered species, and even then, it's very, very rare. No one gets hold of that kind of thing any more!" she cried.

"Desperate women who want their own babies do!" Replied Leah in soft menacing tones.

Rachel sat back in her chair and shook her head. What was she doing here with her sister, talking about insane ideas of fertility drugs?

Leah carried on talking. "It can be obtained. I know someone who can get it. And as you so rightly said, it is expensive, outrageously expensive—almost exclusively expensive! But it can be acquired. If you are interested."

Rachel's heart was racing, and she realised that she still wanted her own child. Wanted it enough to be sitting here listening to her sister talking her into buying a 'love drug'. She licked her dry lips. "What kind of price are we talking about?" She asked.

"Oh, it's a very special price. Very special indeed." She stopped suddenly, as if having a second thought. "I know! Why don't you go home and discuss it with Jacob, and if he agrees, you can get back to me. We can talk about the price then. What do you think, hmm?" She put her head to one side and looked at her sister as if she were indulging a small child. Then she stood up and pulled some money from her purse.

"I must be going. Have this one on me." She walked away from the table and then looked back. "Call me."

Rachel sat by herself for a full hour drinking strong black coffee. Eventually, she left the restaurant and went back to her car. She drove away quickly until she was lost on a narrow lane in the countryside. She pulled the car off the road and switched off the engine, and began to cry—softly at first and then, when she was sure she was alone, released a flood of tears that had been embedded in her soul for years, crying aloud and beating her fists on the steering wheel until they were bruised.

CHAPTER

40

Rachel was virtually living two lives. When Jacob and the children were around, she was blissfully happy. But when she was by herself, she was tortured. Weighing up the pros and cons of Leah's offer, she realised that she had already put Jacob through more than enough already, and he deserved some peace in his life. She just couldn't talk to him about it. She would just have to live with it.

When he came home to her, she wanted nothing more than to please him, but unknown to her he was beginning to see through the facade.

Jacob had a free weekend and decided to spend it at home. On the Saturday morning, Rachel shooed the boys out of the room and gave them over to the part-time nanny. She came back into the bedroom, taking off her silk dressing gown and slipped back in between the sheets with Jacob.

"Oh, why do Saturdays go quicker than any other day of the week?" She nuzzled up to him, kissing his neck.

He turned and stroked her arms. "You're such a puzzle to me at times," he said, his mind miles away.

She looked up quickly as she spoke. "What do you mean by that? That's a strange thing to say!" Her cheeks flushed and she found herself looking away from him.

His fingers continued to caress her, gradually moving up her arms and lightly across her breasts. He was wondering how to ask her if there was anything wrong.

"Well," he continued, "you've had a fairly hard week, and yet here you are at the weekend—as bright as a button."

She giggled at him. "Jacob, are you saying that you are puzzled because I'm happy? Don't you know how happy you make me?" She moved even nearer and snuggled up to him.

He responded naturally and circled her with his arms. "No, it's not that. It's just that ... somehow you seem a little too happy." He smiled down at her wickedly. "You've not started taking any housewife 'pick-me-ups' have you?"

She slapped him playfully. "Jacob! What is this!" She grinned back. "Am I going to get the third degree all morning—or have you something more interesting in mind?"

Jacob put all other thoughts on 'hold' and pulled Rachel over to him.

*   *   *

It was nearly mid-day when they finally got up. Jacob showered and started to dress. Rachel sat by her mirror, combing her hair. And he saw it again. That distant look—what was it? He went over and sat on the edge of the bed and spoke to her reflection.

"Rachel?"

She carried on doing her hair. "Mm?"

He tried again. "Darling. Is anything bothering you?" He spoke lovingly, not knowing what this question would bring to the surface, but knowing that sooner or later they had to talk about it. The hair-brushing continued, so he reached out and took the brush from her. She turned round in surprise. And he tried again. "Darling, what's the matter? There's something you're not telling me. I need to know, Rachel."

She smiled meakly. "Oh, it's nothing. I just let Leah get to me, that's all."

Jacob looked annoyed. "Leah? When?" Would they never be free of this wretched woman?

"Oh, I bumped into her the other week when I was in Henley. We found ourselves in the same restaurant—I could hardly ignore her, so we ended up having lunch together." She looked resigned and tried to brighten. "You know what she's like—never misses an opportunity."

It was Jacob's turn to be down-hearted. He touched her hair. "Why didn't you tell me?"

"There was nothing to tell, really. I'm OK." Her voice was sounding smaller, and he began to feel concerned. "Rachel." There was a warning in his voice.

"Jacob, I can't let her ruin my life. I just have to let her words run off me like water off a duck's back. Don't get involved in this." She was trying to act sensibly, as if she could handle it.

Jacob held Rachel's shoulders, and looked straight at her.

"Darling, I am involved. I'm your husband, remember? I think you'd better tell me what's been going on."

"I don't want to tell you, Jay. It's not worth it. Let it lie." Her lips pleaded, but her eyes were heavy.

"Come here." He pulled her over and she sat on his lap. "Now listen to me Rachel Lindstein. I have never kept secrets from you, however bad things get, you know I always come to you. Now, if you are going to start storing up problems and not telling me about them, I am going to be very upset—much more upset than I would be if you told me whatever it is you won't tell me about."

It was such a long jumbled statement, delivered so seriously, that Rachel's lips curved in a small smile. He saw it and joined in. They bent their heads together and she knew she had to tell him.

"Don't be cross," she whispered.

"Promise," he replied.

And she proceeded to tell him about the conversation in the restaurant. As he nodded sympathetically, she felt more confident and gradually told him how the whole thing had made her feel.

"I honestly didn't know I still felt like that!" She sighed. "I was so sure it had passed. I had Dan and Nathan, and I was so proud of them ... and then these feelings ... these terrible aching feelings ... they just came back. I ... I can't explain it Jay, the emptiness was still there ... "

He didn't know what to say to her. He had never felt so helpless in his life. It was as if everything was his fault.

"What can I say to you, darling?" He rocked her in his arms. "What can I do?"

Rachel was burning to ask him if she could follow-up the offer that Leah had held out to her.

"Do you think she really knows someone who can help?" Her tiny pathetic voice cut into him..

"Rachel, why should she help you?" It was a good argument, but Rachel tossed it aside.

"Maybe she needs the money. She said the price would be outlandishly high. Maybe she just wants to feel that she is still taking from us." Her hopes were rising.

Jacob ran a hand through his shiny hair. "Oh, I don't know. It's tantamount to purchasing illegal drugs ... "

"Well, we have tried other ways that were not exactly above board ... " Rachel didn't want to hurt her husband, but she had to make him see that they had taken risks before. "Jay ... if this works—if I become fertile—we could still have our own child." She started to say more but realised that she was going to cry. She got up off his lap and ran into the bathroom. Following her quickly, he found her wiping her eyes. He stood by the wall, defeated.

"Whatever it takes, darling," he said. "Whatever it takes."

She turned her wet, blue eyes towards him. "You shouldn't have asked me Jacob."

* * *

Leah's circle of friends had widened considerably since Jacob left home. Her moral standard was never that high, but now it seemed there was nothing she wouldn't do.

When Jacob first left, she nearly turned to the comfort of the bottle, but decided to seek solace elsewhere. She started frequenting a few exclusive nightclubs and soon had her eyes opened by some of the things she saw going on. It seemed if you were rich enough, then any pleasure was yours. She had been fascinated by the lengths a man would go to woo another man—but this was the 'elite' darling, and you kept your mouth tightly shut about what you saw. It was understood in these haunts, that everyone had secrets—or you wouldn't be there. She soon found out who the famous were, who couldn't kick their habits—and how much they were willing to pay to get 'high' again. Rent boys and prostitutes were all in a night's work, and the whole thing was so suave, so sophisticated and oh! so acceptable. If 'high profile' personalities could get away with it, then ...?

It was in such a place that Leah had first made her connections with some gruesome dealers. She wasn't stupid—she could see what drugs did to people and had no inclination to try them, but the dealers made a fortune. It was well worth making friends with a few of them. Thus, she added a couple of unwholesome characters to her list of 'acquaintances'. Laban would have been beside himself with fury if he had known about this.

Leah had been making a few tentative phone calls and one of them, to a guy named Michael, had proved successful. He knew where he could get what Leah needed, but the asking price was sky-high.

"I don't suppose I get my money back if it doesn't work?" she said smoothly.

She heard Michael's dirty laugh on the other end of the phone.

"Forget the money—this stuff's so hot, you may never see me again!"

Leah thought to herself that that wouldn't be such a bad idea anyway. A thought struck her. "Michael. This stuff is clean, isn't it? I mean, there are no side effects . . .?"

"Nothing at all sweetheart. This is rich housewife's play dough—nothing to worry about on that score."

"OK, that's all I need to know." She dismissed him briefly, like one of her staff.

As she put the phone down, it rang again. She looked at it in surprise and picked it back up.

"Leah Monklaast." She reverted to her maiden name almost immediately Jacob walked out. It still cut her to hear his name.

"Leah, it's me." She heard Rachel's familiar soft voice on the phone. She smirked to herself and licked her lips in anticipation.

"My little sister! How nice! What can I do for you?" She purred.

Rachel so nearly put the receiver down. Could she go through with this? Begging to Leah? She swallowed hard. "Please Leah, don't be awkward, you know why I've phoned."

"Have you talked to Jacob?" Leah sounded cold and calculating. She was tapping her nails on the table as she talked.

"Yes. I have," answered her sister.

"And ... ?" Leah was enjoying lengthening this out.

"And, we would like to know what kind of money we are talking about, before we go any further." Rachel tried to keep calm. She looked across to Jacob who was still unsure.

She heard Leah start to speak again. "Money? Who mentioned money?" Oh, this was great, she was loving every minute.

Rachel was flustered by Leah's attitude. "I thought you said the price was astronomical?"

"It is, darling." Leah replied.

"But if you don't want money ... " Rachel glanced across to

Jacob again and shrugged her shoulders at him. "What do you
want ?"

She would never, ever forget Leah's answer . . .

"I want a night with Jacob. Just one night. That's all. It's not
too high a price for your own little baby now, is it Rachel?"

CHAPTER

41

Rachel's face was void of colour. The phone still in her hand as she stared blankly in front of her. This could not be real, her life could never be this bizarre. Why her? Had she been so terrible that God just wanted to laugh at her—watch her while she suffered? She felt someone take the phone from her and replace it. Jacob stood next to her.

"So ... she wants even more than we were thinking of," he stated.

Rachel just nodded dumbly, unable to reply. She felt physically sick at what she had just heard. How could Leah even think of something so despicable?

"How much?" Jacob asked flatly.

"She doesn't want money," answered Rachel, looking away. She could almost see her own life fading in front of her.

"The house? The company? What is she after?" Jacob threw his arms in the air in desperation.

Rachel swung round and faced him. Her eyes were dull and her arms hung listlessly by her side.

"She wants you."

He laughed with shock and sarcasm. "Oh right! You get a baby and I go back to Leah! What is the matter with the woman?"

Rachel went to him, an expression on her face that he didn't recognise.

"Not for ever. Just for one night."

Again the shocked laughter rang from Jacob and he slumped into the armchair behind him. He opened his arms wide and his gaze was incredulous. Rachel thought how handsome and desirable he looked and could understand why Leah wanted him—if only for one night.

"Well, I hope you told her what to do with her 'price'!"

He shook his head in disbelief. He was still chuckling at the idea when he noticed that Rachel had not said anything to him. He beckoned to her.

"Come here, darling. Don't worry, I promise not to go! She's obviously out of her mind. She probably doesn't even know where to get this ... aphrodisiac." He saw Rachel's disappointed face and took it to mean that she felt let down. He kissed her lips and brushed her hair away from her downcast eyes. "It was a long-shot, Rachel. We knew that." He felt her tremble and pulled her closer. "I don't know what else we can do. You know I'd do any-thing to help you stop feeling like this." He whispered to her.

"Would you?" Her voice trembled as she asked.

He looked at her in surprise. "Of course I would."

"No, I mean would you spend the night with Leah?" The long curved black lashes blinked in his direction, and the deep blue eyes spoke volumes.

Jacob's reaction was immediate. He put her back from him. "Rachel, you can't be serious!" He was searching her face as if he had never seen her before.

She grabbed hold of his shirt with both hands. "But what if it works? What if this potion gives us the child we know we are both desperate for?" she cried. "Jacob! This could be our very final chance!"

"Have you any idea what you're saying?" Jacob's voice was raised now. In all the time they had been together, he had never, ever shouted at her. She flinched from him.

"Rachel, you are asking me to sleep with your sister! My ex-wife! The woman who kept me away from you for seven years!" He couldn't believe she would even consider something so base. He wiped his hand across his mouth, trying to get his breath back.

"Just once. That's all she wants, and then we have our freedom and our child." It never entered Rachel's head for a moment that Jacob might enjoy the experience. She just saw this as a line to a drowning man. Just one night and it would all be over—surely he could see that? After all these years, she still loved him desperately. Nothing could harm what they had.

"Rachel ... I ... " There were no words left. Jacob walked resignedly from the room and made his way through the house and out into the garden. He walked away from the house and down a small pathway. His thoughts were tearing him apart.

Had Rachel any idea what she was asking? If the situation were the other way round, he would have been outraged by the thought of her sleeping with another man—even for one second! One night. 'Just one night'. So simple to say. He began to think of Leah and the way she had used them both. He could see her now, her figure larger than it had been, she was quite buxom these days. Her face always carried that 'temptress' look when he was in her company. Her eyes seducing him as they followed him around the room. He loathed her. He remembered how she used to try everything in her power to coax him to her bed. Crawling over him, under him, biting him, calling him names. He swallowed hard as he suddenly realised how arousing these thoughts were. He lashed out at the nearest tree. 'Damn that woman!'

He gradually made his way back to the house.

Rachel was still where he had left her. The room was silent and the mood pensive. She heard him enter, but didn't look up. She knew what she had asked of him was wrong, unforgivable, but she didn't know what else to do. She felt him walk past her and pick up the phone.

"It's me." Jacob's voice was thick. She heard Leah's shrill tone on the other end. Rachel began to shake violently. 'What am I doing to him?' she thought to herself.

"Stop talking and listen," she heard him say. His curt attitude to Leah came over strongly. "I am doing this for Rachel." He pulled the phone from his ear as she shrieked with laughter. "Leah. Listen. This is a one-night stand—but then I suppose you know all about those."

Rachel gasped, worried that Jacob might put her sister off with his insults. But she didn't know Leah as well as Jacob knew her. Leah had learned to love the rough way he dealt with her and her desire mounted as he spoke.

"I will be there at midnight tonight. No! Midnight or nothing!" His temper was mounting. "I don't care! Wear what you like!" He slammed the phone down, and rubbed his eyes.

Rachel ran over to him to comfort him. He drew away from her, holding his hands out of reach.

"No, Rachel! No! I don't want you near me until this is over!"

Rachel's eyes widened and she gasped.

Once again, Jacob made for the door.

"I'm going out ... now. I won't be back until the morning."

He left her staring after him. She heard his car as it swept out of the drive—but she didn't watch him go. This was the worst day of her life, and it was of her own volition. She had no one else to blame.

*   *   *

Leah's home was her castle and she ruled the roost. Once she knew that Jacob was on his way, she got rid of everyone. The children were banished to the other side of the now-very large house with promises of a special party if they were good while mummy sorted out 'some business'. The maids were instructed to enter-

EPILOGUE

Joseph was born in March the following year. He grew to be a handsome boy, with blue eyes and black hair. He had inherited all the finer qualities of his proud parents, and made them his own. While he was still a young boy the family bade farewell to England and moved to Australia.

Shortly after arriving, Rachel gave birth to their second son. Jacob named him Ben.

Rachel died soon after after he was born.

Genesis 35:16–20

tain the children, and no one but no one was allowed anywhere near her private wing. The household staff were used to this kind of treatment, and just assumed that Ms Monklaast had a 'friend' to stay over.

Jacob parked his car in town and used a taxi to take him to 'Seventh Heaven'. He instructed the cab-driver where to park, knowing he could walk in unseen from the side entrance. He booked the car to pick him up at six the following morning and entered the house with his own key.

Leah was already standing in the hall waiting for him. She was fully dressed, which surprised him, and had obviously taken care to look her best. The cashmere sweater was wide at the neck and slid towards one shoulder as she moved. She made no attempt to adjust it, but smiled seductively at him. He could smell her expensive perfume, heavy and musky—it clouded his thoughts.

"You seem surprised to see me like this! What did you expect? A naïve little girl running around in a negligee?" She walked towards him, then stopped.

Jacob was drunk. She could smell the alcohol and as she took another look, noticed how unsteady he was. His black jacket was immaculate, but his shirt was unbuttoned and his loose tie at an angle.

She tossed her head and laughed. "I wondered why you came by cab." She raised an eyebrow at him, turned and walked down the hall. He followed her without saying a word, and was puzzled when she led him to the sitting room adjoining her bedroom, rather then the bedroom itself.

She went over to the drinks cabinet and poured herself some white wine. "As you've already started without me," she smirked. "I'll have to catch up a little. Just a little, you understand, I want to remember everything in the morning."

Jacob spoke for the first time. "Why? Leah. Why are you doing this?"

"Oh, lighten up Jacob, for goodness sake! As you said, it's only a one-night stand! A bit of fun!" She walked over to where he stood, and closed in on him. "Come on!" She whispered "We've only got the night!"

The many whiskies he had earlier in town, began to affect him. He looked her up and down. "As a matter of interest, why are you dressed? Going out on the town was not part of the deal."

"Oh, we're not going far, my love," she breathed. "Only a few feet—but I want you, from start ... " She ran her finger down his shirt. "... to finish ... " she nodded towards the bedroom, "and I think it starts here." She began to release the rest of the buttons of his shirt as she continued to talk to him. "It's funny really, don't you think, that you always were the reluctant one—to start with. Always the one who didn't want to 'play'. Hmm?" She didn't attempt to kiss him, but gradually pulled the sleeves of his shirt downwards until the garment slid from his body. He really was a magnificent sight, even when his dark eyes were filled with loathing and his lips curled in disgust. She ran a fingernail teasingly down his chest, walked over to the bedroom door and turned round. Still keeping her eyes fixed tightly on him, she removed the soft sweater to reveal her naked body.

When she disappeared into the bedroom, he followed.

Lust was the only feeling Jacob had for Leah, and it disgusted him to be here. He hated himself for his weakness, and the torment he felt when he thought what this must be doing to Rachel. But Leah played 'the mistress' well, and by dawn he was exhausted and she was triumphant.

He left her bed while she was still sleeping and ran a shower. He stood beneath the hot steaming water, trying to wash away the effects of the night. As the water stung the scratches on his back he realised he would be taking home a visual reminder of the most expensive contract he had ever been involved in. He stepped from the shower and towelled himself dry. As he rubbed his hair, he saw his reflection in the bathroom mirror. The bites on his neck were already turning blue. He dressed quickly and left without a backward glance at the woman who had brought nothing but pain to his life. In the hall he noticed a package with his name on it— he picked it up, walked out of the house to the main road and waited for the taxi to take him home. He didn't know how he would cope with the guilt he was feeling, especially as Rachel was part of it. In fact, he didn't know how to feel at all. Emotions seemed to be a thing of the past.

* * *

As soon as Jacob had left the house, Rachel knew how terribly wrong the whole thing was. Her craving for a child had led her into a devious mess. She searched her soul to find any reason that would satisfy her, for the misery she had brought on herself and the people around her. But for her greed and selfishness, Jacob would be here with her now, loving her and giving her everything she could dream of. But for her greed, Leah would not have Jacob in her arms—and Billie Jean would not have the secret longings for the two sons that were no longer hers.

'I've driven Jacob into my sister's bed!' She tortured herself. 'It would serve me right it if he never came back!' The thought brought uncontrollable weeping as she fled to their room and collapsed on the bed. She cried solidly for hours, till the pillow was wet through.

"I'm sorry! I'm so sorry!" she murmured time and time again. In her own way she was praying, but knew she didn't deserve to be heard. Her belief as a small child was that God wasn't interested in the personal details of your life—just in world situations. Her mother had gently chided her and explained that God wanted to hear every minute detail of everything she did.

"Please, please Lord! Please bring him back!! I know I don't deserve him ... but please, I beg you, bring him back to me!"

She gradually fell into an exhausted sleep, still muttering 'I'm so sorry ... sorry'.

She was woken some time later, by something being thrown on the bed. She sat up startled, her tear-stained face still sleepy. A brown paper package lay by her side, with Jacob, standing, looking over her. His face was blank. His shirt open, hands in his pockets and his head to one side.

"Well—there it is!" He nodded at the parcel and moved towards her. "The 'answer to our prayers'." His voice was thick with sarcasm. "Well? It's 'paid for'. Let's get on with it, shall we?"

Rachel was terrified as she looked into his eyes. She sat upright and tried to move away from him.

"Jacob! What are you doing?!"

His laugh had a sneering sound. "My duty, I think!" He replied.

She sat mesmerised as he quickly threw his clothes off and came to the bed. He reached out and caught her round her waist. She saw the marks on his neck and back, and pushed herself away from him, but his strong hand caught her wrist. She heard herself scream, "Jacob! No! Not like this!!"

CHAPTER

42

It was her scream that brought him back to his senses. He drew back from her, as the truth hit him. The truth—he was just about to rape his wife—sobered him.

He sat back on the sheets and held his head in his hands.

"I'm going mad," he muttered. Rachel came to him putting her arms around his shoulders and laid her head on his back.

"How can you ever forgive me?"she whispered. "What have I done to us?"

"I think we should forget the whole episode, otherwise it will rip us both apart," she heard him say.

She traced the scars that Leah had made with her nails—first with her own fingers, then with her lips. She had no idea whether they had caused Jacob pleasure or pain—she only knew she wanted to heal the divide that was threatening to come between them.

"Do ... do you still love me, Jay?" The words were hard to say, because never in a million years had she ever thought she would have to ask them.

Jacob twisted himself round to face her. "Please don't ask such an absurd question. You are not the one on trial here," he said. " It's me—and I have the marks to prove it. I should never have used your moment of weakness to ... to ... oh, I don't know! Please

Rachel, can we try and put all this behind us? Accept that we've both been stupid and blind?"

Rachel nodded, not knowing how to answer. This kind of experience was outside her knowledge, and she had nothing to draw on. She didn't know what to do next.

"Shall we ... do you want to ... stay here?" Her innocent eyes looked at the crumpled sheets and then at her husband.

He took her hand and pulled her to her feet, "I don't think so."

They walked away from the room together.

*   *   *

They had months and months to heal the wounds. Needless to say, the aphrodisiac didn't solve the problem. Every time they made love, Rachel tried not to think about becoming pregnant, and Jacob did everything he could to forget his night with Leah.

It was an almost impossible situation, and were both striving to come to terms with it in their own way.

Rachel was privately relieved when she discovered that the potion hadn't worked—the baby would have had Leah's mark on it. Jacob felt exactly the same, but didn't mention it. So they continued—never discussing their emotions, never sharing their secrets. They were still deeply in love, but the divide was gradually taking its toll.

Leah, meanwhile, was looking for a house away from Buckinghamshire. That night with Jacob was her last attempt to lure him back, and she had finally resigned herself to the fact that Jacob was never going to love her.

Her mother had been right. You can never have enough love for two. And while she still broke her heart over Jacob—to him she didn't exist. Even when she gave him everything—he just took what he wanted and left. She was heartbroken. Her life now was constantly changing. She even prayed from time to time.

Maybe the God she had used (as Jacob had used her) would be willing to forgive and listen. Maybe if she took the love He offered, and gave a little back—it might not be too late. She could still start again, in a new place, with new people and maybe even someone to love her?

Jacob and Rachel felt a cloud lift from their lives when they heard that Leah was moving away. It helped.

"We've had a stormy time, haven't we?" Jacob asked Rachel soon after. It was a glorious day—the boys were playing football in the garden and Jacob and Rachel sat watching them from a swing chair on the patio.

Rachel's hand found her husbands', and she smiled at him. "Do you remember when we used to meet on the 'blue bridge'?" she asked.

Jacob gazed up at the clear blue sky, "I thought you were the most beautiful thing I had ever seen. Do you remember the day we got in the taxi and neither of us knew where we were going?" He laughed aloud at the thought.

Rachel remembered well. "What did you say to the driver?"

" 'We want to see London, the long way round!' You know, I can't recall seeing a single thing!"

She looked up at him, the sun shining in her face.

Jacob smiled wickedly, "I can't even remember coming up for air!"

She dug his ribs and he yelled. "Hey! You were never so rough then!" The seat was swinging wildly. The day was perfect, and the hot sunny weather was lasting. They continued to gaze at the scenery, and Rachel gave a long sigh.

"What was that for?" he asked.

"I was just thinking how nice it would be to start again. To do it all, without the mistakes ... " she replied.

"Oh, no. The mistakes are supposed to give us strength of character!" he mocked.

She laughed at him and kissed his cheek. "You know what I mean! We had such a beautiful start ..."

"Ah yes, of course! I seem to remember a sleepy blue-eyed blonde trying to pour a jug of coffee on me, by way of an introduction!" he teased.

"Jacob!" she protested. "You're not taking this seriously!"

"All right!" Jacob jumped off the swing and Rachel screamed as she held on to the sides.

"Jay! What are you doing?" She giggled as he picked her up and walked towards the house.

"Put me down!" she cried gleefully.

"Not until you've answered a few questions, Miss!" he continued, as he carried her up the stairs.

"What questions?" She put her arms around his neck and held on tight.

"Will you go out with me?" he asked.

"Yes! Put me down!" she laughed.

"Do you love me?" He was walking towards their room now.

"Yes, yes of course! Jay! What are you doing?"

"Will you marry me?" he stopped for a moment.

"Yes, yes, yes!" she responded to his kiss.

"Last question ... " Still carrying her he stopped at the bed.

"Will you make love to me?" Their eyes met and a new flame kindled between them.

"Can you put me down first?" she asked timidly.

"Oh, Rachel!" he exclaimed in mock frustration, and threw her carelessly onto the bed. "I'm trying to be romantic—I'm starting again!"

The pillow she threw at him hit him squarely on the side of the head. Their squeals of laughter could be heard halfway down the rose garden. But somehow it didn't matter. The two boys continued to play football, the sun continued to shine ... and Rachel and Jacob made love.

*   *   *

Two months later, Rachel collapsed in a department store in Oxford Street. The manager recognised her, and arranged for her to be driven home in one of the company cars. When Jacob came home that night, he found his wife crying by herself in the lounge.

His heart leapt into his mouth. Surely they couldn't have any more troubles? He was by her side in an instant, cradling her and calling her name. She clung to him and cried even more. He tentatively put his hand under her chin and raised her head so that he could see her face.

She was smiling. "Oh Jay! I fainted in Oxford Street today and Doctor Mortimer has been to see me ... and oh, Jacob ... I'm pregnant!"

She fell into his arms again still crying. Jacob was stunned. But when Rachel's words had sunk in he went totally wild with delight.

He picked up the phone and ordered champagne to be delivered to the house immediately. He picked the phone up again and ordered enough flowers to fill a greenhouse. He turned round in circles confused to what to do next, then he ran into the bedroom, brought out a duvet and put it around Rachel.

"Darling! What are you doing?" Rachel's voice was still rather breathless.

"I ... er ... you need to rest ... put your feet on the couch ... keep warm ... don't lift anything ... Rachel! I don't know what I'm doing!" He dropped beside her and scooped her up, duvet and all, into his arms. He stroked her hair lightly. "Are you sure—I mean absolutely?"

She nodded. "Absolutely!"

Jacob looked concernedly around the room. "Where is the doctor anyway? Who said he could leave? Don't I pay him enough to look after you?"

Rachel snuggled into the duvet and laughed, "I don't think he needs to be here constantly for the next seven months—do you?"

Jacob calmed down and shook his head in amazement.

"Rachel, I just can't believe it! After all this time! What did Dr Mortimer say?"

"He said, 'What did I tell you?' No, honestly, he did!" she said giggling at Jacob's doubtful face. He still couldn't take it in.

"We're pregnant!" he whispered. "I can't get over it!"

They spent the rest of the evening bundled up in the duvet, talking quietly and planning out the next months of their lives.

"I shall take leave from work," said Jacob determinedly. "I don't want to miss a moment of this!"

"You will go to work everyday until I say so!" replied Rachel. "You'll drive me crazy if you stay at home! Look at you!"

During the course of the evening, the champagne and flowers arrived. Jacob made short work of the bubbly, even playfully admonishing Rachel for wanting some, and teasingly allowing her to have a small sip from a teaspoon. They fell asleep exhausted, in each others arms—still wrapped in the duvet—shortly afterwards, and didn't wake until early the following morning.

The first rays of the day brought a new dawn to their lives.